P9-CFV-839

# IMPOSTOR SYNDROME

## ALSO BY KATHY WANG

*Family Trust*

# IMPOSTOR SYNDROME

**A NOVEL**

# KATHY WANG

CUSTOM
HOUSE

HarperCollins books may be purchased for educational, business, or sales promotional use. For information, please email the Special Markets Department at SPsales@harpercollins.com.

FIRST EDITION

*Designed by Nancy Singer*

Library of Congress Cataloging-in-Publication Data

Names: Wang, Kathy, author.
Title: Impostor syndrome : a novel / Kathy Wang.
Description: First edition. | New York, NY : Custom House, [2021]
Identifiers: LCCN 2021006379 (print) | LCCN 2021006380 (ebook) | ISBN 9780062855282 (hardcover) | ISBN 9780062855299 (trade paperback) | ISBN 9780063090378 (large print) | ISBN 9780062855305 (ebook)
Subjects: GSAFD: Satire. | Suspense fiction.
Classification: LCC PS3623.A45694 I47 2021 (print) | LCC PS3623.A45694 (ebook) | DDC 813/.6—dc23
LC record available at https://lccn.loc.gov/2021006379
LC ebook record available at https://lccn.loc.gov/2021006380

ISBN 978-0-06-285528-2

21  22  23  24  25   LSC   10  9  8  7  6  5  4  3  2  1

For Tom

# IMPOSTOR SYNDROME

# JUNE 2006

## 1

# LEO

Whenever Leo Guskov met a person of interest, he liked to ask about his or her parents. If the response was cagey, he made note, and if he thought he'd go further, then he was careful to ensure the subject's family-history paperwork was complete. Though it wasn't that Leo believed you needed good parents to be productive. In fact, in his line of work, bad parents were often an advance indicator of success. An early acquaintanceship with adversity, of conquering that high mountain of disappointment and dread; the desire to serve, to be loyal and exceed expectations, if only to garner the approval earlier denied.

Where he sat now, inside a university auditorium by the Moskva River, Leo was surrounded by mothers and fathers (likely most good, some bad). He slouched and let wash over him the flotsam of idle complaint that comprised the background of Moscow life: a two-hour delay on the MKAD; expensive cucumbers at the grocer; a callous dermatologist at the state clinic, who'd refused to stay late and do a body check—*there was alcohol on his breath and he said he had to bring home dinner. Just because his wife cannot keep house, so I have to die . . . ?*

Years earlier Leo had stood onstage in a similar auditorium, his mother in a back row, clutching tulips. A week later he'd arrived for his first day of work, at a twenty-story concrete skyscraper in the Moscow city line. Inside the lobby, a brass plaque with initials: SPB. State Protection Bureau. The best of Russia's three intelligence agencies.

Now the weather outside was warm, which meant the auditorium was near stifling. Peter Stepanov, Leo's colleague from Directorate Eight, fidgeted to his right. Peter was tall and thin, and in the slim seat he was reminiscent of a pocket tool knife, his scissory arms and corkscrew legs all neatly confined in the space. "How about that one?" Peter asked, subtly pointing, though Leo already knew to whom he gestured. The blonde in front, with hair down to her waist.

"No."

"Why not?"

"I need more than just a pretty face."

"You think I'm only scanning for the faces?" Peter looked insulted. "Look at her colors." Meaning the blue-and-yellow sash over her shoulder. Leo's own was in a box, on a high shelf in his closet.

"I don't need a top graduate."

"Oh, so a simpleminded one." Peter leaned forward. "Then the possibilities widen. Over there, the redhead on the right. Better looking than the blonde, and even under that loose gown, you can still tell she has a substantial rack."

Leo had seen the redhead when they first entered, noting her for the same reasons as Peter, though he didn't say this. Last Friday, as he'd prepared to leave work, he'd been cajoled by Peter into a "quick stop" at a fashionable hotel bar; there Leo had nursed the cheapest drink, a bottle of Georgian mineral water, while Peter trawled awkwardly for haughty women. Leo had returned home after midnight, somehow still having gotten drunk, only to find his girlfriend, Vera Rustamova, waiting in the kitchen. Vera was a correspondent for

Russia Central Media, or RCM, the state-owned news group. She had a newscaster's voice, low and rounded, which she could adjust to the precise desired pitch of disapproval. "No, not her."

"What, not beautiful enough? If you want something more, I don't know if the computer science department is where we hunt."

"I don't need beautiful. Don't want it, in fact."

Peter thought about this. "So you want dumb and bad-looking, is that it? I don't know what you're working at, but the next time you take me on one of your scouting trips . . ."

Leo didn't hear the rest. He'd asked Peter along only to be sociable, to share an excuse to leave the office—Leo had little pressure to recruit, as he'd had a good run this year, had already advanced multiple assets. One, a Bashkir, was still in training, while the other two, a pair of siblings, were active: the brother, a trained chef, now worked in London at a hotel frequented by Saudi royals, while the sister was engaged to a corporate lawyer in St. Louis. Leo had awoken this morning with a bad headache and had nearly elected not to come.

But now he was glad he'd made the effort. Back of the stage: fourth row, on the left. Limp auburn hair, pale skin, which, combined with small, sharp dark eyes, gave her a look of feral alertness. How long had it been? Nine years? Ten? And yet he knew her.

Julia. From the institute.

THEY CALLED THEM INSTITUTES BUT what they really were was orphanages, landing zones for unwanted children. Large low-slung buildings with rusted fixtures and faded carpets; visible on the floors were the paths worn by heavy boots and wheelchairs, their adolescent owners wielding the machines like skaters on ice. The institutes were mostly located in larger towns, occasionally on the outskirts of big cities. It was on a trip to one of these that Leo first saw Julia.

He'd been in search of a boy. An older one, which was difficult, because if robust, boys were usually adopted young. The task was both delicate and important, involving the Canadian ambassador and his wife. They were religious people, the wife in particular, who'd made known her wishes to adopt before they permanently returned to Ottawa: to answer God's call and grant some unwanted soul another chance.

But also, you know, they really wanted a boy.

So Leo was sent to seek an acceptable candidate. A child old enough, clever enough to be groomed.

The children were gathered by this institute's director, a brittle matron of unverifiable age named Maria, into lines in the community room. Leo asked Maria to instruct each to introduce themselves, and to repeat a sentence from a favorite book.

One by one they spoke. *Hello, sir, my name is . . .*

Raisa.
Julia.
Svetlana.
Misha.

*My favorite book is the Bible, and here is the part that has meant so much to me, blah blah blah.*

By the ninth introduction, Leo's focus began to drift. He kept his face attentive, maintained eye contact, and when the one he'd earlier identified as most promising moved forward, the boy with straw-colored hair who came up to Leo's chest, he returned to full attention.

"My name is Pavel," the boy began. "My favorite book is the one with the man in blue who has muscles and can fly." Pavel closed his eyes, as if summoning the image. "I don't remember any of the words."

Leo knew the man to whom Pavel referred. A Western fabrication, with Western values.

Bye-bye, Pavel. Have a nice life.

As Leo prepared to depart, he felt a tap and turned to find a girl. She was short, with long thin eyelashes that drooped toward sloped cheeks and an even flatter nose; her eyebrows, which were fat and unruly, lent a somewhat deranged note to her appearance. "You could take me."

"I was looking for something else today," Leo said, inwardly grimacing as he realized he sounded as if he were at the butcher, declining a cut of meat. "I'm sorry. Perhaps next time."

"I can be very good," she said, not moving. "I am very, very interested in doing a good job. I would not say what Pavel did. You were right to leave him behind."

"How did you know I was interested in Pavel?" A little curious now.

"They talked about it before you came. That you wanted a boy. The adults here speak as if none of us have ears."

He was amused by her phrasing. "Pavel is not the only boy."

"You make a fist when you are paying attention. You did it in the beginning, when Sophia bent for the tea. She only wears that sweater when we have visitors, you know."

Instantly, Leo thrust his hand behind his back. He slowly loosened his grip, feeling absurd. He knelt and said in a low voice: "You say you would do a good job. But you don't even know what sort of job it is I would ask."

Her face scrunched as she thought. "Well whatever it is, I am interested."

"What's your name?" He could see Sophia of the famous V-neck hovering near, looking both wary and hopeful; she knew he sought a male, but the institute was compensated for every child taken by Directorate Eight, regardless of gender.

"Julia."

"Julia." He nodded, as if committing the name to a mental ledger. "And how long have you been here?"

"Since I was little."

"Oh? So you do not remember your time before?"

A shadow flicked across her face. "I have been here my whole life." She cleared her throat. "You know, I can also sing."

He rocked on his heels. "Go ahead, then. Sing me a song."

She closed her eyes. "I'm so happy . . ."

"An American song?"

Her eyes opened. "I'm sorry—"

"Don't be. It's never wrong to practice other languages. A very good idea, actually." He rose, and then after a hesitation patted her on the head. "Perhaps I'll see you later."

She took a small step, deftly rejecting his touch. "When?"

"I don't know. Perhaps next year. Or the next."

Julia settled on him a hard look. "You won't come. We will never see each other again."

THEY SAT ACROSS FROM EACH other now, in a room in the back of a mechanical parts warehouse owned by the SPB. The space was unofficially Leo's—no one else from the department liked to use it, because it was far away, in Mitino. Over the years he'd rearranged the decor: he'd kept a campaign photo of the current president, in case he ever were to visit, which he wouldn't; the Gorbachev junk he'd removed, though he'd left up a single poster, of a cartoon alcoholic mistakenly chugging silver polish. *Evil for your body and soul* was printed on the bottom, which Leo would occasionally chant as he poured for himself and Vera. *Glug glug glug.*

"Do you remember meeting me?" He shifted, and his chair made an ugly noise against the floor. "It was a long time ago."

"Yes," Julia said, and Leo took the moment to study her up close. Unfortunately, Julia was not one of those plain children who grew into their features (though from Leo's experience it was never the perfect tens who worked hardest, anyway). She wore a red wool dress with a dirndl collar, as a younger girl might, and had brought along with her a paper sack of food, from which Leo could discern the smell of hot bread and cheese. Sloykas, he guessed. His stomach rumbled.

"When we first met, you said you did not know your parents."

"Yes."

"Is that still the case?" Though he knew the answer, as by now—a week after the graduation—he had assembled her complete file.

"Yes. I do not know them. Or think of them."

"And you understand what the SPB does." Watching her carefully, as here was where some of his potentials flamed out. Though they were initially drawn by the excitement, something about hearing the actual name, the initials, seemed to move them to reconsider. As if by not working for the SPB they might exist farther from its eye, their sins unrecorded.

Julia shrugged. "As much as anyone else."

"You understand our country is under attack. From our enemies, and even our supposed friends."

"Uh-huh."

"And that any harm done to the West is a benefit to us."

"Right. So what do you want?" Her voice brusque, as if she were busy, had many other people to meet, interviews to complete, though Leo knew better. If Julia had graduated with top marks she might have been able to land a job at a telecom, perhaps even a multinational, but her university transcript confirmed such avenues were closed.

"Nothing right now. You'll have to finish the security paperwork, complete introductory training. Then I believe the first order of business will be a voice coach."

"A voice coach?" She sneered. "What do I need *that* for?"

Over Leo's career he'd managed dozens of men and women who mistakenly equated unpleasant behavior with an expression of power; by now he knew it was best to extinguish such beliefs right away. "The way you speak, it's intolerable."

Julia flinched. There was silence, and she glared at the floor. "If you think my speaking is so bad, then why did you request me?" she asked at last, her face reddening. "Because it wasn't for my looks."

Ah, he thought. So you want to take that away before it can be used.

"I believe you are a woman with tenacity," Leo said, deliberately using the word *woman*. "That, plus creativity, is what I search for."

She snorted and flushed deeper. "And what does a voice coach have to do with creativity?"

"What I do for my job is construct a package. A human package, for a specific purpose. I need you to be convincing beyond doubt; it's not your voice that's so much the issue as the way you speak. No elegance. Perhaps the problem came after so much time in the institute. Because when we first met, it was not so bad."

"I sang that song," she said, and Leo knew she must recall nearly every detail of their first interaction. That perhaps she'd nursed hopes of his reappearance for years after. "In English."

"Yes, and your command of language was already decent. With a coach to refine the pronunciation you could become nearly fluent. You'll never get rid of your accent entirely, but you'd be surprised what focused training can accomplish."

He waited for Julia to ask why English was important, but she refrained. "And say I do the voice coach and learn the good English. Then what?"

"Perhaps we do acting training. There are no guarantees. During each step your performance would be evaluated."

"And after?" Her fingers drummed. "A piano teacher, and then gymnastics, and I go join the circus?"

He shook his head. "If you were ready, you'd begin the next phase. To serve our country, in secret, abroad . . ."

Julia perked at this. She began to tick off fingers. "New York, Shanghai, Paris . . ."

"Not any of those."

"Cairo, Munich, Sydney . . ."

"None of those, either."

"All right, where?" Eager in her curiosity. She's just a child, Leo thought. A rude one, but a child nonetheless.

"Silicon Valley."

"Silicon Valley," Julia repeated, not entirely disappointed. "You mean San Francisco?"

"We can determine the right city later. We have people at both Berkeley and Stanford. You'll need to be enrolled in a graduate program, for the visa."

"And what would you have me do?"

He laced his fingers. "You have heard of the start-up culture there?"

"Yes." Her voice held an edge of derision.

"What, you don't think the internet is interesting?"

"I'm not the sort to stare at a computer all day."

"Well, perhaps you could add a hobby. Another boom is coming. I want you to start a technology company. A true Silicon Valley one, based locally."

"A company," Julia repeated uncertainly.

"Yes. One viable enough to attract good investors. The investors will be key, especially in the beginning. From them you will receive introductions to other entrepreneurs, partners—become part of the local ecosystem, as it were. What we refer to as a bridge."

From outside came the beeps and clangs of construction. Maybe the Metro, Leo thought, which they were forever promising would be built. He waited for Julia's response, which he assumed would be positive. He recalled the first time he'd breathed the air outside San Francisco, its sweetness in his lungs—which he'd quickly become used to, and then taken for granted, until he was back on the plane.

But instead of a quick smile or other signs of enthusiasm, Julia only tugged at her collar. Both hands fiddled with the cotton; her eyes were wide and she kept her gaze on the table. "You have seen my grades," she said.

So that was the problem. "Yes."

"Well," she huffed. "Then you already know I don't have much talent. For a while I thought that even if I didn't like my classes, I could still work hard. But it wasn't enough."

Leo was surprised: he had not thought she'd acknowledge her own deficiencies. But this meant only that he was all the more correct about her suitability as an asset. Yes, it'd be good to have a computer genius, but such a person wouldn't necessarily want the job—and above average at home was close to brilliant in America, anyway.

"I don't need an expert. Just some technical proficiency. A hard worker, which you've just told me you are."

"So am I going to have help? A technical coach?"

"No."

"A team of programmers?"

"No. You're going to do it all. Create the company, and lead it."

"But I already told you, I can't manage the technical portion."

"Don't worry about that." He checked his watch. The metal chair was numbing his back. He wanted to start home, stop at the butcher's before returning to Vera.

"But isn't the whole point of a start-up to have a product?" She rocked back and forth in her chair. "It has to have an offering. A reason for its existence."

"Yes, you're right."

"Then I don't understand! Where is it going to come from?"

And finally they had arrived at the heart of the matter. A queer feeling overtook Leo and he felt himself hoping she'd prove worthwhile. I could change your life, he thought.

He let the quiet settle. Watched her face.

"We'll steal it."

# JUNE 2018

# 2

# JULIA

Julia Kall was getting married.

Though Kall wouldn't be her last name, not for long; after the events of the afternoon she'd be known as Julia Lerner, wife of Charlie Lerner. Julia knew that in Silicon Valley, and especially at the levels on which she operated, changing one's last name was considered passé, an incline of the head to the patriarchy: why not ask for an allowance while she was at it, let her husband manage the money; carry out munchies for the boys on poker night, squealing at the ass slap on her way back to the kitchen. It was the expected thing, to keep one's last name, especially given her career. But that was why Julia was changing her own. To hint at an inner traditionalist. She already courted that market, subtly; when giving speeches, she usually mentioned that while her job as *the second-highest executive* at one of the world's *most valuable technology companies* was tremendously difficult, it was nothing compared to that of a mother, so bravo, bravo, let's hear it for the mothers. The audience dutiful in its applause, like junior congressmen saluting veterans, and then she would press forward: balance, childcare, empower. Her (subtly) enhanced red hair, cut to the shoulders, rounding out the image—her heels high, sweaters tight, though with conservative necklines.

Once married, Julia planned to add some bits about her and Charlie to the mix, reflections on her good taste in landing the perfect partner. And then, once they had kids—because naturally kids would follow—she would post about the whole family. I used to think what I did at work, you know, managing billions of dollars at one of the world's most valuable companies—I used to think that was the important thing! But it wasn't until I became a mother that I understood it's what I do at home that truly matters. Raising our next generation. Our future.

You know, all that stupid shit.

Plus, Kall wasn't even her real last name, anyway.

The temperature outside was in the high seventies, the sun's flame reduced by a thin gauze of clouds: a perfect Saturday afternoon in Napa Valley. Though Eisner Gardens had not been her first choice of venue. Originally Julia had thought Napa too basic: yes there were the nice parts, the private estates and wine caves, but there were also the factory wineries stuffed with tour groups, the traffic on Route 29; all the slurring Marina bros and escaped housewives, cheeks fat from bad fillers. Julia's first choice had been Indonesia—not Kuta or Seminyak, but rather a private resort in Borobudur. Her boss, Pierre Roy, the CEO and founder of the social media and internet giant Tangerine, had done something similar, flying all his guests, Julia included, on his 767 to the Caribbean. She'd already asked to borrow the plane, knowing Pierre would agree, but had then been informed that the wedding was not to take place overseas.

The wedding should be in California, Leo said. In California, more people would come.

At least Eisner was undeniably magnificent, with acres of meticulously attended gardens. A popular historical drama had been filmed on-site, the protagonist galloping up on his polo pony to be met by an umbrella-wielding servant (this always fascinated Julia about Americans, how prideful they were about their democracy while worshipping those who lived like kings). She stood now on the second floor of the same mansion as a seamstress buttoned her into the gown (Ralph & Russo, she'd spent a boatload, and now felt as if she might keel over from the weight of the beading). "You're doing a wonderful job," she said to the girl, who appeared thrilled to have received such praise from Julia herself.

Holding her train, taking tiny steps, Julia looked out the window at the view below. The food was circulating, which was good; she'd requested the hors d'oeuvres begin as soon as the first guests arrived. Julia hated parties where the food was served late, the hostess (it was always a hostess) entering triumphantly to the pent-up demand, like a captor doling out warm showers to a pack of hostages with Stockholm syndrome. She scanned the crowd. It appeared most of the two hundred were already here. There was Alan Mark, a Microsoft executive who frequently announced he had no interest in being Tangerine's next CEO, which meant only that he did. Then there was Pierre himself, with his new girlfriend (despite the Caribbean wedding, the bride herself had not stuck); clearly Pierre was going through one of his Japan-worshipping phases again. His date, in one of those tacky jersey dresses cut to the navel, tossed her black hair and laughingly cajoled Pierre to take a selfie. At the last second, with expert agility, Pierre pulled away, said hi to someone just out of the camera's reach.

Finally, Julia sighted him. Leo, in a charcoal suit, in the shade by Rebecca Mosley, the wife of a Tangerine board member. Rebecca was one of those older intellectual housewives with something to prove—who, whenever she encountered Julia, liked to pose all sorts of middling questions on Russia, as if it were not a global power with twice America's landmass but rather one of those minor landlocked countries with a hilarious McDonald's menu. Chances were she was subjecting Leo to the same abuse, since he was here as

Julia's "uncle"—poor Julia, with no other living family to speak of, and represented solely by this humble, well-formed former water bureau manager. How was he finding the first world, Rebecca was likely pressing, did he love California? Wasn't it nice here, because as everyone knew, Russia was so cold, all the time?

Though Julia did, in fact, love California. Imagine if they'd sent her to one of those other states—and she knew the SPB occasionally did do this, seeding assets to small politicians, hoping they might one day become big ones. What would she be doing then? Attending the openings of car dealerships, frying chicken nuggets, falling asleep in church. Shopping on the weekends for wooden plaques to hang on her wall: *The Conner Family, Est. 2011!*

The wedding planner was back in the room. "Are you excited?" Libby Rosenberg was one of those competent former sorority girls Julia liked to hire into marketing. Though Libby had been clipping between the gardens in a full suit, her makeup was still perfectly matte. "*I'm* getting excited."

"Of course."

"You eat? You should have something in your stomach before you go out. Michael, why doesn't Julia have a plate? It's her food, you know."

She's right, Julia thought. It is my food. I'm the one paying for it. And then she returned to the window, to enjoy the view a while longer.

OF COURSE, JULIA WASN'T FOOLISH enough to believe she'd achieved everything on her own merit. There was help, especially in the beginning. Arriving at her depressive studio in San Carlos, initially stunned by the strip malls and sheer ugliness of the place, only to visit Stanford University days later and fall in love, because here—amid the Romanesque architecture and towering palms and lopsided wealth—was the California of her dreams. A PhD candidate in electrical engineering, she'd been set up with Kurt Marshall, described by Leo as a "friendly" professor, who proceeded to match her with another "accommodating" company, at which the ancient Marshall was paid a quarter million a year as an advisor. The company sponsored her visa, no one in Immigration Services curious why a small business repackaging USB keys was navigating the hurdles of an H1-B for an analyst; she'd worked there a year before Leo returned to California and presented her with a laptop. "Now you go fundraise."

She stroked the machine, chunky and metallic. "What is it?"

"Facial recognition software. I assume you still recall enough of your studies to give a convincing demo. I made up the working name, VisionMatch, but change it if you like. It's your company."

She disliked the name but sensed he was proud of his creative output. "Face recognition?"

"Properly deployed, it can match each face in a crowd of thousands in seconds. Such technology has also been on the SPB's wish list. So why not multitask?" He laughed.

"Where did you get it?"

He named an American technology giant, the sort that sponsored stadiums.

"And they won't realize we took it?" Julia was surprised that such a thing could be lifted without consequence. At the institute, if someone stole even an apple, blood was drawn, the accumulation and tracking of possessions being of chief interest among the residents.

"These companies have so much, they probably won't ever use it. It's not their chief business, only one of hundreds of side projects. Something to remember about America: waste is part of their culture."

Just a year after she launched VisionMatch, Tangerine—the social network already frequented by half of all Americans—came to call. Pierre Roy, who'd started as a freshman at Waterloo at fifteen, had at one point, due to his semi-dreamy looks and a habit of grandiose announcements, been referred to in the press as the "Frat Genius." A nickname Pierre hated, because he thought it undercut the fact that he really was, you know, a genius. By twenty-eight, he'd built Tangerine to deca-unicorn status and no longer cared what the media said. He held 88 percent of the outstanding voting shares and was thus not subject to the hedging and consensus building of lesser entrepreneurs; he made brash declarations and dated a string of minor actresses and very good-looking academics. Pierre wanted VisionMatch's facial identification software—Tangerine could do it in-house, he informed Julia, but this was just easier.

"There's another company that's got something similar, you know," Pierre murmured during their closing dinner at Alexander's. Bankers on both sides, ordering the A5 Wagyu because they could. "But the company's one of those big bad corporations, so they'd never give it to me. Hopefully yours is as good."

Oh oh oh, Julia thought. You have no idea.

And now she was chief operating officer of Tangerine, second only to Pierre. Total comp last fiscal year: $39 million.

Julia knew she had a reputation—what was her latest nickname? It used to be the Sweetheart of Silicon Valley, but that was when she was doing the stuff that embarrassed her to think of now: baking cookies for reporters, giving interviews on her twelve-step skin-care routine. While publicly railing against gender inequality, she'd quietly torched the path of any rising female at Tangerine, the same as any man would have done to his own competition. As Tangerine's user count continued to explode, journalists sought a female executive to quote—please, any woman! And then they found Julia, her finger in the dam just in time, before male hubris overflowed and drowned them all . . .

She looked back out at the crowd. She could sense Libby hovering behind, waiting to speak.

Leo had separated himself from Rebecca and was now by the bar, his face tilted at the windows.

Julia waved and blew him a kiss, and he tapped a finger against his watch. *Don't waste time.*

She turned to the room, to the assistants, the planner. Weeks later each would receive a handwritten note thanking them for their contribution. In the room were no bridesmaids, no sisters clutching at modest bouquets.

"I'm ready," she said.

THE NEXT AFTERNOON, JULIA SAT with Leo.

The wedding had been lovely, of course. Lovely, charming, inspiring—Julia's frequently deployed descriptors, used for everything from baby showers to politicians. Her nuptials conducted beneath two willows, the pool's midafternoon reflection casting a gleam. The party afterward, the dinner, the dancing (Julia hated dancing), the fireworks, which she'd watched with utter joy, tracking the arc of each light as it shattered in the sky.

It'd been a month since she and Leo last met. A year earlier, when Leo announced he was moving, Julia was alarmed. She'd not wanted a local handler, one available to observe at close range the vast perks of being free and rich in California. But since his arrival, Leo had mostly left her alone. Their meetings were brief, quiet lunches at her house or empty restaurants, as she passed interesting gossip.

She'd rented the entirety of the Golden Rock Ranch for the weekend, set on its own hill in Stags Leap. She and Leo sat on the deck outside her suite, a table between them. Leo was drooped with his head against the chair's back, eyes ringed with red. His left hand slowly stroked his stomach, as if easing some inner queasiness.

"Drink too much last night?" Julia asked, amused.

He shifted uncomfortably. "I'm getting older, yes? I know that's your implication."

"You should probably wait until the evening to indulge again. If you do." She rose and retrieved a pitcher of water.

"Thank you," Leo said as she poured. "Charlie seems nice," he added. Julia's new husband was at the airport, seeing off his mother and father, the former who had worn an insane red sequined ball gown last night, designed to steal attention.

"He is nice," she agreed.

Leo set down the glass. "*Very* American."

Julia suppressed a smile. Two years earlier she'd been informed she ought to get a husband—*time to establish family ties* was what Leo said, and instantly Julia had understood. She pretended to be insulted, resistant, but secretly began her endeavor immediately. She knew the SPB had likely already begun to strategize; she was not going to be controlled, told to spread her legs for some septuagenarian with a high security clearance or a closeted CEO with a secret phone line.

She met Charlie through a friend, because she now had friends, because guess what? Once your company was acquired and your net worth climbed into nine digits, you became more interesting not only to yourself but also to others. Like magic! Athena, an Israeli biologist who ran a gene-mapping company, had come up to her at a party. Murmuring: "*Have I got a man for you.*"

At the time, Julia already had a semi-boyfriend. Zack Stein, venture capitalist on the rise, excessive hair product, obnoxious car, but he was decent-looking and not too short and seemed willing to learn and improve. By now Julia had undergone her own modifications: gone were the bad clothes, lurid makeup, clumsy hair color and cut. When she recalled how she'd first appeared in California, wearing her neon tracksuit (tracksuit!) as she hiked Rancho San Antonio, mascara clumped around her eyes—she wanted to die. Why hadn't Leo helped? Why get a voice coach and an acting teacher but not a stylist? But men didn't think of such things.

Zack was fine, and Julia could picture herself married to him— maybe. The only problem was that lately his communications had assumed a certain tenor, as if she were not an executive who out-earned him twelve to one but rather one of his firm's many analysts, some young nubile recent grad:

- I find it sexy when a woman is always THRILLED to see me
- Happy to mentor you ;)
- Really busy this month, you know how intense I am about work . . .

So okay, Julia told Athena, let's meet him—not expecting much. And then Athena brought over Charlie. Charlie: dark blond hair, perfect American teeth, like a white picket fence in his mouth. Julia was five nine and he was half a head taller, even when she was in heels.

"You have a bit of a sunburn," Julia had said, spotting a patch of red behind his temple.

"Really?" He touched the area. "Right. From surfing."

"Is that what you do?"

"Do I surf professionally, you mean?" He laughed. "No. I'm a doctor. Cardiologist."

Cardiologist. Julia liked doctors as a rule: they earned less than her, as nearly all men did, but didn't have a complex about it.

"I would ask what you do, if only to be polite," Charlie said, still smiling, still friendly. "But I already know."

That had been the start. The draw was that he did not care. Did not pretend otherwise, went and said out loud what so many men would not, that she was who she was. It was as if the champagne she held spilled into the air between them—that heady mixture of interest and lust that was so delicious and yet totally unexpected. Because how often in life did you get exactly what you want? How rare was it not only to find love, but for the person to love you back?

Charlie. Charlie Charlie Charlie. She had chosen him. He was perfect.

But instead of rolling around in bed, eating breakfast with her flawless new husband, Julia was stuck outside with this old, hung-over, and frequently tedious man.

Leo was fussing about with a fork, hovering over the food. Ear-lier that morning the manager had delivered a charcuterie platter and sliced fruit; Julia had taken some bites of pineapple, but the rest was untouched. Leo speared into the dragon fruit, nibbling suspi-ciously at its edges.

"It's good," Julia said. "Even better in Thailand."

He wagged a finger. "Don't forget we come from the same place."

Julia kicked the table. "How's business?" she asked, before re-gretting the question. She didn't want Leo to think she was nosing about his work—she knew very little of his cover in California. From what she understood, he worked out of an office, one of those sad single-man consulting shops, as befitting a minor relative riding on her coattails.

"It's fine." He crumpled a piece of bresaola into his mouth. "Busy."

"Good." She considered asking some polite follow-ups, but was afraid there was no way of doing so without sounding disingenuous, like when she was forced to compliment toddlers during the annual Take Your Kids to Tangerine event. "Perhaps you can share some thoughts about marriage," she said instead. "Any guidance, tips for success." Julia was actually curious to hear his answer. They rarely spoke about personal matters, Leo dodging her probes while simul-taneously pressing for details on Tangerine's organizational chart.

"Guidance," Leo repeated. He made another pass at the meats, his fork darting for the duck confit. "What's to say? Marriage is just power constantly being renegotiated."

This? This was all he had to offer? Sometimes Julia thought Leo might be losing it. His random confidences on various failings of the SPB, like an attempt to implant Scottish fold kittens with listen-ing devices, intended for the daughter of a Japanese executive, only for the cats to disappear into the streets of Osaka ("Even our animals," he mused, "want to defect"); the way he would occasionally lapse into gloom without provocation or warning, sulking his way through the last course of dinner. Late forties wasn't too young for a midlife crisis, right?

"Well, you're not married, anyway," she teased. "Yet."

He ignored this. "What we do is important. Sometimes I wonder if you forget. Who you truly work for."

Julia bristled. "I've done everything you've asked. The wedding was exactly as you wanted."

"Right." Leo cut a banana into neat slivers. "And now that the wedding's finished, we'll be asking more of you."

She fought her temper. "More? Please be fair. I've contributed. Have *been* contributing." How much dirt had she passed along over the years? A tech CEO's drug problem. The Lockheed executive sleeping with his brother's wife. An attorney general with real estate dreams and credit card debt. Wallet fantasies, Leo called them. Zipper problems.

"As you should. As you will continue to do."

*I just got married yesterday, dickhead.* She wondered why he was being such a hard-ass. What did Leo want? Fine, she would get out and eavesdrop more; even though it was technically her wedding week she would attend Sarah Kleiner's boutique opening next Tuesday, since her husband was CEO of CyberSoft, and purchase one of Sarah's hideous handbags.

"We want you to run a deep search on some people."

*"What?"*

"We need information," Leo said. Depositing a slice of banana into his mouth. "On a group of individuals. All their Tangerine data: messages, browsing, search activity."

Julia dug her nails into her thigh. What Leo was asking was an enormous breach of the trust and privacy Tangerine's entire business model was based upon. Users would never browse, message, search, or upload if they believed someone was watching—machines, fine;

algorithms, maybe; but never humans. No one person sitting in judgment over their Valtrex, their porn, their gambling, their shopping; the stalking of their ex from high school, and his wife, and whether she was fat now after the twins, going to the album and then clicking again, click click click click click.

Though it wasn't the privacy that was her main concern.

"I can't get caught. If I'm caught, my career's over."

"So don't get caught."

"It's harder than that, you understand? What you want, it isn't easy. Otherwise everyone would do it."

"If I believed my requests easy, I could send anyone. Train any nobody from off the street." *But instead I picked you*, being unsaid. *I picked you, and now it's time for payment.*

"I—I'll see what's possible."

Leo nodded. They both knew this meant she would do it. With a short grunt he stood and reached for the coffee. "We also want you to start transferring data from Tangerine's servers."

The hot pit of temper inside her gut instantly re-flared. "This was never part of the arrangement. It places me at risk."

"We don't want *all* the server data," Leo argued as he poured. As if this were even possible. "Our requests would be specific. All queries coming from Tel Aviv over a certain weekend, for example."

Julia shook her head, more violently this time. She realized that despite her earlier training she had not truly thought this day would come—when she would have to risk something important, an accomplishment she alone had achieved, for a bunch of old generals she'd never met and who likely knew nothing about technology. And what would they do if she were caught? What responsibility would they take, other than to say that yet again a woman had messed up?

"Is there anything else you're planning to request?" she fumed. "If so, tell it to me now. All of it."

Leo blinked at her. "We also want access to FreeTalk. Messages and location."

For a moment Julia was unable to speak. Though the air outside was warm her hands were cold and when she looked down they were leached of color. "No," she said. "No. *No.* Absolutely impossible."

FreeTalk, a five-year-old app through which users could send messages and photos, was Pierre's latest acquisition and darling; the service was enormously popular, ostensibly for its encryption features. The two founders, Sean Dara and Johan Frandsen, who'd frequently stated that privacy was their highest priority, that they could never sell the company, had nevertheless in the end sold, to Tangerine, for $9 billion—upon which they'd moved into Tangerine's headquarters, faces flush with embarrassment and money. Julia didn't like Sean or Johan, but better two dudes than one woman. She had yet to see any large company support more than one high-profile female executive at a time—it was as if too many might suck up all the oxygen, causing the entity to collapse in on itself like a dying star.

"What's impossible about it?" Leo actually looked curious.

"Pierre promised Sean and Johan total autonomy. FreeTalk's technical infrastructure is separate from Tangerine's. As is its management. It was one of the key deal points of the acquisition."

"You'll change their mind. You're good at that."

"This isn't something you can propel me to deliver through flattery. I can't."

"Yes you can." And then quietly: "You will."

A bubble of hate, for his humiliating her with a direct order. "What's it all for? Some kind of grand plan?"

"You've been watching too many movies. This isn't a one-time request. There will be an ongoing expectation."

"It must be for something."

"You have development cycles at work, do you not? Periods where you invest, spend to create products. Eventually though, your goal is for such products to earn money."

Not in the Valley, Julia thought, recalling an autonomous start-up she'd met with last week, which projected it would need to lose at least $4 billion before turning profitable. She'd thanked them for coming and then directed Tangerine's venture arm not to invest; later the CEO had emailed Pierre, complaining of her "catty" demeanor.

Taking her silence for assent, Leo continued: "All our rivals are investing in technology. The political situation in the West is, at best, unstable. You understand you've already been extended a long period of dormancy? For years, I pushed the SPB to leave you alone, let you rise. And now you have. They're impatient, Julia. It's only fair they see some return."

She shoved her legs against the chair. "I like my life. I've earned it."

"No one's taking away your life. In fact, it would only please me if you flew even higher. What a lot of fun that'd be, yes? All we're asking is that you share some back. With the country that brought you here."

"You think that's all it is, that you drop me in California and this is what automatically happens? That you take—how did you put it?—any *nobody* off the street, and they end up as COO? Twelve-hour days, seven days a week, for years. Hundreds of others, working just as hard to try and take my position."

"What do you want me to say, thank you? I thank you. Your country thanks you in advance."

Julia pushed away from the table and stood. "Are we done?"

Leo gaped at her, surprised. In all their years together, Julia had never ended a conversation. It had always been Leo who called, Leo who asked, Leo who left and came. She thought he might object, order her to sit, but instead he exclaimed: "Look!"

She looked. In her haste, she had jolted the table, and the carafe was on its side, coffee pouring from its beak. If this were her home, she would already be running for a napkin; scrubbing at the linen with soap, her fingernails digging out the stain.

"You clean up," Julia said, and then went inside and shut the door.

# DECEMBER 2018

# 3

# ALICE

Alice Lu was on her hands and knees, crouched under a table.

The table—custom built and the size of a queen mattress— was in the office of Sean Dara and Johan Frandsen, the founders of FreeTalk. The two men shared a single office (one of Tangerine's largest) as a testament to their first headquarters, a guesthouse in Cupertino. Alice, who was there to fix their phones, had just started to work when she was suddenly paralyzed by a cold fear.

On the ground, a nest of cables in her hands, she was level with the men's legs and feet. Alice concentrated on breathing, her field of vision contracting and sharpening, as she focused on what appeared to be the hardened spiral end of a burrito. Having suffered earlier panic attacks, she theoretically understood that the headache, sweating hands, violent drumming in her chest, these would all pass—and though she was currently convinced of an impending and unavoidable doom, that such doom would not occur, unless there was, like, an earthquake or something. There'd been that time in AP Calculus when she thought she'd bombed her final and would thus fall short of the 4.5 GPA necessary for East Asians to qualify for the Ivy League's holy trifecta, H-Y-P (Harvard, Yale,

Princeton); the one-week period when she'd been rejected by all three anyway, and the agonizing wait for the remaining choice not devastating to her parents, MIT. These, Alice knew now, had been stupid reasons to panic, whereas her present justifications were more reasonable.

These were, in chronological order:

1. that just six months prior, she'd actually been employed on the FreeTalk team, in a more senior position than the one she held now, where she had worked alongside her boyfriend of ten years, Jimmy Chiang, and;

2. following a series of sexual harassment suits, Tangerine announced a policy by which employees in a relationship could no longer work on the same team, triggering Alice to apply for a transfer, and;

3. due to a cultural propensity for rule following, which had also prompted her haste to transfer, Alice had accepted a role within technical support, generally acknowledged to be the lowest caste of engineering, but this was no problem, because inspired by the entrepreneurial zest of Sean and Johan, Jimmy planned to start his own company, at which Alice would serve as employee number 2, upon which:

4. Jimmy had left to start his own company, but had also dumped Alice at the same time, stranding her with a two-bedroom apartment in one of the most inflated rental markets in the country, meaning:

5. that despite worrying for so many years about the grades and the recruiting and the résumé-ing Alice had still managed to mess up her career, for the dumbest reason of all, and:

6. when she'd walked into their office just now, neither Sean nor Johan had recognized her, even though she'd personally presented to them twice.

In Alice's estimation, the last point was the least objectionable—the founders were considered princes of a sort within Tangerine, with the fleeting attention span accorded to celebrities, and she'd been a late transfer onto their team, following Jimmy's lead. Her ex-boyfriend had been enamored with Sean and Johan, who seemed to inspire a near-religious devotion among the male engineer set: the former in his mid-thirties, a vaper who collected Harley-Davidsons and referred to watches as *timepieces*; the latter forty-something, ex-eBay, a Scandinavian with five children and chickens in his backyard.

Sometime that morning Johan had entered the office and, attempting to make a call, found no dial tone. Johan had then texted Bryce Childs, the CTO, who directed the problem to the only woman on his team, Tara Lopez, upon which Tara had done the same.

"It's quite possibly an excellent opportunity for networking" was how Tara presented things. "It's really in the chance encounters that personal connections are made."

Alice knew Tara likely didn't recall that Alice had already enjoyed months of proximity to Sean and Johan, which had clearly not served her career to any great benefit; additionally, were there any opportunities to be had Alice knew it would be Tara swooping in, instead of dispatching a reliable minion. Though Alice hadn't argued. First, because she rarely pushed against authority, but also because weeks earlier she'd had her biannual review, seated across from Tara in the same office from which she'd been ordered to Sean and Johan's.

"I don't like to give a bad rating to *anyone*," Tara saying, even though Tangerine's stack ranking meant she had to do exactly this, twice a year. Her bracelets clacking as she spoke, a framed certificate from Stanford Business School's Executive Education Program equidistant between them on her desk. "Especially not the only woman on my team."

"Can I ask why I'm not meeting expectations?" Alice had asked meekly.

Tara nodded. "You might be surprised. As obviously you're technically proficient." Which Alice understood to be neutral to negative in Tara's universe, as Tara did not respect technical proficiency, given that she had none herself. She had come from human resources, was rotating through the company via its Female Leadership Program (internally referred to as FLIP, as in FLIP! the gender ratios). "Engineering acumen is valuable. But to thrive on my team, you must also demonstrate what's referred to as *soft skills.*"

"Is this because I didn't attend the last team builder?" Which had been the Monday after Jimmy left; Alice had spent it at home, watching *Grave of the Fireflies.*

"This isn't about one thing," Tara said crossly. "It's more a question of cultural fit." It's cultural: that explanation all liberal Americans were obligated to accept without question, which Alice had deployed for years to get out of eating turkey on Thanksgiving and wearing swimsuits in public.

Alice knew the next question expected from her. "How do I improve?"

"Be more present. Empower yourself!" Tara liked positivity, and words like *empowerment* and *aware*; when she spoke them it was as if she imagined herself onstage, in front of a participatory audience.

Now Alice was inches from Johan's Birkenstocks; from the way he was freely scratching at his upper thighs and even higher, he had definitely forgotten she was here. She desperately wished for some guidance on how to *empower* herself in this situation.

"Did you see this latest from Julia?" Sean called. He had a seamless voice, the kind used for voice-over work in commercials. "She's making the case that we should report to her, that FreeTalk should be in her organization. She claims it'll be more efficient. From an *engineering* perspective. I think half the time the bitch doesn't understand what she's talking about."

"Sean. You cannot say words like 'bitch' anymore."

"You know Pierre's going to cave. We can get out. Do a new thing. I hate this corporate shit."

"We don't fully vest for another year." Johan's voice was crisp and robotic. "It is not much to wait, in the scheme of life."

"Oh, *Jesus*." Sean's boots batted each other in agitation. "What do you need the stock for? I thought you were all about modest living. Driving around in your minivan."

"That doesn't mean I don't respect money," Johan said primly. "As I recall, you made the final decision to sell."

"I know, I know. I was greedy. But now I've got regrets, okay? So how do I fucking repent?"

From underneath the desk, Alice briefly pondered whether she was doing something in her own life equivalent to bitching about a nine-figure stock grant—if working at Tangerine automatically notched her on a sliding scale of privilege and offense. Each month, as penitence for her corporate-paid lunch and on-campus juice bar, she made an automatic donation to Médecins Sans Frontières; in exchange she was deluged by phone calls and mailers containing preprinted address labels that guilted her into donating even more.

There was a pause in the chatter, and she forced herself out from under the table. "Okay," she said in her most confident tone, the one she used to negotiate her Comcast bill. "Does one of you have a dog?"

It was obvious she'd been forgotten: Sean was studying her with a mix of calculation and concern, while twin daubs of rose had bloomed on Johan's cheeks. "A dog," Alice repeated loudly, which she thought might make her seem innocuous, a slow sort cheered by large animals.

"A dog?" Johan finally echoed, still struggling to make eye

contact. "Yes, I have a dog. A mountain dog." Then, as if this were an embarrassing revelation: "I bought him for my children."

"Do you bring it to work?"

"Sometimes."

"Well, it's been chewing on the cords. It ate the phone cord down to the wire, so that's why it doesn't work."

"Oh," Johan said. "Okaaaay."

"So I suggest that if you want to bring your dog in the future, you keep it away from electronics." Alice gestured with both hands toward the frayed wire, as if she were a game-show host. "I can order a tube, if you want. It'll go around the wires so that a dog can't chew through them."

"But then won't the dog just chew through the tube?" Johan asked.

"How big is it?"

"*He* is a good size," Johan said, holding a hand level with his waist. "In America, dogs are too small."

"Housing is expensive," Alice said. "Not everyone has the space."

The two men exchanged a look, as if silently conferring over the source of a foul odor.

"Okay," Alice said. She was already regretting her comment about housing; she knew from her limited interactions with the rich and powerful that it was nearly impossible to say anything without having it come out worse than in your head. "You can tell your admin if you change your mind about the tube. I'll have a new cord sent." She gathered her laptop, her pen, the notepad she had uselessly taken out and not opened.

"Jesus," she heard Sean exhale as she left. "*Wow.*"

"*Sean*," Johan warned, and then the door shut, and the rest of their conversation was lost.

ALICE RETURNED TO HER DESK. With the exception of executives, all Tangerine employees worked from "open seating": long tables split by acrylic dividers set five feet apart. To Alice's left sat Sam Diaz, who ran a side business designing skateboards and scheduled fake "working groups" at four P.M. to beat the traffic home to Scotts Valley. To her right was Larry Chan, whom she suspected of an extended campaign of shifting the divider between them millimeters at a time, until he'd acquired enough space for a third LCD. It was late afternoon, which meant the sun had mostly fled, along with the parents who announced they had school pickup or swim meets to attend. Work-life balance and all that, which coincidentally was one of Tara's favorite topics, except that Alice didn't have children or, if she was being honest, much of a life. Instead, in the evenings she would work until seven and then drive home. Greet her roommate, Cheri, if she was around, and then hasten to her room and eat dinner while watching TV on her computer. Alice liked this routine. It was what she'd done when she was in a relationship, except the TV watching had been in the living room, her and Jimmy on the couch with their laptops.

Her computer chimed. Before Alice had left for Sean and Johan's she'd begun a scan of a random block of servers. This was housekeeping each of Tara's employees was supposed to perform, but rarely actually did, just one cohort of an entire legion of neglected activities. When she'd first started in support Alice had been surprised by the laxity of Tangerine's protocols, how much of the back end was just a bunch of crappy code strung together. After her review with Tara, however, Alice had begun performing the scans with furious regularity.

She checked the report. There was high activity in one of the servers, the graph spiking in a jagged Matterhorn. Server 251, located in the Dublin data center. Alice closed her eyes for a few seconds, hoping that the issue, whatever it was, might resolve itself. Sometimes that happened—the systems were like humans, in that occasionally they behaved out of character and then stopped on their own.

Alice opened her eyes. Server 251's grid reflected back the same high activity.

"Hey," she said to Larry. Larry also reported to Tara, and he and Alice were supposedly on friendlier terms due to sheer proximity, though in reality Larry wasn't close to Alice or anyone else on the team. The infrequent times Alice saw him with others it was always the same Chinese and Pakistani engineers, huddled in gloomy circles in the break rooms; occasionally they power walked around campus, arms swinging in tandem. Once, when Larry was feeling chatty, he'd leaned over and informed Alice in Mandarin that he believed she and he to be a similar type of person, given that they were both Chinese and held degrees from prestigious universities that in the hands of an assertive white man would have already landed them in upper management. "What sort of person?" Alice had replied weakly, and Larry said: "Difficulty in social interactions." Looking proud, like a doctor nailing an esoteric diagnosis.

"Hey," Alice said again. She tapped him on the shoulder. "Hey. Hello?"

Larry, who she knew had been deliberately ignoring her, flinched at this unwelcome contact. "What?"

"Look." She nodded at her screen, which displayed the current loads of 251. The activity levels were even higher now, with steep spikes, as if the server were experiencing a heart attack.

"So?" Larry reached back and snatched a bag of dried plums off his desk. He chewed and then spat a seed into his hand, flinging it into her garbage.

Alice suppressed the urge to verify that the seed had actually made it into the bin. "There's a lot of data being transferred. Doesn't look automatic, either. Does that seem off to you?"

"I don't know. Maybe."

"Well, should I do something about it?"

"No."

"Why not?"

"Because who cares?" Larry turned back to his desk.

Alice scowled. Another infuriating Larry Chan response, though he was probably right that it wasn't a big deal—likely she was simply witnessing the birth or death of some project. The usual Tangerine life cycle, where executives were hired and products developed. Products were then canceled and executives fired, and everything saved, for potential lawsuits.

Yet something about 251 nagged at her. It was the amount of data, as well as its timing. It was close to six; there usually wasn't much activity at this hour.

Alice turned to Larry again. She could tell he knew she was looking at him; he kept his eyes locked on his screen as his fingers crawled for more plums. "Can we check who's doing the transfer?"

"Use the report," he said, not looking at her.

"Can you do it for me? I'm not supposed to." To run specific reports required a higher level of access than Alice had been approved for.

Larry rotated in his chair. "You cannot?"

"No. I'm not senior enough."

He paused, as if considering all the various scenarios that could have led Alice to such a fate that at the advanced age of thirty-five, she was still a junior analyst with no social plans to preclude her presence in the office on a Friday night, and lacking the seniority to run high-level reports. "I'm busy. This not emergency. You wait, I do on Monday."

"Uh-huh." Though Alice was now performing her own calculations. She knew that if she allowed an entire weekend to lapse, the question of the server would only hang over her, poking its way into her subconscious like a cracked sidewalk taunting an obsessive-compulsive. Plus Larry would then pretend he'd forgotten the conversation altogether, and refuse to run the reports anyway. "How about after you're done? I'll wait."

"Why you not going home?" he demanded. "Home to your husband."

"I'm not married."

"You live nearby?"

"Yes, in Cupertino." Where she'd spent the last two years. Her building was notable in that it resembled a low-budget Italian palace, with red-carpeted halls and rows of oversize columns. Rent at the Palermo was just beyond affordable given her salary—the apartment was two bedrooms, which was the biggest problem. At the time of lease she'd thought the space was fine, the money fine, everything fine—it was Jimmy's idea, Jimmy who would have the start-up, and what better place to work out of than one's own home? She'd thought he was going to propose, that's how stupid she was: that despite many hints to the contrary she'd allowed the allure of forever being done with dating to override her greater instincts, and if she was being honest she had loved him, had truly loved him, with all the knowing intent of someone entering a relationship in which they felt like crap a third of the time and still very much wanted the other two-thirds anyway.

Instead, during that dinner—the "serious conversation" dinner, which took place at Kenzo's, the Japanese curry restaurant that had become "their" place—he announced that he was moving to Seattle, where the business conditions were better suited for his start-up.

"I don't know if I could do a long-distance relationship," Alice said.

"That's not," Jimmy said, swooping in with his fork to claim the last potato croquette, "what I was going to suggest."

Among the many indignities of Bay Area life was that after the surprise departure of a live-in boyfriend, one immediate consideration—near simultaneous with the packing and negotiation of furniture—was how to sustain a newly doubled rent; Alice now lived with her cousin Cheri Lu, who possessed the dual irritations of being both younger than her and extremely beautiful. Cheri was half-white, which meant their relatives would spend hours at family gatherings debating the pros and cons of Caucasian blood: you often got a very pretty result this was true, but then you also had to deal with the unpredictable downsides, like a propensity to purchase houseboats and sink money into unreasonable projects like in-ground swimming pools.

Cheri mostly spent her weekends preparing for and then attending lavish parties in the Bay Area and beyond. She was invited on yacht holidays to Croatia, ski breaks in Deer Valley. She'd once been referenced by name in a *Vanity Fair* piece on start-up girlfriends, and was part of a loose pack of friends whose numbers swelled and shrank as its members were dropped or impregnated.

"I live with a roommate," Alice said to Larry, to preempt his next question. But Larry didn't say anything, just cocked his head with a look that edged close to sympathy, and then swung back to his desk.

"I help you in five minutes," he muttered.

"Thanks!" Alice manually flagged both the server and the data center, to mark them so she could easily return. She knew that when Larry said five minutes he meant closer to ten, and she went to the nearest break room. It was late, so there were only a few pieces of coconut cake left on a tray; she placed the largest piece in a compostable box, along with a banana and two clementines. Technically, taking food home was discouraged at Tangerine—it was not considered "Tangy" behavior, slotted in the same column as praising the *New York Times* or actually sleeping in the nap pods—but Alice often did so anyway, one of the many tactics she utilized to manage her budget post-Jimmy.

When she returned to her chair, Larry was gone.

The edge of the box bit against her palm. "Crap," she said in a low voice.

Alice looked at his desk. It was messy, as usual, with stacks of printouts and half-eaten bags of nuts. Paranoid that Tangerine might end its free food program at any moment, Larry hoarded dozens of snacks in the metal rolling cabinet by his chair. All day long Alice would hear the drawer's screech as Larry deposited another bag of sugared almonds or dried apricots and then reopened the drawer to nibble away at his treasure. He was stereotypically Chinese in that he was compelled to deposit more than he depleted; the stash had grown until he'd been forced to reorganize, repatriating a box of orange highlighters next to his headset.

Alice sat back at her desk. After a brief deliberation she opened the network tool, the one she was not senior enough to use; it was typical of Tangerine's messy back end that she was not actually blocked from running it. She checked other servers at random: on each was a flat wriggle, the usual hum of files being written and re-written. She returned to 251 and found it lit up, an outline of neon skyscrapers against black sky.

It was almost artistic, reminiscent of the test pattern Alice would run on the TV for background when there was nothing better available when she was a kid. Her family had moved from Beijing when she was five, squatting in Monterey Park with a cousin until her parents could afford to move north. Because June and Lincoln had always worked long hours—first at the battery plant in Milpitas, and then later at the cleaners—Alice spent most of her childhood with a series of inattentive Chinese nannies, who traded low wages for room and board. Alice mostly played by herself, drop-kicking a set of cloth sacks of rice into a basket, and rotating the same three videos her mother had purchased on clearance at Blockbuster (*The Sword and the Stone*, *Lady and the Tramp*, and *Congo*).

If Alice found a bug in the server, that would certainly be a case of *empowerment*; it might even elevate her to another one of Tara's favorites: *achievement*.

In the network tool, Alice clicked on 251, which brought up a set of diagnostics. She chose one that displayed all eighty-six de-vices currently connected to the server. Only one device was drawing an abnormal amount of data—nearly two hundred times more than the others. Alice selected it. She expected the report to return the device's information, in this format:

```
John Doe—Apple MacBook Air—User ID# 12345678
```

But instead, the screen read:

```
Unknown—Device Unknown—User 555
```

Alice frowned and sat back.

In all her time in support, Alice had never encountered an unknown device in the network. An unknown device was an employee phone or laptop procured from some outside source, and thus not outfitted with Tangerine's monitoring software. A big no-no.

She went to the employee database and entered User 555 in the ID field.

```
No results found.
```

What the hell? Alice considered the situation. She could go home, she knew. Change into sweats, eat coconut cake. It was already past seven; leaving after eight on a Friday would be an especially pitiful start to the weekend.

But if she did discover something—if, say, she managed to find a bug, or an outside attempt at infiltration . . .

Alice packed her box of food into her backpack. She reexamined Larry's desk and, on impulse, swiped an unopened bag of dark chocolate almonds. Craning her neck, swiveling revolutions in her chair, she stared at the ceiling until it blurred.

She sighed. The feeling was loneliness, she knew. Even though it was late, she wasn't ready to go home. Sometimes Alice thought the worst part about Jimmy being gone was that when he had been there, she hadn't been alone—by leaving, he had made her lonesome.

She returned to her screen. It was an open secret within support that out of both carelessness and convenience Tangerine automatically saved most employee passwords into a plain text file. Like at any hot Valley company, there was high turnover and occasionally the need to retrieve files from a poached engineer.

Alice found the file and ran a query for User 555.

Password: Kombinator637.

Next, Alice navigated to the main Tangerine site. Here was where two billion people went each day for their news and entertainment; in this place—this *community*, per Tangerine—its visitors read, watched, searched, and clicked. For each of Tangerine's thirty thousand employees, it was also where they logged in to access their work calendars and email, and post the entries tacitly obligatory in their job, to share how much they were loving this new feature! If User 555 was missing from the employee database, then likely their Tangerine account was also empty. There might be something though—a friend, a photo—to hint at their identity.

Alice logged in as User 555. Password: Kombinator637.

She blinked and looked at the screen.

IN 2011, CAMERON EKSTROM, THEN a senior vice president of business development at Tangerine, was going through a divorce. His wife, Elaine, said she'd had enough, that he neglected her, that he was obsessed with work, and also there were other things going on, things hinted to be far worse than what was stated in filings, but which Elaine would not say because of The Children, because after all Cameron was still The Father. And given this thoughtful treatment, and also because Elaine had quit a reasonably compensated, semi-fulfilling job at Stanford to raise The Children—thus enabling Cameron to jet around the world to close deals for Pierre Roy, who was then very happy with Cameron, so pleased in fact that after one particularly fruitful trip to South Korea, Pierre had shown his approval with an additional $6 million in stock—Elaine deserved half.

"But you signed a postnup," Cameron said. Seated across from his soon-to-be ex at Gary Danko, where they'd had their first date. Though he was currently enduring a life event often described in online articles as more stressful than death, Cameron appeared unaged. He ran a palm over his still full hair. "Please. Let's be reasonable."

"Fuck the postnup," said Elaine, who unfortunately did look older. She speared into her branzino and then pointed the fork at him, white flesh dangling from its tongs. "*Fuck* reason."

The Ekstrom split escalated. There was a screaming match outside their home in Old Palo Alto: three-year-old Luke rocking on the front lawn with hands over his ears, while seven-year-old Kara, in the den with chocolate ice cream, played clips from Cameron's stash of vintage Japanese slasher films; private investigators on both sides, the possible murder of Cameron's Siamese fighting fish. And then the blow: Cameron's claim of Elaine's cocaine abuse, and the assertion that she'd actually been high during multiple drop-offs at the Zany School, including the morning she'd chaperoned a Porsche SUV filled with preschoolers to the Bay Area Discovery Museum. He had proof, Cameron added. But really, was fighting over such unpleasantries what was best for The Children?

After Elaine lost in arbitration, she showed up drunk to her ex's thirty-ninth birthday dinner at the Village Pub in Woodside. And it was here, exhausted after a protracted negotiation with Unilever, that Cameron lost it.

"I've seen your messages!" he shouted, spittle landing on the head of Leena Das, a Tangerine director seated to his right. Meaning Elaine's messages in her Tangerine email, which was how she communicated with her dealer, who was also apparently her Pilates instructor, so, like, what the fuck? "I also know you meet your dealer at Mitchell Park," he added, his voice growing louder, a tenor Elaine's attorneys would later characterize as *menacing*. "And all those posts in your sad women's divorce support forum, so just watch who you're calling pathetic . . ."

It was a lucky guess, Cameron said at first. And then, no, a well-meaning friend, a secret sympathizer. Until finally he was forced to admit that he'd accessed Elaine's records through Tangerine: that he was one of thirty or so executives who possessed "God Mode," which allowed them to see everything—messages, browsing, posting—on the network. And that because of the company's proprietary "heart" button, which by now was ubiquitous across the web, God Mode could track nearly all online activity.

For which users, a reporter asked. As it was still those early days when employees could speak with journalists, when their phones weren't monitored for calls and messages to the *New York Times*, the *Wall Street Journal*.

"Uh. Well. For every user," Cameron said.

At first, Pierre was pissed by the uproar. He'd already fired Cameron, after all—had lopped off and delivered to the masses their obligatory rich white male head—so why were they still screaming? This is a *free service*, he kept repeating: one without which many of you would not have your friends, partners, professions, lives. And now you want to complain? Oh, but you don't want terrorists on the site, right, not to mention the pedophiles, the perverts messaging the children you so callously allow online unsupervised. Their privacy isn't a big deal, right? He stewed and raged and then allowed PR to draft him notes for a statement:

> We are sorry. We are a good company. We are a learning company. There will be no more God Mode again. Ever. For anyone.

Except that seven years later, Alice was looking at God Mode. Its screen flickered as if it were alive; she stared at it, unbelieving.

Alice looked around. The office was empty apart from a cleaner on the other side of the floor. She returned to the screen. The interface was clunky and old, with a single search bar.

She typed: Alice Lu.

```
Name: Alice Lu

Age: 35

Marital status: Single

Member of Tangerine: 1298 days

Frequently visited websites: Reddit,
Readingsex, The New York Times

Frequently visited profiles: Jimmy Chiang,
Cheri Lu

Last video seen: Homeland Quinn and Carrie Kiss

Last search query: Why do farts smell on period

Select here for earlier searches

Select here for activity path

Select here for communications (Tangerine
Messenger, Tangerine Mail)
```

Alice sucked in her breath.

At first, she thought Readingsex was the worst part: she'd been lazily using private browsing to access her erotica, believing it would shield her somehow, even though she knew better. She tried to extinguish her memories of all the stories she'd read on the site, many of which were about terrible things. But as she stared and the text unwound, Alice realized it was actually the rest that was most painful—until presented in aggregate, she hadn't realized how meager the components were that made up her daily life.

After Jimmy, Alice had managed to function during the weekdays, but once Saturday morning arrived the same leaden dread would descend that another forty-eight hours now existed before she had a purpose. She hadn't known you could mess up your life like that—that you could make one bad decision, like changing your job for a guy, and have everything go wrong. She didn't know you could make a choice that at the time seemed okay—dating Jimmy—and only at the end learn it was rotten, and waste ten years of your life.

But there was a ringing now, cutting through the low depression that had been her steadfast companion these last months. A sensation not new but nearly lost, an object she'd set down and only now recalled the location of.

Curiosity. Excitement.

Her mouse hovered over the search bar. She hesitated, and then typed: User 555. She chose the first available link, the one that showed the last ten searches.

The screen flashed, populated.

*Oh shit oh shit oh shit oh shit.*

# JANUARY 2019

# 4

# JULIA

Everyone always agreed that it was very sad that Julia's parents were dead. The first time she mentioned it to Charlie he almost teared up: *But that's awful / I just can't imagine / My mother is my rock*—the latter of which, come to think of it, Julia really should have paid more attention to, as a harbinger of the sort of in-laws she'd have to manage down the line. The two magazine profiles Julia had allowed in the last year—both flattering, both conducted after she'd hired Candace Perry to manage her personal media with an iron fist—had each contained a paragraph dedicated to the fact that she was an orphan, raised by loving relatives (ha!). When pressed about her parents Julia would turn down her lips and drop her head. It was so long ago, she would murmur. It was all so unclear.

Though Julia did remember her parents, recalled their details very well, actually. She'd been born in Makhalino, a rural town where the largest employer was a candy factory, which every afternoon belched odorless steam into a flat gray sky. Julia's mother, Nina, worked at the factory, and at one point, so had her father, Karl—though due to some earlier accident, of which no physical effect could be discerned, Karl no longer worked at the factory or at all. Instead, while Nina rose each morning and bicycled to her shift, Karl woke closer to noon and began his day with tea, performing a ritual where he poured boiling water into a mug containing the damp leaves from the evening before, viciously stabbing to release the last dregs of flavor. He then moved on to vodka. Karl's chief responsibilities were to purchase vegetables and dried fish and occasionally cigarettes from the mobile peddler; he frequently purchased poorly, diverting grocery funds into notebooks and cheap tool sets.

One winter morning when Julia was seven, Karl discovered he'd accidentally discarded his tea leaves the night before, and made an early transition to vodka. Once finished with lunch, he abruptly rose and, only slightly teetering, announced he would meet the peddler. After a hesitation Julia shouted after him that it was the wrong day; she risked this even though just weeks earlier, she had commented that his latest purchase, a black plastic digital wristwatch, was not worth the equivalent of a week's groceries, and had paid a steep price—she was tied with a rope to a pine tree and left outside, snow falling onto her hair and clothes, until Nina came home hours later. Seeing Julia, her mother had startled but continued to walk toward the house. And then, at the last minute, she returned to the tree and loosened the knots. "You have such little responsibility, all you have to do is not be stupid," Nina commented as she watched Julia frantically strip her sodden clothes. "You can't even manage that."

So when Karl ignored her shouting, Julia did not follow; she stood and watched as he wobbled and took a shortcut through a heavily wooded area and then passed out of sight. She was later told that somewhere along the way he fell through a patch of ice into a pond and froze to death.

Afterward, Nina quit her job at the factory and refused to leave the house. She was only twenty-six and already a widow; that she was not the youngest or even the second-youngest widow in their community brought little comfort. As for Julia, her mourning was uncertain, uneven, her memories of Karl scattershot, like the rays of a fast-moving prism: his red wool sweater and the way the house would smell of animal when it was washed once a season; Karl declaring himself brilliant as he played both sides of a chessboard.

Nina cried and cried when Karl died and couldn't understand why Julia didn't. "But he was your father," she bayed, as if Julia needed reminding. Julia didn't understand why her mother sobbed so much: Nina had barely spoken to Karl when he was alive, and it often seemed as if she genuinely hated him, and wasn't Julia the most reliable to remark on such a thing, given that she was in the house all day? Yet Nina only grew more hysterical. A week after the body was found, she came to Julia's bed and pulled down the blanket. She lay next to Julia, almost an idyllic parent-child portrait, until Nina's hand moved to Julia's elbow and pinched. When Julia didn't react, she did it again, harder, until Julia yelped. "So you *can* cry," Nina said. She sat and covered her mouth. "My God, what's wrong with you?" She began to weep and ran from the room. The next morning, when Julia reached for her mug, she saw her mother stare at the bruise on her lower arm, and went into her room and put on a sweater.

They moved out of the house and to Mytishchi, where they temporarily settled with Nina's parents. Julia's grandmother Zora was short and thickset and typical of the women of her generation in that her days consisted of brief breaks between cooking and cleaning—if not grocery shopping or preparing a meal, she could be found scrubbing the Khrushchyovka apartment with great fanaticism. Zora believed women should be quiet and docile, with herself as the sole exception, and had married smartly, choosing a taciturn security guard. When he returned home from work each night, Nina's father, Anatoly, liked to take his dinner on a tray and sit in front of the television, where he would remain for the rest of the evening.

Julia could feel her grandmother's eyes upon her as she moved through the apartment. "She's just like her father," Zora remark-ing, after Julia switched channels on the yellow Yunost. "Only cares about herself, no matter that this show is our favorite." Zora had not approved of Karl; he was the root cause, she believed, of all of Nina's miseries. And how unfortunate, Zora continued, that out of tragedy her daughter had finally been freed from her life's worst decision, only to be still so encumbered . . .

Besides Julia, Nina had other troubles. No money. No job. A husband or boyfriend could possibly help, but here, too, there was a worrisome lack of progress. Her mother's problems were no se-cret to Julia, and though she didn't understand how they might be resolved, she was old enough to intuit that her presence, or possibly lack thereof, played an integral role. At night, Julia heard the voices:

"You can start over. You are still young. There are places," Zora urging.

"I could never!" Nina cried. Over the years, Julia would recall this exact line. *I could never.* The fervor with which her mother had said and believed. How easily anyone could set aside their convic-tions, given the right levers.

It began with a trial. One little-known fact about the institutes was that some parents used them as emergency reprieve—maybe they worked long hours, or had to go away for school, or simply didn't have enough money. This was how Nina rationalized it, Julia knew. That the fact she could bear to leave her own child must mean it was a major emergency indeed.

"Mother's just taking you here so she can work," Nina said that first morning as they entered, even though she had no job, at least not yet. Announcing such in a loud voice, as if afraid Julia might con-tradict her otherwise. "Here are your food and clothes. I'll be back on Friday."

Still stunned, Julia didn't respond. The worker who greeted them motioned for Julia to follow her to a room filled with rows of elevated mattresses, and placed her bag on a table in between two cots next to the wall. "You'll share this space with Raisa," the woman said.

A girl slightly older than Julia lay prostrate on the other cot. At the sound of her name, she turned.

"Raisa," the woman said. "Be nice."

Raisa propped herself up on an elbow and smiled. Her eyelashes were so light as to be nearly transparent, and her teeth were yellow and uneven. She had an appealing expression, like that of a friendly dog. She pointed to Julia's bag.

"You want me to move it?" Julia sat on what she assumed to be her own bed, across from Raisa. Raisa shook her head and made a sweeping motion with her hand that Julia interpreted as a gesture of welcome.

This isn't so bad, Julia thought. At least here there wouldn't be the constant looming specter of her grandmother, lurching about with her ancient duster, glaring after Julia as if she were a fleck of shit that had escaped from the toilet. She could stay until Friday and then go home, and by then absence should have done its work in making Nina's heart grow fonder.

She opened her bag and removed one of Nina's lunches, braised cabbage with a slice of rye, wrapped in wax paper. On impulse, she asked, "You want?"

"Thank you very much." Raisa's voice was high and tinny. She rose and Julia saw she wore a blue smock down to her ankles. Then, at a speed that inspired some concern over the institute's meal portions, Raisa began to eat. As she watched, Julia became aware of a boy observing them from farther down the wall. Go ahead and stare, she thought. You're not getting any. She had only one lunch per day, and already she'd given today's to Raisa, though she wasn't hungry anyway, out of nerves.

Raisa ate neatly and completely, in a manner of which Julia's grandmother would have approved, and brushed off the crumbs and then pressed the wax paper into a square. She smiled, and Julia prepared to receive some thanks or a compliment—Nina was no chef, but Julia supposed compared to a government institution's her mother's food might seem gourmet—when Raisa widened her mouth to a round O. Still keeping eye contact, she jammed a finger down her throat. As she retched, the regurgitated bread and cabbage spilled onto her smock and bed. She then began to eat again.

"She's doing it to taste the sweetness," the boy commented. Julia had earlier vowed to ignore him, to establish her own social superiority, but given current events she hastily abandoned this stance. Up close she could see he used to have a cleft lip: the bottom half of his nose was flattened, as if the air had been let out of his nostrils. Seeing her look, he blushed and repeated himself. "She does it sometimes. She likes to eat candy, but we never have it. So she does that instead. I'm Misha."

"Julia." She was fascinated by his lip and didn't bother to hide her staring. It was as if by entering the institute she had automatically shed some outer layer of civility. "Is this where we sleep?" The thought was dawning that the bed by Raisa had been available for a reason.

"Yes. And I won't switch with you. Besides, you look big," he added, eyeing her appraisingly. "You can manage Raisa."

Julia knew she should ask, but at the moment couldn't bear hearing what size had to do with her situation. "I don't care," she said airily. "I'm used to it."

"She also does it with poop," Misha offered.

"She *eats* it?"

"No. She shits and then wipes. Mostly on the walls, though she will also do it on beds. Sometimes other people, if she can catch them. We have not been able to predict when or why. Sometimes she is having a good day, and then still does it."

"I don't believe you."

Misha shrugged. "Believe what you want."

On Wednesday, Julia prepared herself for the possibility that

Nina might not return. It would be fine, she thought. Wasn't she adaptable? And it wasn't as if her life was so great: her father dead, her mother sobbing in bed each night, tearing out her own hair in clumps. By Friday, Julia was glancing at the clock every few minutes, her nails bitten to the pink, her stomach roiling each time there was a noise at the front entrance.

Nina came back.

At home, Julia concentrated on being personable. She said *thank you* when Zora announced dinner, and preemptively set the table; she dusted the apartment as ostentatiously as she dared, with a wad of napkins she'd fashioned into a blunt fan. The night of her return she went to the television hutch, where, after some effort, she pulled out a cheap plastic chess set and arranged the board, all the pieces in their starting position, by her mother's cot. She hoped the sight might inspire some nostalgia for the old house in Makhalino, Nina's life with Karl, and by extension, Julia. But her mother passed the set without comment. And the same problems remained.

No job. No money. No man.

On Monday, Nina returned her to the institute. This time Julia didn't offer Raisa any of her food. During a lull in activity, she snuck to the bathroom, where she'd stowed her bag behind the metal trash bin. It was only when she was in a stall with the door locked that she opened the sack and counted the wrapped meals inside.

Last week, there had been five. Now Julia counted three.

On Tuesday, Julia went to the worker Sophia, the one who wore a strong vanilla perfume, whom Julia believed to be in charge. She asked if Sophia might help her call Nina.

"What for?" Sophia asked. Pretty Sophia, with her singsong voice and clear complexion and plaited yellow hair. Her employment at the institute—where the rest of the helpers notched between ancient and miserable—was the subject of much debate among the children, the theories ranging from altruism to murder.

"I want to ask what time she plans to arrive. On Friday."

"Huh," said Sophia as she used a knife to slice open a box containing donations from overseas. "She didn't say anything when she brought you," she added as she unearthed a set of soft baby slippers, light beige with a delicate lace trim. "Your mother is busy, you know? Best not to bother her."

Julia was distracted by the slippers, which were new with tags attached, in contrast to the rest of the clothes, which were mostly faded and featured the logos of out-of-date sporting competitions. Who had donated the slippers? What kind of life did some little girl have, that she could just give up such shoes? Julia was plotting how she might distract Sophia so she could stow them in her shirt when Sophia dropped them into a bag to be resold and they disappeared.

Julia blinked. "If I don't bother my mother, you think she can find a job?"

Sophia ceased her sorting. "She is not working?" she asked, still not looking at Julia.

"No."

"Does she have a man?"

"No. Well, perhaps now. Maybe a job, too."

"Huh," Sophia said again. Another pause, and she returned to her excavation. "Well, it is always best to think positively. Someone once told me our country's a mess because we are negative thinkers. So now I always try to believe good things will happen."

Over the following days, Julia tried to live by this counsel. On Wednesday, ignoring her stomach's moans, she forced herself to offer her last piece of rye to Misha, who had shown her the hiding place in the bathroom. To make a true show to the universe that she believed she would soon return home, where there was always at least bread on the table.

On Thursday, Julia voluntarily helped clean Raisa's latest subversion, fist-sized balls Raisa had crafted out of her own corn-tinged shit, which she had then smashed on half of the blankets in the sleeping room. Standing at the sink next to Sophia, who'd kindly procured for her a pair of gloves, Julia scrubbed and scrubbed and then hung the blankets to dry. As the hours passed, the dead-fishy odor was slowly swallowed by the industrial scent of patchouli; the sun through the windows was cozy, and a victorious feeling began to grow, buttressed from the approval she sensed from Sophia. She had done it, Julia thought. She had willed a positive event into existence.

And then Friday came, and Nina didn't come back.

JULIA WAS IN SHOCK, THE first few weeks. She lay fetal, drifting through her memories, where her grandmother's apartment now hovered as an oasis. Even the butt-freezing toilet, located in an unheated stall outside the front door, elicited tears; the thought of Nina's stew—a thin combination of carrots, duck, celery, and old bread of which Julia was never awarded any of the meat—brought on a full crying jag. Raisa, sensing the extension in Julia's residency, tried to strangle her the following Saturday—but finally let go when Julia kicked, hard, in between her legs.

I don't belong here, Julia thought. I have to get out.

There were only a few routes she knew of. Adoption, but from what she'd heard that was rare; you could pray and pray to land a rich Western couple, but chances were you'd get a local farming family instead, the sort desirous of free labor and repressed enough that the father crept into your room at night. Supposedly the state occasionally took some children, but that was even rarer—and Julia would rather bet on a pair of local bumpkins than some government agency.

Even though it meant staying at the institute, it was the last option, Julia would come to believe, that offered the best odds for survival: to be identified as an "exception," the state's designation for those wards who possessed some combination of intelligence or athleticism or looks. *Exceptions* had access to better food and a doctor's visit each year; were officially entitled to a primary and secondary education, academic materials and textbooks.

The problem: How to be selected? She'd first learned of the classification via Misha, who, if not exactly her friend by now, was at least whatever it was that passed for acquaintances among children. "You could try and convince the directors you are qualified," he said, with the easy confidence of a casino boss wishing good luck to a bettor.

In the end, it was the phone that saved her.

The institute had one telephone, a beige handset in the administrative office. As was the rule with all electronics, the phone was off-limits, though it was little policed, because who were the children going to call? But still Julia found herself drawn to the machine, its thin yet unassailable connection to the outside world. When the weather was bad or Misha inexplicably unhappy or she herself depressed, Julia liked to linger near the office and eavesdrop. I am a spy, she told herself. I am gathering secrets.

One morning, Julia watched as Maria, the beak-nosed matriarch whom by now she'd identified as the true director of the institute, attempted to call her mother. Maria spent little time with her charges, instead marching about the building, engaged in mysterious tasks—though she did pass through, greeting each child by name, when there were visiting church groups or clusters of Americans. Julia did not consider Maria a hypocrite because she did not pretend to be soft, merely efficient.

Maria dialed and after a few seconds glared at the keypad in frustration. She dialed again and pressed the phone to her ear and swore.

Julia decided to chance it. "It's 459–8555," she called out. "Not 459–8755."

Maria swiveled her head like an owl tracking prey. "What?"

"You have the fifth digit wrong."

"Do you dare spy on me?"

Maria's eyes were narrow and her nostrils were beginning to flare; Julia was frightened but knew she'd gone too far not to continue. "No. I'm just telling you."

"How did you know the number I wanted?"

"You always call your mother at this time. You greet her, and ask about her health and what she has eaten so far."

"And how did you know about the wrong digits?"

"You called yesterday. I could tell what the numbers were by where you placed your hand." And then Julia pressed her own palm against her forehead, as if working to suppress some constantly surging genius. Julia had seen Maria write the number on a floral notepad months earlier, and had promptly stolen the top pages, which she stored along with a handful of millefiori glass beads in the pencil box in which she kept her most treasured possessions. "I've always been good at recalling numbers, long strings of them." Also a lie, or at least, untested.

Maria set down the phone. She left the room and for a moment Julia wondered if she might return with the wooden back scratcher used to mete out beatings. But instead she held a folder. "You are not educated," Maria said, reading from it, and Julia knew this must be her file.

"Yes I am. I went to school." She did not mention it had been for two hours a week, and run by a demented man-child whose parents had bribed local officials for the position. "I can write, too."

"Any other skills?" Maria looked up. "Do not lie."

Julia had just been debating which special talent to fabricate. Quick, she thought. *Quick!* Yes, Maria was authoritative and frightening, but she also could not recall a basic phone number; would she test Julia? Or accept her statement as fact, because at a base level most humans were uncaring and lazy . . .

"I'm excellent at chess."

The director returned to the folder. "Interesting," she murmured, a finger to her lips. "A successful application could bring an extra two thousand a month . . . and the father's background could easily be revised . . ."

And so Julia's first great piece of luck: she won an *exception* designation. It was not the last time she would use this trick of rote memorization to affect some loftier genius—years later she would wonder how many of the "brilliant" executives she met were truly so, versus simply hardworking. When after graduation Leo asked her to meet, she had thought here was her second good fortune; she'd vowed then she would do whatever he wanted, that she'd work tirelessly to exceed whatever it was he asked. Julia knew it was important to be useful. To always be useful.

"WE WANT TO ATTACK TANGERINE," said Leo.

"What?" Julia said, even though she'd heard clearly. She was in her office after a long afternoon with advertisers—had loosened her pump off her right foot and was massaging her heel when Leo called.

"The SPB is in the early stages of planning an intrusion," Leo repeated. "Are you certain you're clear?"

He meant was she private, unmonitored. "Yes." In an ironic turn, her Tangerine office was often the safest place to speak, as it was scanned for bugs twice a week by internal security.

"It should be simple," Leo went on. As usual with their Free-Talk calls, his voice was breezy, almost loud, and Julia pressed the phone against her ear. "We've identified a vulnerability in the back end of your email servers. We need you to download the source code so we can complete the intrusion."

A roiling heat rose and burred itself in her side. The Tangerine email service, unimaginatively called Tangerine Mail, was a product Julia had personally redesigned and grown to a billion users. "Why?"

"Why not? We'd be able to access the emails of your users en masse. Why wouldn't we take advantage?"

"Haven't I done enough?" Julia demanded, with the feeling that had been creeping in as of late, that she was underappreciated. That she'd finally managed the FreeTalk merge had been received with sparse congratulatory words, whereas she thought forcing a $9 billion start-up to cede user data was considerably more impressive than, say, some slut blackmailing a doddering old technician for the schematics of a power plant. And that wasn't even taking into account the recent headache with Sean Dara, who had flamboyantly quit last week, leaving behind $40 million in stock; afterward publishing a blog post in which he railed against Tangerine, making dark accusations about the company's plans to mine private messages for data (true). Julia wasn't so upset about his call to arms to delete Tangerine—people were always trying to marshal up for this, with negligible results. What Julia really resented was that Sean had personally named *her* in the post, calling her a liar and deceitful, both characteristics she worked hard to avoid association with, as they were suicide for any powerful woman in America.

Over the phone there was the rustling of paper. "Please respond this week with an estimate," Leo said primly. "As to when you can procure the code."

"I'll be blamed when the attack is discovered," she warned. "The product is associated with me."

"Why does it have to be discovered at all?"

"Because I can't cover our entire security organization. We have teams of engineers scanning the system's integrity. I'll be lucky to survive a week before the attack's discovered. And then the other executives will call for my head."

"Ah." Leo sounded unconcerned.

She pressed the nib of her pen against her notebook. "So I'm just to be *sacrificed*?"

"You will survive. It is expected that occasionally you may take hits to your persona."

Julia didn't like this at all. For weeks she'd been transferring server data—the most recent being all searches originating from Sydney during a twelve-hour period. She followed the standard process each time, signing in with her User 555 credentials, messaging a FreeTalk account she knew only as HELPER once the transfer was complete. Afterward driving to the designated drop point, this last instance a park bathroom in Woodside, where she left the USB drive in a zipped plastic bag in the trash.

"You can't keep pushing," she warned. "You've already asked for dozens of names, and then the server downloads, and now this. If you keep escalating, I could be caught. Do you understand the potential damage if the public learns Tangerine Mail was compromised? That their affairs, emails to friends, applications for jobs were exposed? It would endanger my position. It would risk my work!"

"What did you say your work was?" Leo asked.

She threw her pen against the wall.

After they hung up, Julia sat in her office, rage ballooning. She checked her screen: sixty-five new messages in the last half hour, all on Tangerine Mail. Her success with relaunching the product was why she'd finally been named COO; its $10 billion in annual revenue served as the moat her competition found impossible to penetrate, capitalist politics a bureaucratic dinosaur like Leo couldn't possibly understand.

She went to the employee database. After a second she found the phone number of Jon Fall, her VP of engineering. In person he was quiet—often during her staff meetings he would not speak at all, except to answer a direct question.

Jon was there in minutes. Julia was massaging her foot again when he arrived; something else she hated, how the executive offices had glass walls, a dopey literal nod to "transparency." He knocked and she motioned for him to enter. Average height, green eyes. Younger than her by a few years. Not gorgeous but not unattractive, the sort of man a clever plain girl would work hard to lock down.

"There's going to be an attack on our network," she said. Jon wasn't the sort for small talk. "Targeting Tangerine Mail."

He looked thoughtful. "A test?"

"No. A real attempt. We were informed by some government sources." Not technically a lie.

"When?"

"I'm not certain. But they've identified a zero-day exploit in our code. Can you find it?"

As she waited, Julia yanked at the hem of her dress. Jon was taking too long, to the point where her impatience was near overflow—

"Yes," Jon said. "I'm sure. But I'll need some time."

She relaxed. "I'll also want to shore up our defenses. Install some employee safeguards, especially for those with developer access. All of their emails, browsing, needs to be vetted."

"Do we publicize? Or do it quietly?"

"No." This was important. "Keep it quiet. Do it internally, with a small team."

"Will do."

"Very good," she said. Impressed by his confidence, pleased because she knew it came from ability and not showmanship. He was actually handsome, she thought. Aquiline nose, full lips, hair not unlike Charlie's, down to a stray kiss curl on the left side. "Keep me informed. Only in person, not email." Jon nodded.

There was a chance Leo would find out, Julia knew. He might discover she'd defied him, and then what would he do? But she couldn't continue to simply take his orders; not when the intent was to cripple something she'd built. How many hours of her life had been spent testing, tweaking Tangerine Mail? She remembered the party they'd thrown when the product finally hit its first one hundred million users—and then a billion, and by the end of the year it was on track to hit two billion. Julia was expecting another party for that milestone: a bigger one, and a nice stock award, too.

After Jon left, she doodled a series of circles into her notebook. She thought again of his face, how much she liked it. Usually when Julia was drawn to a man she could easily shake off the attraction; it was like porn in that when it disappeared from your screen, the people ceased to exist. Yet there was something about Jon that tugged. It was the way he held himself, how his body had an assurance of gentleness.

He reminded her of Misha.

Toward the end Misha had been her best friend at the institute, not that she'd ever told him. Misha, who'd somehow learned that most who aged out of the institute ended up homeless, was obsessed with housekeeping and order. "You have to have discipline," he'd lectured once, after they'd found a stash of chocolate bars at the bottom of a donation bin, both of them going silent at the sight of the bulk ten-pack like Galahad before the Holy Grail. They'd hid their candy in the usual place in the bathroom, and while Julia had gobbled hers within a week, Misha made his last, maintaining a careful inventory down to the fraction of the bars remaining. "You have to learn how to preserve what you have, work hard. Like migrants, do you understand how hard they work?" And then, with a sigh, passing her one of his bars of milk chocolate.

Julia knew she could hire an investigator to find Misha, or some of his history, but she never had. Sometimes she thought if she knew too much of him, her heart would break.

Her stomach hurt. When she descended into these spirals her stress spiked; she rocked in her chair and concentrated on breathing. Placed her open hand on the throbbing of her stomach, as she used to when Raisa kicked her, to manage the pain.

She spread her fingers and summoned their heat. Pressed her hand in harder.

The baby kicked back.

# 5

# ALICE

Here was the rule at Tangerine: You don't mess with the individual.

Especially the important individual.

Individuals with influence, individuals with money, or God forbid, individuals with that ultimate power, both online and in physical life: celebrity.

Better to expose the Social Security numbers of 300 million than snoop through the messages of a model/photographer/influencer; better to store a billion passwords in plain text than "mistakenly" ban the account of a white supremacist. Better not to be Cameron Ekstrom. And thus when the corporate voice of Tangerine spoke, there was an emphasis on the individual—we care about our *users*, Pierre saying, that being *you*—we would never violate our *users'* rights, because we love you. Occasionally, yes, mistakes were made, terabytes of data exposed—but it wasn't personal, it wasn't that Tangerine was after you as a person, and probably no one would see or care anyway, which was why you never bothered to change your password or check your credit report. Tangerine would never deliberately share your secrets, and truly, you understood this, you knew it deep in your soul, which was why you spent so much time with it each day.

And yet, these had been the last searches by User 555 on God Mode:

- The current U.S. secretary of defense
- A senator from Delaware, the ranking member of the Senate Intelligence Committee
- The chairman of the Chemistry Department at Caltech
- The wife of the CEO of Lockheed Martin
- Two members of the Apple board of directors
- A Stanford professor
- A former undersecretary in the Obama administration

As well as a few other names Alice hadn't recognized. She could have looked them up, but by then was freaked out; she no longer wished to learn the identity of User 555, and was instead paranoid that User 555 might somehow learn about her. Back home, opening her laptop halfway, she had pressed the power key until the screen went black. And had not logged in to God Mode again.

It wasn't as if she weren't curious, Alice thought as she drove—it was Sunday morning, the only time she took the 101, because traffic was light—and in the past weeks she had indeed found herself tempted. When her mother phoned, announcing yet another twenty-something cousin's engagement, the nuptials planned for the Ritz-Carlton in Half Moon Bay; her last meeting with Tara, in which Alice's lack of "human" initiative had once again been reviewed. If she were confident of safe access to God Mode, Alice might have already examined the inner lives of Tara Lopez and Ginny Leo, Stanford graduate and bride-to-be; it was so much easier not to be jealous or angry when you knew what people wrote and searched.

She exited the freeway. Her parents still lived in the same townhome in which she'd grown up, and each of the curves, stoplights, and Mexican and Indian grocers along the way was as familiar as water. She parked at the curb and entered the house to find her father watching the news. Lincoln was usually watching TV; it was like white noise, but for his waking hours.

"Where's Mom?" Alice asked. As with the rest of the house, the living room was barely altered from her childhood. The same brown thatched couch and chair, the black plastic cat clock on the wall, where the eyes rolled and the curved tail swung every hour.

"Outside," Lincoln answered. He smiled at her and then made a pushing motion—*You're in front of the TV.*

Alice went out back, to the small patch of green buttressed on the other end by their carport. The garden was a rainbow: red tomatoes, a fig tree, Chinese pumpkin plants, multiple flowers that June nurtured but simultaneously considered an indulgence, because too many attracted wasps and bees.

"I thought after you retired, you guys would leave the house more," Alice said, pausing to stroke the figs. She was interested in the fruit but kept quiet, because she knew if she said anything June would immediately begin to harvest, shoving upon her an entire box.

"We were never *in* the house before," June said, not bothering to turn. She carefully placed a net over the kumquat tree, a low-grade weapon in her ongoing war against squirrels and birds. "Now we don't work, we stay in." She stood and shook the dirt from her hands. "Besides, we go out now, don't we?"

They went to Alice's Honda, each carrying a large cooler. June had started selling her homemade noodles at the Mountain View Farmers' Market ostensibly to make money, but after everything her mother spent on ingredients and the modest fee for the market, Alice wondered if she took any profit at all. June made liang pi, a cold flat noodle with cucumbers, minced garlic, chili oil, and vinegar. The dish was a popular street food in China, and Alice still had memories of eating it at her grandmother's, the old woman

negotiating a refill just as soon as Alice choked down another bite
of stewed eggplant. June made the noodles using the traditional,
more meticulous method, kneading flour and water and then rins-
ing the dough in a bowl of water until the water was heavy with
starch. She then removed the dough and let the water sit until the
next morning, when she settled the remaining paste into pans. June
charged five dollars per serving, which Alice suspected brought
her near break-even, though Alice knew June's reluctance to price
higher wasn't born from some greater altruism but rather a conviction that big margins were for those who spoke good English—
those Americans with smooth words and stylish packaging.

They weren't officially allowed to start selling until ten A.M.,
so after they unpacked, June went to a produce stall while Alice
dragged two canvas folding chairs from the trunk. She heard June
cackling as she inspected a pod of French peas; she already knew
her mother wouldn't buy any, as she was suspicious of vegetables
that didn't need to be cooked. Plus they had an Ethiopian neighbor, Zeni, with whom June traded alteration services for vegetables
from her garden.

Alice sank into the chair. It was unsupportive but wholly plea-
surable, like a waterbed at a sleepover. She pitched back and shut
her eyes. Last night Cheri had returned home at three A.M. after
some undoubtedly lavish party. She'd stumbled about the kitchen,
from which there emerged the sound of a pan being yanked from
other pans, eggs cracking, the kettle hissing—all indicators she was
making ramen, likely using one of the Neoguris Alice purchased
from the Korean market. Awakened by the noise, Alice had rolled
onto her side, pressing her ear to the bed. Eventually she'd been
forced to paw through her dresser for her silicone earplugs, which
she ripped in half to lengthen the life of the pack ($8 at CVS). In
the morning she found a pot in the sink, red soup scum on its sides;
the door to Jimmy's former office closed, Cheri inside snoring del-
icately.

Alice was dreaming now. She was at a party. A civilized one: low music, cheese on platters. A man took the empty seat next to her. He was Chinese and earnest and clear-skinned.

"I'm sorry," he said. "I'm embarrassed. I think I love you."

There was noise coming from the outside. She tried to block it out, hang on to the dregs. This could be her real life, she thought, if she could just stay in the mist, it was all so *nice*—

"Hello, hello!" Her mother stood before her. "What are you doing? You sleeping?"

As Alice struggled to rise, she could see June's expression downgrade from curiosity to a mild disapproval. "I'm only resting." She swatted away a fly. "Has it started?"

"No. It is nine fifty." June's hair fell evenly over both sides of her face like the curtain on a short window. It was newly cut, and lay in blunt layers at the neck. Zeni's work, Alice suspected.

Alice clasped her hands behind her head. "If we have ten more minutes, I'm going to sleep."

June eyed her. "You are not getting enough rest. Why do you come? I don't need you."

"I came to help."

"But you look like a slug. If you want to nap, maybe you can move by the sidewalk. In the shade, so you do not get hot. Really, I do not need help. How long did I manage the cleaners? Almost twenty years!"

Alice stood with a groan. It hurt her feelings that June said she didn't need her, though she suspected it might be true. Sometimes she thought her presence in the booth actually hindered June's success, as shoppers crowded around and made mention of China, Japan, the Orient, do you know Jocelyn Liu, another Chinese lady who makes the most darling potstickers? Do *you* make potstickers? Are these organic? After they left, Alice often had the feeling she hadn't been enough—nice enough, thankful enough—reassuring such shoppers that they were multicultural, that they were in fact doing a very good thing by purchasing the noodles her mother spent days assembling and charged five dollars for.

"I'm your only child. I thought you'd want to spend time to-gether."

June regarded her flatly. "What do you think of the noodles today. Good?"

"Yes. Very good."

June sniffed the air. "There's something strange about the tex-ture. Maybe I didn't wait long enough for it to settle. Your father, you think he is so quiet, but when it is him and I alone, he is always talking, distracting. Talk, talk, talk."

"You can tell him to call me at work."

"No! Tangerine is not paying you to do this! You must concen-trate!"

"Okay," Alice said quickly, though June still looked agitated. Alice wondered if she still allowed her mother any form of face—if Tangerine was her last bastion of accomplishment, given that for all of June and Lincoln's hard work Alice was thirty-five, not thin, and still single. The last point being one in which she'd unfortunately misled them both, an omission that began from being too trauma-tized to discuss the breakup, but which over the following months had assumed a life of its own, one where she began to conjure all sorts of half-truths and full-out lies about her and Jimmy, includ-ing the very real event of his moving to Seattle, but also turning their relationship into a long-distance arrangement, from which she hoped to eventually execute some sort of soft landing. Only to be discovered when Jimmy abruptly changed his relationship status on Tangerine to *Single*, provoking the curiosity of one Cindy Leo, June's older sister, who managed an active Tangerine presence for her real estate business in Alhambra.

She had to keep her job at Tangerine, Alice thought. She needed to stay the hell away from User 555 and God Mode.

A bell clanged; the market had begun. Alice stood and helped

June arrange noodles into the plastic sauce cups they used for samples.

A mother and her toddler approached. "Are these spicy?" the woman asked. Her son wore a hat with a propeller on it, like Dennis the Menace.

"A little bit," Alice said. "I don't know if it's best for kids." Although she had eaten far spicier in her grandmother's kitchen.

"I want it!" the boy shouted.

"No, no," the mother said, directing a glare at Alice, as if she were to blame for both selling a spicy food and then declaring it to be so in front of children. "They are spicy. You don't *like* spice. Hot. Hot. HOT!"

"But I *want* the noodles."

"Now, Oliver," the woman said, kneeling. "What did we say about being polite?"

"Give me the food!"

"Fine." The woman grabbed a handful of samples. "I'll rinse these at the fountain." June smiled at them as they left, as if she thought they might return.

Alice watched the crowd. The market's traffic was unpredictable in that sometimes the walkways were packed, strollers wielded like battering rams; other times it was calm, like now. She would sometimes encounter former classmates from Magdalena High, now married with kids, living in their parents' old houses or the houses their parents had helped purchase for them. They rarely recognized her, and when they did, were overly cordial.

Alice was about to sneak away for some empanadas when a couple strolled near. They were sampling the cherry tomatoes from the booth across the walkway, but the woman had glanced over, and Alice recognized the trapped interest exhibited by certain shoppers when they accidentally locked eyes with her or June. They didn't want to visit but, worried about being perceived as racist, usually did; they rarely bought noodles, though the samples were always proclaimed delicious. The woman, who wore a light yellow sundress and golden sandals, held hands with a man who still faced the produce. He wore a plaid shirt and his brown hair was long and curling against his neck. Alice's breath caught and she thought that it couldn't be him, likely it was just someone similar. It was another person. A stranger. It wasn't.

He turned, and Alice knew that it was.

IT HAD HAPPENED WHEN SHE was eight. Their last Cantonese nanny had just abruptly departed; unable to secure alternate after-school care, June compromised by leaving the cleaners each afternoon to retrieve Alice from Oak Elementary, parking the old Chrysler along the curb. Afterward they returned to the cleaners, where Alice was installed inside in the back. She was never allowed near the equipment, and had been given strict instructions not to touch anything: the clothes, the machines, and especially the solvents. "Your hands will fall off" was June's warning, and while this was before June and Lincoln's own cancer diagnoses—and though at the age of eight Alice was already beginning to suspect that her parents lied, that in fact they lied *often*—the threat was still menacing. To supplement Alice's homework, June took her to the library on weekends, where they checked out stacks of books. These were carefully laid on top of a blanket in the back room of the cleaners, next to a table where Alice ate.

One afternoon, when they arrived at the store, June presented to Alice a puzzle still in shrink wrap.

"One thousand pieces?" Alice asked in alarm.

"Yes, you can do it for a long time." When Alice got new clothes, they were always at least a size or two larger.

Alice inspected the box, slowly reading. "World War Two planes?"

"It was on the sale table," June said. "Barnes & Noble."

Alice was piecing together the left wing of the Messerschmitt when the door chimed. She looked at the clock, which read 6:30 P.M., exactly closing. Most of the other cleaners in the area shut at 6:00 P.M.: June and Lincoln stayed open the extra half hour for the office crowd.

"Drop off," Alice heard June confirm, in her accented English. She could tell her mother wanted a quick transaction; no query about alterations or shoe shine.

"Open the register." The voice was young and male.

"What?" June replied. Though Alice sensed danger, at this point her alarm was mild: the faint scream of a fire engine as it sped down a faraway road. Her chief concern was that they'd be late returning home, which might result in her bath being taken away. Alice liked baths. She had a trick of running a tiny stream of hot water so the temperature remained constant; it was just quiet enough that her parents couldn't hear and scold her for wasting water.

"Don't you fucking understand English? Open the register and hand over the cash."

And then another voice: "Lie on the ground."

For some reason, it was the second voice that carried with it an escalation of danger. Alice clutched the puzzle piece in her hand; suddenly she had trouble breathing.

She recognized the sound of the register opening. Then the murmuring of voices: "That's all? Forty?"

"My husband," June replied nervously. "My husband, he take the rest."

This was true. Throughout the day June and Lincoln stowed cash in a green pleather envelope kept hidden in the back behind the microwave. After June returned from school with Alice, Lincoln would depart for the bank with the envelope, leaving behind only small bills for making change.

"Are you . . ." June said, cutting through the quiet, "are you going to sexually harass me?"

Later, when she was older and understood its meaning, this

was always the memory Alice would work to suppress most: her mother's thick accent, how it was obvious June had not known what harassment meant but rather was repeating a known action, like dialing 911. Each week when they visited the library her mother would borrow movies—it was only after college that Alice began to question June's selections, which often had a thrilling, sexual theme. What would it be like, Alice thought, if you were a woman in a foreign country, and while the Chinese video rental shop on Union Street did have a section cordoned off, only men were ever seen browsing its shelves, their faces hidden behind its curtain? So instead June resorted to the library and its R-rated titles. The latest pick, one where a boss stalked his direct report, had been watched by the whole family, Alice on the carpet, sorting beads. She'd been sent to bed right as the boss began to menace his second target: "He's sexually harassing me," the girl complained to her roommate. Despite her fright there was a heavy undertone of musk: the dim lighting, the sinister yet sensual score, the way the camera lingered on the girl's chest, heaving in a strapless gingham dress.

But in this moment Alice knew her mother didn't understand the meaning of the words; she instinctively grasped that they were uttered from terror, a blunder constructed from fright.

"Sexually harass—what the fuck? Like I'd enjoy that," one said, and they both laughed.

"I will give you my bracelet—" June then tried, referring to her jade bangle, which she always wore. Alice loved the bangle, which was bright green and whorled with flecks of cream. She was already mourning its loss when suddenly there came a cry, a deep, guttural noise of pain. Alice strained, as if the noise might repeat itself—she thought it'd been female, but she could not recall ever hearing such a sound from June.

"Shit," said the first voice, now higher. "Why'd you do that?"

"I don't know. I hate how they talk. Fucking gooks."

"She's not moving."

"It wasn't that bad. She's faking, right? Whatever, fuck it, let's go."

After they left, the store was silent. Alice forced herself to count to twenty. She recalled a character from one of her books, a girl detective, having done the same. "Mama?" she then called. She felt a dampness on her pants and thought perhaps she'd been murdered. But then she touched the spot and knew she had wet herself; she did not feel shame but rather only fear that June would be disappointed, and then she remembered June.

When she ran out, her mother was on the floor. Her mouth and the side of her face were a smear of blood.

Alice thought she was dead. Oddly, she did not scream or cry but instead moved to action, as June had always taught. She began to drag the heavy stool from the back, to reach the telephone on the high counter.

"Don't. Go find a big person." June's eyes were open.

"What happened?" Alice was crying now.

"Go. Go ask for help."

Alice ran next door, to the convenience mart. The shop, not a chain but an individual bodega, had been there as long as the cleaners. June and Lincoln rarely visited, because the few American staples they regularly purchased—milk, eggs, orange juice—were priced lower in the discount supermarket, and this was not something in their household budget, to purchase for "convenience." The store was owned and operated by a man named Aman. Aman was skinny and tall, and moved as if constructed from heavy material; in the mornings he and Lincoln would exchange greetings, and Alice had seen him smoking a few times by the dumpsters.

Alice passed through the automatic door. She saw Aman recognize her, and then his gaze moved to the dark patch on her leg.

"My mother," she said, and he came swiftly from behind the register.

When the ambulance arrived, followed by the police, Aman locked his front door and came out and sat with Alice on the curb.

June hunched in the back of the ambulance, a hand pressed to her face, insisting she only needed bandages; a translator was eventually summoned, who assured June in clipped Mandarin that she would not be charged, either legally or financially, and eventually June agreed to go to a hospital once Lincoln arrived an hour later. After he parked, Lincoln went first to the police, loping forward in that apologetic manner he adopted whenever near authority—and Alice experienced a wave of disgust toward him, a shameful feeling she then quickly buried.

The voices were caught that night. Logan Schiller and Vince Mays, both seniors at Magdalena High, the same school with good test scores Alice would attend years later. Her parents used the address of the cleaners to enroll her in Saratoga's school district; when the traffic on the 101 was snarled, which was often, Alice's commute neared ninety minutes each way. Magdalena's student parking was filled with German coupes and open-top Jeeps, and half the kids came from up in the hills, from homes with gates and housekeepers. Even though Alice tried to find friends whose backgrounds approximated her own—whose parents were service workers instead of technology managers and real estate developers—when they went to the mall, her friends would order without regard to budget, charging entrées at California Pizza Kitchen. Twice a week Alice would eat by herself in the school library, where she discovered the archive of Magdalena yearbooks. Flipping through the senior portraits, she would count the Asians, the numbers decreasing linearly the earlier the edition. She was leisurely marking off the Mings and Mas in the 1993 volume, eating a tuna sandwich she'd packed that morning, when she came upon Vince Mays.

Alice stopped. She rested a finger on Vince's blond hair. After a few seconds she skipped forward, to Logan Schiller. And then went to the index and found the rest of their pages, moving through and memorizing their faces.

It was Vince who eventually explained what happened. Having ditched school that morning, he and Logan had spent the day at the mall and then taken a bag of Wendy's to the creek. There, idling between diluted Everclear and burgers and baked potatoes, they somehow decided to try a robbery, an easy one. They began at Safeway, Logan dropping two unlocked bottles of Stoli into his backpack. Next they'd walked a few blocks, intending to go to the convenience store, but detouring to Lucky Cleaners. Giddy and drunk, Logan had impulsively swung the backpack containing the Stoli into June's face, knocking her into the sharp corner of the counter. There was so much blood, Vince said. And it all occurred so quickly. It really scared them. They hadn't known what to do.

As he spoke, his voice grew soft and he began to cry. Alice was almost disappointed to hear in his speech none of the evil she'd earlier ascribed, and she realized the scraping drawl that occasionally floated into her consciousness did not belong to Vince, but rather Logan.

*Why a dry cleaner?* Lincoln had asked. June silent in the chair next to him, her jaw still in braces. Vince had come to the townhome for the official apology, squashed on the couch in between his parents and their family lawyer. Alice was not supposed to be listening, though her parents had been so stressed the day of the visit that none of her rules had been enforced. She had eaten gummy candy for dinner and then crept to the living room to eavesdrop.

It was just an impulse, Vince explained, based on the cleaners' appearance. The faded roof paint, something with the sign's font: it was clearly owned by a foreigner. The Asians and Indians at school never participated in anything: they sat together at lunch, didn't play team sports. Their clothes were bad and when you went to their house the furniture always had a weird smell. He'd heard his parents talk about how after graduation they might move to someplace with fewer immigrants in the neighborhood. As Vince spoke, he left long pauses, as if making space for someone to enter: words words, pause. Words words, pause. But each time, no one else said anything.

IT WAS LOGAN. HE WAS coming toward them now, led by the woman.

"What's this?" he asked, drawing up, and because Alice knew his face so well, for a moment she was surprised he didn't know hers.

June glanced at Alice. It was usually her job to speak to anyone under fifty. In horror Alice realized she had not considered what encountering Logan would do to her mother, but June appeared unbothered. When Alice was silent, June prompted: "Chinese noodles. Try them! You'll like."

"Do they have gluten?" the woman asked.

"Yes," Alice said.

"Why are you asking?" Logan said, turning. "You don't have an allergy."

"I just want to know." She pinched a cup, and as she dangled the noodles into her mouth Alice registered the stacks of gold and diamonds that crawled up her fingers.

"Do you like it?" Logan asked.

The woman swallowed. "The kids certainly won't have it. But it's fine. Reminds me of Tokyo." She smiled silkily. Alice could tell she was the sort who carefully considered how to treat service workers when they came to her home, eventually settling on pretending they didn't exist.

"I'll get one," Logan said. He grinned, the easy smile of someone used to having his overtures returned. He paid and then he and his wife slid past, the plastic bag dangling from his fingers.

June flattened the five-dollar bill against the table, readying it for the zipped Clinique pouch they used for cash. Alice knew she shouldn't say something. That actually it would be hideously selfish to say anything at all.

"Do you know who that was?" she blurted.

"Who?" Yet there was *something*—a flick of the voice. June opened another box of noodles and began to ladle out more samples.

"That man. It was the kid. From back in the cleaners."

"Hmm?" June wiped a splash of sauce. "The kid?"

"The one who *hit* you. Who went to Magdalena."

"Oh." June shook her shoulders. "I don't pay attention."

Alice dropped into the chair.

"Why you down there?" June asked. "You tired again?"

Alice shook her head, waving her away. To her great shame—especially since she'd never seen June do so, after—she had begun to cry.

"You sick?" June sounded concerned now.

Alice dropped her head into her hands. "Why didn't you ever do anything, back then?"

"What to do? The police, they do their job." Logan and Vince had each attended a weekend class and completed twenty hours of community service.

"You could have asked for something. From the parents. You couldn't work after surgery for weeks! They never even paid your medical deductible! They were obviously wealthy."

June knelt to face her. "Are you needing money?" she asked in a serious voice.

"No! I was asking for you. Look at their families! Their life! You can *tell*."

"It is its own difficulty to be rich," June said, a statement Alice found particularly implausible coming from her mother. "People like that, they will get a lesson later."

Did they really? From what Alice had observed, it seemed to be the shittiest people to whom good things happened—the loud-mouths and self-promoters, who made outsize promises and never checked back to see whether any of it got done. They learned no lesson except to be even worse the next time, and so they networked up the ladder of life. She sighed, and June made the rare gesture of placing a hand on her shoulder. "I want you to be a happy *person*," she said.

Alice could feel the tears again. She had spent so long polishing her shame; she had so much anger and didn't know why. Her parents never complained, instead finding delight in such small favors, like dinner at a new Chinese restaurant or a surprise rain shower watering their garden. Alice knew that all June and Lincoln wanted was for her to do better than they had. She owed it to them to be happy, it was really such a simple thing, and yet still she was failing.

THEY SOLD OUT EARLIER THAN usual. The last five boxes were bought all at once, by a programmer at a start-up that was having its employees work the weekend. Alice selected a bag of white peaches from a nearby stall to take home, while June bought three bags of barbecue almonds.

"Next time I'll make another fifty," June mused in the car, carefully rubbing her fingers so she didn't crumb the barbecue seasoning. "Maybe I can get your father to help, even though he is useless in the kitchen."

"You could also raise prices," Alice said, but June pooh-poohed, as if Alice didn't know anything.

When she arrived home, it was early evening. As soon as Alice entered, she knew Cheri was out; the apartment had that stale air of abandonment, quiet except for the low hum of inert electronics.

Alice contemplated drinking. She had a bottle of merlot that had been given to her and Jimmy; since they rarely consumed alcohol, they'd simply accumulated bottles and saved them to regift. After the breakup, however, Alice had stopped being invited to dinners. Locating the corkscrew at the back of the utensils drawer, Alice then tried to open the bottle, but was so unfamiliar with the process that she broke off the top half of the cork.

Fuck it, she thought. She poured herself a glass of water and took it into her room.

And then opened her laptop and signed into God Mode and entered the name Logan Schiller.

# 6

# LEO

A secret, which at times Leo found painful to admit even to himself: he liked California.

Oh, he knew all the bad things about the state—it was too left-wing; the state tax criminal; the men and women near depressive in their attire, marching about in their black fleece like a trail of polyester pill bugs. In his residency so far he had been both impressed and enraged by the place: yes, there was the good sushi, ripe apricots, beautiful people (at least in Los Angeles). But simultaneously it was so wasteful, of *everything*—talent, money, clean air, and coast—the natives ruined it with their quick talk and idle boasting and lack of follow-through, and when the sun began to drop and he could watch the stars come out in just a T-shirt in January, he thought both that he hated it here, and also that he loved it, and either way this was to be endured, because it was now his home.

He'd lived here a year already. Had kept count of his time, from the morning eighteen months earlier when he'd been called into the office of Colonel Ivan Litvin, chief of Directorate Eight.

"MINERVA will be transitioning to an active position," Ivan had said, rising heavily to greet Leo from behind his desk. A pudgy finger to the ceiling, as if to say: *Orders from the top*. MINERVA was Julia's cryptonym: only a few knew her actual identity, and her case files were kept in a closed office, firewalled physically and electronically from the rest of the bureau.

"When?" Leo asked, sounding surprised, though in reality he'd been expecting such news. The last few months there'd been an outsize amount of press on both Julia and Tangerine, the latter having surpassed Google to become the most visited site in North America. In celebration, Julia had given interview after interview in which she was both strident ("*Why* are there not more female CEOs?") and artificially modest ("Tangerine's accomplishments belong not just to me or Pierre, but to all employees").

"Soon. I know you've wanted to give her room—"

"To maximize her outcome," Leo interrupted. "For the bureau."

"Yes, yes, for the bureau. I know you've always looked after our interests. But now that MINERVA is already so senior . . . what did they call her on that show, the wunderkind? And the director and the chief, they want some new goodies to wave. It's promotion time for some." Ivan sighed. He was a decade older than Leo, half a head shorter but heavier, with a cherub face and a vast collection of cashmere sweaters. Unlike other directorate heads, the majority of whom could be sorted in a Venn diagram between toady and sadist with broad overlap, Ivan was inherently good-natured. He floated through his days buttressed by the mere existence of his father, a former general who remained a mentor to the president. As a teenager, Ivan had spent his summers with his mother in Avignon, and his continuing admiration for France's food, culture, and clothing had earned him the nickname "the Frog."

"Do they know what they want?" Leo asked. "Is there a plan?" The SPB was no different from many organizations in that its edicts typically began with vague challenges and predictions of glory, only to sputter on the details, upon which the serfs who'd failed to execute were stomped and eliminated. So Leo was surprised when

Ivan reached for a sheet from which he began to list the specific asks: server downloads, deep searches, potential alterations to the algorithm.

"The safety of MINERVA will need to be carefully managed," Ivan noted. "So we'd like to send a handler to California. Someone who's never been on a diplomatic posting, who won't show up on watch lists. While on the ground they can also develop new sources; we've lacked local manpower since they closed the San Francisco consulate."

"The focus should remain MINERVA," Leo said. "Any handler you send must ensure that she is protected."

"Of course." Ivan smiled at him. "So wouldn't it be best if that handler was you?"

On the beige business cards now in his wallet: *Leonid (Leo) Guskov, President, Founder, and Chairman of Russo Import/Export Advisory.* The title deliberately clunky, the sort favored by an Eastern European whose closet contained long black leather coats, still worn on occasion.

Most mornings Leo worked from a small office in a tower off of Lawrence Expressway. His building resembled a moderately priced chain hotel, with a round atrium and a waterfall spanning the bottom levels. There Leo met with various would-be entrepreneurs with dreams of importing alcohol, toys, or—as was increasingly common—claiming some new billion-dollar technology.

Though he was not in his office today.

Seated across from Leo on a stained hotel couch was Ned Daly, senior vice president of architecture at one of the world's largest semiconductor companies, a PhD from Illinois who specialized in circuit design. Ned was the first semiconductor engineer Leo had ever encountered in person, though Leo felt as if they'd met before; the man was one of those people whose physical appearance perfectly matched his job, like a fat pastry chef. Thin silver glasses, curly hair, his heaviness clustered around his middle, as if he wore a pool inflatable underneath his clothes. He'd been silent since Leo entered, and Leo guessed the man had read someplace that whoever spoke first in a negotiation was the loser.

You're going to need a lot better than some internet articles, Leo thought. You're going to need something nuclear, given what I have.

They'd picked Ned up through one of Leo's local assets, a woman referred to as Trisha who regularly advertised herself on a popular escort site. Originally brought over as a programmer, Trisha had quickly discovered that she preferred going on dates and talking dirty to supply chain executives over troubleshooting production issues. By her third month at Google she'd begun moonlighting on CanBuyLove, until her poor attendance was noticed and she was placed on a "performance improvement plan." Now Trisha didn't work at all in tech, and Leo had no quarrel with this as she was furnishing far better intelligence than when she'd been a Grade 5 on AdWords. When she received Ned's initial request, Trisha had done a search, as she did on all her prospective clients—she noted his job title and company (LinkedIn being a wonderful tool for espionage) and messaged Leo. Was he interested? The next day, he replied: Yes.

And so arrangements were made, between Trisha and Ned and Trisha and Leo. Trisha met Ned a few times alone—it was important to establish rapport, an independent relationship.

One hour earlier Leo had sat in the adjoining room of the Crowne Plaza Suites in Milpitas as Trisha and Ned began their latest assignation—the Crowne was where Ned always made his reservations, Trisha said, as it was near LinkTel's headquarters. Next to Leo was Alexey Kaverine, a low-level operative whom Leo often used as a second man on jobs. Alexey had chosen his American name himself—the ridiculous Chester—but was otherwise reliable. He was six foot four, with a blocky muscular physique and a refined face; he resembled an intellectual wrestler, the sort who might pen simple poetry in his free time. His primary employment was as a waiter at the Madera restaurant in the Rosewood Hotel off of Sand

Hill, where he eavesdropped on venture capitalists. He had also discovered a secondary talent, not so dissimilar to Trisha's: at the end of the night, when there were still some cougars left alone at the bar, Chester was often welcome consolation. "The crumbs that ex-wives drop," he'd once commented, "when they are angry."

Each month, when Julia had data to pass, she sent a single icon to a FreeTalk account, which she knew only as HELPER; HELPER was managed and checked twice daily by Chester. Depending on the icon, of which there were twenty-four predetermined options, Chester would then make his way to the specified drop point, retrieving the USB drive and sending it on in the diplomatic pouch. Leo had repeatedly requested that Julia use a physical marker rather than electronic messaging to signal pickups, but she'd refused, citing her schedule: "I'm not going to Philz to be stared at by a bunch of nobodies to shove a pin on a bulletin board."

"What if the network is compromised?" he'd asked. Meaning FreeTalk.

"You forget," Julia had said, "that I *own* the network."

Because the air-conditioning was either broken or rigged at a high temperature, Leo had sent Chester out earlier for ice; now it sat on the table, heavily sweating, as Chester flicked pieces of it back into the white plastic bucket. "This place is disgusting," he said, no doubt recalling the service standards of the Rosewood. "The machine, I don't think it's ever been cleaned."

"At least your head is cool," Leo remarked. While Chester was disguised only by a cap pulled low over his face, Leo wore a combination of dentures, puffy cheeks (achieved with cotton balls), and a sand-colored wig—which, in spite of its cotton liner, still tickled the side of his head. All this, plus his hunched posture, was aligned with the passport photo of one Henk Van Tiel, a chubby Dutchman ostensibly working in London as a sports equipment distributor, whose documents Leo used when needing to travel discreetly abroad. He rarely directly involved himself in such operations anymore, the risk being too great, but Ned was considered a significant enough get that he'd wanted to manage the initial contact.

Chester fanned himself again. "Jesus," he said. "Shit."

Leo put a finger to his lips and pointed to the laptop playing the feed from next door. The video was high-definition: you could see even the birthmark on Trisha's cheek. She wasn't truly beautiful, or even particularly kempt—sometimes when they met, Leo wondered when she'd last bathed—yet she had a certain appeal, arising from the combination of her low voice and delicate waist, that made her seem both sweet and bawdy. She had already changed into the requested outfit, a navy pleated skirt and white shirt, her hair in a high ponytail. The skirt and shirt were not revealing but rather oversize, as if she'd inherited them from an older sibling.

"Oh gosh," Trisha was saying in an American accent. "Oh gosh . . . I really don't know . . ."

Ned walked to the bed, where he removed from his laptop bag a green chopping board. He set it down and then, carefully unzipping a small plastic pouch, laid the powder in neat lines.

"Snort it," he said.

"Mr. Daly, I can't, I'm only thirteen, I wouldn't know how . . ."

"Do you want me to show you?"

"Now, Mr. Daly, they always tell us in school to say *no* to drugs . . ."

Ned stroked her hair. "I think we should stop the 'mister' stuff, don't you? Next week I'm going to be marrying your mother. But you understand"—breathing—"that soon I'll be calling in my special privileges . . . We're going to be one close, very"—heavy breathing—"very, very"—breathing—"happy family . . ."

"That's enough," Leo said.

Chester went in first, standard protocol—two meaty hands and a Slavic accent were miraculous for setting a mood. Leo was next: We have photos, we have videos, you have a family, etc. etc. etc. Half the time the subject started to cry. Occasionally you could tell they hadn't cried for a long time, and as they sobbed they would look to Leo: I am *crying*, there are *tears*, don't you see? Where is my kindness, my attention?

The other half didn't cry. Ned wasn't a crier.

"What would you like our relationship to look like?" Leo began. They were alone, Trisha and Chester having left through the connecting door. Trisha likely already on her way home to eat pancakes, as was her routine after client appointments.

Ned didn't respond. From the articles he'd read, Leo knew Ned was a ballroom dancer, that he went to tango class every Saturday and often brought along his nine-year-old daughter. He was the sort of man women could easily imagine falling in love with them, writing letters, sending flowers. And then gracefully retreating back into friendship when they were inevitably rejected, eventually settling for someone homely.

Though this had not been his behavior with Trisha.

"I want to be clear," Ned said at last, pushing up his glasses. "I don't intend to have *any* kind of relationship with you."

"That is possible," Leo said mildly.

A hesitation. "Yes?"

"At this stage, anything is possible."

Ned eyed him, almost sniffing the air, as if attempting to detect the shitty part of this hand. And of course there was one. "What do you want?"

"Why don't you tell me first what it is that you'd like. Please. Be thorough."

"Obviously it's simple. I would like the videos and photographs and whatever else you have of me destroyed. They could do great damage . . . they could ruin a lot of innocent lives."

"Okay," Leo said, and then directed toward Ned a look of such genuine fondness that out of reflex the man actually smiled back before catching himself. "I'm glad you say this. It means you have an understanding of what is important in this situation." Upon which

Leo explained the situation. LinkTel had a product line named Tigertail, comprising microchips and motherboards; the line was hugely successful, shipped in everything from servers to refrigerators to planes. The chips and boards were difficult to infiltrate, nearly impossible to insert back doors into, unless you owned the supply chain. Which LinkTel did. The next generation of Tigertail was set to launch in two years; Ned would work, as he had been doing, to ensure its success. But going forward he would also report to the SPB.

"This isn't okay," Ned said, shaking his head. "This isn't fair."

Ah, Leo thought. Fairness. That old song.

THAT AFTERNOON, LEO DROVE TO Julia's.

Today, as he entered her home (Atherton, surprisingly ornate given what he'd assumed were her personal aesthetics), he found her in an especially foul mood. Leo thought a sign that Julia had truly assimilated as an American was that she seemed to consider herself the first woman to ever become pregnant, complaining endlessly of the weight gain, the backaches, the cramps. Her public face was of course far different: she'd revealed her pregnancy in the manner of a rock star, wearing loose sweaters and coats for months, until the afternoon of Tangerine's developer conference, when she'd strolled onstage in a clingy black dress, hands cradling her bump. "I'm just thankful to be employed at Tangerine, which so values working mothers," she said, before making a little frown, presumably thinking of all the unvalued mothers at lesser companies.

Leo was surprised to find Charlie's parents also present. "A last-minute visit," Julia explained, with a slight grimace. The Lerners, who were from somewhere in Texas, were polite and assumed, like most Americans, that Leo was interested in the backstory of every Russian and Eastern European in their social circle. They were informing him of a Slovak translator they'd met on the plane—"Did you know they call it *Central* Europe"—when Julia yanked him away.

"Charlie's mother especially, I have dreams of strangling her," she said to him now. They were in her office, where they usually spoke. It was the most isolated room in the house, situated at the end of a hall and nearly impossible to approach without the floor creaking.

"What's wrong with Betsy?" Leo rather liked Charlie's mother, whom he'd identified at first meet as one of those older women conducting a synchronized assault against aging on multiple fronts. Her forehead was smooth plaster, her wardrobe tight and colorful, and this afternoon when she greeted him she'd already been wielding a cocktail, explaining that she was "no fun" without one.

"She talks too much. And when she sees me she is always trying to have, what do you call it, *girl chat*. It's been worse since the pregnancy. She says I'll be a different person once the baby comes. That I won't want to work, that I'll spend all day staring at the children, as she did."

"Obviously you won't."

"No, never." She exhaled. "But she'd like that. I know what she thinks. That each time I order takeout I'm insulting Charlie. As if I've never cooked or washed a dish in my life."

Interesting. Though from what Leo had observed, neither Julia nor her husband did much in the domestic sphere, their home instead maintained by a small army of cleaners, gardeners, chefs, and housekeepers. He knew Charlie had not been raised in such splendor; the Lerners hovered a fraction above middle class, the sort of Americans who saved for their anniversary cruise to Spain and upon their return loudly ordered the Rioja at restaurants.

"Be gentle with Betsy," he advised. "It can be difficult, this stage in a woman's life."

"Like I care."

"Does Charlie know you feel this way?"

Julia wriggled and pressed her hands against her stomach. "I tell him she annoys me. But he is a nonconfrontational person."

Which you'd have to be, Leo thought, to be successfully married to Julia. "How does Betsy think you can pay for all this without Tangerine?"

Julia snorted and threw her feet onto the ottoman. She was chewing gum—one of her newly acquired pregnancy habits, along with orange soda—and blew a bubble. Leo watched with fascination as the balloon grew larger and more sheer. The gum of his childhood was hard, nonpliable, as if it had come premixed with ice water; the chocolate crumbly and chalklike, white flakes marring its surface.

The bubble popped, and Julia began to chew again. "She thinks Charlie makes enough. He's a *doctor*, she says. It is Betsy's favorite topic, how Charlie is a doctor. How many junior cardiologists are living in this neighborhood, I want to ask. Chartering planes? But women like her have no idea of money."

"Really." Leo had a natural interest in this topic, given what so many of his targets wept: *I'm in debt, I want a good life for my family, my wife has no idea.*

Julia sagged in her chair. "She also talks about her dreams."

"Americans love to discuss their dreams. They assume everyone is interested in them. You told me about your dream, remember? The one of strangling her."

"That was only for a few seconds. She'll go for an hour if you allow her. Her theories on symbolism, yammering on—" Her fist opened and closed, as if independently imagining Betsy's neck. "She speaks as if Charlie's the most wonderful person on earth. The greatest son, the best husband."

"She's his *mother*. You're the one who married him, remember?"

Silence.

Ah, all this tireless conversation, and now he understood: the old familiar story and apparently it was no different in America than any other place. Two young people, who believe that since they are both intelligent, both beautiful, together they might form an even more exceptional union—only to get married and sink into the same tedium as everyone else. But no, Leo reminded himself, Julia and Charlie had been wed for less than a year; they should still be enjoying their choice.

Leo cast an uneasy eye at Julia's stomach. "It is," he ventured, "it is going well with Charlie, is it not?"

She glared. "Of course. It's nothing. Women's stuff."

Women's stuff. Which Leo didn't wish to hear anything about, but unfortunately he'd long learned that the problems of women usually became the problems of all. "Such as?"

Julia sighed. "I feel unattractive, for one." She absentmindedly picked at her dress. "I know, the miracle of life, growing a human, but my feet are turning into fat little boats while I'm at it. I can't sleep. And Charlie, he can't understand why I'm having such a hard time. Billions of women have given birth before, he keeps saying."

"I'm sure he cares."

Julia paused. "Yes. And anyway, all the suffering will be over once I give birth." She perked up at this thought. "I've told Charlie he has to do half the work when the baby arrives. Though truly it'll be more. I have two launches the week I'm due, and it's going to be war with the other executives swooping for crumbs. Do you understand what the women are like now, how vicious they are? If I were a man, for sure I'd have already been accused of harassment. The first time in my career I've been glad to have a vagina."

"And what does Charlie say? About his expected participation. He has concerns?"

She regarded Leo with pity. "No. He's fine. It's his child, too. He is a modern man."

"Well, good for you." Julia was even more naive about men than he'd assumed, Leo thought, if she truly believed Charlie would do half. Likely Charlie even thought this, but really in such matters it was less about the man himself and more about his parents. Was his mother independent, did she control her retirement; when she made dinner, did his father clean up after? Even when a man thought himself a certain way, it was a different matter to circumvent a young lifetime of convenience. At the wedding, Charlie's father had given a toast: "May your wife bake as well as mine. May your wife shop less than mine." Betsy laughing the loudest.

Though Leo stayed quiet. It was never a good idea to let assets speak of their emotions too long. Then they would expect it always, and you would never have any peace.

IN THE EVENING, THEY GATHERED in the dining room. The Lerners were departing Friday—were combining their stay with a weekend in Napa, though Leo had not inquired too closely about their itinerary, not wishing to bear the conversational tax of being mistaken for an oenophile. At one point during the wedding he'd told Betsy and Paul he enjoyed steak, and Paul in particular had latched on to this: "How's the steak business going?" he chortled when they met again. "You all eating a lot of BEEF?" Julia had either decided to further this farce or forgotten it was made up altogether, and had arranged for a traditional prime rib dinner. The housekeeper, Magda, brought out salad, loaves of warm sourdough, Yorkshire pudding, Brussels sprouts. The chef rolled out the meat to carve tableside, recommending medium rare, and then rolled it back to the kitchen, like a spring-loaded toy.

"In my day it just wasn't done, having a cook," Betsy observed as she served herself salad. She wore large hoop earrings and a blouse with slits along the sleeves, the sort of garment that technically showed none of the important parts yet seemed all the more provocative for it.

"Jesús isn't our regular chef," Julia said pleasantly. "Usually it's Tyler, but he said Jesús was better with prime rib. They're with the same management concierge. Most families in our position use a chef."

"I've never heard of somebody with one."

"Perhaps it's a regional thing."

"Oh, Houston is extremely metropolitan. Maybe a little too much, for my taste. All our friends have cleaners. And housekeepers. Do you know Colt Granville, the CEO of Oiler's Bank? His wife Doreen is in my book club. She roasts her own chickens."

Leo looked at Charlie. Even if he was a particularly insensitive sort, which Leo found most physicians were, he should still be attuned to major shifts in mood: already in choppy conversational waters, an iceberg now loomed ahead. But Charlie said nothing, only raised his beer and licked its foam.

Betsy was also imbibing. For dinner she had mixed a new cocktail, something with rum and lemon juice that had come out the color of amber. "I thought you enjoyed cooking," she said, stirring. "I read it in one of those interviews you like to do."

"I don't *like* to do those interviews. I'm asked to do them and I participate because it's my job."

"My goodness, you do so many things for that company." Betsy took a long sip. "As soon as you're off a plane, it seems like you're on another. I'm not sure I could manage it all."

"Yes," said Julia evenly. "It's not for everyone."

"Coming through," Paul said. He spooned a mass of Yorkshire pudding onto his plate, making appreciative noises while keeping his head low. Charlie had finally set down his beer and was observing his mother.

"Once you're on maternity leave, you might have some time to experiment in the kitchen," Betsy said as she extended a pearly-painted finger to snag a brown tear of gravy from Paul's plate before it fell. "I know that when Charlie was young, he just loved my lemon chicken. Wouldn't take anything else, was the pickiest eater, but that chicken kept him healthy. No special seasoning, either. He barely got sick when he was little. You'll see what I'm talking about once you have your own. Some kids get sick all the time. It isn't natural."

"Mom," Charlie said, "Julia's too busy to spend time cooking."

If Betsy had hurt feelings, she hid them well. "I just remember reading in so many of those articles how Julia loved cooking and baking . . . I swore I read it was one of her favorite hobbies."

"I don't actually like to cook," Julia cut in. Chef Jesús and Magda, perhaps sensing danger, had not reentered the room. "It's just one of the things I say, because otherwise I would be unpalatable to women, even though were a man to be asked if he cooked and cleaned it'd absolutely be considered an idiotic question, and since we're discussing this I might add that Charlie is an *extremely* unenthusiastic tidier, and I have often wondered what kind of household he grew up in, that he believes he can simply drop his boxers on the floor—"

"Excuse me." Leo stood. "I just recalled I had some family photos to show Julia."

The three original Lerners stared after them as they left: Charlie and Paul with the same flat confusion, Betsy with relieved pleasure, as if she'd just peeled loose a scab.

"What did I tell you about being careful?" Leo hissed once they were back inside the office.

Julia waddled through and closed the door. "Do you really have pictures of my mother?"

"No!" Was she losing her mind? He'd been told pregnancy messed with the female brain, but had always assumed it one of those made-up American concepts, like being "unable to manage stress" or "bad at test taking."

"Oh. So you are not in contact with her?"

"No!" Leo said again. He clamped his palms against his forehead. "I only wanted to remove you from the table. The talk was going in the entirely wrong direction." He crossed his arms and then, even though he preferred to stand, sat across from her on the sofa. "I wouldn't be pleased if my wife spoke to my mother like that."

"Oh? So you think your theoretical wife would be pleased if your mother came to her home and ate her food and guzzled her liquor and then interrogated her about her housekeeping?"

"You have to keep Charlie happy. A good marriage is important. Americans don't like it when women have relationship problems. Especially with a new baby." Leo recalled Julia's file, the history of Karl and Nina. Julia had likely never even seen any kind of functional marriage, he reminded himself.

Julia harrumphed. "Charlie has to keep *me* happy." Then, in response to his look: "Oh, I'm an excellent wife. And I told you, Charlie is on my side."

For now, Leo thought. You are newly wed and rich; you don't yet know what it is like to be together longer, to watch each other become heavier, angrier, tired. He'd always known Julia didn't understand men, but had hoped it wouldn't pose a major problem, as long as she held her position.

Her job. Her job, and all of its access, was key.

Leo removed from his pocket a sheet of lined paper. He'd been procrastinating, hoping for a better mood, but the opportunity hadn't come. "For you."

She made him wait before she reached. "What's this?"

"A list. If there's no mark next to the name, then all I need is a basic search. What you've already been doing—messages, sites visited, any unusual activity."

She scanned the paper. "Ned Daly? The LinkTel exec? Pierre tried to hire him once. And Dmitri Marin, I thought he was anti-Kremlin, that he'd gone all rogue."

Leo shifted uneasily. Julia would sometimes do this, ask him about the names, even though he never answered any of her queries. Dmitri—the former CFO of Gazprom, now known in the West as the "rogue oligarch," who posted tabloid-style videos detailing the Kremlin's corruptions—was in reality executing a long-range plan with the SPB, though Dmitri had wrangled himself a plum deal in the process. Two billion he'd been allowed to keep, from that great stew of privatization into which decades earlier he'd thrust his hands, and with these funds he'd now reinvented himself as a venture capitalist in Silicon Valley. The legend of a reformed oligarch, one who'd fled Russia and all its nefarious influences, had been enough for a good handful of established unicorns to not only accept Dmitri's money, but name him to their boards.

"We run searches for a variety of reasons. How have you been managing those, by the way?" he asked, changing the topic. "You never told me." Because she was always careful to reveal as little as possible—*as if I don't know your game, Julia.*

She studied him and exhaled, as if smoking an invisible cigarette. "I use an internal tool called God Mode. Pierre was supposed to have disabled it, but he never did. Kicked all the executives off, though, except me and him."

"Does Pierre know you're using it?"

"No. But either way my login is anonymous. The same as for my FreeTalk account. User 555." She looked again at the list. "Why's this one highlighted?"

He leaned forward. "For that one we'll need location data." He spoke casually, easily. As if it were only a small task, of passing concern.

"Jefferson Caine. Who's that?"

"How am I to know? I receive the list from above, same as you."

"And this Jefferson, the SPB wants to know where he is?"

"Yes." Then: "You may have to transmit his location real-time, using FreeTalk. Do you have access yet?"

"I should," she said, still studying the paper, but now one hand was on her stomach and he knew her attention was fading. "Soon. The second founder looks to be on his way out. I've been pushing to finalize the data merge; after that's done, I can access location. I'm targeting for after I give birth."

"It can't be done before?"

"No."

"Why not?"

She looked amused at his persistence. "Because it's actually an incredible violation of user privacy. What Pierre and I make speeches about, promising the public and Congress we would never, ever do."

"Then how do you know you'll succeed in merging the data?"

"I'll make the final argument right before I go to the hospital. Americans, they have a thing for new mothers. I'll be untouchable then."

"All right." Leo knew he couldn't push further. "You've been doing good work," he added. "Like with the source code for Tangerine Mail." Which Julia had passed days earlier. He'd anticipated a bigger fuss, but in the end she'd delivered without complaint.

"You are welcome," she said lightly. Years earlier, whenever Leo had issued Julia a compliment, she would redden and stammer, which he'd informed her was unacceptable. To succeed was to have confidence: it was the underpinning of all achievement, both fraudulent and earned. Yet the ease with which she now took his praise brought forth a wave of melancholy.

"Are you taking a long leave?" Leo eyed Julia's feet, which she'd tossed up next to him on the couch. They were indeed bloated and pained-looking, and the toes were bright red.

"Likely not. I'll have to find a way to keep track of Pierre while not returning too early. I've been told working mothers are paying close attention to the length of my maternity leave." She smiled silkily. "Do you care?"

"No, as long as you are not replaced while you're away."

"Don't worry about my job. Worry about yours."

Your job is my job, Leo thought. But he didn't continue. He

wanted to leave; suddenly he found himself disliking her, for no specific reason.

By the next morning the feeling had mostly subsided. Still, he took a day trip by himself to Half Moon Bay as a distraction. The roads curving and twisting, the expanse of the Pacific just on the other side; no barriers between the road and the cliff's drop to the water, and it amazed him that in a society as litigious as America's, such dangerous beauty could still exist.

The following week he received notice that Julia had gone into labor. *It's a girl*, Charlie shouted over the phone. Leo made all the right noises, said all the necessary words, but they felt muffled in his head, as if he were speaking into a tin can. After they hung up, as he sat in his office in Santa Clara, he was struck with the urge to cry—it just seemed so sad, a new soul coming into this dirty world.

# FEBRUARY 2019

# 7

# JULIA

**G**iving birth was terrible. Terrible, really, wasn't enough to describe it. A better term might be crushing, for despite what Julia claimed in interviews she had barely prepared for birth, had not gone to any of the breathing courses, and it wasn't the sort of thing about which stories were swapped at Sun Valley (at least in her sessions), so she'd been unprepared for the pain that engulfed her. Twenty hours of excruciating labor because she had wanted to do it naturally, did not want chemicals sullying her precious baby, the useless doula waving essential oils, massaging her back with a gnat's strength—upon which Julia had shoved the mantra-chanting Autumn to the side and screamed for the epidural. The anesthesiologist finally arriving after a seeming eternity, some humorless Nigerian, and at that moment he held all the power, and Julia none, because she was willing to do whatever he asked, give up everything she possessed, to have what he held.

And then he'd given it.

*Oh*, she'd thought. And understood for the first time the necessity of pain, if only to appreciate the bliss that came from its absence.

After, there were difficulties. They'd had to do an episiotomy at the last minute, which meant she couldn't sit for a week. She found herself urinating randomly, the wetness appearing like a surprise rain shower, and then she'd go change her underwear, all while crying to herself that perhaps this would never end, that one day her "recovery" would continue its rocky descent into full incontinence. She sobbed for hours. For the first time she found herself despising nearly everything about Charlie—his attempts to comfort her with medical factoids, his slow waking, his immediate suggestion of a second nanny, to go with the regular nanny and the newly added night nurse, so that they might never be without coverage. Why not, he argued. Why not, when they were both important people and possessed the resources? And by resources she knew he meant: *hers*.

He was used to the money now, she knew—the boy who raked leaves to buy a Schwinn, whose garage now contained three vehicles each retailing into the six figures. Who took boys' trips to Aspen, was planning a family reunion at Kruger Park, Lufthansa First Class for his parents. In the morning, Julia watched as he left for work, one hand grasping a steel thermos filled with coffee. He wore green scrubs and a shawl-collar cardigan, which she found even more attractive than a suit, for the same reason firefighters look better in uniform. Julia knew that when Charlie arrived, the nurses would chide: Are you sleeping, you need to rest, is that adorable baby keeping you up? He would stretch, joke, wash his hands; there was a time when just watching him complete such tasks brought her pleasure.

Yesterday, Charlie had entered the bathroom while she was in the shower. She'd already finished with her hair and had been standing with her eyes closed under the water, letting the heat beat her shoulders, her body loose in that way she only allowed when truly alone, her stomach hanging over its own waist, as if she wore a belt of extra flesh. When Julia heard the door she turned to face the wall, but she was too slow, and she knew he'd seen. After a second, he said: "You're always beautiful."

But it wasn't convincing.

Julia rose from her chair in the nursery and went to the crib. Picked up Emily, who had been awake but quiet, staring at the shadows. Brought her to the rocker, cradling the soft body against her own.

There was the head and the scent; each time she thought of Emily her breasts would ache and milk would fall, like water from a broken faucet. There might have been a time when Nina had held her in such a way—and when Julia imagined this, she both hated and better understood her own mother. How in the end it might have been necessary for Nina to draw a border around herself. To say, I can only love you so much. As Nina had so little as it was.

From atop the dresser, Julia's phone began to ring. She shut her eyes, willing the device to stop. Two weeks earlier, the night of the dinner with Charlie's parents, Julia had waited until the rest of the house was asleep and gone to her office. Opened her notebook, removing from the inner flap Leo's sheet of names. And searched for Jefferson Caine. She'd been surprised to find in Jefferson's email none of the utility bills or alumni newsletters she usually parsed. His credit cards were paid online, and the required address listed a PO box in South Dakota. His history seemed to have begun as abruptly as hers, and from his search queries and pirated documentaries, she knew he was Russian.

She stewed and slept and then called Leo the next morning.

"What you're asking isn't possible," she said.

Silence. She knew he was thinking, calculating.

"It was my understanding," Leo said, his voice thin with static, "that user location would be possible after you gave birth."

"I was speaking purely of the technology." She scratched at the paper with her nail. "It's reckless, what you want. You're asking for real-time data. I'd have to be on the platform, tracking this man's position. It could be traced back to me."

"Then make sure it isn't," he said, calm as always. "It is your product, isn't it?"

There arose a frustration not dissimilar to when she presented to Wall Street—the immense pressure to deliver short-term gains, balanced with long-term survival. "The company is forty thousand employees, and I'm not the CEO. There are limits to what is safe."

"It's not even a phone call," Leo said reassuringly. "You just have to send a few messages with his location."

She'd known what Leo wanted when he first asked for access to FreeTalk, Julia realized. Had understood in her heart what the end point would be. "I haven't done anything like this." She was surprised to find her voice shaking. "Before, all I gave you was information, things that were already true." Which was how she'd justified matters. If the CEO of Airbus didn't want to be black-mailed, then he shouldn't have claimed to have a PhD; if a three-star general didn't want to relax certain purchasing standards, then maybe he shouldn't have paid for his girlfriend's abortion. "I haven't done this before. Actively helped target someone, an innocent person."

"How do you know he is innocent?"

And then she knew that he'd won, because they both understood she would not want to answer as to whether she herself was innocent.

THE PHONE CONTINUED TO RING, one of those attempts where the caller is determined to reach voicemail before hanging up. The ringtone was "Another Day in Paradise" by Phil Collins. Leo's favorite. It was his fifth attempt today—she was supposed to have transmitted Jefferson's location in the morning.

On the wall, the clock read ten P.M.

It was more a negotiation than outright defiance, Julia consoled herself. She'd told Leo she didn't want to do the Jefferson ask, so now it was his job to return with something else. And hadn't she earned the right to some flexibility? She wondered how many assets Leo handled, if there were others of her caliber, though she doubted it. She was like a prime Thoroughbred: the jockey raced the horse, but there was no question as to whose value was greater. Right?

To calm herself, she paced the hall until Emily fell asleep. Julia stood for a while, enjoying the soft weight in her arms, and then swaddled Emily and set her in her crib.

Back in their bedroom Charlie was already on his side of the bed, in the dead sleep she was enraged by his ability to enter at will. After Emily there'd been times she thought she hated him, a new and frightening feeling she justified as hormones—the quick temper that had arisen just yesterday, when he said it was her idea to have the baby and disrupt their lives, to try before they were even married. It was technically true: she'd been thirty-seven, and who knew she'd get pregnant on their first attempt? But it was also because she'd wanted to join herself to him, permanently, and now that Charlie was asleep her anger receded and she found herself recalling all the things about him she loved. His willingness to converse with strangers, his extreme fondness for cats. How he always made a big deal about her birthday, insisting on a cake and candles, even though she said she didn't care. It was normal to feel out of sorts after having a baby, wasn't it? Even for those in the best of marriages, and she had worked hard for this marriage, as she had worked hard for this life . . .

She swept his hair from his face. She could see he was wearing his favorite pajamas, an old marled gray T-shirt with a Duke logo on the back. Julia liked to hear about Charlie's college years: the basketball games watched from the bar, the girls he'd dated (and how they were dumped). The summer he'd spent in Italy before junior year. All of this, his very *Americanness*, brought her a wide feeling of security. That she was safe, that here in this house she was untouchable and could do as she wanted.

With the certainty of this thought Julia sank into bed. She wrapped herself in her blanket and quickly dropped off to sleep.

THE NEXT MORNING, JULIA WOKE up refreshed.

The feeling of satiation, of being almost fully rested (with one nursing interruption), was unusual. Julia knew she'd overslept because she so rarely did, despite the eight hours of "self-care" she claimed to achieve each night in various lifestyle publications. In reality she rarely slept more than four or five hours—how else did people think she got everything done? Fucking magic? And truly, it was incredible how young people these days seemed to think exceptional results could be had between their hours of sifting through Tangerine videos, leaving at four for drinks—though to be fair, most could never achieve greatness even if they worked every minute. It was simply the sad kind of truth Americans seemed so ill equipped to handle: how unspecial most of them were.

Charlie emerged from the bathroom. He glanced at her, still under the duvet, in amusement. "Sleepyhead."

She stretched. "Slept late."

"You never do that." He bent and powdered his feet. She watched the powder spilling onto the floor, determined to ignore it. *You will not be ordinary; you will not nag and bitch.*

Charlie stood and pulled on a clean pair of shorts. "I'm going for a run, and then over to meet Connors." Tim Connors was an old college friend of Charlie's who lived three miles away. "We'll get some lunch and he can give me a ride back. You want anything?"

"No, I'm fine." Then, even though she knew she shouldn't: "Have you played with Emily today?"

He paused in his dressing. "You know she's two weeks old, right? We can't exactly shoot hoops."

"I meant reading to her, talking, the books say singing . . ."

"She's just a baby," he repeated, enunciating each word, as if communicating to someone of low mental capacity. "She's not thinking about anything except that she's hungry or tired."

"Okay," Julia said brightly. "Have fun."

She went down for a bowl of oatmeal and then returned to her bed to monitor emails. By late afternoon Julia was hungry again, and in the kitchen happened upon Luna, who was reading to Emily from an illustrated book of constellations. Julia had hired Luna after interviewing two dozen other candidates—she held a degree in early childhood education and spoke both Spanish and German.

After finishing her salad, Julia went to her office, where she stubbed her toe against a stack of boxes. Given her fondness for online shopping, Julia had always received packages, but after Emily their numbers had multiplied, to where the opening and disposal of cardboard was now a daily chore. Magda was supposed to tend to the boxes, but she was off and Julia had not wanted a stranger from the agency. Irritated, she retrieved a cutter from her desk. Within minutes she'd unearthed two boxes of baby toys, a Jacadi cardigan set, an Hermès baby blanket, and from their French sales director, Thierry Catroux, an enormous wheel of cheese. She paused after each to log the item and gifter into a spreadsheet; she would write thank-you notes while nursing.

Finally, Julia reached the last package. It was the size of a shoebox, with a handwritten label, no postage. Slightly breathless, she cut the tape. Inside there were delicate folds of yellow tissue, which she tore away.

She lifted them to the light. A set of soft woolen baby slippers, the color of flax. A thin leather sole, little bobbles of wool circling the ankle.

Julia went cold.

She'd told Leo about the slippers, once. Back in Moscow, before she'd ever seen an airport or set foot on a plane, as she described for him her years at the institute. In their sessions, Julia sometimes had the feeling that Leo thought he already knew everything about her; that's when she would reach, search for a surprise detail. The casual manner in which Sophia had unpacked the slippers; how much Julia had wanted them, before they disappeared. "You'll have the opportunity for much more than that." Leo had laughed as they sat in the training room. "In America, you can purchase a thousand slippers."

"Those are *adorable*," Luna cooed from the doorway, Emily in her arms. Julia scrambled, shoved her hands between her knees to stop their shaking. As she reached for the box to reexamine its label, Emily made a gurgling sound and Julia looked up to see a fat foot kick toward the shoes. Surely it was an involuntary spasm; Charlie said it wouldn't be until the second month that deliberate movements were made.

But Luna was already rapt with praise: "Good baby! She knows what she likes!" And, before Julia could stop her, she had snatched the slippers and shelved them on Emily's feet.

"These from a friend?" Luna asked, her fingers stroking the wool. "A good friend?" Which Julia took to mean they were obviously personal, in contrast to the stack of caviar and Tiffany boxes in the corner.

"Yes," Julia said.

"You can tell, when something is made with this." Luna tapped a hand against her heart. Julia watched her retreat with Emily, the oversize shoes dangling on her daughter's feet.

After Luna left, Julia crept into the nursery. Emily was sleeping in her swaddle, and Luna had changed her into pajamas and removed the booties, placing them atop the dresser. Pinching the shoes between her fingers, Julia wrapped them in one of the many blankets that lay in a folded pile, ironed and smelling of lavender; the lump was hot and seemed to shift in her arms, as if it were alive. She walked into her office and dumped the bundle into the back of her filing cabinet, after which she immediately felt better. The cabinet was cheap and plastic and out of sight in a closet; there were six vertical drawers, each containing folders with labels like *Property Tax* and *Medical*.

She dropped into her chair with a groan. Charlie had gone back out to the bike shop, so Julia felt free to indulge in a favorite habit of peeling the dead skin from her heels. She flicked the pieces into a corner; she used to feel bad about this, but now assumed all women were dirtier when no one was watching.

DIG, PULL, FLICK. DIG, PULL, roll, roll, flick. The slippers were a message, that much Julia understood. That she could not be this Julia now, this Julia after, and leave behind the Julia before. To the SPB they were one and the same, and if she needed reminding, well, here was her reminder.

But when had Leo come? She thought of his calls, how any time yesterday he could have just brought the package and knocked on her door. But no, he'd wanted her to be surprised—to know he could reach her, though just in this instance, he'd chosen not to.

Julia checked the baby monitor, squinting at Emily's form until she could confirm the rise and fall of her chest. The new night nurse had arrived, a woman named Claire whose employment had also been managed solely by Julia, who was paid an incredible sum to sit by the crib and wash bottles. Though Julia would pay any amount, any price, to ensure Emily's safety.

The house was quiet, and the office seemed smaller, eerie and devoid of air. Julia opened a window and then reached into her desk for her notebook. She removed the sheet from Leo, pressing flat the paper. With her other hand, she opened her laptop and navigated to God Mode. And entered the name Jefferson Caine.

A green dot appeared: Jefferson's location. Incredible that on a tool designed years earlier, they'd thought to put in location tracking. This was the power of Tangerine, Julia thought. All those brilliant minds, working as a hive, obeying the commands from above. And her, seated at the top like a queen.

Julia watched the dot as it moved. A favorite tag line of Tangerine's marketing was that it was a company by and for humans—the company was connecting people, they said. They were changing lives.

Before her on the screen, a light. A person, a life.

Julia sighed.

# 8

# JEFFERSON

Jefferson Caine was on the 195, heading east. His face to the sun, and though he wore sunglasses the heat still beat against his neck and cheeks.

He lived in Palm Beach but not *the* Palm Beach—wasn't in one of those airy mansions on the North End, but rather a one-bedroom off of Ocean Boulevard. Usually in the morning he made the drive to Little Havana, occasionally Wynwood; today he was headed to Chicago, but his flight wasn't until late afternoon. So he pulled into a favorite Cuban spot and took out his phone.

His stocks were doing well. That was good. Usually they weren't.

CIA resettlement. There was a time when the idea would have made Jefferson both laugh and cross himself out of superstition. He'd been in charge of Russia's largest automotive concern then, and honestly there were times he thought maybe they didn't even need their own automotive concern, given all that was already being done by the Japanese and Americans and Germans. Let them spend the money for R&D, right? But given the recent dissolution, Russia had been going through a period of intense national pride (well, they were always going through these)—this one even had an official slogan: "Our Country." And Our Country needed cars made by Our Hands. So Jefferson managed the automotive company, and then he grew the automotive company, and given his success he was allowed to win, in various privatization auctions: an electric utility, shoe manufacturing, two of the smaller banks. He divorced, met a new wife. Upon which Irina, his first one—as encouraged by a business competitor—took him to court. He lost, but the settlement was moderate, and in six months he'd earned back the money again and more. His life continued in its vertical orbit.

And then, things had changed.

He'd pissed off the president, that was the main problem—well really, the only problem. It was funny, from afar now the president seemed like such a sinister, omniscient being, but he hadn't been so earlier. They'd grown up in the same apartment block, had practiced martial arts with a whole gang of boys. Jefferson hadn't been his name then. It was only when he came over, when the situation turned so damning that he'd asked for the S visa, that he became his new self.

The Canadian border, in a hidden office behind a gas station two miles from the Detroit-Windsor Tunnel. Jefferson in a folding chair, being handed a stack of documents.

His fingernails had dirt underneath them, he noticed. He opened the passport and read: *Clemson Sanders*.

"Fuck. I really look like a Clemson to you? You want everyone to think I'm a, what do you call it here, a cousin fucker?"

His handler on the FBI end, a man named Scott Seton who Jefferson thought looked exactly like a Scott, thick russet hair and a face crowded with freckles, had sighed with a deep intensity that Jefferson knew was a signal he was getting sick of his shit. "You know you're lucky you can even have an American name. Most people in your situation, they've got some thick accent, we have to give them a Russian one off the bat. You know how conspicuous that is? Whereas you, you've got options."

"You mean I *worked* to have options," Jefferson shot back. As it wasn't the Americans who'd paid for his English lessons. He'd had a tutor come weekly to his house for years, until Irina got wind of his and Eugenie's other extracurriculars and smashed a tea service to the ground.

Another sigh. "What name do you want?"

"I can choose?"

"Sure, within reason," Scott said. Translated: *I don't care anymore.*

In the end, he chose Jefferson. Yes, after the president. Ha, ha, ha ha ha. He thought it would be funny to be named after someone on hard currency (the two-dollar bill, but still).

Jefferson could still recall the exact day his life began to turn. He must have asked himself a hundred times why he'd done it, why he'd pushed back on that specific request with the car company. But over his tenure he'd become familiar with the industry, had begun to shape the manufacturer into one that could possibly, someday, bring fame and respect to Russia, associate the country with a product of quality. Because really, when had you ever heard of a high-caliber Russian anything? They could *do* stuff, that was for sure; they had the raw brains, they could launch a man into space and fight wars and design bombs, but it was always done so rough, without that final 10 percent of care necessary for real excellence. But Jefferson, he and his team tried hard, and they produced a car model, and it was *good*.

And then the state began asking for favors.

The requests started minor: hire this guy here, give him a salary there. And then the asks grew: hand over manufacturing, we want to sweeten relations with this district, open a plant there . . .

Jefferson didn't want to manufacture in the district. For starters, the governor was a moron, and Jefferson knew he would soon have his whole family's hands in the till. And they didn't have the talent; they were far from the trade schools, half the town was inbred, and it would put production behind at least two years, an absolute eternity . . .

He said no.

It wasn't the first time Jefferson said no to the president. It was, however, the first time the president remembered, and this Jefferson knew was his fault because he just couldn't keep his mouth shut. Instead opting to spout off on *why* the company couldn't manufacture, going as far as to criticize the governor, and then offering some advice about education reform as well. He knew he had done it because he was proud of his team's achievements, especially given the macro view: at the time Moscow was in the midst of a ten-week blackout, two million impacted, all because of (big surprise) shitty infrastructure and poor planning. Blackouts had become so common that people joked they were traveling back in time, to candlelight. "Don't worry, they will never say we'll be needing the horse and buggy," he joked, and his friend's face clouded, and then he realized the president had entered the delusion zone, that place where even the most honeyed of criticisms soon soured to paranoia.

It came quick after that: the cancellation of meetings, the phone calls never returned, the sudden hostility of various hangers-on. Jefferson should have apologized right away, but his pride sabotaged him, prompting him to escalate. He granted an interview to an international news channel and offered his thoughts on the energy crisis—they should not be constructing billion-dollar shopping malls, he said, when there wasn't enough electricity for the people.

He grew popular. In the West, his name appeared in articles. When his friends (the numbers dwindling) exhorted him to be careful, he waved them off. Me and the president, we're old friends. And besides, Jefferson wasn't delusional. He had safe-deposit boxes in London and Switzerland, each filled with records of the Kremlin's financial dealings. Some of which he knew of only because he'd been in on the deals, too, and like he said, he wasn't crazy, he knew it'd be impossible to rid the country of all the thieves and the siloviki. All he wanted was a little progress. The safe-deposit boxes were a last resort.

In the end, it was only what was inside those boxes that saved him. That brought him to Florida.

Now Jefferson was always lonely. Over the years he'd been warned ("ordered") not to contact prior acquaintances, but that was near impossible. In many ways they were like siblings, having grown up in the same regime, the same womb. Yes, some of them owned 747s and sports teams, but none of it mattered, none of it held any meaning, unless you understood from where they'd come. And you couldn't explain it unless you'd been in it—to have made your bones in an era when half the men ended up dead and the other half billionaires. To have government officials, ministers of democracies who decried you in newspapers, come in private and kiss the ring.

Jefferson was careful: He never called or emailed. Instead, he used FreeTalk, since it was encrypted and he liked the founders, who spoke so much of a man's right to privacy. He usually wrote only to Mikhail, his best friend of decades, though lately he'd made contact with a few others. Jefferson understood that each new person was a risk, but so was loneliness. And who was he, anyway? Not a spy or a troublemaker, merely a man who had gotten a little rich and who for a brief period had stretched his mouth too big.

*How is life?* his friends asked.

*Oh, good.*

*What're you doing, wherever you are?* Though he suspected they all knew he lived in America.

*I am good. I am thinking of you.*

Jefferson drove to the airport. He had a BMW, a 3 Series convertible, which in certain parts of Miami was considered a car for high schoolers. In front of him in the security line was a Hispanic family with three child-monsters, and directly behind was a Black lady, one of those older women not irritated by children. "Isn't that nice," she said, smiling at the toddlers as one smacked him in the leg with a truck. Jefferson was never too upset about all the money he'd left behind except for when traveling. That's when he thought it would have been better to keep his mouth shut, stay rich. Fly private.

He passed through security. He didn't even fly first class these days, but rather economy. He'd forgotten to pack nuts, and wandered into one of the identical snack shops.

Two men, the sort Jefferson liked to refer to in his head as *American white*—young but balding, plaid shirts—drifted to the display he browsed. He moved away, toward the liquor.

A nip at his ear, as if a mosquito had flown into it. He slapped, and on his hand was liquid.

At the same second, the first rush of pain.

Out of reflex he reached. His hand met fabric and he grabbed, but now the pain had overtaken him; he felt his heart might burst, and his grip weakened and the person twisted free. Jefferson's vision was still clear; he could see the men running, the rest of the store looking after them.

There should be a medical station near. It was something he researched, as part of his new life: how many paths to safe harbor in any given space. Right as he reached the store's entrance, he fell.

It was painful. Oh God, the pain.

A boy had noticed him, was pointing and shouting. Jefferson could not recall where they had sprayed. He wanted to push, scream, but his mind was numb. He watched as the woman from the security line approached. "Get away," he rasped, finding his voice. She waved him off and, kneeling, took his other hand.

Get off me, get the hell away, oh God, please hold me. Someone hold me. He wished to die. He knew he'd have to die now, for it to stop.

She was murmuring something Jefferson didn't recognize, was it prayers? He was not religious, had never been. Americans, so ignorant and yet so beautiful. Americans, in all their thrilling, boastful glory. From close up he could smell her. Almond mixed with something. Basil?

He hoped they wouldn't use his American name. The newspapers, the internet blogs back home, they would use his real name, wouldn't they? His Russian name. Because otherwise no one who'd known him before would ever know where he'd gone. In the end it was all he had. Otherwise he was not important, he was nothing, just an ordinary man, and still they had done this . . .

"I'm nobody," he whispered.

*It's okay, honey. Just breathe.*

"I'm nobody. Nobody special."

*Hold on hold on hold on hold on.*

"I'm sorry." He let go of her fingers and slid away.

# 9

# LEO

Leo was already changed, ready for bed, when his phone rang.

"Your passenger was retrieved. At the airport." The voice was familiar but unknown.

Leo hung up. His bedroom was empty, the walls creamy and blank. Besides the bed, the only furniture was a wooden table and chair, both of which he'd assembled the first weekend of his arrival.

"Okay," he said to himself, as he was alone in the room. He felt an odd pang of regret, though the news was positive: Jefferson had been on the wish list for over a decade. Directorate Eight had learned his American identity years earlier, via a compromised translator out of Langley. The woman lacked access to case files however, and they'd been unable to determine his location. Until Julia.

On Leo's table were the remnants of dinner: chicken soup with bread, and stuffed cabbage he'd driven forty minutes to a Hungarian bakery in Morgan Hill to buy.

"Okay," he said again. "Very good." His voice weak and faraway.

THE FIRST TIME LEO SAW Natalia was in a house.

Not his and Vera's, which was an apartment. But a mansion, a leeringly baroque residence off Zachatyevsky Lane. Leo had only been invited to the party because of Vera: they were married by then, and she promoted to a full anchor at RCM, leaving at five each morning for hair and makeup.

At the event Leo had stood on his own in a corner, amiably biding his wife's socializing. There were at least a dozen others from RCM circulating in the rooms; though they were always polite, Leo had the impression that Vera's colleagues thought little of him. After all, here were the real men, the opinion makers, some with yellow phones on their desks, direct lines to the Kremlin. How could a simple water bureau manager compare?

After his wine was nearly gone, Vera disentangled herself and floated back to his side. She breathed: "Look."

"What?"

"There." Making a quick movement with her chin toward a knot of people. "Natalia Vishneva. You know, the journalist? It's crazy that she's here. I wonder who brought her."

The name was familiar, though Leo couldn't place it. He glanced at the group, in which Natalia was the only woman. She looked to be in her forties, and was wearing the kind of shapeless garment Leo had come to associate with women who wished to be taken seriously and asked about their work.

"She's an employee at RCM?" Given her appearance, he pegged her as a researcher.

Vera snorted. "No. Though that would be funny. Don't you know her? She works for the New Press." The pro-opposition media company, the last in Moscow still to publish a daily paper. And then, in a low voice: "The one suing the SPB."

Ah, Leo thought, keeping his face steady. That Natalia. Her lawsuit against the SPB, sparingly covered by the international press, was either ingenious or idiotic, depending on your politics and practicality, though Natalia's considerable legal expenses were paid not by her but rather by Alexander Mironov, a self-proclaimed "kingmaker" and energy oligarch now in exile from the president he professed to have throned. Alexander, bored and rich in his home in Knightsbridge, had at any given time at least a dozen projects in flight—Natalia being merely a small quiver in an arsenal of attempts to irritate, complicate, and otherwise infuriate the Kremlin. Natalia had been working as a Moscow correspondent for Agence France-Presse when her sister was killed in an apartment bombing in '99. The attack, attributed to Chechen separatists, was now publicly asserted by Natalia to have been organized by the SPB.

As he finished the last of his wine, Leo observed Natalia. She was wearing all black: shoes, dress, stockings; the only color came from a pair of cut-glass earrings, which dangled in drops of pinks and reds. Surprisingly—for Leo had found that most public moralists exhibited a good deal of ethical flexibility in the face of material rewards—she appeared true to her persona. No surreptitious scans for the wealthy and important who might benefit her career; instead Natalia was animatedly engaged with a gray-suited academic type, and Leo overheard the phrase "disgusting thugs." Likely speaking of the SPB, though Leo bore her no enmity. He could not imagine suing the bureau—to him it seemed akin to pelting ice cubes at the sun—and, as a junior officer, the activities of the Alexander Mironovs of the world did not touch him, but for the rare times the aftereffects seeped to his level in the form of paperwork.

Vera tapped his back. "Ready?"

"Yes." He set down his glass. Relieved, as always, to depart from one of these events. Though as they neared the front he was compelled to turn for another look. Natalia was still standing in the same place, gesturing with both hands in the air—either not noticing or not caring that her companions were no longer paying attention.

TWO YEARS PASSED. LEO BEGAN to travel to Turkey, to make contact with a source within the ongoing if reduced Chechen insurgency, a minor criminal named Artur Dimayev. Artur, a Vedeno-born weapons trader currently based in Istanbul, loved foreign cars and prostitutes but lacked the funds to procure either in the quantities he desired; in exchange for the envelopes of cash Leo brought with him each visit, Artur shared updates on weapons orders and operational positions. Normally they met at a hotel, but in this instance Artur suggested they try a restaurant specializing in Chechen cuisine. When Leo arrived, Artur whispered to a server, and the girl led them to a private room to drink.

The restaurant was new, garish with neon lighting, qualities reflected in Artur's own wardrobe. As Artur passed his latest intelligence, Leo entertained the suspicion that his asset was, if not outright playing him, at least taking advantage: their last few meetings his information had been negligible, names Leo already knew, general statements that could not be traced or confirmed. There was a tacit understanding that the bill was Leo's responsibility, and by the end of the night, Artur was fully intoxicated.

As they exited the restaurant, Leo reluctantly supporting Artur under his shoulder, they passed the Chechen separatist field commander Halid Yusopov as he entered. Halid, possibly recognizing Artur, gave him a nod, his lips turning as he noted the stench of drink—and then, after a glance at Leo, he continued inside.

Faced with one of the SPB's top targets, his hand still on the door, Leo briefly entertained lunatic acts of heroism. Trailing Halid were six bodyguards, one with a Borz submachine gun half visible under his jacket. In the midst of this group Leo also noticed a slighter figure, a scarf over her head.

It took Leo a second to place her. "Is that Natalia?" he asked, once they'd passed. "Natalia Vishneva," he added in a low voice.

"What?" Artur said. "Who?" But it was clear he understood—for a moment his eyes lost their glassiness and a tremor moved through his face, as if he were experiencing a light aftershock.

Back in Moscow, Leo debated whether to report the sighting. That Natalia was in contact with Halid was a concern—besides the

SPB's natural interest in the commander, Halid also claimed to hold evidence of Russian war violations, mountains of civilian bodies. Leo knew his job was not to make judgments. But rather only to collect all available facts and package them for another person to decide.

But he was hesitant.

"If I saw someone of interest," Leo said to Vera that evening, "do you think I should report it?"

Vera set down her spoon and looked at him. They were eating sorrel soup for dinner, her favorite—on his way home he'd stopped at the market and purchased fresh dill. Vera liked it when Leo cooked. She bragged about his willingness to her friends, though carefully, in a way he knew was meant not to emasculate him.

"Are they a bad influence?" Vera was always careful to keep to generalities, and Leo occasionally wondered if she believed their apartment was bugged.

"No." Then, thinking better of it: "It is debatable."

"Would Vlad be interested?" Meaning Vladimir Klebanov, the head of the SPB, who Vera had once interviewed on-camera.

"Yes."

"Then report it."

So Leo did. Wrote up the Natalia sighting, along with the rest of the trip. He assumed it was Halid who would be of most interest; the prevalent thinking was that the commander had gone underground, so the discovery that he was openly dining in Istanbul, Leo knew, would be enough to earn Artur another cash-filled envelope or two, despite his negligible contributions in the matter.

Two days after Leo filed the report, Ivan called him into his office. Did he recognize anyone else, Ivan asked, was Leo certain it was Natalia who'd been with Halid? Did he observe documents being passed? Did they seem to know each other well, appear comfortable?

And then, after: nothing. Nothing because it meant nothing, which he should have known. Leo chided himself for even hesitating, for being afraid—of what?

A week later, back in Moscow, Natalia left the apartment she shared with her husband, Joseph, and their son, Erik. Erik, who was eight, had stayed home from school that day, complaining of a headache. Their space heater was broken, and so Natalia left to purchase a replacement. Upon returning to the apartment, as she searched for her keys, the new heater in a bag on the ground by her feet, a man came around the corner and shot her in the head.

THE SHOOTING MADE THE NEWS that night. Leo saw the photos, the blanket pulled over the body—the TV was on RCM, as was custom in their household, though Vera wasn't reporting but rather one of her colleagues, Ekaterina Golubeva. The police were investigating, Ekaterina said, though the range of potential suspects was wide. *When you are reckless, there are risks*, she added, and Leo stared at her mouth, the coral O's it made as she spoke. Vera wore a similar color, he realized.

The next morning, Leo woke to a powerful inertia. He left a message stating he was sick on the answering service that was purportedly the water utility's employee help line. He then slept until late afternoon, and repeated this routine the next day. The third morning, Leo upgraded his illness to pneumonia, after which Ivan called. "You don't sound well," he said, hearing Leo's greeting.

Leo cleared his throat, in which there was a web of phlegm, as if he were actually sick. "I'm sure it is nothing."

"Don't play the tough man. Stay home and recover. We don't always need you, I can manage some things on my own, you hear?" From the laughter in Ivan's voice, Leo understood that Natalia's shooting had indeed been ordered—and though such a hit would have been executed not via Directorate Eight but rather Directorate

Four, the "Executive Action" group tasked with such wet work, Leo knew that his boss had claimed his share of recognition.

On the fourth morning, Leo drove to their dacha in Voronezh. Over their marriage he and Vera had amassed a handful of the accessories of good living: opera tickets, a wine collection, extended holidays twice a year, in which they'd evolved from Thai and Turkish package tours to places like Marseille and Bali. They had two cars—a Volvo and a BMW—and twice a week employed a Filipino housekeeper to cook and clean. All these things, these accomplishments, and still sometimes there would come crawling a little man up Leo's spine, whispering that there was something terrible about his life.

This sensation rose full force in the dacha. Leo lay against the progressively grimier sheets, napping during the day and sleeping long stretches at night.

He was pathetic, he understood. He'd known from the beginning the bureau's charter. Had applied to the academy, because like so many others he'd associated an SPB job with excitement—had envisioned himself skulking undercover and foiling plots to disrupt country and state, upon which he was wildly successful and pursued by a bevy of gorgeous women. And even when he outgrew such ideals, Leo still held in his head the idea of a man with a gun: a man taking charge, changing history and saving lives. And now here had come someone, presumably a man, a gun, one life—of a woman he'd seen only twice and never spoken to—and he had gone to pieces. A woman presumably friendly with Halid Yusopov, a violent terrorist who'd be first to claim the loss of human life as relative, and certainly when it came to war.

On his third day in Voronezh, Vera came to see him. From the bedroom Leo heard the engine of the Volvo and, like a child whose parents have returned unexpectedly early, hurriedly began to straighten. There was the sound of the front door opening, the tap running in the kitchen, followed by the efficient strides of his wife.

Who, until this moment, he had not realized was more competent than he was. "You are sick," she said, entering the bedroom.

"Yes."

Vera looked healthy and had on full makeup, as if she'd come directly from work. Normally Leo's routine upon entering the dacha was to air it out, opening doors and windows—but he'd not possessed the energy, and he belatedly realized that the room bore the damp, decayed odor of a neglected basement. Vera sniffed the air and then fanned herself. "With what?"

"A fever."

She touched his forehead with the back of her hand. "You don't feel sick."

"I was."

"Well, likely you are better now. It's been nearly a week, hasn't it?"

When he didn't answer, she sighed and went to the kitchen, from which she returned with a cup of milk, as if he were a baby. He sipped and found it near scalding.

Vera circled the bed, stopping to wipe some dust from the dresser with a tissue. "Is it to do with Natalia?"

He felt a jolt at the name. "No."

"I saw the news. I remember our conversation, over dinner. I'm the one who first pointed her out to you, right?"

"It isn't to do with any of that."

Vera gave him the tissue. "You've always been soft when it comes to women. Of course it's appreciated, but you can't let it become a serious weakness. Do you understand women are just like men, capable of terrible things? Natalia's a good example. It isn't as if she cared who she harmed when writing her articles—"

"I don't want to talk about it," he said sharply.

Vera pursed her lips, a look she assumed only when extremely disappointed. Between them was a length of quiet, and he reached for her.

"Yours isn't a job you can quit."

Leo nodded and dropped his hand. "I know."

Vera stroked his hair.

It wasn't really Natalia who ruined their marriage. Her death was more a distraction, spilled wine on a piece of clothing, a jacket you'd loved when you first bought it but which hadn't fit you quite right for years. In the early period of their relationship, Vera would occasionally return home and tell him about the politicians and oligarchs she'd interviewed. "We are so lucky," she'd say. "To have proximity to such success, such people, so we can learn all their lessons."

Later, Leo would sometimes find Vera waiting after such anecdotes, studying him with a quizzical expression. "Don't you want to be like that?" she'd asked once.

"No."

"Why not?"

He didn't have a good answer. "I'm happy where I am."

"But that's the *problem*," Vera said. "Because you're *not*."

Had Jefferson suffered, Leo wondered now. Had he felt any pain?

Leo had seen him once, early in his career. At a Spaso House function even a minor if well-connected water bureaucrat might conceivably attend. There Jefferson had orated, resplendent in a well-cut charcoal suit, to a crowd of admirers and sycophants. Leo had watched with passive interest while a redhead in a green dress, a translator with the foreign service, circled for his attention—he'd brought her home that evening, and had not thought of Jefferson again until the Florida operation. He knew that at a stage in his life when a man might dream of retirement, Jefferson had instead made an ideological stand and paid dearly. And though everyone knew that the things he said were logical, the only question they all asked was: *Why?* Why do this, why say that, why risk it all? Why not keep it in your head, as the rest of them did?

Ah, Leo thought, climbing into bed: I'm ashamed. I'm ashamed and yet I'm alive and I would not change the circumstances.

THE NEXT MORNING, HE WOKE up hungover.

Leo had a vague recollection of drinking the night before. He'd gradually lessened these binges over the years; the last time he'd been drunk was Julia's wedding. All the dazzling people, gladhanding, *whatdoyoudo wheredoyoulive*—by the end of the first hour he'd begun to feel increasingly anxious, and so spent most of the evening at the bar, instead of by the admittedly alluring though simultaneously frightening tech mogul's widow he'd been seated next to.

Leo went to the kitchen and started breakfast, stirring oats and dropping a single sausage into the frying pan. While he waited for his food to cook, he returned to his desk and opened his laptop. He first searched for "Fort Lauderdale," and, finding nothing, tried "Miami Airport," which brought up the articles. No identity. *A local resident* was all the pieces said. Possibly a health issue. A few remarks from onlookers, one who insisted that Jefferson had shown signs of Ebola, which was why there'd been so many police. And then another statement, from a woman they said had spoken to him, had even touched him right before he died, who'd been checked by the authorities and released:

"He was a lovely-seeming person," she said. "But one thing stuck with me. He kept saying, *I'm nobody. I'm nobody special.*"

I'm nobody. I'm nobody special. The words wobbled in Leo's head.

HE HAD TO LEAVE. HE needed to get away from his apartment. The atmosphere inside was suddenly so heavy and airless—he had to go somewhere, and as he stared at his room, the plain white walls, the dark marks on the floor from renters past, Leo decided on IKEA.

Inside, he wound through the aisles. He selected objects at random: a wall clock, okay; an oversize teak bowl, why not? There was still a part of him that found a well-stocked store thrilling, since for years the shelves at home had held nearly nothing, and he'd been taught to purchase any object of quality regardless of utility. Which was how in his twenties he'd found himself with a box of canned tomatoes, six bottles of soy sauce, a package of maxi pads, and two packs of shoelaces in his pantry. The shoelaces came to use months later, when the department store received a shipment of sneakers from Korea—there'd been a long line for those, stretching blocks.

Leo pushed his cart to the register. Here were the extras, the brilliantly colored candies, all the cleverly priced trinkets designed to separate you from your money. To his right was a baby hat with embroidered giraffes, which reminded Leo of his gift to Julia. The slippers had been an impulse purchase: returning from the bathrooms at Nordstrom, he'd made a wrong turn and ended up in the children's section. The shoes were five times what he'd pay in Moscow, but that was the deal with America, where some things were less and others much more. He'd intended to bring them on his next visit, only for Julia to go dark that Friday and refuse his calls.

He'd known what she was doing, of course. At some point most assets attempted it: the proverbial "drawing of the line." Leo had pondered the issue overnight and then the next morning taken the package from his closet and driven to Julia's. He'd been to her home enough to know when the mail was delivered; had waved to the courier, named Oscar, several times, whom that afternoon Leo politely asked to include an additional package in the day's deliveries. At home, Leo contemplated whether to report Oscar as a security hole and decided against it; the man was only doing his job, after all.

"Would you like help out to the car?" the cashier asked. Her face was bare and her chin marked with acne. Her unpainted hands took his credit card, and now part of Leo fell in love, because of her competence. Sometimes he thought the worst thing about his job was how it made you disappointed in people: it was so hard to respect life when you saw how poorly most of it operated. The revered statesman-like star (Tim Gersh, winner of two Oscars, most recently for his portrayal of Lyndon Johnson in *The Baffler*) and his frantic cover-up of the teenage actress drowned in his pool; the elder politician campaigning against the deep state, the abortionists, the gays—all while messaging for his favorite young men to come spit in his mouth at night (Ted Bunk, Senate Majority Whip, Kentucky). All the terrible things people were capable of, to the point where a young woman simply doing her job, moving things back and forth, could appear the most noble thing in the world . . .

"No thank you," Leo said.

At his apartment complex, he found a line of cars waiting to turn. The Wisteria had seventy units, and shared an aboveground parking lot with a commercial development. Leo's assigned parking space was in a convenient location, near the front lobby, and turning in to his spot, he abruptly braked upon seeing an orange Porsche already in it. That there were two empty guest spaces within sight— usually occupied—only compounded the insult.

Leo had just begun to veer away when the door of the Porsche opened. He stopped and rolled down his window. "Hey!" he said. He expected to see an older man, the well-fed sort who dressed poorly on holiday, or else someone young, the greased son of some real estate developer. In another second, it was revealed to be the former. "I believe you are in my spot," Leo called. "You may not know, but there is guest parking."

"Yeah," the man said, and turned and disappeared through the front doors of the lobby.

Rage swept over him. Leo shoved his hands against his lap to fight against the impulse now coursing through, of following Porsche Jerk and punching him out. Clearly a man like this had never actually been threatened with physical violence in his life, and instinctually Leo knew such an act would change him. Never again would he move with the same blithe confidence; he would think of his humiliation, and the world would never again seem so secure . . .

The air inside his car was hot, and Leo realized he wasn't breathing.

*Stop*. He exhaled.

A delivery truck honked, and automatically Leo drove forward and parked in a guest space. Leaving his car, he found his anger undiminished. Why couldn't Porsche Jerk have parked here? Why couldn't he have more consideration for the others sharing this world? The air was cool and his apartment stuffiest in the late afternoon, so he decided to linger outside; there was a bench facing the shared green, and he sat and faced the scenery.

In between two of the office buildings was a small patch of grass with an adjoining playground, currently filled with children. There was a skinny boy with brown hair running too close to the swings, who looked soon to have his head kicked in. At the last moment, the boy veered away with a loud scream. Leo's neighbor Mrs. Jeffries darted a nasty look at the noise, and instantly Leo was on the boy's side. Mrs. Jeffries was a retiree who hated Hillary Clinton; she had once cornered him for his thoughts on the 2016 election, and, not satisfied with his response, now studied him in the halls as if he were a banana accumulating brown spots. On the other side of the playground, supervising her brood, was his downstairs neighbor Jenny Sugimoto, who from Leo's observations was a depressed albeit highly productive housewife. The children's hysteria reached a pitch and again fear fell through him—was this self-pity? Or perhaps there was something wrong with his brain.

*STOP.*

But his heart only beat harder.

Another woman was walking back and forth, who Leo belatedly recognized as the mother of the boy who'd run by the swings. Her hair was piled atop her head, and she wore a shawl that looked as if it had been painted by someone on drugs. "Patrick," she called. "Let's go." Leo had never seen her husband. Was he around? A workaholic? Divorced? Dead?

Really, it was so easy to die. Not only in his job, but in any. Or just walking down the street. The human body, so soft and vulnerable to the weather, falling objects, a gun, anything.

*I'm nobody.*

Leo hit the air as if this phrase—which had popped into his head with sudden force—were an insect, one to be swatted. Too late, he saw that the woman had noticed his movement, and after a hesitation, she began to walk in his direction. Their eyes met and he dropped his head.

He didn't belong here, Leo knew. He had not chosen to come. How had he ended up here, his life tethered to Julia, a woman for whom he'd done everything yet who begrudged him every little bit she had to give in return? He wanted to rise, but as soon as he bent forward he found he wanted nothing more than to be back on the bench, and there was a pain in his chest, and was he having a heart attack?

The woman was almost next to him. "Hey," she said, but Leo was already staggering. The sky took on a strange hue and the world grew dim and then black.

# 10

# ALICE

Alice had found enough on Logan Schiller in five minutes on God Mode to ruin him.

Logan's profile photo was of a Mercedes GLS 550, with an old Memorial Day *Celebrate the Fallen* banner on top; he lived in Willow Glen, in a 4,000-square-foot home purchased in 2015 for $2.8 million. He had 563 friends on Tangerine and was married with two kids, though there were no photos of his wife in public view. But then Alice wasn't bound by Logan's privacy limitations, so next she skipped to Carolyn Schiller's Tangerine page, where she'd been initially nonplussed by a profile photo of Logan's wife dressed as a fairy queen, her twin daughters as princesses, while a depressed-looking white horse stood between them with a unicorn horn strapped to its head. Carolyn had dozens of photos of Logan—*We are SO fortunate to have you, my wild and loving husband, the ultimate father, partner, and provider,* she'd written on the latest—though a perusal of their bank documents proved the latter wasn't technically true. It was actually Carolyn through whom the money flowed, via her father, Tony Lukas, who ran a business subcontracting employees with security clearances to companies bidding on federal work. To assure his only daughter of a lifestyle in which she could continue to purchase from Restoration Hardware at will, Tony had hired his son-in-law into a vice president position.

After a review of Carolyn's wedding portraits, Alice had then returned to Logan, broadening her search to all online activity. She found he regularly posted on the subreddit TAM - TRUE AMERICAN MALE, which touted its support of the men's rights movement; he used his Tangerine credentials to log in, with an anonymous screen name: YouGonnaMakeIt. But Alice didn't linger, as by then she'd discovered his FreeTalk messages with Chloe Kirkpatrick. A junior at Magdalena, Chloe worked part-time at a florist downtown, which was where she and Logan met:

**LOGAN:** You thinking about college admissions?

**CHLOE:** Not yet. But it's all my brother and his friends talk about they're sooo stressed

**LOGAN:** You ever think about internships? We've got them at Icon. Looks good on an application

**CHLOE:** LOL I can't. I'm really bad at computer stuff I'm not a geek but I wish I was

**LOGAN:** I'm not a geek either.

**CHLOE:** Geeks are cool

**LOGAN:** OK, so maybe I am. Think about the internship. $25 an hour

**CHLOE:** Maybe I could help cook or something

**LOGAN:** You and your friends ever drink?

**CHLOE:** Yea sometimes

**LOGAN:** You ever need help getting stuff, let me know

**CHLOE:** OK

**LOGAN:** What would you think if I said you were sexy?

From his blunt confidence, the bit with the internship, Alice thought Logan must have prior experience—so she'd tunneled further, collecting more girls, prior and present. Navigated to Tangerine Cloud, where Logan kept a folder labeled *Trash*. From the file type she knew it contained photos, though she hadn't been able to stomach opening it.

That'd been a month earlier. Since that first sighting at the market, Alice had gone into Logan's email and FreeTalk a dozen more times. Logan was in regular correspondence with five or six women, all in their early twenties, and given its relative dormancy, Alice thought perhaps his flirtation with Chloe had ceased. But then this morning, Alice had found at the top of Logan's FreeTalk messages Chloe's latest reply. And in fact Chloe appeared to have visited the Willow Glen house just last Saturday, while Carolyn was with the children in San Diego. The two had watched a Harry Potter movie and then Logan had given Chloe a $300 Visa gift card, at which point her mother had called twice, totally freaking Chloe out, and then she'd gone home. *I know a great hotel in Carmel*, Logan wrote to her the next morning, and Chloe sent back a winky face. *Fun!*

What to do, Alice asked herself. What to do, who to tell. Yes, Chloe was a minor, but nothing physical seemed to have occurred— and also the girl didn't seem stupid, had in fact demurred at Logan's multiple attempts to secure a weekend date for the Carmel getaway, all while hinting that she'd like a new iPhone for her upcoming birthday: *mine is sooo slow.* Alice wondered how User 555 would manage things. What did they do, after they searched for those names? How did they use what they found?

Who is User 555? Alice thought. How do I find you?

LOTUS GARDEN WAS ONE OF the best restaurants at Tangerine, serving high-end dim sum: barbecue pork buns and shrimp dumplings and delicate mango pudding. Unlike Tangerine's other restaurants, which ran cafeteria style, Lotus Garden had a set menu: when you entered you marked your dietary preference (everything, vegan, vegetarian, pescatarian), and then, minutes later, a platter of bamboo steamers was brought to the table. Everything was supposed to be excellent. Though Alice had never been.

To dine at Lotus Garden required an advance reservation, which Alice never bothered to make; when she did think to try she would log on to the booking site, only to find all the slots already filled. Alice had recently been informed by Sam, however, that Larry ate at Lotus Garden every day: "He's obsessed," Sam had confided in his Valley boy drawl, and Alice had taken care to note this, because as of late it had become very difficult to speak with Larry. It was almost as if her seatmate sensed her desire to interact, and in response had begun to minimize his time at his desk; when he was there, he always wore a set of oversize red headphones, which circled his ears like tire rims. Alice stalked the reservation tool until a cancellation appeared at 12:00—she knew Larry liked to leave at 11:45 and return at 1:15, thus extending his lunch an extra half hour—and now she was inside, breezing past the host with her QR code, her triumph complete when she sighted Larry in a booth against the wall.

"How do you find an anonymous user on the network?" Alice asked as she approached, not bothering with pleasantries as she knew Larry didn't respect those, anyway. On the wall behind his head was an enormous rendition of the Chinese character for "double happiness" in bright gold. "I need their actual identity."

Larry, who'd been reading on his phone, slammed the device facedown on the table and eyed her with dismay. "You have reservation?"

"Yes." Alice poured herself a cup of chrysanthemum tea from the metal pot on the table. From behind she could hear groups arriving, giddily chatting—this was how other people managed life, she thought. Making lunch dates, blowing off an extra half hour of work. Taking your pleasures where you could find them, because in the end your happiness was up to you.

"Yuh," Larry grunted. "I'm expecting friends." And then crossed his arms and waited for her to leave. He was using her expected politeness toward elders against her, Alice knew. It was a strategy frequently employed by the grandmothers at 99 Ranch as they rammed their carts against her legs to cut in front at the fish counter. Alice looked pointedly at the table, which was small, seating at maximum two. Larry sighed.

She slung her backpack over her chair. "If you really have friends coming, fine. I just need your help for a few seconds."

"Be. Precise."

"Ten minutes. Or twenty."

Larry pressed his lips and craned his neck at the ceiling. "This is not work hour."

"Technically it is. We're at Tangerine, aren't we?"

The food arrived. Alice felt a pang of victory, as the server had clearly assumed they were dining together, having brought two portions. Now she could really stay. "If I want to find someone on the internal network, what can I do?" She poured out more tea, making sure to serve Larry first. "An employee with an anonymous login. I want to know who they are."

Larry peeled off the chopstick wrapper, viciously rubbing the sticks against each other to remove splinters. "Anonymous employee? You try their username?"

"Yes." She'd already searched for information on User 555 numerous times, to no avail. They'd firewalled nearly all their activity, including emails and messages. The only data available was their search history; Alice couldn't decide whether or not this was accidental, like the messy blood splatter of a careless serial killer. "I can't find anything. The person barely goes online. And when they do, I can't see any information. Employee ID, name, where they are in the building, nothing."

Larry spooned a mass of pickled jellyfish into his mouth. Alice stared at the dish, which she had loved as a kid, found disturbing in her teens, and now in her thirties enjoyed again. She knew without trying it that this version wouldn't compare to June's. Her mother made a special marinade and always added sesame seeds on top.

Larry continued to chew, his jaws moving like a horse masticating low-quality hay. "You have MAC address?"

MAC address. She should have thought of that. It was the unique identifier assigned to every piece of hardware with a network interface card around the world, anything from phones to printers, an alphanumeric string that looked like this: 00-15-E9-2B-99-3C. If User 555 was using the same laptop or phone to do other work at Tangerine, it might register.

"MAC address difficult to hide," Larry added. "It hardware. Solid."

"Can I find that from a prior report?" Alice reached with her chopsticks for a square of turnip cake.

"Yes. If you saved. It's in the last tab. The one you run, even though you're not supposed to."

Startled, Alice dropped her food. She inhaled and directed a measuring look at Larry. "You aren't going to tell Tara," she breathed.

Larry's spindly hand settled on a taro bun. "I eat this."

"Are you going to tell Tara?"

"Tara," Larry said, biting down, "is *stupid*."

"That's not very nice."

His eyes widened. "But she *is*. I thought you *know*."

"I *do* know."

"Then why you complain, if it is the truth?"

Alice left this. "You think the information's there even if the report was run months earlier?"

"Why you ask things you can check yourself?" Larry waved for a refill.

Alice unzipped her bag and took out her laptop. She went to her saved report, the one with Server 251. Maddeningly, the MAC address was there, as Larry had said it would be. "You want to see?" She rotated the screen.

He shook his head, pushing it back. "Why you do this?" he said instead. "Why you want to know?"

Alice paused. She'd already asked herself this same question multiple times, as there seemed few positive outcomes. She would either (a) fail to find User 555's identity, or (b) find it, and then have to decide whether to expose them, upon which Alice might be fired herself. After using God Mode, however, Alice had to know who User 555 was; she wanted to know what kind of person could wield such a tool, and what happened after. What did you do, with all that power? What *could* you do?

"I'm just curious," she said lamely. "They're up to something weird."

"You not doing anything bad?"

"No."

"You need job," Larry stated, not looking at her.

"Yes, I need job." She realized she was imitating his accent and stopped. "I'm not doing anything wrong. I'll be sitting next to you for a long time, okay?" *Probably until I die.*

Larry's arm snaked past, reaching for the chili paste by her elbow. "I stay in my business," he said, as if he'd known she was lying all along.

ALICE WAS EAGER TO RUN the report when she returned to her desk, but the area was crowded, with little chance for privacy. She made herself do real work instead, crafting two mindless presentations for Tara.

When she arrived home, Alice shouted a cursory greeting before realizing Cheri was out, and hurried into her room. She arranged on her desk her laptop and phone, as well as a slightly bruised banana she'd dropped into her bag on the way out. And then, finally, Alice launched the locator report on User 555. While the report ran she debated thank-you gifts for Larry: a new set of wireless headphones versus the corresponding amount in a gift card to Costco (June and Lincoln, she knew, would prefer the latter).

But the report returned nothing.

Alice stared at her screen for several beats and then got up and went to the kitchen. After retrieving an unopened Toblerone kept hidden for emergencies, she went back to her room, where the blank report greeted her. Depressed, she logged in to God Mode. Logan had little activity for the day, a Visa charge at a gas station, a short message to Chloe on FreeTalk: *What's up?* Chloe hadn't replied, but to be certain, Alice went to Logan's email—

*Ding.*

It was the locator report, Alice realized. It had been running in the background.

She left Logan's profile and went to the window. User 555's MAC address—their phone or laptop—had been online, though while she was in the kitchen, it had left the network.

Was there anything else? Sometimes there was *something*, a location in the building, but here she saw only:

Locator Record: Yes
7:45 PM.

It was 8:05 now. Damn. Damn damn damn!

She would stop obsessing and close the report, Alice decided. She would wash the dishes and then finish another presentation for Tara. But she didn't move.

After two minutes there was another chime. It was the MAC address; the device was on, it was live. Where was it, she had to focus, she had to search while it was still connected . . .

There! It was being used right now, to connect to a printer, Epson-INK 9872. And here at last some good luck, for Tangerine kept a record of everything printed off its network. Selecting the icon, she opened another window, showing a job at 8:08 P.M.

Alice clicked.

**THE BEST CHICKEN MUSHROOM**
**CASSEROLE YOU'VE EVER MADE!**

Okay guys, I know I said I was going to stop
sharing one-pot meals. But this is one of little
Mason's FAVORITE recipes, and it's so yummy and
easy and I've had so many requests for recipes
that can easily be adapted for vegetarians!

I first came upon this recipe when visiting
my friend Harmony in Portland . . .

What the hell? Alice refreshed the page. Next to the list of jobs was a map, showing Epson-INK 9872's location on the floor.

Alice's heart began to race. She touched a finger to the screen. Her skin left a faint trail of oil, which she normally hated, but she was not thinking of that now because she realized she knew where Epson-INK 9872 was. Had passed that space many times, when she still worked at FreeTalk. Back then Sean and Johan would go almost daily, and occasionally Alice would be asked to sit in an adjoining room, her laptop primed with backup slides. She would wait, both excited and nervous that she might be called in, though she never was.

Julia Lerner. The printer was in Julia Lerner's office.

## 11

# JULIA

The corner office, with all its flex; the glass walls through which continued her domain, its surface flecked with chairs and computer displays. The workers hunched at their terminals, pretending not to watch her but of course doing so. It was what Julia had done for years: watching, waiting, noting, adjusting. Shedding time, until an opportunity arose, and it was only because she had won a sort of karmic lottery, in a country where karma seemed to fuck so many others, that she was here.

It was good to be back at work.

She had almost waited too long. She'd been a fool to think daily calls to Pierre would be enough—that it'd be sufficient for her to "check in" from bed, and that her throne would be kept empty for her return. In Julia's absence a nest of vipers had sprung up, chief among them one Lara Conrad, totally unqualified, an operations VP who often complained she was the "lone female in the room," even though she was only in the room because she was female, and usually the stupidest as well. Lara's mousy looks were deceptive: she had fucked at least two executives at Tangerine, as well as that asshole Sean Dara, who had almost certainly promoted her because of it before he left. Lara was fortunate the current political climate favored her, Julia thought: it was like affirmative action for sluts.

Julia pondered Lara and her numerous other headaches as Emily nuzzled her breast. Julia hated to pump, finding it barbaric, and instead had Emily brought to her every four hours for feedings. She'd requisitioned a private conference room for this purpose, in which she would remove her top, undo her pants, let her flesh spill as she reclined; relishing the relief of the milk as it flowed, that feeling of freedom, mild ecstasy.

Lara was nothing, she thought, softly patting Emily on the back. Easily managed through a quick word to Pierre. Pierre, who was still on her side. Nearly running to her, her first day back, as if they were lovers parted by tragic terms. Shouting: "I missed you so much!" even though he could have visited her at home anytime (he hadn't). They'd spent two minutes discussing Emily, which Julia knew was all he could bear of another's spotlight, and then she pivoted—"How's the business?"—and he'd moved on, augmented reality and the shits in Congress and some development with lidar.

All of which had been heaped on her, on top of other issues. A head of R&D who'd just quit, leaving their nascent autonomous team in shambles; Gary Halperin—Tangerine's gnomelike CFO— was upset she'd returned earlier than expected, and in retaliation had directed Finance to reject all new head count in her organization. The problems were endless, and through it all she'd been forced to graciously absorb the compliments, usually lobbed from young women, some variant of: *You look so amazing! I don't know how you do it!* Of course I look good, she wanted to scream, of course I am doing it, because I have to! As if she *liked* sleeping four hours a night, wearing fitted dresses and sucking in her gut all day; as if she enjoyed having her face injected, because any article invariably featured some horrific blown-up candid photo, taken from below. Julia always publicly said aging was the best thing that could happen to a woman, but really what she meant was that she'd love to have her thirty-eight-year-old brain in her twenty-year-old body. Her first stop this morning had been at the dermatologist's, where she'd browsed a brochure touting a "mini" facelift; she'd turned the pages with interest, reading the copy.

Emily finished. Julia gave her a few firm pats, efficiently ejecting a burp, and then buttoned up her blouse and brought Emily to Luna, who sat in the waiting area. As she passed her daughter over, Julia checked to see who was watching, as she'd been informed of some resistance from the greater workforce about her childcare arrangements. Why does Julia get to bring her baby? they cawed. Why is she allowed to see her child? Though nothing was said of Tangerine's F1 sponsorship (Ferrari), or Pierre's private meditation rooms on each campus; the Boeing 787 on order, another Gulfstream G650, eight of Pierre's college buddies currently drawing Tangerine salaries to fuck with the product and tell him he was right about everything. And yet it was Julia's baby who seemed to enrage.

A symbol, they called it.

Julia returned to her office, examining her blouse for spots of spit-up. Reviewing her day's schedule, she saw her next meeting was with Jon Fall. The engineering lead had given his congratulations her first day back, though not in that leering way of most men, where they pumped your hand while eye-fucking your postpartum breasts. He'd offered a few sentences, and then Joanna Weaver had inserted herself, the human resources VP who'd planned Julia's baby shower and sent sycophantic emails throughout her leave (*Thinking of you!*), and so they hadn't spoken further.

"Hello," Jon greeted her now. He made no additional mention of the birth, which satisfied Julia; she still wanted to be seen as someone separate from children. She used to walk into a room and assess her competition: pretty but dumb, married, married with kids—the latter always being the ultimate mood killer.

The check-in went as usual: milestones review, an update on

user engagement numbers. Julia pushed herself to imagine unin-
tended impacts, the contrarian position. Before Tangerine, she
hadn't understood how fragile a company was—how quickly things
could fall apart if someone didn't care. If an executive was negligent
or lazy. She let Jon finish his current topic, some issue with operations for which Lara Conrad was also to blame. Julia wondered if
she could fire Lara. Or, more conveniently, shove her off onto Google or Microsoft through one of their executive diversity recruiters.
She made a note of this on her "B level" checklist and then moved to
her primary concern. "The zero-day exploit," she said. "In Tangerine Mail's source code. Did you find it?"

"Yes. There was a hole in the scripting engine."

"Were any outside parties able to use it?"

"No. We got to it early. I've also asked that the team examine
similar vulnerabilities. In the mobile app as well as desktop."

Perfect. Julia had fretted about the exploit the two weeks she'd
officially been on leave, but had been nervous to call Jon, paranoid
her phone might be monitored. Having shed this weight, Julia felt
buoyed; she thought this afternoon she would shop for some new
glassware, Bergdorf had some darling Murano tumblers . . .

"Did you notice anything else during your review?" she asked,
right as Jon was at the door. Another thing she liked: he wasn't a
time waster. "Any unusual activity on the servers?"

Jon turned. "It's interesting you mention it," he said slowly. "I
did see a flag."

"A flag?"

"Yes, but it wasn't an external approach. The flag came from our
side."

"What do you mean?"

"An alert someone placed on one of our servers. I wouldn't normally have noticed, but they also flagged the data center and so I
got curious and checked. Usually such a thing would have auto-

matically disappeared in twenty-four hours, but this was manually added, which is likely why it didn't drop off."

"When was it placed?"

"Two months ago."

Which was when she'd started downloading search data for Leo, Julia realized. She should have known the high transfer rate might alert the system. Another area where Leo had needlessly, thoughtlessly put her at risk.

"Why would an employee have flagged a server?"

"It could be anything. Maybe a detected intrusion attempt. Or unusual transfer activity. It's a good thing," Jon said, noting her expression. "Means our security and tech support are doing their jobs."

"So it's a regular thing, these alerts?" She should know this, she had to know everything. "Does, say, a high transfer rate automatically trigger one?"

He began to answer and then stopped. "No. It's the first time I've seen it, actually."

"So it's a person, then? Who placed it?"

"That would be my guess. Or maybe they're testing a new program. Support is always trying these things; their management is somewhat disorganized."

"Could you get me their name? The person who placed the alert?"

His look was hooded, a little confused, and Julia was glad she was known for bouts of micromanagement. "Sure." He smiled. "Whatever you want."

AFTER JON LEFT, JULIA WENT through her emails, deleting with little discrimination. She chugged her iced coffee and yawned. This week, Emily had wanted to feed at night what seemed like every hour—Julia had to figure out how to get her to sleep more; really, how the fuck did people do this? In response, Charlie had tempo-rarily relocated to one of the guest bedrooms, a division of suffering that alternately enraged and puzzled her. He didn't do well when sleep deprived, Charlie said. Adding: "It's important to take care of yourself." Which Julia agreed with, but the problem was that every-thing was important. So then what did you do?

What was that advice other mothers liked to bray at her? *Date night. You've got to have date nights.* There was no way she was starting a gratitude journal or setting a recurring sex appointment, but she could find a new restaurant to try. San Francisco appeared to be adding establishments at a startling pace, and she scrolled to a high-end sushi bar said to be the most difficult reservation in the city. She would request a corner, face the wall—otherwise some-one would say hello, wanting a photograph or to pitch, which used to amuse Charlie but now seemed to drive him crazy.

*Ding.* Jon's email had arrived. Julia sent a note to her assis-tant Nicole, asking her to make a reservation at Suki-Ya, and then opened Jon's message. Perhaps their conversation had made him cautious, because he'd added this comment at the end:

> . . . The employee who placed the alert is Alice Lu. She works in technical support, as I thought. Again, I believe this was a random check, it's what everyone on her team is supposed to be doing, though most don't bother, which is why I noticed it in the first place. I would be pleased if I were her manager.

Alice Lu. The name had a pleasing sound to it. Julia scanned the employee profile, zooming in on the photo, though she already knew she wouldn't recognize her.

*Alice Lu, Alice Lu.* Are you something? Or nothing? There had been something odd the other day, with God Mode. When she'd logged in as User 555, she'd found a name she didn't recognize in her search history. Logan Schiller. Julia had originally thought it a fluke—given that the interface was old, occasionally things went screwy—but she'd recorded the name as a precaution.

Julia added Alice's name to her notebook underneath Logan's, her pen making loops out of the *L*'s.

## 12

# LEO

As Leo opened his eyes he was startled by a brilliant flash of gold; thinking it was the sun, he squinted and the object became a dangling pendant. This surprise was followed by the realization that he was not upright, or even sitting, but rather flat on his back, prostrate on the bench. Worried he'd been injured, he brought his hand to his head and touched something soft behind it.

"It's my shawl," the woman said. She was about his age, dramatic looking with big eyes and thick hair. "I put it under your head when you passed out. I'm Miriam." By her side was her son, who stared at Leo with alarm. While most of the playground was deliberately ignoring them, two others had come near: another woman Leo recognized from the building, who was already edging back, and a man looking at his phone. Since moving to California Leo had never had so much attention on him; he needed to get away, to be in a private space, but his body was weak and also there were too many people. *Damned American do-gooders!*

"Are you all right?" the man asked, dropping his phone into

his pocket. His face was familiar yet remote, and for a second Leo feared this was an operation. But then the man moved out of the sun's glare and Leo realized it was Porsche Jerk.

"It's getting cold out," Miriam said. "I think you should lie somewhere else." She hesitated. "Why don't you come with me and Patrick? My apartment is right there on the ground floor."

"I—*I live here*," Leo whispered. He tried to say it again, louder, but could not—was worried if he spared the oxygen, he would once again pass out.

"Yes," Miriam said. "I know. That's why I invited you." She spoke with placation, the way a person might to a child unrelated to them who is in the midst of an inappropriate tantrum.

Leo didn't want to go with Miriam. He didn't even *know* this woman, and he especially wished to avoid any unnecessary neighborly interactions, given all he'd done to sequester himself from the terrible Mrs. Jeffries and Jenny Sugimoto. But before he could extricate himself, Porsche Jerk spoke:

"We should call the police. Or an ambulance."

Leo was seized by a desire to throttle him. This degenerate, who could not even respect a written sign marking a personal parking spot, now thought to summon a cadre of authorities? Though a greater concern then broke—Leo did not want to be interviewed by some medic or policeman, his name entered into an American system. The wonks in the SPB might catch it, and then he'd have to explain, and likely be subjected to all sorts of physical tests on his next return to Moscow.

He tried to rise but was still shaky, and so lay back and evaluated his options. Miriam had her boy with her, and Americans were mostly guileless when children were involved.

Leo summoned the energy to speak. "I'll go." His breath, the act of steady breathing, felt near impossible. He raised a hand to Miriam. "I—I'll go with you, let's go."

HER APARTMENT WAS CLOSE. STILL, on the short walk, Leo felt exposed—as if there were people observing from above, and he had the intense desire to seek closed quarters. Once inside her apartment he was unceremoniously dropped onto a couch: "Lie down," Miriam ordered. The couch was comfortable, made out of a soft tiger-print velvet, and Leo brushed it with his hand as he might a real animal.

Am I going crazy, he thought. Am I dying?

The apartment's layout was congruous to his own, only in reverse. The ceilings were speckled, and if he turned his head, he could see the sliding door leading to the balcony. He heard movement behind him; after another minute, Miriam returned from the kitchen with water.

"So," she said, sitting on the coffee table. "You've had a panic attack."

"What?" He understood the individual words, but together they were incomprehensible.

"Yup. A panic attack. At least I'm fairly certain. You can say anxiety attack, if that makes you feel better. Some men don't like the word 'anxiety.' Wait, don't say anything, first take ten breaths. Measured. In and out."

*In, out.* "A panic attack," he echoed.

"Yes. Have you had one before?"

"No."

"Never?"

"No," he said with emphasis, although now Leo thought of the first night he'd spent in the dacha after Natalia. For dinner, he'd boiled himself frozen pelmeni and then sat at the kitchen table, a fork and spoon in hand. Only to wake on the floor minutes later, a lump on the back of his head. "When I was younger, maybe."

"Right," Miriam said. He was relieved she did not inquire further. Her hair had almost completely escaped its ties and was now sprung about her face as if she'd gone down a slide with static electricity. Her apartment was in similar disarray: half the cabinets in the kitchen were open, and scattered about the living room were stacks of unopened boxes and toys in clear plastic containers.

She passed him the water. "I warmed it on the stove, so it'll go down easy. Drink. But not too fast."

Leo gulped, greedy for the liquid. Afterward he felt as if he might vomit, and lay on the couch on his side. His head was inches from the now-empty cup, made out of a wispy porcelain, on which there was a tawny spotted jaguar leaping over a wash of blue. He was surprised that such a messy person could own such an elegant item, and allow a stranger to use it.

"I am having a problem at work," he said. It slipped out in a monotone and instantly he regretted it.

Miriam surveyed him. "You are stressed," she said, as if confirming a prior statement.

"Yes."

"Do you want to talk about it?"

His first thought was a resolute *no*—it was already lunacy that he was on her couch. Although, having confessed the problem, he could admit he now felt more at ease; he'd already said the worst of it, so was it so terrible to share a little more?

"I—have some stressful projects." Thinking of Jefferson. "There's also a . . . subordinate of sorts, who is causing some trouble."

"Subordinate. That's an interesting word. Man or woman?"

He debated whether this was too nosy, but settled on it being one of those annoying yet harmless questions asked by California liberals when they'd already decided you were a certain sort, anyway. "Woman."

"Can't you just fire her?"

"What she does is hard to hire for."

Miriam thought about this. "Like a specialized engineer."

"Exactly. Her expertise is . . . hard to source. And would be difficult to replace."

"Right," Miriam said. "Right, right." And in fact she appeared sincere, as if she truly meant what she said—the opposite of most interactions he had with Americans, who liked to pretend a conversation was a relationship when really it was only a mirror, one in which to admire their own labored self-reflections.

Bolstered, he added: "She's been with me a long time. There's a certain amount of loyalty."

"How is she causing you trouble?"

Leo paused. "She's not *listening* to me."

"What if you tell her she has to listen? That there are consequences if she doesn't?"

"I think"—though now Leo could not recall if he'd had that conversation with Julia, at least recently—"I think she would just do what she wants, anyway."

"Hmm," Miriam said. Taking the beautiful cup with her as she returned to the kitchen. "That is a real problem."

LATER, AFTER LEO FINISHED ANOTHER cup of water, he felt strong enough to sit and immediately had to urinate. When he returned, Patrick was on the ground by the sofa, opening one of the plastic boxes. "Do you want to show me?" Leo asked, not meaning it, and to his horror the boy nodded. They played for an hour, constructing elaborate towers from plastic bricks.

"Are you a psychiatrist?" Leo asked as Miriam came toward them with a plate of cut fruit. A furtive expression crossed her face. My God, she's one of those, he then thought. A hypochondriac whose greatest joy was the diagnoses of extreme conditions in others. Perhaps she was going to say she could smell that he had cancer next, or that his cooking pans were poison.

"No," Miriam said flatly. She wore an apron, a beige pullover with a giant pocket, out of which drooped a wooden spatula.

"Oh," Leo said.

Miriam sighed and kicked an enormous stuffed bear upright. "I was a therapist," she explained, dropping onto the lap of the bear. "Before. Had my own practice, but gave it up after my divorce. Please don't think I'm *hitting* on you!" she cried, one of those unbelievably forward statements Americans occasionally favored. "I'm just *explaining*, because when you give up a healthy business, people have all kinds of theories. Like maybe you're a drug addict or an embezzler. Anyway, I work in video games now. I enjoy my job. Sometimes I even help the designers with dialogue. You wouldn't believe how little these people know about a woman's interior process. Or a man's, for that matter."

"Wow," Leo said dumbly. To him it was incredible that a divorce should bring someone to give up their job, one he assumed they enjoyed and were richly compensated for. In Moscow nearly half the people he knew were divorced, and he'd read that in the United States the percentage was similar, so why did they all make such a big deal out of it here? "Do you miss it? Your practice," he added, in case she thought he meant her husband.

She sighed again. "I was good at it. But it got to be too much. I had clients tell me they were going to kill themselves if I went on vacation. When I had my C-section, I came out of surgery to forty messages, all from the same woman promising that if I didn't answer she was going to come to my house. And the thing is, I know I had some talent. But I couldn't handle it anymore. And then one day I realized that somehow months had passed since me and my husband had bothered to eat a meal together." Her laugh was low. "I mean, here I am supposedly helping people, but at a certain point I couldn't even manage my own affairs." She met his eyes. "Does that sound crazy to you?"

"Not really," said Leo.

A WEEK LATER, LEO FLEW to Moscow.

A considerable benefit of Russo Import/Export was how it simplified travel—no need for him to construct an elaborate cover, to strap on Henk Van Tiel's sandy wig and prepare the fat Dutchman's documents and Samsonite trolley. Every six months when he returned he could simply be Leo, struggling logistics consultant operating out of Santa Clara; at SFO he stood before the immigration officer, patiently waiting for his passport to be scanned, while behind him a mass of passengers heaved with messy energy. The airport official, her auburn hair tied back, looked at him for less than a second. "Have a nice trip," she said, and turned to the horde.

Per routine, Leo spent his first two days conducting real work for his fake job. He arranged a meeting with the uncle of a client, one looking to import what was pitched as the best honey vodka from Primorsky Krai. Leo met the uncle, a tall, furry man with childish eyes named Konstantin, at the Star—an overpriced café near St. Peter's Cathedral that bore a depressingly similar menu and pricing to the coffee shops in San Francisco. Leo had hoped to discharge his responsibilities there, but had not been able to escape being taken to Kotelniki to visit the distributor: "There are big margins in alcohol," Konstantin bellowing as he pressed another sample on Leo, come on, have another, don't be a sissy! "Money, that's the universal, isn't it so?"

Now it was the third day, and Leo was at an apartment building in Shchukino. Though the complex was SPB owned, its units were rented publicly, as even the SPB couldn't pull off an entire building remaining vacant in the local real estate market without unwanted scrutiny. On the seventh floor, two apartments were occupied by what were marked in the building's plans as "storage equipment and telecommunications," while another three were furnished but empty, allegedly an extended pied-à-terre for a wealthy factory owner in Kazakhstan. Leo went to the apartment at the end of the hall. He knocked twice, deliberately not looking at the lamp hanging adjacent, which contained a motion-activated video recorder. After a few seconds Ivan answered. The chief of Directorate Eight was rosy faced, wearing a suit with no tie. He waved at Leo to enter and then returned to the kitchen, where he was arranging smoked salmon on bread.

The apartment was one bedroom, with an open kitchen separated from the seating area by a long counter. Leo sat on the couch, where he fought a low drowsiness. As was generally the case when he traveled, it was only on his last day that he'd finally had his first good night's rest.

"I have an update on Florida," Leo began while Ivan fussed with his food. At the end of the counter was a wicker basket of the sort used to collect mushrooms. On this one was printed the name of an expensive local deli, and Ivan reached inside and removed a jar of roe, using a small spoon to sprinkle the caviar over his plate. He'd begun to assemble progressively more elaborate and calorie-rich meals during their meetings—Leo had heard Ivan's wife was strict, and he wondered if his superior was secretly violating some agreed-upon diet. "The Jefferson job," Leo added. "I have the final report."

"Good!" Ivan came around. "So it was clean?"

"Yes. It appears one woman was taken to the hospital but released hours later."

"Are the Americans allowing his name to be published?"

"No." As of yesterday, Leo had yet to see the name Jefferson Caine in print. "They'll likely conceal it, don't want the embarrassment." *I'm nobody special.* His heart thumped, and he recalled Miriam's instructions should he feel light-headed again. Above Ivan's head Leo now imagined a five-pointed star—he started at the top and then, each time the line bent, breathed in and out. His pulse returned to normal. "Why was he targeted?"

"Who knows. Someone in the Kremlin wanted a victory. Timor, most likely." Timor Poliakov was the head of all three intelligence services; he sat on the Security Council and met with the president weekly. "Timor's been clocking off a whole list of them in London.

Each time there's a success, his wife's construction company re-
ceives another contract." Ivan opened his mouth, as if to add more,
but instead went to the kitchen and returned with espressos.

They drank and traded gossip. Leo was entertained to learn that
Peter had remarried: "To a *dentist*!" Ivan exclaimed, and they both
laughed, even though neither could explain precisely why it was
funny. Leo shared the latest on Ned Daly: Ned was cooperating, as
Leo had known he would. Had already passed sensitive engineering papers detailing LinkTel's next launch, with promises that he'd
design a back door within the hardware.

"Is he truly cooperative?" Ivan touched his fingers together.
"Not fooling us? He hasn't gone to the authorities?"

"Not per the latest from MINERVA. Ned spends a lot of time on
FreeTalk; he seems to use it for nearly all his private communications." Including with his latest girlfriend, who'd once again been
sourced through CanBuyLove, though Leo didn't tell Ivan this. Just
as Julia managed information to him, so Leo also managed information upward. And so it went, and went, until the people on top had
an entirely different view of things from the people on the bottom.

"MINERVA, she's doing good work." Ivan offered the last piece
of smoked salmon to Leo. Leo waved him off and Ivan happily sailed
it into his mouth.

"Yes," Leo agreed. Then: "I think she needs a break."

"Oh?"

"A short one," Leo caveated. "She needs to rest, recover. She is
a new mother."

"Interesting," Ivan said, and Leo could not discern what his superior was pronouncing *interesting*: his suggestion about Julia, or
Julia's becoming a mother. Ivan returned to the kitchen, where he
removed from the wicker basket a round covered tray. As he sliced
its contents, he called: "I leave it to you. From an operational stand-
point, you have full oversight."

"Of course I will still manage any requests from the bureau."

Leo suddenly felt he'd been too hasty. He didn't know what had prompted him to ask this favor, especially since Julia hadn't even been particularly forthcoming as of late. Still, she'd ended up tracking Jefferson, hadn't she? And a break for Julia meant one for himself, some *breathing room*, as they liked to say in California. "Not a full stoppage. Just a temporary lessening of responsibilities. We'll continue to execute any special requests, like with the Tangerine Mail source code."

"Right, the code . . ." Ivan returned with a wedge of Black Forest cake. "That was something I meant to mention. It seems there was an error."

Leo was instantly alert. "What sort?"

"Oh," Ivan said, waving a blobby hand. "I don't know. The cyber team said the vulnerability was no longer there. So they were unable to complete. But what do they know? Likely they messed up from the start."

Leo wanted to believe this. "Do you have details?"

"Let's see . . ." Ivan reached for his briefcase. "I'm sure I brought it—here, here it is." He passed Leo a folder. "You know, there's a good chance it is the computer men on our end who are making problems," he said as he ate. "Perhaps there was never a vulnerability to begin with. Or they ruined something, entered a wrong password too many times. So instead they come back to us and complain, something's wrong, data is corrupted, oh no!"

"Maybe," Leo said. *But I don't think so.*

BACK ON THE PLANE, IT took Leo an hour to review the papers. By the end, not only was he certain that the vulnerability had been fixed by Tangerine, but that given the timing, it was Julia who'd instigated it.

Leo set down the notes and let out a deep sigh. Julia was lucky, he thought. She was lucky her company had been purchased for millions and that she could fly private. She was lucky that Ivan both liked her and had a rich and powerful father, which meant he was more laissez-faire than nearly any other SPB directorate head. And because Julia knew this—because she couldn't help but dig and chip when before her was a weakness to exploit—she'd gone and done this.

Of course, she would have to be taught a serious lesson.

It was as he was waiting to be picked up that Leo thought of it. As he stood on the curb outside San Francisco Airport's arrivals terminal he turned the idea over in his head: it was always satisfying when a solution was elegant. Though there would be difficulties. Julia would be difficult.

A blue Mazda slowly curved to a stop. The driver popped the trunk but did not emerge, and after depositing his bag, Leo opened the passenger door. He knew it wasn't totally secure for Chester to retrieve him—it went against recommended procedure, especially if Chester was somehow compromised—but at the last minute Leo hadn't wanted to be picked up by a stranger. Had wished to be like the other returning travelers, craning their necks for specific cars and faces.

"How was your trip?" Chester asked. He sat straight with both hands on the wheel, at ten and two, as if he were a driving student. "You have a good time?"

"I did," Leo said. He passed to Chester the bottle of honey vodka he'd saved for him, as well as a porcelain jar of paprika he'd purchased from duty free. Outside, the sun was a highlighter to the sky. Leo pressed his cheek against the glass and they set off for home.

# MARCH 2019

# 13

# ALICE

**W**hat do you think of Julia Lerner?" Alice asked.

It was late Saturday morning, and she and Cheri were in the apartment having breakfast: Alice dipping her Chinese doughnut in the soy milk she'd purchased fresh yesterday, while Cheri peeled back the lid on her second Scandinavian yogurt. As she watched her cousin eat, Alice reminded herself that Cheri didn't deliberately consume her food to be annoying; that over Cheri's years of cohabitation with a string of high-net-worth admirers she'd grown removed from the payment of necessities such as rent or car insurance. Each month, when Alice calculated and wrote down Cheri's share of the utilities, Cheri would receive the sticky note in wonder: "So interesting," she'd remark. "Crazy how the electricity costs so much in winter."

"Julia Lerner?" Cheri repeated as she scooped a mouthful of vanilla coconut, Alice's favorite. The yogurts came in a four-pack that also contained blueberry, strawberry, and banana; as per habit, Alice ate the flavors she disliked first, saving the best for last, which was usually when Cheri swooped.

"Yeah, you know who that is?" Alice ripped off another piece of doughnut.

"Yes. I do read. A ton of articles." Cheri scraped the edges of the cup. "The Tangerine exec, right? I mean, I don't know that much about her. I didn't read her book."

"She doesn't have a book."

"Oh. I mean, her TED talk."

"She doesn't have a TED talk. At least I don't think," Alice said, as if she weren't sure, though she was. When she'd first realized User 555's identity, Alice had backed away from the laptop, hands apart as if in surrender; she'd intended to stop there, to delete all her reports and searches, but had somehow entered a Julia Lerner internet rat hole instead, one in which endless material was available on her quarry. Julia Lerner on the glass ceiling. Julia Lerner on women and power. Julia Lerner on holiday entertaining, double standards, marriage and house chores. And, as of the last weeks, Julia Lerner on motherhood.

It was something in Julia's manner, Alice had thought just earlier this morning, as she'd scanned yet another piece—one in which she was assured she would simply not believe What Julia Lerner Has To Say About THIS!, in which the THIS! was revealed to be a speech titled "Balancing Personal Ambition with Corporate Objectives," given at Duke's commencement—a self-aware, performative quality, which Alice instinctively disliked. After finishing the article, Alice had scrolled to the comments:

Remember she only got where she is because she fucked Pierre Roy

This feminazi discriminates against all men! I see a coming male purge, and then a revolt! Shareholders will not stand, especially when she doesn't deliver!

Anyone else think she's a crazy fucking cunt?

As she read, Alice's disgust had been undermined by a shallow, guilty pleasure; she knew that as a thirty-five-year-old Chinese American woman with moderate if vague ambitions she should actually be cheering the self-promotional activities of Julia Lerner. After all, didn't that ubiquitous argument apply: that the men were awful, too? As if it were acceptable for Pierre to threaten to take Tangerine private (it was just idle *conjecture*, Pierre said, though you know if he wanted he *totally could*); as if he didn't bear equal or greater responsibility for God Mode, and a world where it was acceptable for a thirty-four-year-old to be worth billions and purchase entire neighborhoods in Palo Alto.

"Are these from your mom?" Cheri held up a pack of pineapple cakes, which June had pressed upon Alice along with fried noodle leftovers last Sunday.

"Yes."

Cheri turned over the pack, studying the foreign kcal nutritional data before setting it down with a sigh. "Your mom is so cute." An esteem Alice knew was reciprocated by June. It'd been June who suggested Alice call her cousin, after learning of Jimmy's desertion. Cheri was living at home, June said, she had just broken up with her boyfriend, he would not propose, and she would not stand for it! That June framed Cheri's predicament in such favorable terms was not lost on Alice; the boyfriend, a thirty-eight-year-old CEO of a payments-processing unicorn, was considered one of the better-looking bachelors in the Valley. Prior to him, Cheri had dated the CFO of one of his competitors, and before him a richly compensated Israeli engineering VP at Google. "She needs to settle," Jimmy had once commented. "Stop aiming for the top guys. She's just going to get older and then have to drop her standards even lower. It's the basic yield curve."

Alice made a surreptitious inspection of Cheri. Her cousin was bare-faced, and dressed in leggings and a cropped tee. She had that appearance of certain mixed-race Asians, where from specific angles they just looked like a slightly exotic, extremely attractive Caucasian person. In the sun, her hair was near blond, and her eyes were a mix of hazel and flecks of green, which brought to mind the admiring discussions their Chinese relatives would have over Cheri's features, fussing over her enormous eyes and high nose bridge; a written transcript of these conversations might read to an unfamiliar audience as a meeting of white supremacists.

"I do think it's cool, you know, that she's a woman," Cheri said. "I mean, it's hard, right?"

"You think that because she's female, she should get extra credit," Alice said. "That we should go easier on her."

"Well yeah," Cheri said automatically as she turned to the fridge, where Alice knew—just *knew*!—she was going to go for the expensive dark chocolate mousse. "Don't you?"

"I don't know."

"You know she just had a baby." Cheri was still holding open the fridge door, oblivious to the cold draining out.

"Yes. Everyone knows."

Cheri shut the fridge without taking anything. She lifted an ankle to the counter and stretched, effortlessly touching her head to her toes. "You think she's kind of a fake," she remarked as she rose.

"Maybe. Or that she's a bitch." Saying the word out loud felt strange; Alice wasn't used to it. In college, she'd admired girls who could shout it as an endearment: *Heyyyyy, bitch!*

"Everyone's a bitch. At least she's a good person."

"Why do you think that? Because she *says* so?"

Cheri switched legs. "Why think something terrible about someone when you can believe the best?"

"Because people aren't nice," Alice said, voice breaking. "They aren't nice at all."

"Oh, Alice." Cheri slid her leg off the counter and, before Alice could escape, had already come around and trapped her in a hug.

After a second, Alice placed an arm stiffly around Cheri's back; she then broke the embrace and began to clear the counter of dishes.

"Let me do mine," Cheri said, snatching up her empty yogurt cup and spoon. She dropped the spoon into the sink with a clang and threw the cup toward the recycling bin—it bounced off the side and rolled underneath the shoe rack, where Alice eventually retrieved it.

MONTHLY BUDGET

Fed. loans: $2,100
Rent: $1,600
Food and utilities: $800
Other: $100

Seated at her desk, the pen spinning between her fingers, Alice stared at the numbers until they blurred. Here, on this sheet, were the monthly obligations she risked by continuing her obsession with one of the most important executives in her company.

Alice was aware that on the topic of "corporate responsibility" she held a particularly flimsy claim; she had never even considered the ethics of any company she worked for, instead opting to prioritize attributes such as salary, free meals, and proximity to the 280. It was her parents' contention that a company's dissemination of authoritarian propaganda, its right to monetize user data, were subjects for white people to worry about—specifically, white people with funded retirements and paid-off mortgages. Who'd never had to weigh each decision on that internal scale of financial levy: how much in gas and parking to drive to San Francisco in traffic, was ordering water okay on a "coffee" date, did you really have to press 20 percent tip just for getting a muffin when they tilted at you that little screen? White people, white *Americans*, June said, were to be admired: they adopted children from all over, and when had you ever seen a Japanese person with a Rwandan baby or vice versa? Yes, there were some bad ones, but the good examples were what made the country so admirable.

But Chinese people, immigrants: their job was to survive.

Alice logged back in to God Mode. After a brief deliberation, she printed Logan's messages with Chloe Kirkpatrick. This, she promised herself, would be the last time she used the tool.

Her email chimed. Alice ignored it. Having made the decision about God Mode, she now felt at peace; she considered painting her nails and browsed Gap online for pajamas. She added two pairs of loose cotton pants to her cart and opened Tangerine Mail.

And then, seconds later, began to panic.

To: Alice Lu
From: Nicole Wallace
Subject: Invite: Roundtable with Julia Lerner

Dear Alice,

I am pleased to inform you that you have been personally selected to join the next roundtable with Julia Lerner. As you may know, Julia conducts very few of these intimate ten-person roundtables throughout the year, and personally invites only those employees she believes to be rising talents within Tangerine.

While the roundtables are invite-only, there is high demand for the slots. If you cannot make it, please let me know as soon as possible so that another woman might have the opportunity.

Best regards,

Nicole Wallace

Executive Assistant to Julia Lerner

# 14

# JULIA

Once, the meeting rooms at Tangerine had been named after inventors; in the beginning the entire hundred-person staff had worked out of the bottom floor of a warehouse, the meeting rooms along the walls, Pierre's office across from Woods and between Curie and Franklin. As the company ballooned they'd moved multiple times, eventually settling for good at Tangerine's ninety-acre Herzog & de Meuron–designed campus in Mountain View. But by then the topic of inventors itself had become controversial, because of questions like how many women and minorities, and it was just a great big bummer, at least to the executive team, so the decree came down from Pierre that no, they'd ruined the concept, and frankly he was disappointed about the complaining, given that they now had Food Truck Tuesdays and a dog grooming salon and so what else did they want? What else were they going to demand, in this utopia he had built at great expense—and Pierre was normally someone who was all about the youth, because he too was a young person, he was super young in fact, had just turned thirty-two, though he was very much starting to see what the older people (forty plus) meant when they spoke of the thanklessness of the younger generation. So fuck the inventors, going forward the meeting rooms would be named after animals. And, if an employee with too much time—hours that should be spent in pursuit of innovation and not the social justice bean counting that'd been on display earlier—should go and analyze the names of the rooms, what was the worst they could say, that there were too many based on *large cats*? Like, you've got a leopard and a tiger but no dementor wasp? What are you, biased against insects of the order Hymenoptera? And even then Pierre could say: *Yeah, I just really prefer cats.* And that would be the end of it.

And thus it was in the sixteen-person-capacity Bowhead Whale, her private meeting room, that Julia now faced her assembled roundtable.

Okay, she thought. Let's get this shit over with.

She'd been up since three A.M. Had been dreaming she was at the institute, playing chess with Misha, when abruptly she was back in California, awake and in pain from a clogged duct. After calling to Charlie—who, while having returned from the guest bedroom, had also adopted a mild deafness when it came to night noise—Julia had ended up pushing him, hard, using the opposite arm from the angry breast, and then he'd woken, angry himself. "A lot of women have problems with latching," he'd murmured once he understood the issue, and his eyes had fluttered in that way she knew meant he was trying to fall back asleep. Which had then inspired a hot rage, and if she'd held in her hands the cast-iron skillet that just hours prior she'd used to make his favorite meal, some chicken casserole mess she'd printed the recipe for ages earlier, which had required two sticks of butter and an entire pack of bread crumbs, she might have swung it at his head. That he thought he could ignore her! After she had fucking cooked! All through dinner she'd waited for a compliment, some acknowledgment of her actually preparing him a meal, but Charlie had simply shoveled in the food as usual, dousing the dish in Parmesan and then depositing the cheese-scaled bowl into the middle of the table for Magda to retrieve. In the morning

Charlie left early for work, and so it had been the night nurse, Claire, who'd comforted her, pushing a hot compress against her chest.

"You know, husbands can be clueless," Claire had said, in a rare gesture of initiated conversation, and Julia thought that perhaps last night's hissing match hadn't been so silent. "Nearly all my clients go through a period where they loathe their partners," she added with a laugh. Claire was in her fifties, large boned, the sort of woman whom back home they said was easier to go over than around. There was an earthiness to her, accented by her short, undyed hair and a wardrobe that seemed comprised mostly of sackcloth. Julia wondered where she spent her money, as her weekly fee was usurious.

"Oh?" Julia murmured, not wishing to share her thoughts on the topic of useless husbands, though Claire had signed a nondisclosure agreement, as did all their staff. She did wish to hear about these other women who hated their spouses, however, and so offered a tepid: "Well. It is tough."

"Yes, you can say that." Without warning, Claire bore down with both hands. "You have to breathe through the pain, dear. I know you can do it." Julia grimaced.

"I had this one client," Claire continued. She briefly let up on the pressure and Julia clamped her teeth and sucked in air, hoping it might be over. "The husband, he wouldn't do anything. Said it was how he'd been raised. So it was the wife who got up at night, rocked the baby, brought up the older children, cleaned house. I saw that *60 Minutes* interview you did, where you said women were born stronger than men. It's true, completely true." She rose and wiped her hands on a towel.

"Right," said Julia. Though in reality she didn't believe this at all. Sometimes she hated the women who repeated her own inanity back to her—the men too, but especially the women, who really ought to know better. Who should intuitively understand that her business was not the furthering of womankind but only the appearance of such while still remaining palatable to men, who after all comprised 50 percent of her audience and 100 percent of her up-ward reporting structure. Women were just born stronger? *Really?*

She had looked at the clock: eight A.M., an hour past Claire's usual leaving time, and for sure she would charge extra for it—charge *her*, Julia thought.

"Charlie is a great father," Claire said, screwing a cap onto a clean bottle. "Believe me, I would know. I've seen all sorts."

"He could do more," Julia said, handing the woman her bag. *Leave.*

"Oh honey, you've got to see where they started. Most of them, they've got good hearts. And they're working hard to support the family . . ." Here Claire had faded, recalling she was speaking not to one of her usual clients, some aspiring makeup artist turned soft-ware geek's arm candy, but Julia. "They're doing their best."

Taking her silence for assent, Claire went on: "And that's life, that women should suffer more . . ."

No, Julia thought. Not my life.

She'd had only a few hours of relief before the lump had re-turned, hard and hot; after two sessions in a bathroom stall press-ing, massaging, dabbing toilet paper at the leaking milk, she'd made little progress. By four P.M. she had already packed her things, was anticipating a hot bath, when Nicole informed her of the roundtable.

"Roundtable?" For a moment Julia thought her perfect assis-tant was mistaken. She'd found Nicole years earlier, one of those rare jewels who never went on vacation and kept meticulous men-tal records of everyone Julia liked and disliked, slotting them into her schedule accordingly. Julia had not done a roundtable in half a year, for the simple reason that she hated them—she'd started the program only as an offensive measure, to obstruct cretins like Lara Conrad who'd otherwise start bitching about "pulling up the ladder" behind her. But then Julia retrieved a hazy memory, of impulsively deciding to suss out the server-tagging Alice Lu.

Goddammit! She'd completely lost interest; the girl was nothing, had not cropped up on any more of Jon's reports. She briefly entertained canceling the event but had acquired a reputation for being punctual and rarely missing meetings ("To Gain Respect, You Must Give Respect"), and certainly a room full of petty millennials was not the audience to blow off.

Julia brought her coat and bag with her. The room was already full, as she knew it would be.

"I'm thrilled to be here today. Why don't we do introductions?" Julia smiled. "Let's start with your name and group. I'd especially love to hear something you're passionate about outside of work." And then she zoned out, making sporadic eye contact while her brain snoozed. All the usuals were there: the fancy-schools lady, the engineer lady, the marketing lady, the person-of-color lady, the complaining lady. When the circle reached Alice, Julia was jolted from her reverie; there was really nothing remarkable about the girl, she saw. Merely one of the zillion Asian nerds who dotted Tangerine's landscape but were rarely sighted at her level, the dark-haired grunts who made the wheels turn. When Alice mumbled her role— *technical support*—it was all in a jumble, as if she was trying to eject the information as quickly as possible.

Ugh. For this stale piece of bread, Julia was having to suffer an entire hour?

The introductions concluded, and Julia opened the floor to questions. The first concerned Tangerine's recent abandonment of a government surveillance contract, a stance encouraged by Leo, which Julia had therefore executed. The question was pure softball—the asker, a frizzy user experience researcher in the games division, said that what Julia did was *admirable*, that she was standing up for *their rights*, which Julia understood to actually be a call for her to stand up for the girl's rights, her rights to a swift promotion and personal recognition.

"But shouldn't the government *have* this technology?" the

complainer interjected. *Wah wah wah, bitch, bitch, bitch.* "What makes Tangerine a better arbiter than the leaders we elect?"

"These are all excellent points." Julia imagined a pair of demon horns over the complainer and faintly smirked. The girl frowned, and Julia beamed at her an encouraging look until she returned an uncertain smile. *Careful.* It was always the unlikable ones who saw through her outer glaze.

The rest of the conversation was light, stupid—Katy Rao, who had gone to Harvard and Princeton and whose employment was a favor to her father, Ravi Rao, the CTO of CloudWare, interrogating Julia about what she was going to do about her privilege, her shameful white privilege. Another productivity question, any "hacks" she could share. When you asked a supermodel what she ate for breakfast, did you think you could look like one, too?

With only minutes remaining, the complainer hijacked the conversation once more, something about how men were the enemy, and, like, why wasn't Julia doing *more* about them?

"Alice," Julia called out, "we haven't heard from you in a while. What do you think? Are men the enemy?"

Alice reddened. She should part her hair on the side, Julia thought as she waited out Alice's fumbling; she could tell the girl knew nothing of grooming, had likely parted her hair down the middle all her life, even though it made her look like a horse. "Men?" Alice finally repeated. "All of them?"

"Well, not the ones you like," Julia said teasingly, so it wouldn't appear she was being mean-spirited. She was about to add *not your husband*, but could not imagine this girl married.

"I think anyone can be the enemy," Alice said quietly, and for a moment there was *something*, an instinct within Julia that rang. Did Alice know something? It seemed impossible, and yet there was the strange activity with the server, that name in God Mode . . .

She would have to do something, Julia decided. Even if it was nothing, the chance that it was something meant she'd have to take care of it. The session ended, and the women swarmed like carp in a small pond at feeding: *That was such a great point* and *Maybe we can meet once a quarter* and *I loved what you said about this.* Julia caught the back of Alice's head as she slipped through the door. Pity, as their female engineer numbers were such a trouble spot, but what could you do?

Her phone vibrated. "Yes," Julia answered flatly as she reached into her tote to retrieve her lower-tier business cards, the ones she handed out at conferences, which had no phone number and a secondary email address managed by Nicole.

"Julia." It was Leo. She was surprised to hear his voice, as he rarely called without prior arrangement. "Can we speak?"

"What is it?" she asked, as she tossed her cards to the remaining brown-nosers. Her chest was on fire: she was not in the mood for a list of demands or another request to sabotage her product. "I'm busy. Perhaps we can arrange a time to talk."

"Please find yourself some privacy," Leo said, as if she hadn't just told him she was busy. "I have some news. We're bringing another asset to Tangerine."

JULIA KICKED SHUT THE DOOR to her office. She'd nearly run back from the Bowhead, murmuring sorry, she had to go, next meeting. The pain in her breast now temporarily forgotten, and she set down her bag and retrieved her phone. The call with Leo was still active, and she could hear him clicking his pen over the line.

"*Okay,*" he said, with a slight note of impatience. "Are you alone now?"

Julia was still stunned by the news and silent at first. In their entire relationship, not once had Leo asked to place anyone into her company. To install someone else at Tangerine, a person with actual knowledge of her—*Why would you do this*, she wanted to scream.

"Who is it?" she finally asked. Forcing her voice out calm as she bashed an employee tchotchke, a key chain in the shape of a tangerine, against her desk. The fruit had a GPS tracker inside, so you could always find your keys—one of her personal inspirations, as she'd seen how the local hirelings paraded about in their corporate swag.

"Another patriot," Leo said. For once the connection was clear of static. "Like you."

"Someone important?" The president had four sons, and the youngest had a supposed interest in technology—now *that* would be a nice challenge, one with many possibilities . . .

"No, another asset. He's worked with me for years."

Her knuckles went white around the orange casing. "Why are you sending him?"

"We think he'd be good on the ground. Another pair of eyes. We don't want all the pressure on you, Julia, we know how much work you have." All these words, so many *we*s.

"And you expect him to do . . ."

"Oh, he's very versatile. I'm not sending someone unqualified. He was top in his class for computer science." He coughed, and she knew they were both thinking of her own mediocre grades. "But since then he's worked in the industry. A lot of good experience."

"What's deemed *good* in your world may not fly over here."

"Shall I send you his résumé? Currently a product executive at Siemens. Prior to that, McKinsey, also in Berlin." He paused. "I would like Aaron placed in a managerial position. Enough so that he has high-level data access, can approve ad campaigns."

Aaron. So that was his name. Though it was good news about the ads: the less her involvement, the better. If you wished to be depressed about the world all you needed was the click-through rates of some of the SPB's widgets—see how many believed they had a 99.9 percent IQ or resembled Julia Roberts. All while the SPB scraped their data and photos. "It won't be so easy to find a position. You understand people wait years to become a vice president here. If they ever get it."

"But surely a chief operating officer has a great deal of auton-omy, no? You can make nearly anything you want happen."

And somehow—in the way two people in a long marriage can argue over a subject without ever directly speaking of it—Julia understood Leo knew she'd disobeyed him, that she'd secretly patched Tangerine Mail's source code and had thus betrayed both him and the SPB.

"I'm doing this to *help*," he then added as a parting shot. "You don't need to worry. Aaron will report to you."

# 15

# ALICE

There was a part of Alice that had worried the roundtable would be—what? An ambush, a hostile conversation: *who are you / how dare you / what do you think you're doing?* Which was delusional, she knew, and yet she couldn't imagine why else she'd been invited. All week she'd fretted over the event, how to prepare, what to say. The stress of it all compounded the morning of by Tara, who enforced a much-hated "open calendars" policy among her staff and had thus spotted the roundtable on Alice's schedule:

"How'd you get on the list?" Tara asked, appearing right as Alice was about to depart for a breakfast croissant, sorely needed for her nerves. "I thought the roundtables were paused."

"Yeah." Alice cast around in case Sam or even Larry might be able to help. "Uh. I don't know."

Tara crouched so they were eye level, a hand on Alice's chair. "Did you email anybody? Talk to someone in her office? Nicole, maybe?"

"Who's Nicole?"

"Julia's *assistant*," Tara said, with sudden disgust. She stood and waved as if shaking off something dirty. Her dress was witchy, with sleeves that widened at the end; as she moved, the fabric brushed Alice's hair.

Hours later, sitting in the Bowhead Whale, Alice would flash back to this moment. Tara's face before her, the mix of longing and displeasure. Understanding it more.

Because she'd discovered that she quite liked Julia Lerner.

She was charming, and smart, and self-deprecating, the latter of which Alice was usually suspicious of, in particular from the beautiful and successful—but Julia appeared truly humble, had told an embarrassing story about botching a presentation to the board, after which she'd not been invited back for a year. And then focused on each of them in the room, asking follow-ups to their comments. The sheer execution of it all! To sustain that interest level, that energy! Julia made you feel special, seen—by the end Alice could even understand how she might have been selected for the roundtable, given Julia's careful explanation of how they'd each been specifically screened, the invites going only to those with "unmet potential."

And really, didn't Alice have quite a lot of unmet potential?

Returning to her desk, Alice had an impulse to walk into Tara's office and gloat, which was so outside of her normal behavior that she knew she had to remove herself from the area. She took her laptop and bag to the "contemplation space" on the other side of the floor. Finding a table at which she was halfway obscured by a lemon tree, she sat and half closed her eyes, reliving the last hour.

At first, as Alice had listened to Julia, she'd been almost depressed. Why even try, when someone else was always going to be better? Why stop buying lattes if you knew you'd never be rich? And in fact another participant, a twitchy product manager named Bea Schumann whom Alice thought Larry might also diagnose as having *difficulty with social interactions*, had asked something similar:

"What if you've got, uh, certain dreams but know you won't ever reach them? Not all of us can be COO or CEO. It's statistically impossible. So then what do you do?"

Julia had begun as expected. You are special, you can do any-thing, a life is very long. As with the rest of her answers, her words were both predictable and fortifying, like a romantic comedy: you left feeling hopeful, but without any practical knowledge that could be applied to your own life. At the end of her response, however, Julia's face took on a pained urgency and she added: "When I was younger, I used to think about how happy I'd be if only certain things in my life could be different. And then one day I simply de-cided to change them myself. You've all got some issue nagging at you. The only reason you haven't done anything is because you're scared or lazy or think it isn't worth the time. But who else is going to care as much? Nobody, that's the truth."

Julia was right, Alice knew. No one was coming to rescue her from anything. She had to do it herself. And in that moment Alice felt so inspired that she went into her backpack and retrieved the conversations between Logan and Chloe and mapped the route to his home.

IT TOOK ALICE TWENTY MINUTES to drive to Willow Glen. She worried she'd be noticed, but the street bustled with a constant stream of gardeners and cleaners and nannies. Across from Logan's house, a white van was departing, and Alice took its spot.

Freshman year at MIT, Alice had been paired in the housing lottery with a girl named Tanya Jenkins. Tanya was one of those girls with naturally dark hair who refused to bear it—Alice would later learn she had her blond retouched every three weeks, charging $200 to her parents' credit card at a salon in Back Bay. Tanya of-ten explained to Alice why her taste in everything from clothing to flowers was wrong. "That's a *McMansion*," she said once, when Alice pointed to a house listing in a broker's window.

"A McMansion?" Alice repeated. They were on Newbury Street, having just finished lunch before going shopping. Alice had splurged, ordering the spaghetti carbonara and then finishing it all, since she already knew she wasn't going to buy any clothes.

"Yeah. It's like, a house that pretends to be fancy, but really isn't."

"How do you know it's pretending?"

Tanya flitted a hand. "Something to do with construction quality."

Alice wasn't sure if Logan's house was a McMansion. But it was the sort of place that as a child she would have found tremendously impressive, which boded poorly for it on the Tanya Jenkins taste meter: It was Spanish style, with multiple roof shapes, and loomed over the houses to the left and right like a bully edging out others for space. The lawn was square and well watered, the mailbox faux stone.

Alice stared at the house number: 424.

She'd told Jimmy once, about what had happened. It had been an impulse, on one of the rare nights they didn't watch TV but sat on the couch and talked. Jimmy spent the first hour speaking nearly exclusively, outlining the next five years of his start-up—and then, perhaps realizing he'd monopolized the conversation, he pressed Alice to speak. Worried her own issues might sound petty, or boring, Alice suddenly reached for an old memory. As she described the boys entering the cleaners, threatening her mother, and then her own discovery of June with blood on her face on the floor, she could see Jimmy's expression creep from indifference to mild interest to distaste—

"What?" Alice finally asked.

He hesitated. "You're not going to like it."

"Tell me."

Jimmy opened his mouth and closed it. Opened it again. "I thought you were going to say she was raped or something."

"Raped? Is that the only way it can be awful?"

"It *is* awful," he agreed. "It *is* horrible." But she could see in his face that he thought it wasn't enough; that it wasn't unlucky enough, or grim enough, to have been given such weight in her head.

On Alice's lap lay an envelope addressed to Carolyn Schiller, into which Alice had neatly slotted the conversations between Logan and Chloe Kirkpatrick back at Tangerine. Alice sat for another minute, pressing the envelope flat between her palms. Then she opened her car door, walked to the Schillers' mailbox, and set the envelope inside.

# APRIL 2019

# 16

# JULIA

Aaron Pina was handsome, with light eyes and dark brows and brown fairy-tale-prince hair. He obviously worked out, and wore shirts designed to show it: a little tight, not so much to be convincingly accused of vanity, but enough so that you could *see*. He used gel in his hair and employed a heavy hand with a sandalwood-based cologne but by far his worst trait—the one that made Julia want to shoot him in the face—was that he knew exactly who she was.

He'd materialized a week earlier, announcing his name and then hers at reception. Julia knew the exact date of his arrival, Leo having dropped this turd during their last call. Julia believed she might not even have warranted this advance notice, had she not been required to conjure the requested job at Tangerine: "And as I said, something in management," Leo reminded her. "I can't imagine it's terribly difficult, is it?"

In the last quarter, Julia's projects had delivered $2 billion in new revenue; she'd been asked to the Bilderberg steering committee and approached for the board of directors of Nvidia, Goldman Sachs, and Starbucks. It wasn't easy to stay at the top, and the fact that Julia did remain here, second only to Pierre, was a testament to her ability and exceptionalism.

And yet here she was, obeying the orders of a public servant, like some dumb little bitch.

Julia had to credit Aaron—since their first meeting, in which he'd arrived wearing a cobalt shirt and black pants that both screamed German polyester, he'd markedly evolved. Gone was the hair mousse, the excessively groomed beard; even his cologne was muted, if not entirely absent. He'd made alarmingly quick inroads into the executive coterie: she'd overheard Raj Singh, their chief of cloud, asking Aaron if he golfed, and seen him flirting with Lara Conrad—Lara braying her big toothy laugh and shoving her tits in his face—at the Burmese café earlier this week. Even Nicole wasn't immune: somehow in the initial walk from the lobby a week earlier, Aaron had learned Julia's assistant liked chocolate, and today had appeared with a box of Christopher Elbow caramels. Nicole had beamed when she brought him in, and Nicole never beamed.

He was, Julia thought, extremely dangerous.

"I trust you're enjoying yourself?" she asked as he entered, not rising from her desk.

"Very much so," Aaron replied, flashing a brilliant smile that made her loathe him all the more. He was tall, which she found particularly unfair, given that she knew quite a few competent short men who would likely have much nicer lives, or at least careers, if only they possessed some extra height. He went to her shelf, where he examined an orange lava lamp, a stray decoration from last year's holiday party. "There's just one minor issue. My office."

Ah. The office. Initially it'd burned when Julia realized that for reasons of discretion, Aaron should have an office—she herself had toiled at those awful open desks for years before qualifying for her own. She'd specifically selected his allocation: on the second floor, in an abnormally cramped and sauna-like cave into which the sun beamed its full powers and that also boasted a direct view of the men's urinals. She knew the layout of the entire headquarters because she'd managed its construction—just one of her many dreadful jobs over the years, which people conveniently forgot when they bemoaned how high she was now.

"You don't like the space? I thought it was nice. A pretty view of the mountains."

"It's too hot," Aaron said, setting down the lamp.

*I bet. I hope you roast.* She clucked in sympathy. "I'll see what we can do with the facilities team. But this is only a temporary assignment, isn't it?"

"Well." He stopped. "Leo didn't say. I hope not."

"Surely Mountain View can't compare to Berlin. Or home."

"I want to live in California. Doesn't everyone? That's why *you're* here."

Julia ignored this. Aaron's shoes were freshly shined, she saw—she could imagine him working carefully at night with black polish, as she once had. "What about your family?" She was curious about this, Leo having given few details.

He shrugged. "I'll go home for a few weeks in the summer. Like the rest of the Russians do."

The rest of the Russians. Naturally, Aaron had already insinuated himself with the Tangerine contingent; there were a good number, most of them engineers. Though Julia rarely socialized. First, because they would immediately hit her up for favors, but also because she didn't want to be questioned about her grandparents' dacha, or her years in university, or how would you like to keynote this year's Eurasian Investment Forum? She knew any information she surrendered would be summarily turned over and examined with a searing ferocity unimaginable to Americans. "How lovely for you. That your family is still there."

Aaron gazed at her. "You had a baby recently, didn't you? I'd like to have one. It would be better for citizenship."

"I didn't know you were married."

Aaron laughed. "That's not the difficult part." He directed at her a warm smile. "I hope you know I'm not here to make your life difficult, Julia. I'm here to *help* you."

Help. She wondered what he could possibly do, if he had any idea of the specifics of her job. Aaron was like most men, in that he could easily envision himself with power but never considered what it took to hold it, which was why they so frequently lost their positions to drugs and blow jobs.

Aaron made another revolution around her office and then sat in one of her chairs. It was new, Le Corbusier; she'd purchased it along with a twelve-person service of Herend the day Leo had informed her of Aaron's arrival. "I've started working to identify a new vulnerability in Tangerine's source code," he said, smoothing a hand over the navy leather. "For Leo."

"Whatever Leo asks of you, you must also inform me," she said sharply.

He blinked. "Of course."

"I'm the second highest in the company, you understand? You must treat me like your manager, because I am. You report to me."

He continued to nod, his face set in amicable lines, even though she'd just used her Superbitch voice, the one she knew men hated. "I report to you," he repeated.

"Correct."

"And you report to Pierre," Aaron added, in the same pleasant drone—a thumb to his lips, as if daydreaming.

She was instantly wary. "Yes."

"And how is he doing?"

What did it matter? Aaron was never going to meet Pierre, that was for sure. "Pierre's well. Busy."

"I saw his interview the other day. On CNBC?"

"Yes." Thankfully Pierre had restrained himself from another exaggeration about their road map. The last few months he'd become increasingly distracted from the business: attending the Met

Gala, flying to Iceland last-minute to observe a satellite launch. His girlfriends, always vapid, had taken a turn toward the outer edge of famous. He hadn't even attended his last two staff meetings, instead delegating to Julia his signatory power. Which suited her just fine.

She turned to her screen. "I have a call. We'll meet again later."

Aaron stood. "You'll let me know about the office?" She gave a curt nod.

He went to her door. He stood, not moving, until she looked up: "Yes? What *is* it?"

"I could just ask Pierre," he said softly. "About the office."

Was he crazy? "You don't go to the CEO with your real estate problems."

"Right. Though I am playing hockey with him on Sunday. Perhaps if it comes up . . ."

"Hockey," Julia repeated, unconsciously pushing herself away from her desk. She could not recall the last time Pierre had asked to see her on a weekend. How had Aaron even met Pierre? How had they been introduced?

"Ice hockey," Aaron elaborated. His face held a fleck of . . . could it be *satisfaction*? "There's a rink in San Jose. We were in the elevator together and got to talking. Of course I'd seen his interviews before, but it's really when you speak to Pierre one-on-one that you can tell he's a genius, isn't it? And even after running Tangerine all day, he still somehow finds time to keep fit. While the rest of us sit on the couch and binge TV." He chuckled.

"Perhaps you could come watch us play sometime," Aaron added. "You know, see the boys." And then, before Julia could recover, he'd closed the door and walked out.

As Aaron went past, Julia watched the usual flunkies turn: there were two junior analysts, a Jamaican girl with acne scars and her friend, a slutty brunette, who acted as quasi beat reporters, noting everyone who came and went from her office. When he reached

Nicole, Aaron stopped—leaned over her desk and spoke a few words, upon which Nicole blushed and offered him a caramel.

She'd been a fool, Julia realized. To assume Aaron was as he appeared. Had nearly forgotten that precept that had ruled her own life starting from the institute, that most of the time you hid what it was you wanted, to get what you truly desired. That to enable the extraordinary, it was best to project mediocrity until you were finally prepared to take.

Julia returned to her screen and logged in as User 555. Aaron was more cautious than she'd assumed: his Tangerine profile had only been opened his first day of work, and even God Mode returned little more than a basic email. Though that didn't mean he was traceless altogether. Since its purchase of VisionMatch years earlier, Tangerine had continued to acquire start-ups with facial recognition software. The technology had developed over the years, to the point where accuracy had been refined to 99.8 percent. Julia opened a fake Tangerine account for Aaron, uploaded the photo from his employee ID (flattering), and then: *pop!*

In under a minute. A few seconds, actually. Drawing from a database of billions, a record of every photo of Aaron that had ever been uploaded to Tangerine, by anyone in the world.

Julia went through the results, almost stroking the screen. And thought: *Interesting.*

# 17

# ALICE

Birthday boozing with my man!

Pics or it never happened, right?! Had an awesome night with my partner in crime at Miller Academy's Winter Ball to support the girl's school! Dress is by DVF!

Does someone want to adopt a puppy? Save this handsome Lab mix from the shelter (we already have THREE)

At the Bierhaus, remembering 9-11! We Will Never Forget!!

The last set of pictures, taken at the First Responders Gala, featured a full-length of Carolyn as the cover image, followed by multiple configurations of her and six similarly attired friends. In the final photo, her lipstick was reapplied, strapless dress straightened and hiked; she held hands with Logan, big smiles, eyes locked on the camera.

Alice looked up the date of the gala. Sunday. Two days earlier. To her right, Larry typed while noisily eating corn chips.

What was Carolyn doing? Why wasn't anything *happening*?

It'd been two weeks since Alice delivered Logan's chat logs. Having promised she would permanently ban herself from God Mode, that she would never again access the tool, Alice had then proceeded to log back in that very same night. And, in breaking her vows, had been rewarded with a series of hastily conducted searches, all via Carolyn's profile, of:

- Chloe Kirkpatrick
- Chloe Kirkpatrick's girlfriends
- Chloe Kirkpatrick's parents, her parents' places of employment, her childhood home, and her junior varsity field hockey scores

But since this initial burst, Alice had seen nothing further: no appointments with a divorce lawyer; no feverish emails to a sister, sorority sister, or faraway best friend. The only suspicious behavior was an influx of logins to Carolyn and Logan's joint Wells Fargo account, though Carolyn had not withdrawn any money. The majority of her financial activity remained on her Nordstrom credit card, to which she had charged $2,800 in the past week.

Alice picked at the dust on her keyboard. Was she missing something? Was there something else she should be searching for? She was about to log back in to God Mode, to attempt another path, when she heard her name.

"Alice?" Tara stood in her doorway. "Could you come in?"

TARA'S DESK HAD A NEW acrylic tray in the corner, with WORK WORK WORK scrawled on its side in red; next to it was a framed print of Tara's recent nomination to the Forbes Fearless & Fabulous 100. While not technically an executive, Tara had still managed to wangle herself an office, citing something to do with data security. Though hers was one of the less coveted locations, facing the afternoon sun.

"Okay," Tara began, and Alice reminded herself to make eye contact, as this had been listed as one of her deficiencies. Tara wore a draped shirt, cropped pants, and high platform sandals; she was also trying something new with a dark lipstick, which Alice would try to compliment later if she thought it could be done sincerely.

Tara clasped her hands. "There's something we need to discuss."

"Sure."

"Have you been running any reports on our servers?"

*Oh shit.* Alice tried to speak, but croaked and then fake-coughed to buy time.

"Alice," Tara repeated, "I asked you a question. Have you run any reports on our servers? And to be clear, I mean reports you do not currently possess the authority to be using?"

Focus, Alice ordered herself. Focus, and don't you dare panic! She understood it was crucial that she answer, and that her answer be both vague and self-assured. That Tara was asking meant she already knew *something*—so now it was a matter of determining what and steering her in an innocuous direction.

"I did run a report. I mean, I run them every day. It's part of my *job*," Alice said. Yes. This was good. Tara didn't actually know what anyone on her team did. If Alice could confuse her, this would add another layer of protection.

"Did you, at any point this past quarter, run a scan of Server 251, based out of the Dublin data center?" Tara looked at her notebook, and alarm clawed at Alice's throat as she realized Tara was reading from a report or update.

"I—" Alice began, and then thought it was best not to lie, as Tara was excellent at detecting these. She was one of those people who, having blundered into their own position, had a talent for discerning fragile spots in other stories; would ask and prod and follow up until you became confused and eventually gave way. "Yes."

"Why?"

"I was curious. I saw some strange activity."

"You were curious," Tara said incredulously.

"Yes. I was, ah, trying to be resourceful. I saw something un-usual, and I wanted to make sure nothing serious was going on."

"Were you near anyone else who could have run it? A superior you could have asked?"

"Well—" Alice paused again, both smarting at the idea of Larry as her superior and debating whether to expose him, especially since just yesterday she'd discovered he had pushed their shared barrier over another half inch. "No. There was no one around. And I was concerned the server issue could impact the whole data center." Highly unlikely, nearly impossible, but Alice was banking on Tara not knowing this—and then by luck, one of those corporate phrases Tara wielded with such ease floated into her head: "I thought there was a business justification. I'm really sorry." Alice congratulated herself for apologizing. No one else on the team would have de-based themselves in this way, and she was certain by now Larry or Sam would have gotten up and left.

Tara was silent. She gazed at Alice, pushing her bracelets up her arm. "You understand there are processes," she said at last. "Correct ways to go about these actions. Such caution is crucial, given the sensitivity of our work."

"I understand," Alice began, but Tara held up a hand. She returned to her notebook, a finger on the page as she read: "I'm espe-cially disappointed given that last quarter we'd already discussed your lack of soft skills." She looked up. "And now I have to worry about your judgment as well?"

And then: "You acknowledge our position is one of privilege. And that what you've done is a violation of our code of conduct."

Oh God, Alice thought, finally understanding. Oh God, it's ac-tually happening.

IT HAD ALWAYS BEEN ONE of Alice's greatest fears that she would lose her job. How amazing she found them, her colleagues who were seemingly so carefree—who said they'd quit when they wanted, that they could find new work, why not follow your passions, because this was your one life and remember one day you're definitely going to die. While Alice thought she understood—at least conceptually—the delights of sightseeing in Santorini or sunning oneself on a lounger in Palawan, she still could not personally imagine a greater long-term happiness than being stably employed, with a recurring paycheck and health insurance. You might be tired or lonely, but with a job such problems at least seemed surmountable: employment was like a best friend or boyfriend, in that it seemed so easy when you had it, but an impossible task when you didn't.

She should have been more careful. She had risked everything. And for what?

Tara had stood, was moving about her office now. Explaining how there'd be documentation of the incident, an official investigation with human resources. It might seem harsh, Tara said, she understood Alice might not have known her actions were such a violation—but it was what had to be done, because after all, personal ambition had to be balanced with corporate objectives.

In the midst of Alice's agony, a faraway light blinked. "Could you repeat that?"

"What?"

"Could you repeat that? What you just said."

Tara frowned. "About balancing personal ambition with corporate objectives? Alice . . . you're normally *such* a good listener."

But Alice didn't respond. Balancing personal ambition with corporate objectives: at first she thought it was a Tangerine mantra, one of those phrases on the intranet site where she checked her pay stubs, but the memory didn't fit. Was it written on a wall somewhere? The bathrooms?

And then it came to her: Julia's commencement speech at Duke, the transcript of which Alice had read weeks earlier.

She'd been stupid, Alice realized. So terribly stupid. And now, as Tara ran on about the code of conduct, Alice recalled the flag she'd placed on Server 251. Server 251, which had led her to God Mode. The server with a flag with her name. Julia must have found it. Perhaps she'd even found Alice's activity on God Mode—while Alice thought she'd been careful, she couldn't be certain, and either way she had abused it, had searched and read without contrition. And then as the pain spread in her stomach Alice knew that at the very least Julia knew she'd been snooping around the servers, and at worst Julia knew *everything*. Julia Lerner, who used God Mode to search for government leaders, military generals. Who as COO of Tangerine was one of the most powerful women in the world.

Alice stood. The air in the office felt tight, as if she'd ascended a high summit; she wobbled and tried to breathe.

"*Alice,*" Tara said, with a note of alarm. "Nothing is happening right now, okay? You aren't getting fired." Then, perhaps not intending to be so comforting: "But this isn't good. It's definitely going to be documented."

Alice grabbed the top of her chair. "I need a few minutes."

"Well . . ." She could see Tara was hesitant, but Alice no longer cared, it was coming fast, the panic—

Alice ran into the bathroom and threw up.

# 18

# LEO

L eo had known Julia would hate Aaron.

It was, he could admit, precisely the point.

It was a crisp, clear Saturday morning, and Leo was driving to see his asset. Leo had originally met Aaron through a contact at the Berlin embassy—while at Siemens, Aaron had come to possess a cache of top secret research documents, and nursed a grievance toward his German bosses, whom he felt looked down on him over his lack of a doctorate. Though creative in the field, at times Aaron displayed an unnecessary recklessness, and occasionally Leo thought the man believed he was in fact not an operative but an actor playing one in a movie, a character destined to survive to the end credits. Like many a movie star, Aaron was more attractive in person than on-screen. And also like most actors Leo knew of, Aaron was both smarter and pettier than he appeared.

"Everything is shit," Aaron complained as soon as Leo was seated. Not even offering a water, though he had directed Leo to a cracked leather chair. Aaron's apartment was cramped and bleak, the sort that came furnished for newly divorced men; in the corner was a wooden folding table, next to a shopping bag from Neiman Marcus.

Thirsty, Leo retrieved a soda from his backpack. As he did, Aaron took out his laptop and began to type, as if he could not waste a minute of active time, slotting in random tasks whenever the opportunity arose. Rather like the advice in a Julia Lerner interview, though Leo kept this thought to himself. Instead, he opened the can and asked, "What's wrong?"

"It's Julia. She's power selfish."

*Big surprise.* "Power hungry, not power selfish. The correct term is 'power hungry.' Or you could just say that she is selfish."

Aaron pushed down his screen. Behind him a guitar lay against the wall; Aaron was a musician, Leo recalled, a fairly talented one. He was the sort of man whose attractiveness to women was particularly irritating to other men, though one-on-one Aaron could make himself likable to nearly anyone. If he felt like it.

"This is what you came here to discuss? My *language*?"

"It's important that you have clean English." Leo had never had to stress this to Julia; she had studied on her own. "We don't want people to hear your accent, remember you're both from Russia. To carry that linkage in their mind. Why do you think Julia has been so successful?"

"Fine," Aaron said mockingly, with a tinge of cowboy. *Fiiiiine.*

Leo wiped his mouth. "Tell me what's wrong with her."

"She's territorial. And deliberately gave me the worst office in the building. All day long I look at men pissing. How do you like this hellhole, by the way? It's because she refuses to release my relocation money."

"Your job is not to take over Julia's projects. You're to help on the technical side, identify gaps in the source code. Also to approve political accounts, understand how we might achieve better value with ad spending." It always was the bean counters, Leo thought, who ran everything in the end. "And to be a voice of support, especially when it comes to any desired positions that might prove controversial."

"Such as?"

"Such as if there's a business decision that would put Julia at risk of scrutiny. Something to do with political censorship, for example. We can't have her seen as lobbying for too many of the SPB's positions. It's best for her to remain aboveboard."

Aaron laughed. "So you want me to take her shits, is what you're saying."

"If that's how you put it," Leo said mildly.

Aaron spread his knees as if preparing to argue. He exhaled. "Fine. I've always been a good soldier. But know that even if I wanted, I couldn't execute your requests. As Julia's cut me off from any major project. Putting on her little angel act, all while kneecapping me in private like a bitch—"

Leo raised a hand. "No more talk like this."

"What is this, some kind of gentlemen's club? 'Let's go blow up America but remember to open doors for the ladies'? You know, I'm the true equalist here. I wouldn't care if Julia were a man. Either way, she's still an asshole."

"I'll talk to her."

Aaron shook his head, releasing a cloud of musk. "You don't *tell* people like Julia anything. You *make* them do what you want."

"As I said earlier, don't be rude."

"But—"

But Leo had heard enough; he was in no mood to console, cajole, or generally endure a poor attitude, especially from a minor engineer he'd brought over to California and settled at considerable cost. He stood and took his leave.

Outside, the sun was oppressive in its brightness: he had the sensation that time was a wave, grinding him to the ground. As he walked to his car, his back became damp with sweat. Just another ordinary man, he thought, dabbing at his neck with a tissue. Nobody special, going about his work for the day.

LEO DROVE DIRECTLY TO JULIA'S.

By now he was used to her neighborhood, the way its residents made pretending they didn't care about money into a blunt art: old Acuras and Subarus on the curbs, mutts urinating in front of $15 million mansions. When he arrived, he knocked and waited for what he thought an inordinate amount of time. When Julia finally answered, her hair was unbrushed and redolent of grease: "It's mad today," she declared, Emily on her hip.

"Where are the others?" Leo asked, taking the baby from her and walking inside. He didn't see Luna or Magda, and from what Leo understood of the world of wealthy women this was akin to a nightmare: that you might be separated from your "staff," that you would not have your "people" to do things for you.

"Everyone's sick or on vacation." It was clear she considered neither a suitable defense.

They went to her library, a light-filled space with potted orchids along the walls. On his way Leo had stopped at an upscale grocer's and purchased a bouquet of dahlias; Julia thanked him and set them on a table. "I'll take Emily," she said, reaching. "Your arms must be tired."

"No, I am fine. And wouldn't you like a break?" Leo wondered where Charlie was, but knew better than to ask.

"Really, you can hand her over. I know how children bore you." A note of anxiety had crept into her voice.

He passed her back. "Well, this one is beautiful." Leo was slightly disturbed by the warmth he felt for Julia and her child. Though was it wrong to be a little happy for her? "Truly, she is perfect."

Julia awarded him a low beam of a smile. She made a lap around the room, pausing under the skylight. "I have a request," she said, kicking off her shoes. She began to rise up and down on the balls of her feet, a low-impact move he guessed was meant to exercise her calf muscles. "A nanny."

"Don't you already have a few?" Though Leo knew the exact number, as each member of Julia's personal staff had to pass an SPB background check. It was something Julia complained about; she said the process took too long, that she lost good candidates this way.

"I have two, as you well know. Not exactly an army. I need some weekend childcare."

"What for?"

"Coverage. I often work on the weekends. This isn't some government job, where I clock in and out."

He let that go. "Can't the housekeeper manage it?"

"A housekeeper manages the *house*. Not the children."

"What about Charlie?"

"What about him?"

"He's not good with babies?"

"No," Julia said softly, and for a moment Leo's heart went out to her. How interesting, he thought. That out of everything in Julia's life, this was what would stress her. What a tragedy, that whatever their resources, all women seemed to suffer in this way.

But then Julia squared her shoulders, and a steeliness Leo was familiar with reentered her voice. "I've been recommended a good candidate. But I have to hire her right away, before she's snatched up."

Leo hesitated. "We still have to do the background check. Each new person is an area of risk. We don't have visibility into the Americans' counterintelligence—a compromised local contact could lead them to you."

"Why do we have HELPER, then?"

"For your security. The dead drop procedure adds a layer of protection. And HELPER doesn't know who you are." Though sometimes Leo suspected Chester knew more than he said.

She crossed her arms. "You know how long it takes to drive to some of these places?"

Leo sighed. If Julia had it her way, it would be Leo who retrieved her intelligence packages, who did *everything*—as if he worked for her, instead of the other way around. But after his morning with Aaron, he was tired of arguing. "I'll think about the nanny."

Julia blinked, surprised by the swift victory. "Thank you."

"But now in return you'll have to do something for me. You have to be nicer to Aaron."

"'*Nicer*'? You sound like one of those journalists, always debating whether I'm nice, as if it matters to do my job. As if the men and women writing those articles aren't nightmares themselves. Would you care if your surgeon was nice?"

"No, but you aren't a surgeon."

"Correct. I'm far more important."

*Careful with that ego.* "You said you'd accepted Aaron. So why not release his housing money?"

A slippery look crossed her face. "He told you about that?"

"I don't need to be told. I know how my assets live."

"His home is still a palace, compared to the institute."

"Yes, but he isn't at the institute, is he?"

She narrowed her eyes. "Has he been complaining?"

"No. But I look after Aaron's well-being, you understand. The same as all my assets."

She smoothed her dress. "Though none are as important as me."

"Correct." He knew that this was her way, to always try to notch a final win. "None are as important as you."

JULIA MADE HIM WAIT WITH her while she packed, Leo reading the spines of books in her office as she tossed cream-colored silks and black exercise clothes into a suitcase. Charlie entered the room as she finished, and Julia retrieved Emily from the nursery. "When's the night nurse coming?" Charlie asked, taking the baby.

Julia checked her watch. "An hour."

"Where are you going?"

"Palo Alto Airport. Quick business trip. Be good," she sang, and kissed Charlie on the cheek.

"I didn't know there was an airport in Palo Alto," Leo remarked as they stood outside.

She directed at him a pitying look: "It's, ah, not commercial," she said, and rolled her bag to the walkway. In Leo's right pocket was a USB drive containing her latest search results. By protocol Julia was supposed to leave it at the dead drop, but in this instance he'd acquiesced, to save both her and Chester the trouble.

Back at the Wisteria, Leo stopped to retrieve his mail. On the lobby door was a new sign, clumsily taped, threatening dire consequences for package thieves. He stopped to read, entertained by its promised violence, and when he turned, Miriam was at the mailboxes.

"How are you feeling?" she asked, sighting him. Against the wall were canvas bags containing French peas and cantaloupe.

"Fine." He made himself smile.

"You doing okay? Any more rushes, feeling light-headed?"

"No."

"You get that bottle I dropped off?"

For a moment Leo was confused. The bottle had been left on his doormat; when he'd first seen the package he'd been wary, but he had eventually taken it inside, assuming it to be an order he'd placed with one of the building's many schoolchildren. That it was considered entirely reasonable for a child you'd never met to stand before you, snot dribbling, inquiring if you'd like to purchase twenty-five-dollar wrapping paper while the parents stood beatifically to the side Leo still thought a beastly practice; he had been advised by Julia, however, that Americans were hopelessly biased when it came to their children and often took it personally when you rejected their dreams. The bottle still sat in a high cabinet, in a plastic bag tied at the top. "I wasn't sure where it came from." And then awkwardly: "Thank you."

"Yes, I thought I should have left a note after. I got it at Whole Foods. What you do is fill it with really cold water and some ice." Miriam stopped to file through her letters, tossing a stack of flyers into the recycling bin.

"Yes," Leo said, already knowing where this was headed. It would make sense that she was one of those eco-warriors, with her farmers' market totes and long shawls. "And then I will no longer use plastic."

"*No.*" Miriam sounded irritated. "Well, although you shouldn't be using that too much, either. Plastic. But what you do with the bottle is keep it filled with ice, right? And over the day it'll melt into cool water. Then if you feel yourself panicking, slowly dribble it over the inside of your wrist. The cold will focus you. And you can also drink some of the water. Slowly, like I said before."

"Wow," Leo said, briefly at a loss for words. That Miriam had done this was both touching and embarrassing. The idea that she had thought of him while going about her daily business made him feel exposed, as if she'd seen him crying or asking for money.

"I saw it and thought it was a good size. Small. Easy to carry." She herself seemed embarrassed now. "I got one for Patrick, too. To put in his lunch bag. It isn't a big deal."

"Still. It was considerate."

He turned, to open his own mailbox, and Miriam called to Patrick, who was running laps around the fountain. As she disappeared through the entrance, she called back: "Well, we're friends, aren't we?" The door shut before he could form a response.

Friends. Leo thought about this now as he stood in his apartment. Was it even possible to be friends with a female in this society? It wasn't as if since his arrival he hadn't yearned for a woman, some steady companionship. But when he thought about what that entailed—the online profile, the dating, the spending—he gave up and settled for being alone. Despite her thoughtfulness Leo had not detected from Miriam any of the shy eye contact or tinkling laughter he was used to from females interested in his greater affections; instead, he sensed only the flavor of a dish he himself had tasted these last years—a sort of narrow loneliness, the kind you tried to fill in between all your other obligations.

Leo went to his cupboard and retrieved the bottle, which was dark green with a metallic glitter. Dribble it over your wrist, Miriam had said. He tried this, catching some cold water in the bottle and then dripping it down. He didn't feel much. But then, he was already calm.

Friends. Leo wondered if Jefferson had managed any of his own, down in Miami. Did he have someone he could call if his power went out, or a friendly clerk at the grocer whose line he always chose?

Leo went to his computer and removed from his pocket the USB drive. On impulse, he'd included Miriam in the last batch of searches. She'd come into his life by such coincidence: had been right there, and perhaps it wasn't a panic attack, but rather something planted, a chemical agent, the SPB used those all the time . . .

He inserted the drive into his laptop and found her folder. Miriam Reyes. Leo skipped the bits about her net worth, her emails— to look through such things after her kindness felt like a violation, though he would return if necessary. If it wasn't kindness at all, but rather something planned.

```
Name: Miriam Reyes

Age: 41

School affiliations: Macalester, Columbia

Graduate school: Columbia

Marital status: (Married) Craig Thompson,
2007-2015
```

```
Recent searches: How to dry fruit, Uber for
kids, best water bottle without BPA . . .
```

In other words: nothing. Nothing because there was nothing. She was simply what she said: a mother who could no longer work a job she was good at and so spent her days helping to design video games. Who, when tired in the evening, had still sat at her computer and thought of a gift for a relative stranger.

He would have to purchase her something in return, Leo thought. That would be what was considered polite. And he would have to remember Patrick; Leo knew children didn't like it when only adults received presents. After another second, he deleted Miriam's files from the drive. He didn't want her name seen by the SPB; they might get the wrong idea.

Leo went to the kitchen, where he set the bottle by the sink. He was surprised by how happy he felt.

# 19

# JULIA

Julia was tired.

She was always tired, but it just seemed so pathetic to complain, to talk of how fatigued you were. Men never said they were tired, which made sense, because compared to women they did fuck-all. But right now, alone in her office, the weekly sales call booming on speaker behind her, Julia could admit she was that most American of all states: *exhausted*.

She'd just returned from London and Amsterdam, where she'd spent five days. Normally after such a trip Julia would go directly home from the airport—she hated how she felt after a red-eye, so shriveled and used—and wash off her makeup and slather herself with creams. Her maternity leave and Aaron's arrival, however, had both served as reminders of that most indispensable of corporate drudgeries, face time: that no matter how smart Pierre was about technology, he remained obtuse about humans themselves, often favoring whichever toady stood in sight at a specific moment. And so Julia had gone in to work and listened to Pierre's ramblings on German cauliflower and the FCC, and could barely pay attention because she was thinking of Emily the entire time. She used to believe those women who talked endlessly about their children were, okay, pathetic: interrupting the meeting, holding the phone at arm's length: *Hi! Hi! Mommy misses!* But after this trip she was a member of the same tribe, that pack of Working Moms who always felt guilty; she was ready to be home, to hold her daughter, to experience a level of joy she thought she'd already achieved, but no, there was even more to be had.

She should write this down, Julia thought. This was the perfect pithy stream of consciousness for a future Tangerine update.

She reached for her tote and extracted the notebook she brought with her everywhere (*Write things down! I begin each morning with a checklist!*). Julia segmented her notebook by date and priority, a typical page of her B-list reading like:

DRINKS WITH PIERRE
CALL EVAN
CALL JON TO DEAL WITH EVAN
LUNCH WITH AD GROUP
TINA DEAL WITH AD GROUP
NEGOTIATE KEVIN PRINCE OFFER
CLOSE KEVIN PRINCE OFFER
FLOWERS FOR SALLY

After locating her notebook, Julia went hunting in her desk for her favorite ballpoint. In her search, she was pleased to discover an errant square of dark chocolate in the back of her drawer.

When she looked up, Aaron stood before her.

She hadn't heard her door, and for a moment Julia thought she'd conjured him out of her exhaustion. He wore his usual ivory shirt with jeans, though she noticed his leather brogues had been swapped for sneakers: he was slowly but surely transforming into his obvious aspiration, the Silicon Valley power dick.

"Why," Aaron said, "was my invitation to Pierre's staff meeting canceled?"

*Because I deleted you, shithead.* She hit the mute button on her call. "You would need to ask Pierre." She decided to hang up on the meeting, which was only a pissing match over who was at fault for poor European ad sales, anyway. "It's his staff."

Aaron held a paper cup of coffee. "You are," he said, lightly crushing its sides, "such a fucking bitch."

Julia was silent. She found she was surprised not by the content of Aaron's statement but by his speed of escalation. She'd thought it would take a year or longer to arrive at this place; that's how it'd always been, before. But then those men had all been American.

"Right." She licked her lips, which were dry; she wished her makeup were at least fresh. "You will be respectful when speaking to me."

"I know it was you who removed me from Pierre's staff. Everyone knows you micromanage his calendar. But why?"

She decided to be honest. "I don't want you too close to him."

"It's not your choice. He's the one who said I could join. At hockey."

"If you're such good friends, why don't you ask him to add you back on yourself? Give him a call. I'm sure Pierre wouldn't mind, given your relationship."

Aaron was less attractive when he sneered, she noted. He moved closer. "You know people talk about you."

She crossed her legs. "Yeah?"

"They say that you are unqualified, that you are a dilettante. That you will run Tangerine into the ground."

She nodded: *yeah yeah yeah.*

"That you're a cunt."

Julia almost laughed. That was all he had? The C-word? She reclined and smoothed her hair. "As I said, you shouldn't be speaking to me like this."

"You shouldn't be sabotaging my career because you don't want your boss to like me. Because you are worried that I will eventually outrank you."

Aaron had a new watch, Julia noticed: a stainless-steel Patek Philippe, she'd purchased the calendar version for Charlie. "The way you're behaving to a superior, I'm not concerned."

"Is that what you believe you are?" Aaron drew closer, near enough that Nicole looked over. "My *superior*?"

Julia's heart beat and her hands went hot; she could not recall being confronted like this before. "It's correct, isn't it?" To her surprise, she was almost excited by the hostility—even in her worst fights with Charlie, she had to censor herself.

"Be careful. I am not a fool, like Leo."

"Leo's not a fool."

"You two seem to have such a *close* relationship. He's really allowed you to do whatever you've wanted, hasn't he? Have fun, play your little games, get rich. And what have you done in exchange? Just some searches. What is your secret, Julia? What could you possibly be doing for Leo to be so . . . positively inclined?" Aaron's face took on a lewd grossness, and Julia was dismayed—to accuse her of screwing her way to her position was elementary stuff, the sort of petty tactic she thought beneath both of them.

All right, all right, she thought. That's about enough.

JULIA HAD BEEN CERTAIN AARON was a deviant. She'd met enough of them to know the type: he was good-looking (not that looks were a prerequisite); he was an egomaniac; he believed the world belonged to him and also was clearly a pervert.

As she'd scanned his facial match results, Julia had discovered the photos were all from the same album, of a German political gathering. Mostly men, serious faces, half of them potbellied or balding. And then she saw the banner in the top background, the white slanted initials, the blocks of blue and orange. The official flag of Independence Alliance, the fourth-largest party in the Bundestag. The fascist group opposing any immigration and in favor of a "celebratory" view of German history. Was it true? Could it possibly be this good? She'd clicked through each photo in the carousel until he appeared.

Fourth row, to the right. Black jacket, white shirt. No identifiers, no names, but Tangerine's algorithm recognized him as Aaron.

Ding ding ding. Even better than a harasser. At least in Silicon Valley.

A racist, baby.

Now Julia reached for her tote, still keeping eye contact with Aaron. Her hand moved through her bag: phone, water, other phone, lipstick, foundation, charger, wet wipes, diaper, tissues. *Fuck!* Why did she have such a big bag? And then she touched the envelope.

She fanned the photos on her desk and watched as Aaron's expression drained from curiosity to dread. "Where did you find these?"

"You haven't been paying attention if you have to ask."

"I did it in service."

"Yes, yes. That's what we tell ourselves. That all we do is in service."

"No, I mean for a job. An operation. Didn't Leo tell you I was in Berlin? It was SPB mandated."

"How tragic," Julia said. And then let silence take over, because it really didn't matter.

"What do you want?" From Aaron's posture she could see he was already defeated, engulfed by the self-pity men seemed to so easily summon. Though Julia derived little pleasure from this. She wasn't a sadist, it was just that it had to be done—as it was only when their egos were punctured and the air let out that men became reasonable.

She sorted the photographs, sliding them back into their envelope. "Nothing." Which was the truth. She wasn't going to threaten, order him to leave; that would anger Leo, which was how she'd landed in this mess to begin with. Better for Aaron to stay on at Tangerine: appropriately neutered, he would serve as ongoing affirmation of her good behavior. Leo never knowing she had infiltrated the watcher. "Only stay out of my way. Let's pretend we like each other, yes? And we'll both have a fine time."

"What about my life here? My job?"

"That can remain. You can remain. As long as you keep to the projects and people I approve. No deviations."

"And my apartment? My compensation?"

"You'll be taken care of." He snorted and rolled his eyes, and Julia held up a hand. "Tomorrow morning when you wake, you'll have already received email confirmation of an additional grant of stock. While that vests, if, say, you decide you want a house, Tangerine can lend you the down payment at no interest." She saw his surprise: Yes, I have this power, I have more than you could imagine, and if you'd understood this earlier I wouldn't have had to dredge up your pathetic old photos to begin with. "All I ask is that you know your place. No more meetings with Pierre or the other executives. Do your job and stay out of my sight, and you can stay. That's what you want, right? To stay?"

Aaron stared at the floor, as if angry or ashamed or some mix of it all. After a minute he looked up and nodded. *Good.*

AFTER AARON LEFT, JULIA PACKED to go home. As she shut her door, she said goodbye to Nicole. And on impulse added: "I'll be in late tomorrow." She would sleep in. Why the hell not?

"You've got that meeting with Tara Lopez," Nicole called back. "In ten minutes. Should I cancel?" Seeing Julia's confusion, she added, "Alice Lu's manager. You met with her right before your trip. She's since sent multiple emails asking for a follow-up."

Ugh. Now Julia remembered. That Tara Lopez.

To be honest, the woman had kind of creeped her out—Julia had initially sent a polite request that Tara "drop by sometime for a chat," minutes after which she'd been interrupted by the woman maniacally knocking at her office door. Julia, who had not expected Tara to appear but rather to reply like a regular person with manners, had quickly waved her in and shut her screen. "You weren't busy?"

Tara paused. "I was in a staff," she said. "*My* staff, I'm a people manager. But I, ah, left to see you when I received your message."

So the woman had abandoned her own team, presumably still seated in a conference room, when she received the summons from Julia. Not terribly considerate, but certainly helpful for Julia's purposes. They'd concluded their business quickly, Julia explaining how an access violation had been detected in one of the servers; how it was best that the employee responsible for such violation find a place outside of engineering, and eventually Tangerine altogether. Tara was a fast study, had agreed without much questioning. "And I'd love to have some time with *you*," she'd trilled. "Some words of advice for a minority woman trying to succeed."

Julia knew she'd have to meet with Tara. First, because the words *minority woman* were like chemical weapons of a sort within Tangerine—once used by a party, they could not be left unaddressed—but also because Julia had requested that she and Tara meet once more before Tara took any permanent action. Julia had been concerned that otherwise Tara might return to her desk and—in an effort to further lodge herself up Julia's ass—fire Alice on the spot. Julia did not want a lawsuit or another screamy online blog à la Sean Dara.

By now Tara had presumably begun the documentation process, which meant Alice was fair game. To take care of the problem this afternoon with Tara would be the Julia thing to do: she could still leave by six, go home, greet Emily, supervise dinner, read bedtime stories, send emails, have obligatory sex with Charlie, wake up early, go for a run, and come back to work, during which time the cogs on Alice Lu's termination would already have begun to turn.

Fuck it. "Reschedule the appointment," Julia said to Nicole. She would take care of the Alice situation later. Even she had to allow herself some slack somewhere.

# MAY 2019

## 20

# ALICE

The mansion was steel and glass and light, a box of electricity set high in the hills of Los Altos. From the passenger seat of Cheri's Audi, Alice watched the brake lights of the car in front, a Tesla with a custom green paint job, wink on and off; every twenty seconds or so the car would lurch forward as the inhabitants of another vehicle alighted and went in. It was only when they drew closer that Alice could make out details of some of the guests: a man with blond hair, dressed in loose shorts with a dangling drawstring, clasping the hand of a woman in a red bandage dress. "Yes!" the woman was shouting. "Fucking awesome!"

Oh God, Alice thought. Please let me get through this.

It was ten days earlier that Alice had hit upon her idea: how she might resolve the issue of Julia and God Mode, all while conveniently transferring the moral burden to another person to boot. To wait and see was no longer viable, after her meeting with Tara; Alice had to assume Julia knew who she was, and at least attempt to protect herself. That Alice's plan had certain flaws, some major gaping assumptions, was outweighed by the fact that any alternate route she'd considered was even worse—and all involved the Tangerine employee whistleblower hotline in some fashion, a corporate tool of which the last known users had found themselves either fired or sued by the company or both. That same day, Alice had walked the quarter mile to Building Eight for lunch. There was a burrito purveyor there with two thousand Yelp reviews that for twenty years had been based out of Oakland until Pierre paid the owner to move. She asked for a to-go box, and after she returned home from work set her bait on the kitchen counter.

Cheri came out of her room minutes later. "The smell," she said. "It's driving me craaaazy." She immediately went to the food.

"Hey," Cheri said, once half the carne asada was gone, "did you want some? This isn't your dinner, right?"

"No. I'm fine." Alice needed the whole burrito to keep Cheri sated and at her most cooperative. Though on the drive home the car had filled with the most delicious scent; she had cursed herself then for not getting two.

"How's it going?" Cheri asked. There was a drop of avocado on her chin, which to Alice's dismay was almost adorable, as if Cheri were the fun-loving mother in a commercial.

"I was wondering. If I could come with you to a party."

Cheri gasped. "A *party*?"

"Yeah. If you could manage it." Alice fingered the box. "Spare a plus-one."

"A plus-one," Cheri repeated in wonder. "*Any* party?"

Better to just say it: even when she was a kid, Alice had never been the type to peel off a bandage slowly. "A Smash Bash."

Cheri dropped the burrito. "My God, I feel like I'm dreaming. A Smash Bash—*I* didn't even go to the last one! Alice, are you okay?"

Smash Bashes were the impossibly embarrassing name for the bacchanals regularly thrown by the venture capitalist Barry Levine at his ultramodernist mansion; the parties were a poorly held secret within the higher echelons of the tech community, though Alice had come into her knowledge not through some social back channel but rather via Cheri, after she'd returned home one evening from yet another event. Still drunk, Cheri had kicked off her heels and then, sprawled on the couch, begun to narrate to a rapt Alice the ecosystem of Silicon Valley parties. At the top were the private gatherings, like the "Billionaire Huddles" organized by Fort Capital. These were difficult to score invites to if you were not currently a billionaire or sleeping with one, and sometimes, as Cheri hinted, the scrutiny incited by a mostly sober small-group atmosphere was not conducive to certain dating goals, if you know what I mean. In Cheri's rant, she'd described the Smash Bashes as occupying a middle tier; there were a lot of prime candidates for sure, but also a bunch of model types and old dudes, a drag on both supply and demand. But the food was great, the house spectacular if modern design was your thing and still, like, a really expensive house if not. And there was always the chance you could corner the lonely rider of some rising unicorn—the guest list, Cheri said, was usually *excellent*.

And more important, for Alice's purposes: Sean Dara was known to be a regular attendee.

"A Smash Bash," Cheri said again. Her gaze slipped, and Alice was afraid: that her roommate might laugh, or say no, she couldn't possibly bring her. Instead Cheri chuckled and got ready to cram the rest of the burrito into her mouth. "Oh *yeah*," she said. "This will be fun."

THEY WERE ONLY A FEW cars away now. Close up the house looked respectable, a little Southern California inspired, though Alice had never actually seen a mansion in Los Angeles. With its angular boxiness and lights flooded through glass she thought it resembled an Apple store.

"I'm so excited," Cheri said. "You never want to come to these things. A Smash Bash! Wow!"

Alice grunted. She was itchy and constrained, in a black skirt and tight top, both closet rejects of Cheri's. Alice had originally planned on wearing jeans and a loose blouse before Cheri came into her room.

"You can't," Cheri had said, assessing her up and down, "wear that."

"What's wrong with this?" Alice was a little hurt about the top, which had small lace insets on the sleeves. It was one of the prettier items in her closet, which her mother would describe as *suh bu duh*—too precious to use.

"You look like a sister wife," Cheri said, demolishing in a single second one of Alice's favorite wardrobe items. "You have to wear something like this." Gesturing to herself. She was encased in a fitted gold dress with long sleeves, the V of the neckline landing a few inches above her navel.

"No."

"Come on," Cheri wheedled. "You have to at least make an effort. Do you know the kinds of people at these parties? Otherwise they might think you're a journalist."

The green Tesla in front of them had ejected its passengers; next it would be their turn. Cheri opened the door and had already bounded out by the time Alice unbuckled her seat belt. "Cheri Lu," she announced to a sleepy-looking security guard. "I'm on the list. I brought a friend, hope that's okay."

"Oh yeah?" the guard said, as Alice nervously rounded the corner of the car. The valet hovered, waiting to give Cheri the ticket; after a moment, Alice took it from him instead. The guard cast an unimpressed eye at Alice and then scanned Cheri's ID. "Bag."

"Sure." Cheri passed over her clutch, a slim contraption made from two conch shells that had been purchased for her from the Amanpuri gift shop in Thailand. The guard sifted through its contents, pressed a sticker over the phone's camera, and handed it back.

"I need to see your bag, too," he told Alice.

"I don't have one."

"Where's your phone?"

"In my pocket," Alice said, removing it from her skirt. The pockets were the garment's best feature.

The guard gaped at the side of her skirt in surprise, as if she'd revealed it to be a wizard's cloak. "Anything else in there?" he asked, stickering her camera.

She removed the remaining items. A few receipts of Cheri's, one of her Tangerine business cards, the valet ticket, a mint lip balm.

He waved them in.

Inside, the house was both sterile and palatial, with white marble walls and light fixtures resembling constellations. They passed a huddle of Asian girls near the entrance, rail thin with winged eyeliner—the sort that lamented their high metabolisms and said things like "Please don't call me cute!" all while working to accentuate this very cuteness, throwing kawaii signs and marveling at how much food they'd ordered. The girls glanced at Alice and then their eyes passed to Cheri, surveying her as they might an apex predator.

They passed to another room, where a fit, near-elderly man in a tight shirt reclined on a couch, bracketed by two very young, very good-looking men with weary faces. A buffet of fried chicken was set up in a corner, and Alice's stomach growled. She yanked on Cheri's hand to pull her to the table, and then stopped.

It was Julia. Julia Lerner was at this party. She'd just entered the room from the other side and was in conversation with a man Alice thought vaguely familiar; Julia laughed and then looked over at the men on the couches.

IGNORING CHERI'S PROTESTS, ALICE PULLED her back toward the front, away from Julia; when Cheri resisted, Alice panicked and let go of her hand and ran into what she thought was the bathroom but turned out to be the nanny's quarters, of a size and lavishness exceeding her entire apartment. She darted right, upon which she did discover a bathroom; she shut the door and then sat on the toilet lid, flicking on the light.

Fluorescence rained from above. Alice pressed her head into her hands and concentrated on breathing. She was being overdramatic, she reasoned. After all, Julia hadn't seen her. And even if she had, there was no guarantee Julia would recognize her, especially in the environs of a Smash Bash.

After another minute Alice rose and washed her hands, pausing to sniff at the Diptyque candle. Instead of hiding from Julia, she should actually be following her, she then thought. A Smash Bash wasn't exactly on brand for Supermom COO, so why was she here?

Alice returned to where she'd left Cheri, only to find both her and Julia vanished. A growing hysteria in her chest, Alice walked through room after room, scanning for not only Cheri, but also: Sean Dara.

Alice wasn't sure what had initially brought Sean to mind to assist with Julia. It wasn't like they were friends, or even acquaintances, and in their last interaction he'd been kind of a dick. What she did know, however, was that for a person to help he needed to possess both a great dislike of Julia and a good deal of "fuck-you money," and while it might be feasible to locate the former, the combination of both did not exist in her social sphere. Sean was the only "important" person Alice had ever heard say anything negative about Julia—before asking Cheri to take her to the Smash Bash, Alice had first tried Sean's Tangerine email, which bounced back, and then his FreeTalk ID, which did the same. His tweets were months apart and mentioned only the Warriors, and he did not respond to the burner account she'd created: *@SeanDara can you please check your DMs, I promise I am not a scammer.*

Alice passed into a room that contained a dark purple love seat and a round glass table, on which macarons were arranged in a concentric rainbow. An obese man was on the love seat, a girl with lavender hair straddling him and lapping at his face, and Alice considered the possibility that Sean might not even be at this party, that the *Wired* profile in which his attendance at such gatherings had been so teasingly detailed ("There is enough collective hair gel to pose a fire hazard; Sean orders his fourth Japanese whiskey and speculates on whether it'd be better to date someone hot or someone famous") might have been his swan song. She left this room and entered the next, where against the wall there was a photo booth, in front of which a curly-haired man was holding court, speaking of crypto. Alice was edging closer—she had a hopeful fascination with get-rich-quick schemes, though she was too much of a fiscal coward to enact any—when she sighted Sean.

Far left, in a white chair pressed into a corner. He was unshaven and wore a faded green shirt. Next to him, her head against his armpit, was a blonde in a silver dress.

Alice's relief at seeing him overwhelmed her anxiety. She hurried over. "I need to talk to you."

Sean blinked at her. "Hey. Yeah, no thanks."

The blonde's face was a mix of curiosity and triumph. Alice ordered herself to stand firm, to tamp down the shame and press forward. "No, I need to talk to you about work."

"You've got the wrong Indian."

"You're half-Indian," the blonde corrected, smacking him on the shoulder. "And you *barely* look it."

There was a moment of silence as Sean regarded his companion with an inscrutable heavy-lidded look. He returned to Alice. "Who cares. I don't have a job."

"You're Sean Dara, right? We used to work together."

He peered at her. His eyes were the same color as Cheri's, light brown with green. He shook his head. "Don't remember."

Alice forced herself to address the blonde. "Could you please give us a few minutes?" The girl sat up and looked at Sean. "I'm just going to *talk* to him," Alice said. "It'll be really quick and then you can come back."

"Jesus," Sean muttered. He exhaled, as if this were an everyday nuisance, a stream of female acolytes competing for his attention. The blonde rose, removing her phone from her clutch.

"I used to work for you," Alice said once the girl was out of hearing. She debated sitting on the floor, as her feet were sore from her sandals, but didn't want to lose her height advantage. "I worked in the FreeTalk group for half a year."

"After the acquisition?"

"Yes."

"Figures." Which Alice took to mean she was clearly a stooge, a keyboard monkey, someone who'd never be found at a hot early-stage start-up but rather only in some large, unimaginative corporation.

"I worked on the classifiers project. I presented to you?"

Sean studied his fingers in the light. "I have blocked every memory of my time there."

"Okay. So you don't remember me."

He sneered. "Absolutely not."

She hit him, quickly, across the face.

"Ow!" Sean shouted, and Alice turned to check if anyone had seen. The blonde was looking up from her phone, but appeared to have missed the actual strike—the group of crypto-worshippers blocked her view, and there was an overall loud din in the room.

Sean pushed himself up. "What the fuck was that?"

"Listen to me," Alice hissed. Her heart was racing and she was both impressed and frightened that she had hit him. "I still work at Tangerine, okay? I want to talk to you about something there."

"Are you fucking *insane*? I've already told you I don't work there! Go to someone else for your promotion bitching."

Alice made another scan to ensure no one else was near. The

blonde was back to her phone, the Bitcoin dude's crowd even larger now. She turned to Sean. "It's about Julia Lerner."

His face betrayed a flicker of interest. "What's your name?"

"Alice." She dug into her pocket and removed her business card.

He pinched it from her with two fingers and then, without looking, stuffed it underneath the seat. "No comment on Julia."

"You don't even want to hear?"

"No."

"It has to do with God Mode."

"God Mode." His eyes lifted again. "Huh."

"Do you know what that is?"

"Yeah."

"Okay." Alice lowered her voice. "She's using it to *hurt* people."

"What else is God Mode for?" Sean said. He leaned forward, as if to continue, but then reconsidered: "I have no comment on that, either."

"She's going to ruin FreeTalk," Alice said, more desperately now. Even in her worst-case scenarios, she had not imagined Sean would be so difficult; had assumed his interest would naturally materialize after he heard of Julia's involvement.

"FreeTalk used to be my baby," Sean said. His eyes rolled and Alice wondered if he was high. Was this what high people looked like? She was embarrassingly uninitiated with drugs. "It was my baby, those days we worked, just me and Johan. Do *you* have a baby?"

"No."

"Well. Okay then. People say it was a mistake to sell . . . I don't know. Because if we hadn't, Tangerine would have just launched a copycat, crushed us anyway. I mean . . . would I have been as happy then? I guess it's a possibility. *Everything's* a possibility, you know?"

There was a distinct overlap, Alice was realizing, between wealthy-founder blather and plain drunk talk; the problem was she didn't know how to manage either. Even in college, when she'd held back the hair of weeping pukers, she'd never known what to do—was she supposed to say all would be well? That it was going to be fine, they'd definitely pass Commutative Algebra? Or just wait out the crying? "If FreeTalk's your baby, then you should care about it. Don't you want to know what's happening? What about your early users, all those people who depend on your product for privacy?"

"Any FreeTalk user with a few working brain cells should have known the game was up as soon as we sold."

"That's not what you said." She'd been there. Sean and Johan together for her first team update, Sean excitedly pacing, speaking of the revolution. "You said you had earned people's trust and that you were going to keep it."

"Oh fuck, I keep forgetting you were actually there." Sean rubbed his palms against his thighs. "Well, things change. You think it's about more, but really it just comes down to the people. A few people, making all the decisions. None of them you. The day I left was the day I deleted my account." He sighed, and there was a stretch of quiet before he lifted his head and glared. "I don't know what you're doing, Alice whatever-the-fuck. But if I were you, I'd delete your account, too."

And with that, it was as if the air had been let out of his body; he flopped onto the cushions and closed his eyes, and Alice knew then that she'd failed.

IN DESPAIR, ALICE BEGAN TO wander. It had been a mistake not to drive: she'd been lazy, let Cheri lead. She tried to return to a room she'd passed earlier, from which there'd been the most delicious scent of roasting potatoes, but couldn't find it. She left the house and went into the backyard, where large white tents were set up, like at a fancy wedding. In the nearest she found platters of food on heated chargers, and she took a plate and filled it with lamb kebab and moussaka. Aside from the occasional model or model-adjacent who would wander in and then—seeing the food and Alice—promptly exit, she was the only person inside the tent.

After eating, Alice felt more energized. She tried to call Cheri but reached her voicemail. Cheri barely answered when the phone was ringing in her hand, so it was impossible to expect that she'd be responsive here, in the midst of so many high-value targets. No doubt she had already attached herself to some young CEO, and then the guy would want her to move in with him, and then Alice would be alone again, which would be cool, oh, except for the issue of rent, and then she might be fired . . .

Alice decided to drink. She moved to another tent, this one with five or six guests crowded around a bar. She ordered a mojito, the only cocktail she could think of, and then drifted to a table with tall glass jars filled with candy. She was reaching for the cola-shaped gummies when there was a tap on her back.

"I love your skirt," the girl said. She was a few inches shorter than Alice, with dark hair to her waist and eyes eclipsed by silver shadow. "Where'd you get it?"

"I don't know." Surprised by the girl's friendliness and wanting to reciprocate, Alice impulsively offered: "Do you want me to check? I can go to the bathroom."

"Ohmygod you are so nice. I'm Jane, by the way. No, I can look." Alice, not understanding, turned back to the table as Jane reached for her waist and twisted the label toward her.

"Ahh!" Alice yelped.

"Cushnie," Jane said. "*Nice.* Are you eating?" She gestured with her chin. "You shouldn't. They're like those milk tea pearls, too many calories."

"Oh." Alice set down the scoop.

"Are you rolling?"

"What's rolling?"

"Wow! You don't know! You really don't know!"

"No." Alice ordinarily would have been annoyed, but Jane

seemed so guileless, so openly happy in her mood; a welcome contrast from Sean's glowering.

"Here." Jane reached into a glass vase containing dozens of miniature brown envelopes. She removed one and tapped from it a pill. "Wait. Better split, if you haven't before." She bit off half, stuck it back in the envelope, and dropped it into the jar. The other half she held toward Alice: "Go ahead."

Alice hesitated. But Jane was friendly and her night a bust; she was overcome with the feeling that possibly she had wasted her life, that she had stayed home because socializing was inconvenient or she didn't want to wear makeup or because she was frightened of some undefined humiliation, but then the years went by and what had you done? What had you achieved but a dead feeling after you'd spent hours watching videos of people in love or fighting on the internet?

Within thirty minutes Alice began to feel light, airy. The world was not cruel but rather like a person with a mean face: not bad at all once you get to "know" them. She was still with Jane and had the urge to touch random partygoers: to hug a wondrously pretty girl in a lace top, to pet the silken baldness of a man's head. Which she did, and by the time he turned, Alice was already gone. Was this what life was? It wasn't so bad. You could be impulsive, you could touch, people forgave, and the rooms continued . . .

Alice tripped and fell on the floor. This was a situation, like many this evening, where normally she would have been embarrassed—but now it was fine, it was ordinary, who cared? Thank you, Barry Levine! She laughed and was pretty sure she'd done so out loud. She couldn't see Jane any longer but that was okay; she was comfortable where she lay and the lights were bright and she didn't have that empty-parking-garage feeling of imminent assault.

And then Jane was back. "Oh *God*," she said.

"Hi, hi." A mild discomfort was beginning to impinge on her

pleasure—her teeth hurt, Alice realized. She was also thirsty. "I was looking for you."

"For how long? It's been like two hours!"

Alice frowned. Really? She knew she did not currently possess the best idea of time—was it three mojitos she'd downed? But two hours seemed awfully long.

"You're having fun, aren't you?" Jane asked.

"Yesh," said Alice, as another surge of affection went through, toward this stranger who was taking such good care of her.

"You sure you're okay? You know you're on the floor."

"Yeah. But uh, if you're gonna go . . ." The thought lost itself and then looped and returned. "Could you go back to that tent? And get me some of those gummies?"

"What gummies?"

"You know, the cola ones. The ones you said would make me fat." Though at the moment she didn't care about that. The silk skirt from Cheri, which she'd earlier thought so constricting, was now—after she'd undone half the zipper—so comfortable and light . . . Alice thought she was rather like a goddess, floating about in it. Clothes were *better* on fatter people!

"Alice! What the hell are you talking about!"

The voice was sharp, not soft and feathery like Jane's. Alice placed a hand over her eyes, as if shielding herself from a glare, and squinted. The person was familiar, in a spiky sort of way. She was like a gorgeous white version of herself, and then Alice realized it was Cheri.

"Mary. Cherry. I mean Cheri. Hiya."

"Oh God, help me," Cheri said to some guy who had either just appeared or been there the whole time, some fuzzy white person with fuzzier hair. "She's my cousin, she's totally drugged out, help me get her to a car."

"She doesn't look so good," the guy said, not moving.

"No no." Alice waved Cheri away. "Don't bother with me, I'm having fun . . ."

"No you're not, you're in a freaking ecstasy hole."

"You know, she sleeps in her makeup," Alice said, directing a serious look to the man. "She announces her farts after she's done them."

"Ugh! Alice!"

"I don't want to ruin your date, this could be your dream life, I mean this guy could get your dream—" Alice suddenly found her breathing constricted. Cheri's hand was over her mouth.

"She seems fucked up," the guy said.

"She's actually a very lovely person." Cheri was patting around Alice's legs, putting things into her pockets. "Just help me get her into a car, all right?"

"No," Alice said, "I don't need a car, go have fun—"

She blacked out.

# 21

# JULIA

**B**arry Levine's house was fucking disgusting.

This was what happened, Julia thought as she passed a glass case containing a dinosaur skull—next to the bones was a placard clarifying it was *real*, a real dinosaur, a baby *T. rex*—this was the end result, when you were late fifty-something and your dick had a high priority line to your brain: saddling your wife—sorry, let's be clear, your *first* wife—with the five children you'd so enthusiastically bred, all while dumping your slimy Caltech PhD seed all over the Valley. And then settling with your current USC or SCU or whoever it was, a submillennial who wore glasses because you thought it was hot, whose idiotic colloquialisms on female ambition Julia then had to endure at parties. Julia had known Barry a long time, had even gone to a few of his bashes, years back—they'd been held at his Pacific Heights place then, the one with the wraparound view. The catering was always fabulous, and they had these baked potatoes, kept warm and wrapped with aluminum foil: you'd come up with your plate and a server would dollop sour cream and caviar on top. Yum.

There'd been drugs then, too. Subtly served, on silver trays, but

Julia always declined—she'd seen enough of what drugs did at the institute, where sedatives and psychotropics were freely distributed as childcare, to be off pills forever. Though she did drink. Once, after she'd accepted a glass of champagne, she even recalled Barry making a pass—his hand pawing as he gazed at her with the limp eyes of an animal being euthanized, and she'd stared back, like, *Really?* And then he'd groped *harder*, even though First Wife was there, a woman with whom Julia sympathized greatly even though she could no longer remember her name, and wasn't that just an allegory for everything? And now all of it was gone: the Pac Heights mansion, the caviar potatoes, the little Christofle trays. And all that remained was this vulgar cubic house filled with Art Basel castoffs.

Julia descended the staircase, a twisted steel-and-stone monstrosity with suspended slabs for steps. She was arm in arm with Charlie, whose idea it had been to come. They were parents now, he said, and it'd been Julia who'd asked for date nights. She'd tried for another dinner at Suki-Ya, but it was Charlie's turn to choose and so here was his choice.

They reached the ground level. The floor itself was elegant, a rare aesthetic relief set in black and tan marble. On the walls was a series of Aboriginal paintings, the canvases oversize and rendered in spring greens and pinks and reds.

Charlie examined them. "I like these. We need to get more art. Did Barry pick all of them? That's pretty cool if so."

"Uh-huh," said Julia, though she knew the paintings had actually been purchased via Barry's art consultant, a young woman in a black dress paid millions to tell Barry his bad taste was good. She secretly believed most art to be overpriced, but wished to avoid that squabble. Charlie had been very considerate today, had read to Emily for twenty minutes while Julia showered, followed by an idyllic half hour in bed, hands clasped in a family cuddle. "Isn't this incredible?" she'd asked. "Don't you think life couldn't possibly get any better?" And Charlie had agreed that yes, life was indeed very nice . . .

Julia's breasts were straining against her dress, one of the few benefits of postpartum; she'd never had large breasts before. And nursing itself was going well, after she'd recovered from her bout of mastitis. On Friday she'd felt so good about her overall state of affairs that she'd done a surprise swoop-and-poop on Lara Conrad's staff meeting: dropping in unannounced like a visiting liege lord, stabbing holes all over Lara's road map. And then floating back to her office on her favorite Blahniks, where, on impulse, she'd called Taffin and ordered a custom choker with sapphires and ceramic. The necklace was still being made; on her wrists, however, were the jade Verdura bangles she'd purchased during the same spree. "Should we get some paintings later? Or sculptures? Some furniture?"

"Yeah," Charlie said. "All of the above." He liked to shop.

They continued to wander. Julia waved at or was obligated to greet a few guests of note—there always seemed to be another step on that staircase of upward mobility, though lately for Julia it'd been less other executives and more the actual vectors of power, the politicians and the money who backed them. The lists from Leo were usually an interesting entrée: all the scientists, academics, politicians, and executives who were already dirty or whom the SPB was looking to mire. A good dozen or so were at this party. *I know who you are*, she thought. And even better: *You do not know me.*

The buffet was set near the door, and as Julia arranged her plate she surveyed the other guests. In one corner was Ari Cheever, an Israeli entrepreneur who resembled a friendly sheepdog. He waved to Julia, his other hand clapped firmly over the ass of a slim, vacant-eyed woman who could only be one Mary Lim Cheever, forty years his junior. Dan McClaren was by the salad, another one-hit-wonder venture capitalist, known as the "Godfather of Silicon Valley," even though by Julia's standards he'd engendered very little into the world but a string of shitty companies and even dafter progeny. It always amazed Julia when powerful men married dumb models; it was as if they didn't ascribe to biology, simply believed their sperm could magically colonize whichever low-quality receptacle they happened to land in. McClaren had emailed her years earlier, referring his youngest to Tangerine—Bay Area royalty always touting meritocracy, except for their own—and to this day Bennett McClaren remained in brand marketing, no doubt torturing the rest of the team with his unearned self-confidence.

Julia sighed. A party like this was depressing. It was physical proof that you could tell yourself you were extraordinary but really it was to the ordinary that most extraordinary things happened; these ordinary people then accumulated layers of the extraordinary—wealth, houses, art—until their brilliance was blinding.

Ah! But here was good news! The baked potatoes! They were back!

She was behind Charlie, loading up on caviar—it was self-serve now, one of the few improvements from earlier—when she heard: "Charlie?"

Julia turned. The girl was in her mid-twenties, fawn-eyed and wearing a low-cut shirt edged with lace. In one hand she held a wineglass.

"Hey," Charlie said. "Hey." Julia wondered if he'd forgotten her name.

"I know who you are, of course," the girl said, turning to Julia. "You're like, insane. I mean, insanely great."

"Thank you." Aware people were watching, Julia extended her hand.

"I'm Mandy." Mandy's palm was supple and her nails were painted a light violet. "Mandy Lewis."

"I met Mandy when she was doing an intern program at the

hospital," Charlie said. He was looking around, already distracted, craning his neck at the desserts.

"I'm not a *doctor*. I'm a law student at Santa Clara."

"Wonderful," Julia said. She gave a little tilt of her head, to indicate they should get out of the way. Mandy did not move, but pointed at Julia's plate. "What's that?"

"Baked potatoes." Julia turned to the table, relieved to have something to do. "You'll enjoy it. Here, let me put one together for you." She gathered the cheese, the onions, the sour cream, and then added a healthy scoop of Petrossian Special Reserve on top. Why not? It was Barry's money.

"Thanks," Mandy said. She really did seem sweet; she had that naturally wholesome look that Julia both envied and admired. "Honestly, I don't even know if I can eat this. I mean, *Julia Lerner* put this together for me. Maybe I should take it home and frame it."

"Bless your heart," Julia said, and then took Charlie's arm and slid away.

ANOTHER HOUR PASSED. A HANDFUL of networking pests came and introduced themselves: a random Apple executive, two venture capitalists she'd never heard of, a Stanford professor hunting for a board seat. Lilian Aptos floated over, an old software hand who sat on Tangerine's compensation committee. Lilian liked young men, and had two chiefs of staff, whom she rather nauseatingly referred to as CP1 and CP2, Cutie Pie 1 and Cutie Pie 2.

"How's your little sweetheart?" Lilian asked. She was wearing a shift printed with enormous abstract flowers, one of those garments that look simultaneously deranged and expensive.

"She's wonderful." Julia found she couldn't help but feel pleased whenever someone asked about Emily. And Lilian was safe to speak with, given that she was already ancient and rich, in contrast to the other middle managers who constantly circled, waiting for conversational gaps to insert mentions of their twins.

"When are you going to be running the place?" Lilian said. But in an indulgent way, how one might cheer an overweight child about to enter a sporting event.

After sighting a muscled Turkish entrepreneur in his mid-twenties, Lilian quickly moved off. Julia went looking for Charlie, who had disappeared. He hated it when people networked in front of him; it was demeaning, he said, she didn't understand how it made a man feel to be passed over, ignored. At times Julia was surprised to recall all the things she'd thought Charlie didn't care about, only to discover after marriage that he actually cared about very much. She vowed to find him, to be soft and sweet and catering, when after kneeling to adjust her sandal strap, she looked up and saw not Charlie but: Aaron Pina.

Her brain rearranged itself. Aaron. Aaron was across the room. The space was not large, and he should have already seen her, but he was busy, in conversation with a group of men, including Ari Cheever, whom she'd waved to earlier.

How the hell had Aaron met Ari?

Julia shifted her focus to the overweight man on Aaron's left, running him through her mental bank until she'd identified him as Dmitri Marin, the Russian investor she'd once looked up on God Mode for Leo. The former oligarch who now spent his days chucking money at start-ups, calling in to podcasts, and recording his own clips attacking the Kremlin. Julia had seen the videos before—Dmitri speaking from his homes in Woodside, Water Mill, Malibu, narrating the latest conspiracy theories in his meaty accent as palms swayed behind his head. Pierre had come by her office once, after sending a link to one of Dmitri's missives: "How is this guy not dead yet?" Pierre laughed, and she'd ha-ha-ed while rocks tumbled in her stomach. And now she was thinking of Jefferson, and she hated to think about him, the rotting feeling it brought to her chest.

And then—without quite understanding what she was doing—she walked over.

"How are we?" Julia asked, drawing up. Friendly. Brainless. The neglected wife at a business dinner, returning from the bathrooms and tired of being spoken around, deciding that this is it, she's going to insert herself and Make Conversation!

Aaron turned. Instead of the expected fear or surprise, there was a low pleasure on his face, and a ping of fear rang within her.

"Ah you know, the same," Dmitri said. In person he was even larger than in his videos, though he wore his girth not like an American but rather a European, the weight evenly distributed like an expensive overcoat.

Aaron's mouth had assumed the curve of a smirk, which bothered Julia enough that she asked, "How do you all know each other?"

"We don't," Aaron said. "We just met. The Russian connection."

"Right." She turned to Ari. "But you aren't. Russian, I mean."

"I admire the *people*," Ari said, and Dmitri gave a low snigger. Julia automatically chuckled before realizing he was referring to the women, all the lush young Svetlanas and Anastasias, at which point her laughter abruptly died. To dispel the awkwardness, and also out of pettiness and a desire to regain lost ground, she said, "Aaron works for me. At Tangerine."

"Ah, yes." The men exchanged a look of discomfort, as if she'd been rude in announcing this, like a toddler pointing at a disabled person. "Tangerine," Dmitri finally said. "You're really at the center of everything, aren't you." His smile edged on pity.

The talk limped on, but it was clear her entrance had ruined things, as if she were a needle that'd deflated the entire conversation. After a few minutes Julia couldn't stand it anymore and grabbed Aaron—"A contract I had some questions on," she said, nearly yanking, and he was smart enough not to protest. They went through the house, Aaron navigating with seeming familiarity behind. Was this his first time at Barry's? Or had Aaron been before? Would she never be able to relax, to enjoy with abandon this life she had so exactingly crafted?

Finally Julia found an office walled in glass, not completely pri-vate but at least contained, and there were only a few others visible in the adjoining rooms. The space was modestly lit, with a musky scent of dirty breeding that reminded her of her first studio in San Carlos. Julia let Aaron settle in a chair and then turned to face him, hands against the table behind her. "What did I say about staying out of my way?" Her voice low.

"It's a party. Take it easy." *Take it easy.* Like an American would say.

"It's the kind of party I would go to. Thus, given our agreement, you should not."

Aaron raised his eyebrows toward a couple on a couch visible in the next room, a woman with purple hair straddling her partner. "Is it."

She ignored this. "What're you doing with Ari?"

"He was next to me at the bar. We got to talking."

"And Dmitri?"

"I introduced myself. Said I had some classmates who'd worked with him at Gazprom." Because naturally Aaron would have such classmates. Because Aaron had gone to Moscow State, had worked at McKinsey, had had everything go right in his life, and still had to try to take some of hers.

"Dmitri was open to you? He didn't think you were a plant?" Julia realized this was why she'd never spoken to the man, despite their shared commonalities, mainly being rich and Russian and liv-ing in Silicon Valley. She was worried that were she to approach, Dmitri would know who she was somehow, sniff her out, and with his fat hand point—*Traitor!* And her life would be over, for all it took was one person, one convincing accusation, for it to be undone.

Aaron looked at her. His eyes were so clear and his features so symmetrical—no wonder he'd done so well in Dresden, she thought. She waited for his reply and then recoiled when he began to laugh. "Dmitri? You truly believe that 'fled oligarch' shit? Oh *God*." He laughed harder. "Oh God, you don't know he's one of us. You're so goddamned ignorant, you think you're the only one."

"No." But her voice betrayed her. Because as Aaron said it, she knew it must be true—she should have known about Dmitri being an asset, she should have known about many things. But it was so hard to be totally aware when there was so much else to do: managing Tangerine and running six miles in the morning and being a good mother and keeping her marriage intact. Just do more, Leo would say. Work more. Work harder.

She allowed herself the question: "Did Leo tell you about him?"

"No." She couldn't tell if Aaron was lying.

"Then how do you know?"

"I have connections, Julia. Friends. It's something you should try. Besides, you think Dmitri would be *alive* otherwise? With all his money, and traveling as he does?" Aaron laughed again and smiled. When he did this he looked younger, sweet; if not for the SPB she probably would have gone her entire career believing him to be a very pleasant person.

She was losing control, her voice and hands making those miniature vibrations when her anger was near overflow. "I could destroy your career. You think I don't have influence? It'd be very easy for me to show you how much I have."

Aaron ran a hand through his hair. His breathing was heavy but she couldn't tell if it was from the drink, and when he spoke his voice was calm. "Go ahead. Run and tell your *friends* what a bad man I am. What do you think, that everyone will be on your side?" He came forward, so near as to be almost touching her. "I'll tell you a secret. All the men out there? And women? They *hate* you."

Julia was surprised to feel a dull ache. She shrugged, but weakly, and seeing this, Aaron moved closer.

"You've been lucky," he said. "You were here early, the only woman. Pretending to be so nice, but you're quite vicious yourself, aren't you? You can't hide it forever. At your level, it's impossible.

And what you should remember is that there are so many of us, and we're willing to wait. Until you're done, and we've taken back our power." Aaron bent his head, and in a swift movement licked his finger. Then, leaning in, so that to anyone outside it would appear only as if he were whispering into her hair, he quickly touched his finger to the skin behind her ear. Pressed down hard, tracing a curve. She forced herself to smile, in case anyone was watching.

# 22

# ALICE

When Alice woke, her mouth was dry.

She was in her bed, though how she'd arrived was unclear. Her top was off but she still wore Cheri's black skirt, and while her limbs throbbed, it was really her head that hurt most. In college, when she had been hungover, it always took Alice a full day—until she'd sweated and pooped out everything impure—to recover. And now she was over a decade older, and had also done drugs.

Pale yellow leaked through the curtains. Alice hoped that whoever had put her to bed would appear with water. (It must have been Cheri / It couldn't have been Cheri.) "Thirsty," Alice said. Her throat like sandpaper.

She pushed herself upright and hunted for a shirt with her foot, eventually landing on the oversize MIT crewneck she usually slept in. In the bathroom, she turned on the tap and filled the cup she used to hold her toothbrush. After she chugged the water, her throat was still dry, and she refilled the mug twice more before setting it down to pee.

Next, Alice braved the mirror. As expected, the situation was grim: her makeup was smeared and her skin sallow and flaky.

Though in a surprise turn, two pimples on her chin that'd been gen-
erating strength appeared to have been repelled—likely from all the
toxins, she thought.

Alice turned the tap back on and stuck her head underneath.
The cold helped absorb the pain, and she swiveled her mouth and
drank from the flow before toweling off and moving to the kitchen.
The sun, seemingly harmless earlier, was now piercingly bright, and
Alice realized the window was open while the air-conditioning was
on, a great sin in their household. "Cheri," she groaned. She moved
to shut the window and then stopped. Because there, standing in
the courtyard, was Sean Dara.

Alice yelped and reached to yank down the shade. It was too
late: Sean had sighted her, was raising a hand in greeting. "Is this
where you live?" he called.

Alice didn't respond. She continued to stare, confirming his
presence as reality. The sun felt good against her wet hair and she
rested her head against the window.

"Well?" Sean shouted. "Are you going to let me in?"

"Why?" Alice shouted back.

"Didn't you want to talk?"

"Yesterday. But not now. It's, ah . . . not a good time."

He squinted. "Jesus. Are you hungover?"

One particular flaw of the Palermo was that any noise from the
courtyard had a tendency to echo and boom back into the rest of
the units. Alice was suddenly aware she was engaging in the sort of
loud early-morning conversation she herself had been annoyed by,
on many occasions.

"Apartment 228," she hissed. "The elevator code is 987." She answered the door a minute later.

"Wow," Sean said. "You don't look good." He himself appeared
in perfect health.

"You're an asshole," Alice said, the best she could manage. She realized too late that she still wore the MIT shirt and the skirt from last night. "How do you know where I live?"

"I found your card in the chair this morning. It's easy, once you have that. You should know."

"Uh-huh."

She followed his gaze around the apartment. It was messy, with toppled jars of foundation and empty seasoning packets from the ramen Alice now had vague memories of Cheri assembling last night. "Eat!" Cheri barking as she brandished a fork with frighteningly pointy tines, shoving the spiral noodles into Alice's face.

"When did you leave yesterday?" Sean asked.

Her stomach quavered. "I don't remember."

"Who brought you home?"

"Uhhh. My roommate."

"Do you normally go to, ah . . . such events?"

"No." Alice slouched onto the floor. "It was my first time. I went to find you."

Sean nodded and shifted uncomfortably. He had removed his shoes at the door without asking, a small point in his favor. She saw him take in the kitchen counter, where last night Cheri had dumped out the contents of her bag, mainly lipstick and loose bills and a cache of tampons. "So. You want to talk?"

Alice's mouth felt furry. "Why are you here?"

"Come on. I'm sorry for yesterday. Let's go somewhere."

"No, I want to know. Since you blew me off earlier."

"I wasn't ready, all right? Barry Levine's place isn't exactly the setting to contemplate Julia Lerner. I had some time to think, afterwards. Moments under the stars. You were serious about God Mode?"

There was a groan from the second bedroom, and Alice realized she hadn't yet checked on Cheri. "Hold on." She filled a glass from the fridge, dropped in some ice, and carried it into Cheri's room. "Stop talking so loud!" Cheri yelled, one furious mascara-smudged eye darting toward the door. Alice quickly set the water by her bed and backed out.

"Is that your roommate?" Sean asked, craning.

Alice pointed at the couch. "Wait there. I need to change."

AT MCDONALD'S, THEY SAT IN a corner booth far from the other diners. Sean had driven—Alice had intended to drive herself, but once outside had been hit with the full power of the sun, triggering her head pains anew. She'd ordered a large coffee, hash browns, a breakfast sandwich, and hot cakes, had consumed it all, and now contemplated more. Next to her on the booth seat was a bag containing an identical order for Cheri.

"You know she was there last night," Sean said. He himself had ordered only black coffee. "Julia."

Alice shook her empty coffee cup and slumped. "Yeah."

"You saw her? Did you speak with her?"

"I believe Julia Lerner's familiarity with me hovers somewhere around yours."

"Wow." Sean drank. "Passive-aggressive. *Okay.*"

Alice ignored this. At home, after changing, she had removed from her Very Special Hiding Place—the zip-up butt of a hollow stuffed elephant—the piece of paper on which she'd written Julia's searches. She removed the folded square from her hoodie and pushed it across the table.

Sean reached. "What's this?"

"Julia's searches on God Mode."

"Why didn't you just print them?"

"Because they monitor the printers." She sat up. "Did you know that God Mode was still active?"

Sean ate a crumb from her hash brown wrapper. He had yet to open the paper. "No. Well, not exactly. Johan and I heard rumors, but you have to understand that in a company like Tangerine, there's a lot to keep track of."

"Do you think Pierre knows? Or uses it?"

"Yes. Or at least he's aware it's still operational." He wiped his fingers. "Now, I want to ask you something. Why did you come to me?"

Alice considered telling Sean about Tara, Julia's finding out about the servers, but decided against it. Who knew what might scare him off? "I guess I thought you'd be helpful. I'm a Grade Three at Tangerine. I have rent. And debt. You saw I have a roommate. I don't want to ruin my life."

"So you decide to ruin mine," Sean muttered.

"You came to my apartment. You wrote that blog!"

"I never should have published that. The online equivalent of a drunk dial."

Was he saying he didn't mean it? But Sean hadn't deleted the post: it was still the most recent on his Medium profile, preceded by a "state of FreeTalk" update from two years earlier, in which he'd likened himself and Johan to a pair of Olympic-level ice dancers. "It wasn't because of your blog that I thought of you. I was in your office once. You were talking to Johan about Julia. You were, uh, not too nice—"

"And you could hear?" Sean looked thoughtful. "No. I wouldn't have. Not in front of a random."

She let this pass. "I was underneath your table. Fixing your phone." When Sean blushed, she knew he'd remembered. "I thought of a lot of people before you," Alice added, sitting up even straighter. Her headache was fading; she felt nearly at full capacity. "None of them made sense. So why don't you go through the searches and then we can talk."

WHILE SEAN READ, ALICE WENT and ordered a soft serve. She was unexpectedly chipper, the relief of having unloaded God Mode nearly canceling out her hangover. She ate quickly, the ice cream soothing the back of her throat. This was always her favorite part, when the coldness began to combine with crunch; she'd felt happy enough to order an extra cone for Sean, though in contrast to herself, he was now more morose than when they'd arrived. He finished his vanilla swirl without savor, pressing the binder paper into tight folds with his nail. "I can't believe you found this. It's insane. If you hadn't been checking that server . . ."

"But then Julia would have done something else, right?" Alice thought it was best to maintain a positive attitude, one that framed Sean's involvement as inevitable. "And then maybe I would have found that."

"Maybe." He rubbed his arms. "But I don't think so. Jesus, those searches. What do you think she's doing? You know she's foreign."

"I'm foreign."

"Hey." Sean put up his hands in surrender. "My mom's from Chennai. We're on the same side."

"No we're not." Alice was tired of this kind of posturing, especially from someone like Sean, who looked pretty much like a white person and thus lived the reality of one, at least since his company had been acquired for billions. "What is Julia doing? The whole reason I came to you is I can't figure it out."

Sean ran a knuckle across his lip. "She's using the information. Exchanging it."

"You think she's selling it?" Which sounded both crazy and implausible. Sean shook his head.

"Or maybe she's one of those political kooks?" You occasionally came across one of these at Tangerine, usually a male engineer with extreme political positions who planned to retire on the ocean to escape taxes. "An anarchist?"

"Kind of. Closer."

"Say it," Alice said. "Just say it, don't keep making me guess."

No reply. Exasperated, Alice rolled her head back against the booth. The plastic was cold and her stomach newly queasy from the ice cream and she suppressed the urge to vomit.

Sean set down his cup. "I think she's a fucking spy."

# 23

# JULIA

Julia scratched at herself the entire way home from the party. Her nails digging into her arms, her neck, as Charlie drove with the bleary concentration of someone who knows he's a little bit drunk. Occasionally he sang, the radio set to the hair metal Julia thought resembled cats being strangled, but she didn't complain. She continued to scratch and press and abrade long after it stopped feeling good, finally ceasing when she felt the thin damp of blood, upon which she switched to pulling on her coat. By the time they arrived home, she had ruined the lining of her new Max Mara.

The next morning, Julia stretched and saw the dried blood on her arm. Charlie yawned and began to stir, and she quietly rose and went to the bathroom. Locking the door just in case, because she didn't want him to see her distress. Marriage meant that you could plot certain fights in advance: he would start sympathetic, but then become angry. As he had little patience for her "work problems."

"Why don't you just quit Tangerine," he would say. "You can leave, take some time."

"I don't want to," she'd reply. Because they might kill me if I stop. Because they could kill me, and you, too, and it would mean nothing to them, and I've known this all along.

She turned on the shower and slipped under the water. As the stream ran hot, Julia forced herself to recall the slickness of Aaron's finger, the pressure of it as it traced the bone near her brain. She parsed through his words, separating them from her distress—and when she did this, nothing had changed, she was still COO, had been on the covers of *Time* and *Fortune*, would be lunching with the German chancellor at a United Nations dinner in San Francisco next week. And what did Aaron have? Only the satisfaction that he had frightened her, that he had *touched* her, and that he'd done so without consequence . . .

The water was lukewarm now. Soon it would turn cold. Julia pushed it off. When she reentered the bedroom, Charlie was awake, searching his closet.

"Going out?" She could see he was making a mess of his clothes—Magda would have to come and redo everything later.

"Yeah. I'm going to hit the course." He yanked a polo over his head. "Hey. There was a reporter there last night. Did you meet her? She said she was going to find you."

"What for?" Julia hated most journalists. They'd been fine during that brief period when she'd been considered a female pioneer, an "icon"—but ever since the media discovered that exponentially more page views could be had by blasting her job performance and character (*Julia Lerner has carefully crafted her image—so why do anonymous employees still say she's a real bitch?*), they'd morphed into nasty little cockroaches. The last interview she recalled finding tolerable had been years back, with the *Guardian*. The reporter, Asha Jain, had been smart, quick, and though the piece was prevetted, Marcy Clemens from PR only a chair's length away, Asha had still managed to touch on topics that would only emerge as controversial years later. Tangerine and its role as a market maker of information—how between Julia and Pierre, they could theoret-

ically shape public opinion, decide an election, the future of an entire country. Julia had liked Asha, had said more than she normally
would, and then, toward the end, had been about to make a point,
some casual remark about women and men and cancel culture: *I
know this isn't a popular opinion*, she'd started, and then Asha had
opened her mouth and closed it. Given her a tight nod. *No. Then
don't say it.*

So Julia hadn't. And had canceled the rest of the quarter's interviews, for good measure.

"She was proposing a feature," Charlie said. "About both of us.
Kind of a power couple thing. It's nothing big," he added, flushing
slightly. "Just one of those lifestyle magazines. The *Peninsula Digest*?"

"Right," Julia said. She grabbed his water bottle from the top of
the dresser and knelt to zip his bag. "The two of us. Great."

AFTER CHARLIE LEFT, JULIA WENT to her office. She was dismayed, though not surprised, to find more than three hundred new
messages waiting on Tangerine Mail. Her last was from Tara Lopez,
asking when they could reschedule. *I wanted to contact you directly,*
Tara wrote, *given that your assistant does not seem to understand the
urgency of the matter.*

Julia closed it without replying. Next she looked up the *Peninsula Digest*: circulation 40,000, one of those jewelry-ad-stuffed
glossies that seemed to exist only so the wives of executives could
document their charity contributions and gala dresses. Marcy Clemens would have a shit fit if she agreed to the feature, especially
since she'd just said no to the *Wall Street Journal*. Was there a way
to escape it without upsetting Charlie?

A slight headache had bloomed, and Julia massaged her temples
with both hands. At least she'd agreed to go to the Smash Bash,
which Charlie had feigned only mild interest in but she knew he'd
been secretly eager to attend, just as she intuitively knew that he'd

likely enjoyed a light flirtation with that girl, Mandy. He was often a flirt. A week after their wedding, they had gone to a restaurant and upon being informed their table wasn't ready, went to wait at the bar. Charlie had ordered a bottle of Sancerre and, while mostly paying attention to Julia, had directed a casual stream of commentary to a group of women nearby: *Ladies, good choice on the flatbread . . . Are you going to finish ALL those fries?* Each time he spoke, the women had laughed and then looked at Julia.

"Don't do that anymore," she'd told him once they were seated.

"Do what?"

"Talk to women like that in front of me. It makes me look bad."

Charlie's face had been blank, but then there'd been a quick movement behind his eyes, something close to disdain—

What was Mandy's last name? Had she said it?

And now Julia was on God Mode, Charlie's Tangerine profile before her. She'd always promised herself she wouldn't do this, be a wife who spied, who kept her husband's loyalty through playing offense—such measures were pathetic, she thought. She was not pathetic. Though now she found she was not overcome with any major guilt or sense of disloyalty but only a mild acceptance. And really, wasn't it kind of commendable that she hadn't snooped until now?

Charlie's profile was empty but for his first name and last initial, though Julia knew this, as he always made a big deal about how he didn't use Tangerine. "That's *her* thing," he'd say at dinners, and then everyone would laugh, because of course social media was so frivolous and stupid. He didn't use Tangerine Messenger, either, or Tangerine Mail, preferring his alumni email. "I kind of hate technology" was another assertion.

Though, as Julia noted now, that didn't stop him from using FreeTalk.

There was a lot of activity there, actually. With Charlie's medical staff and schedulers. Group chat with the boys, poker night, who's bringing the sushi?

And also: last Wednesday. Julia found the date in her calendar, and saw it was the night she'd been out late for work. A roundtable with alumni of Collège Jean-de-Brébeuf, the Quebec secondary school Pierre had attended, followed by a late dinner with industry executives before Tangerine's developers' conference. She'd been away until nearly midnight, and now she recalled Charlie asking if she was certain she'd be gone. *Why do you ask?* she'd said, thinking he was worried about dinner. *Aren't you taken care of? You want me to ask Tyler to make something?* She couldn't recall his response.

Wednesday, 5:45 PM

**CHARLIE:** Do you know Rose Bar?

**MANDY:** Uh yeah! Love that place.

**CHARLIE:** We can meet at 7. I'll get a table. They have appetizers. You still hanging with friends before?

**MANDY:** I decided to go to barre. What are you doing?

**CHARLIE:** Browsing. Waiting for you. *wink face*

**MANDY:** I'm coming hungry!

Rose Bar. With Mandy.

And now God Mode returned her full name: Mandy Lewis. Short height, long hair, bad school. Mandy liked to bake, owned a fiddle-leaf fig, and messaged both her parents daily, a habit Julia found somewhat disgusting in adults. She was "obsessed" with climbing but still a little fat, though in the manner of extreme youth, the excesses mostly allocated between her breasts and ass. Overall she looked to be precisely the sort of girl Julia knew from extensive research that Charlie had dated prior to her.

She assessed the situation, blood pounding. Julia could predict with fair confidence that Charlie wouldn't ever want a divorce—

something to do with a mix of childhood religion as well as his own parents, who bragged about their forty-year marriage with the righteous air of political prisoners who've undergone considerable torture. Julia even gave it reasonable odds he'd not cheated that night, that instead there'd only been *conversation*, and while Mandy might mash together her tits, touch a hand to his sleeve, Julia put it at only fifty-fifty that he'd responded. Charlie was one of those guys, convinced he was a *good* guy, maybe because he'd always been. But convictions wore down. You outgrew your boyhood dogmas, stopped ordering the cheap wine at restaurants; became accustomed to walking into a room, a party, all the girls already knowing your name. *Charlie Lerner.* The hot husband of Julia Lerner, who would still be something even without her. Now that he'd had her.

Her head was hot and she could feel her insides churning. Julia breathed, slowly, and gripped the arms of her chair.

The feeling of believing yourself savvy, of being smarter than everyone else, of selecting better than everyone else, of being careful, of being exceptional enough to carve a fantasy from the nothing you were bestowed, of choosing who to share this dream with.

Only for that person to choose someone else, and hurt you.

THE BABY MONITOR CAME TO life with a soft cry. Julia automatically stood and went to find Luna, who passed Emily to her for nursing. After Emily finished, Julia returned to her office. The twenty minutes she'd spent with Emily eased her; while still outraged, she no longer had the feeling of her insides cracking, her world splitting apart. The world was not ending. At least not for her.

Julia returned to Mandy. After another minute on God Mode, she discovered in Mandy's cloud storage a few naked selfies. For a second Julia was tempted, but even she found it too distasteful to distribute these, it was—what did they call it? Slut shaming. And though Mandy was indeed a slut, Julia would not shame her in this way. Her ear was suddenly hot and she pressed her palm against it.

*What you should remember is that there are so many of us, and we're willing to wait. Until you're done, and we've taken back our power.*

Julia left God Mode and went to her email and searched her messages. She found the note Asha had sent years back, after the *Guardian* interview was published—a single line of thanks, no add-ons, no sycophanting. No sticky tidings about how Asha might stay in touch, perhaps be considered for Tangerine's own PR team once she'd tired of the modest prestige of journalism.

According to her Twitter bio, Asha was with the *Washington Post* now. Given the *Post*'s coverage of Tangerine, Pierre viewed the paper as an adversary; he'd even once sought to disadvantage their articles through the algorithm. (Julia had later quietly squashed the order: too much downside.)

Julia drafted a message to Asha's *Post* email via one of her anonymous accounts. *Check out Tangerine's latest executive hire*, she wrote. *Photos attached. His name is Aaron Pina.* Her finger hovered over SEND. After another second she pressed it.

She felt her heartbeat slow. A cool tranquility moved over her; she was in control again. She hadn't known any better before—had let them take it from her, use her life as a tool. But things were different now. As with any conflict, there would be difficulties, and she would likely struggle, but what was a life anyway, no matter how perfect, if a man could just come and steal it away?

# JUNE 2019

## 24

# LEO

The Golden Hand Spa in Sunnyvale advertised ninety-minute massages for sixty-nine dollars: not a bargain, but in the Bay Area, believably cheap. The intent was for the business to look operational, but not enticing. Hygienic, yet not pristine. The front window featured a press-on decal of a green bamboo and was otherwise bare with shades drawn.

It wasn't until Leo saw Julia here inside, examining with open disgust a slab of imitation quartz, that he understood he'd summoned her to the Golden Hand deliberately. That he'd *wanted* her here, uneasy and uncertain among the remains of sweat and honeysuckle-scented lotion. That she'd leaked the information on Aaron was disaster enough, but that the photos had been of an SPB operation, previously unknown to the Americans, brought it near treason. After the *Post* article published, Aaron had voluntarily resigned—had traveled under alternate cover to Moscow and was now in debrief, sputtering God knew what. What have I done, Julia? Leo thought. What have I done, for you to behave like such a selfish, reckless little shit?

There was only one "couples" room in the Golden Hand, located in the back, and inside were two massage tables, each wide enough for a single body. Though Julia had chosen not to sit on the other table but rather on a stool in the corner. Her hands were clasped and she wore a lavender scarf so ugly and out of character that Leo thought it must be a deliberate choice. An aesthetic hair shirt of sorts, though he knew better than to believe she was sorry.

"Let's say you're going to a restaurant," he said. "And you give your car to, what do you call it, a valet. Is that what they say here? A valet?"

"Yes," she said, after a slight delay. "That's what they call it. The people who park your car."

"Right." Leo scratched the side of his head. In his haste he had forgotten the cotton liner, though he simply had not bothered with the rest, the dentures and sloped back and mole-spotted neck of Henk Van Tiel.

"So," Leo said, "let's say you're going to this kind of place. A fancy restaurant. Name one." He shifted, and the tissue paper under him made an ugly tearing sound.

"I don't know."

"Please. Expensive, that you and Charlie like."

She pressed her lips into a tight line and touched her scarf. "Benu."

"All right. So say you are going to Benu. And you arrive and drop your car with the valet. It's a nice car, expensive. Like a Porsche. That's what Charlie just bought, right?"

She gave a terse nod.

"Okay, you say to the man, 'Park it for me.' And you give him a hundred dollars, because you're feeling generous. And then, at the end of the night, it's the same man. 'Hello again,' you say. And as he's bringing your car, you look in your bag for another hundred. But the man never returns. In fact it's only hours later, still waiting at the restaurant, the night ruined, all the good memories of your dinner already gone, that you learn the valet actually stole your car.

'But *why*?' you cry to the police. 'I was so generous!' And all they can tell you is that because you were driving a fancy car, and you were eating in an expensive restaurant, he thought he deserved from you even *more*.

"Now what," Leo said, "would you do, with a person like that?"

As he spoke, he'd watched Julia's face flit between bravado and indifference—though she played well at apathy he knew she must be weighing outcomes, whether to attack or defend or play dead. She locked her fingers. "I didn't *do* anything."

"Please. Do not lie."

"I'm not. What did I do? Release some information. It was bound to come out. A racist like that. Extremely difficult to recover from something of that nature, especially in America." She crossed her legs and looked back to the crystals.

When had Julia become like this, Leo thought. Had she always been hard, or had it happened in stages? In Moscow, Leo had occasionally been tasked with debriefing returning Spetsnaz—the special forces operatives, referred to internally as Directorate Y, who conducted everything from hostage retrieval to checkpoint destruction. Leo interviewed the returnees, assessing their mental capacity, assuring his superiors that the operative wouldn't, say, suddenly strip naked in public or impulsively choke a stranger on the Metro. Were they *impacted*, was the phrase. The American version being: Did they have PTSD? Though the problem was that PTSD didn't necessarily mean you blew out your brains or drank yourself to death (occasionally it did); sometimes it was coming home and being a bit of a jerk to everyone, or no longer watching movies with unhappy endings. And if you thought about it this way, nearly everyone could claim PTSD from life, and when you saw things like that, how was anyone's behavior excusable?

"Do you think the Americans don't torture?" he asked quietly. "They do. They love it, in fact. And why wouldn't they, after they discover what you've done? You've *killed* people, Julia, you've killed people they've invested money in, and if there's one thing Americans cannot abide, it's interference in their territory."

For a moment Julia gripped the stool, as if to stop herself from falling. She righted herself and laid her hands in her lap. "Who did I kill? Or harm, even? All I've ever done is pass along the truth. Is it my fault if someone has an affair, or moves to Florida?"

The point was too juvenile for him to acknowledge. "If they discover who you are. If they discover your true identity. They will take you to some place, the Indian Ocean, or an aircraft carrier. They will tie you upside down. They will penetrate you and feed you with a tube up your anal passage. All this will be recorded on video. All of this has already been done to others. Look me in the eyes so I know you understand this."

Her face was red. "Yes."

"Okay." Leo considered what to say next. Should he continue to frighten, or offer a path to absolution? "Now, what we—"

"You should be grateful," Julia blurted. "It's because of me that you are here."

He looked up and let some of his anger burn off before replying. "Grateful?"

"I changed your *life*." Her voice rose, and he made a lowering motion with his hand. "Oh, don't bother saying the rest, I already know. That I wouldn't be here but for you. But what about you, Leo? Would you be here if it weren't for me? We all want to live here. We all want to have this life."

"That depends on what your life was like before," Leo said evenly.

Julia fell silent. In the quiet, the groans and murmured negotiations of the surrounding rooms were amplified. Leo had the depressing thought that he owed much of his career to the fact that humans were deviant and filthy, that they had an inescapable yen for goods and bodies that went far beyond their merit, and that they were willing to travel considerable lengths to procure them.

He released a sigh. "I have been called to Moscow."

Julia drew a sharp breath. "Not permanently."

"It's unclear." Three days earlier, the Venture Suite at the Rosewood had been booked under the name Marilyn Choi, a signal Chester dutifully reported to Leo without knowing its meaning. "I could be recalled. Or you, even."

She blanched. "They couldn't do such a thing."

"Of course they could. You think governments are like machines? That they always make the rational decision? You should have made a bigger effort with Aaron. It was an unreasonable escalation, what you did."

She looked thoughtful. "Will he keep quiet?"

"I wouldn't count on loyalty." But here Leo thought that Julia, as usual, might be more fortunate than she deserved. As Aaron, in all his rage—and certainly Aaron would be expected to rage—might not report their disaccord. MINERVA was a revered name within SPB headquarters; she stood as a powerful symbol of their superior craft, their cleverness and resourcefulness. Of their ability to punch so far above their weight these past decades, and if that was wrong, then what did that say about the rest? The bureau was no different from most government agencies in that when bad news came, self-reflection often took a back seat to looking for a good messenger to shoot. Sometimes literally.

"Aaron threatened me."

He scoffed. "Don't be overdramatic."

"He did. He pressed his finger to my ear. And told me I was a fool for not knowing Dmitri Marin was an asset."

Leo absorbed this. Pressed a *finger* to her ear? It sounded both petty and absurd, though he didn't doubt Aaron was capable of some creative violence. As for Dmitri: his status was highly classified, so much so that Leo thought Aaron's assertion must have been a bluff. He could sense Julia watching him, and so didn't affirm or deny.

Julia twisted her fingers. "Do you remember what you told me when I first moved here? That last night, before you returned to Moscow?"

Leo tried to recall. They'd been sitting in her apartment, a studio not so dissimilar from his own now. Not knowing how to entertain, Julia had served warm tap water and an inexpensive pizza. Nervous or tired or both, when she tried to set the table she leaned too heavily against the side of the box, flipping the pizza to the ground and sending her to the kitchen in hysterics. While Julia floundered for cleaning supplies, Leo dropped to the floor with his napkin. As he gently scooped tomato sauce, he'd been surprised to feel an almost parental ache of concern; and even as he absorbed this, he'd also known that he could not be soft, he could not console her, because soon he would be gone and if she was to survive she had to be better. And now it was as if he were there, back in that apartment, and in his head Leo echoed the words as Julia said them out loud:

*"No one will take better care of yourself than you."*

THE SUN WAS BLAZING WHEN they left, the heat unceasing and harsh, swimming blunt loops in Leo's head. They exited separately, Julia through the back, her hair tied up and hidden in her scarf; Leo through the front, over to the Panera Bread by where he'd parked. The air conditioner in his car was weak, and he waited until he was a distance away and then ripped off his wig and pressed down the window.

As hot air blew against his face he berated himself. It was his fault, he knew. At some point during his time in California, he had let this place contaminate him, ease him unnaturally.

By the time he arrived home his back and neck were drenched with sweat. As he passed through the lobby Leo saw Miriam at the mailboxes, but her back was to him and he didn't greet her. She lingered as he went through his flyers and letters, looking at her phone—he could not tell if she was deliberately waiting or simply distracted.

As he started for the elevators, still looking at his mail, she spoke. "More work troubles?"

"Yes," Leo said curtly.

"You want to have coffee? Or tea? I got a new one. Loose-leaf. From the mall, which I know sounds silly, but I bought it because I'm always drinking their samples."

Leo was tempted. He understood Miriam was being friendly, that she was only trying to be—what did they call it? *Nice.* But it was in the kindness of others that you lost yourself; you forgot what you stood for, all you'd originally wanted.

"I can't," Leo said. And went to his apartment and closed the door.

# 25

# ALICE

So you're saying Julia Lerner is a foreign asset," the FBI agent said.

Leah Connolly's hair was short and dark, and parted deep on one side. She'd asked to meet at the Cheese Board, the pizza restaurant in Berkeley that Alice loved. Alice had been excited to go, especially since Cheese Board was an hour north and Sean had offered to drive—but then the entire way Sean had grumbled and been a total killjoy, tanking the mood. He was annoyed because he'd originally contacted a friend on whose board sat a former director of the FBI; Sean's query had then been punted to the San Francisco office, rolling downhill until it settled with Leah. Which was *fine*, Alice argued. What did it matter who they met with, as long as it was the right person?

"The right person *is* the higher person," Sean said.

"Are you aware," said Alice, "that you often sound incredibly rude?"

Though now, as she sat across from Leah at a square wooden table against a wall in the restaurant, Alice was not so certain Sean had been wrong. Throughout Alice's telling—Server 251! God Mode!—

Leah had only sat in polite silence; she'd yet to write anything in her notebook, and her gaze periodically strayed toward the windows and passersby outside. Alice, always sensitive to the waning interest of others, had struggled to complete her account and limped to the end. "So yeah, that's basically it," she finished.

"Julia Lerner of Tangerine," Leah repeated, glancing again at the exit.

"I think we've established her identity," Sean snapped as he viciously cut his corn and mushroom slice into pieces.

"And both of you are employees of Tangerine."

"I'm a *former* employee." Sean set down his knife. "I would have thought Robbie mentioned in his email? I'm one of the founders of FreeTalk?"

"And again, this is based on some activity you saw on your servers." Leah reached for the bottle of green sauce. As she shook, the liquid plopped out in uneven clumps; she swore and brushed at her slice.

"Not just *servers*," Sean said, glaring at the top of Leah's head. "Not just *activity*. There's a pattern—"

She set down the bottle. "Sorry, but why are you speaking so much? As I understand things, it wasn't even you who found the server activity?"

"My God, a man-hater," Sean breathed, at the same time Alice said, "I asked for his help."

"Right." The agent returned her attention to Alice. Her eyes were ice blue, like those of the monsters in the anime cartoons Alice had watched as a kid. "And why did you approach Mr. Dara? Did you have an existing relationship?"

"No." Below the table, Alice began to anxiously tear a napkin into bits. "I knew Sean disliked Julia, based—based on statements he'd made in the past. I'm a junior employee at Tangerine. My boss worships Julia. I didn't feel that I could speak to someone internally about the issue."

"She approached *me*," Sean interjected. "I was just sitting there, enjoying my retirement, when—"

"Could you please leave?" Leah cut in.

"*What?*"

"For a few minutes." She shook the ice in her drink. "Girl talk."

For a second Alice steeled herself, but then Sean surprised her by setting down his fork and standing. She and Leah watched him lope across the street, to a shop with glass pipes in its window.

"Interesting guy," Leah said, pushing back her hair. Her eyeliner was smudged, as if she'd woken early and already accomplished many things so far that day. "Though I'm used to it. Millionaire by twenty-two, lost his virginity at the same time. Oh, don't worry, I'm not going to *eat* you," she added, clocking Alice's expression. "I only wanted to ask a few questions about Julia. In private. What did you think of her before all of this?"

What was safe to say? "I didn't really have any thoughts."

"And you never had any interactions with her."

"No. None until a month ago, when I was invited to a round-table."

"Right." Leah unwrapped her straw. "I've seen those on her profile. Picture of a bunch of ladies, caption about girl power. Or girls in tech. Not girls, sorry, women. So you went to one?"

"Yes." Alice hesitated. "I sat in the back. But it's not like we were one-on-one."

"Why were you invited?"

"I don't know. I was—I am—worried that she found out I knew about God Mode." For a moment Alice thought to tell Leah about Logan. But that would implicate her own usage, so she kept quiet.

Leah's plate was now slivers of crust; she pinched a crescent, cracking it into pieces. "I did some basic research on you before I came. MIT. Computer science. That's a pretty good résumé, right? You're not too high at the company, though."

Was she trying to insult her? "I'm considered a low- to mid-level employee," Alice said carefully.

"And how much younger are you than Julia?"

"Um. I think two or three years."

"And do you think Julia is a likable person?"

"I'm not sure it matters whether I find her likable."

Leah's smile was wolfish. "Indulge me."

To stall, Alice nibbled her own piece of crust. "Outside of what we just discussed, I believe Julia to be a capable leader, to have risen so high at Tangerine." Or just good at politics and strategy, which Alice figured amounted to the same. "I work there, I know how difficult it is to survive. And I'm sure a good number of people, especially women, find her likable."

Leah leaned in. "Do they really, though?" Her tone husky now, almost seductive. "The women, I mean. After all, you don't. It's fairly obvious. Oh, they *admire* her," she said, overriding Alice's protest. "They photograph themselves with her and defend her to men and say laudatory things in public. When you ask educated women about Julia, they tend to list her accomplishments, as you have, and say what she does is so *hard*. But they don't seem to like her."

Alice's cheeks were hot. "That's not why I came forward. It has nothing to do with likability."

"I didn't think so. You don't seem the sort . . ." Leah's eyes wandered and then returned. "My point is, there's something irritating about Julia. She tries so hard to be relatable, right? Even though we all know she's not."

"I don't know," Alice murmured. "I just think she shouldn't be looking at people's data."

"Right. Data." Leah fell silent, and Alice checked the shop window across the street. Sean had disappeared.

"Hey," Leah said, "want to know something about women? They make bad jurists when it comes to rape cases. Isn't that interesting?"

"Rape?" Alice echoed, a little wary. She had the feeling she was being led, that she had lost control of the conversation.

"Yeah, rape. Like a man holding you down, shoving his dick into you? *That* kind of rape. You get a guy like that in front of a jury of women, more often than not, they vote to acquit."

"Why?" Alice asked, though she didn't really want to hear. She already knew the interview was a disaster. Here Alice thought her life was a failure because she hadn't tried *enough*—and finally she'd forced herself, gone to the Smash Bash, found Sean, met the FBI—and it turned out the results were the same anyway.

"It's to do with how they relate to the victim," Leah said, twirling her straw. "Or victims, most of the time. The defense always tries to get a jury with women, and a specific type. If the victim's young and pretty, they'll go for some old church wives; if she's floozier—tragic past, bad eyeliner—then they try to stack it with a bunch of PTA moms. The sort that could have *been* that floozy, if they hadn't married the insurance agent." A group of students entered, chattering and laughing, and Leah turned. "If it's men on the jury, though?" she continued, swiveling back. "If there's enough dudes in the room? Then the conviction rate climbs. You get a bunch of guys thinking about the stuff they've fantasized about, the real dark nasty material in their heads, and they know the accused is guilty."

"I'm not doing this because I'm jealous of Julia," Alice said angrily. To her horror, her eyes had begun to water. She was upset that Leah assumed she knew everything about her, simply because she was less successful and not beautiful. In agitation she stuffed her hands into her pockets, where they jammed against the square of paper she'd shown Sean at McDonald's. "Here." Nearly throwing it across the table. "I have a list of her searches. Some of the names Julia was looking for on God Mode."

Leah hesitated. "Take it," Alice said, louder. "When a name's underlined, it means it was a search on FreeTalk."

Leah unfolded the paper.

"She's not just spying on people's Tangerine activity," Alice added, "but also using FreeTalk to view their messages."

Leah ran a finger down the sheet. Slowly, evenly, like a teacher checking homework. She stopped. "What's this one?"

Alice looked. "Jefferson Caine? I didn't recognize the name. You see the red star I put next to it, though? That means she looked him up on both FreeTalk and Tangerine."

"And you said she was using FreeTalk to find locations?" Leah's eyes were still on the sheet. There was something new in her voice and posture, however—a certain sharpness, which came off her like perfume.

"I didn't say locations, I said messages, though I suppose she *could*—" Leah let out a long sigh, and Alice stopped. She braced herself for whatever new horrible anecdote the agent was going to share. But Leah didn't say anything. She stared at the paper a second longer and then refolded it.

"Uh. That's my only copy."

"Oh." The agent still seemed in a daze. "Could I take a photo?"

"Is your phone safe?"

"I sure hope so," Leah said, reaching. She took the picture and then continued to look at the paper, which she'd pressed flat against the table. It was soft now, from overhandling, and a corner was torn. Leah ran a finger against it, stopping again at the name Jefferson Caine.

"Ah," she said. "That's a shame."

# 26

# JULIA

Betsy was back.

Charlie's mother had arrived with almost no notice Monday evening (she claimed to have emailed Charlie her itinerary, and *Julia, I thought I had you on copy, but you know, you never respond* . . . ). Rolling with her through the front door two oversize trolleys and a Louis Vuitton tote in which she stored her iPad and reading glasses. Julia had given Betsy the largest guest bedroom, more importantly the most isolated guest bedroom, and, citing her work schedule, had mostly avoided contact. But now the weekend had come, and Charlie wanted a "family brunch," one Julia knew she was expected to endure with good cheer.

"I think the temperature of your home makes it difficult for me to sleep," said Betsy as Julia stood in the kitchen fussing with the French press. On the weekends it was usually Charlie's job to make coffee, and though she'd repeatedly warned him that he was Not! Allowed! To Leave Her Alone With His Mother! he'd still managed to sleep through Julia's waking, her shower, Emily's morning meltdown—which Julia had shushed and rocked Emily through, tiptoeing downstairs, because this was what one did in a loving marriage, except she was fairly certain that (a) Charlie had fucked Mandy Lewis, and (b) he had done so when he claimed to be too busy to attend Emily's six-month checkup. While tight-lipped with rage about Mandy, at times Julia was even angrier about the missed appointment, which she'd thought for Charlie should carry both a personal and professional interest. The mess with Aaron, Leo's fury, her sheer lack of available time, had so far been what kept her from a confrontation.

Betsy was flitting about the kitchen, the sequin flowers on her robe glinting as she selected her creamer. She no longer emerged fully dressed in the mornings as she used to, which alarmed Julia. It was as if Betsy were slowly becoming more comfortable, reveal-ing more of herself—she had also grown more ostentatious with her grocery demands, requesting three different types of probiotics.

"Your house," Betsy remarked. "Brrrrrrrrrrr."

"Yes," Julia said, pretending to not understand. Just yesterday she'd discovered Betsy meddling with the thermostat, a smart de-vice manufactured by Tangerine that Julia was secretly impressed Charlie's mother knew how to operate, as it had scored poorly in the senior citizen use case. Julia had since placed a fingerprint lock on it, and the home's temperature was immovable at 68.

"It has to do with my internal body regulator. I'm very sensi-tive."

"We have blankets. And guest robes."

"Oh, no. I wouldn't want to be any trouble."

Julia sighed. Betsy had arrived solo, which Julia had originally thought preferable from a sheer body count perspective, though now she understood this to be wrong. Without the muffling factor of Paul, the woman was amplified. Besides the business with the thermostat, she had also taken to following Julia throughout the house, making racially tinged observations about Luna and the rest of the household staff (*Very loving to children! But they also believe in ghosts!*).

At last Julia could see Charlie descending, still in his Duke T-shirt and boxers. He laid a friendly hand on her shoulder as he reached for his mug.

"Are we having brunch?" Betsy asked. She moved closer to her son, rubbing a small circle on his back. "I'd love somewhere with good mimosas. And corned beef, but, Charlie, promise you're only going to let me have a little. Red meat is a killer."

"We're definitely having brunch." Charlie turned to Julia. "Where do you think? Village Pub?"

Julia did not respond but instead retrieved Emily from her chair, where she had been staring peacefully at a plastic bird. Julia nuzzled her daughter's neck, breathing in the scent of her hair and head. *I love you.*

"You know, I have a few friends who believe Emily looks like me," Betsy said from behind.

Julia didn't turn. "She does not look like you."

"I've always been interested in genetics. It's why Charlie became a doctor."

"Uh-huh."

"I hope you don't take this the wrong way, naturally you're her actual mother, but one of my friends said she couldn't even see any little bit of Russian or Eastern European in her. There was a lively debate just this morning. You know how I've been taking those photos of Emily? To post on my Tangerine page? Because you never send or post any, and really, dear, you *do* work at the company—"

It took Julia a moment to understand. When she did, she whipped around in a cold fury. "Do not post any photos of my daughter online."

Betsy reared back, a hand over her chest.

Charlie shot Julia a warning look. "What she means," he said to his mother soothingly, "is that we want our lives to be private. Especially Emily's. After all, it's not like she can choose to have her photos on the internet."

"Of course it's *private*. It's just my friends who are looking. What do you think they are, terrorists?"

"You have no idea," Julia said, voice shaking. "You have no idea what you're talking about." And then, still holding Emily, she went upstairs; she closed the door to the nursery and settled into the rocker, having decided she wasn't going to brunch after all.

CHARLIE FOUND HER AN HOUR later.

"You were rude," he said, legs apart and hands on hips, the stance their safari ranger in Botswana had instructed them to assume were they to unexpectedly encounter a predator outside the vehicle. Even from below—lying on the carved stone bench in the backyard Julia had relocated to, after Emily fell asleep in her crib—her husband appeared remarkably clean and pure; Charlie had once told her that out of all the physicians' on the Concierge Health website, it was his photo that received the most clicks.

"You left," Julia said. Charlie and Betsy had departed shortly after Julia went upstairs. She'd heard the sound of the engine starting, the garage opening, the low rumble of the gate, upon which she'd been struck by the brief mad temptation to have the car towed from wherever they'd gone, as some remote expression of her power.

"You wanted us to leave."

"Good point."

Charlie made a sound of exasperation and circled the bench, stopping in a shaded spot by the maple. He held a plastic cup of orange juice, which meant they had not made it to Village Pub; chances were it'd been the local diner, Franken's, which he despised for its grease. "I think you're depressed."

"Nope." Though actually: Was she depressed? Was this what depression looked like? At the institute, depression had been mocked by the children and adults alike: *Oh, Americans*, they would say with comic sourness. *They are depressed.*

"Okay, then why are you being such a bitch? You're making me look like a piece of shit."

A piece of shit, Julia thought. That was it. That was how Charlie's indiscriminate screwing made her feel. And suddenly she'd had it: She was tired of the suppression, the good behavior. Of trying to maintain dignity when the world itself was so undignified.

"I'm not the one having dinner with Mandy Lewis." Julia raised a hand to her forehead to better observe his expression.

Charlie blanched. She could see him recalibrating, reevaluating. He ran a palm through his hair. "Someone saw us eating?"

She had to let him assume this; he couldn't know she'd seen his messages. "Yes."

"She's just a friend from work."

She stretched, toes to the sky. "Right."

"What are you implying? That it's something more?"

The Mandarin Oriental last week, mid-level suite, paid in cash. On the same night Julia was at a fundraiser for the Zany School, which had wrung from her the appearance even though Emily wouldn't attend for another two years. Mandy the morning after: *You're hilarious! Like a drug dealer with your rolls of \*cash emoji\* \*cash emoji\*!* Unlike when she'd first discovered the messages, this time Julia hadn't felt that same hot stream of hate—it was as if she'd already extrapolated herself to this point, from the very first text, and Charlie was only fulfilling his end of a contract.

"Yes." Her voice was a monotone. "I'm saying you're sleeping with her, of course."

"Why? Just because I have a female friend, that means I have to be sleeping with her? Not terribly progressive, Julia. In fact, I think you might even refer to it as *not on brand*."

"Please." Though Julia was almost impressed by his indignation. If it weren't for God Mode, she would likely be doubting herself right now. And then she sat up, suddenly angry, and kicked a wool blanket from the bench onto the ground, where it partially unfurled.

Charlie stood with his arms crossed. "You think I like it when you're out at dinners with a bunch of dudes, or traveling overseas with Pierre? And don't say it's all for work. What about when you gave the graduation speech at Duke?"

She was surprised by this. "I thought you'd be happy for me. You always talk about your time there."

"Yeah, emphasis on *my* time. So why would you think it'd be fun for me to watch my wife onstage years later? While I sit in the audience listening to some shtick on corporate ethics I'm certain you couldn't care less about . . . You know, the chancellor wasn't even aware I'd gone to school there."

"I'm sure I mentioned it in the speech."

"No. You didn't."

Her laugh was strained. "So because you were mad about some random graduation speech, you went and slept with a twenty-year-old. Very original. Does your ego feel better now?"

Charlie shuddered. "You can be so fucking cold." He turned from her and walked toward the house.

"Where are you going?" Julia called, though she wasn't certain he'd heard—her voice seemed to sail halfway and then crash into silence.

Charlie disappeared inside.

After a few minutes, Julia got up from the bench. She patted around herself for her phone. She realized she'd left it inside, but, not wanting to go back in, spread the corners of the blanket flat on the grass instead. And then lay down again. Her favorite part of the house was the backyard, though she didn't spend much time here; the air was crystalline and the sun, filtered through tall oaks, cast on her body slim pinkies and fat thumbs of light. Come spring, birds would begin to caw before six, when she was already on her second cup of coffee; she'd wanted to install a feeder, but her landscaper, Mr. Fujihara, had advised against it. While she loved the garden, the house itself was not her style. She had wanted something older, smaller, and more subdued, but Charlie had seen the listing and insisted they come.

"The estate is being offered for fifteen million," the agent had said, addressing Julia before adjusting herself from some micro-cue to face Charlie. "I've been informed the seller will let it go for thirteen."

Julia had been quiet, let him lead. The evening before, they'd discussed a budget of $8 million.

"I love it," Charlie said.

So she'd bought it for him.

Would she have to give him the house, she wondered now. If they split, would she lose the house?

Julia had never thought she'd get a divorce. Especially once she'd had Emily, once she understood that Charlie was the sole other person who'd love her child as much as she did. There's no better solution than this, she'd thought. But the truth was that marriage was both infuriating and dull; she wanted to kill her husband for having sex with someone else, while at the same time not really wanting to have sex with him herself. At first she had thought this was normal, universal: How many times had she been advised on middle-aged celibacy, sagging bellies, deflated dreams? Followed by the inescapable downhill stumble, upon which you had to adjust all your expectations?

But the men in Julia's orbit didn't suffer. They grew older and grosser and made their conquests and disposed of wives and families; they fucked up, lost *billions*, but kept on with their ascent . . .

If she divorced, it would make the news. There would be articles, debates over whether it was possible to have it all, whether an alpha could marry an alpha or if something would have to give way: some*thing* or somebody. There would be conjectures about her

work, the lifestyle, whether triumph in one area (work) meant failure in another (husband). And she had failed, because when you
chose to love a person, wasn't he supposed to love you back? When
you had a father and a mother, weren't they supposed to want to
*stay*? Julia's face was wet and for a moment she didn't realize she was
crying.

You are so fucking stupid, she thought.

SHE DOZED UNTIL SHE WAS awoken by the low roar of a passing
plane. Julia raised herself halfway, onto her elbows, and then arched
and let her hair fall behind her, like a magazine ad for sunscreen
she'd seen on her first day at her grandmother's. That night, Nina
had retrieved from her luggage a box of chocolate truffles saved
from the factory. At dinner they'd passed the box, Zora impatiently
urging Julia: *Go on, don't be slow!* Julia, acting from some greater
instinct, had chosen the smallest chocolate, a fat button with lines
of white. When she bit in she found the outer layer had hardened;
inside there was not the smooth pleasure of fine chocolate but
rather something like grit, and as she chewed she could sense the
table's cumulative disappointment. Perhaps if the chocolate had
been good, everything might have been different—it was so much
harder to let people go once you'd shared in pleasures together.

Julia sat up the rest of the way and shook the loose grass and
pollen from her shirt. Her job would be fine. Everything would be
fine. She would mend relations with Leo: be obedient, service with
a smile. Start thrice-weekly appointments with Bruce Kim, her personal trainer; call her stylist, buy some new clothes. She would be
an excellent mother to Emily and a good COO to Pierre.

As for Charlie, well. She would decide that later.

There was a noise from the door. Julia turned, thinking it was
Charlie, but instead Betsy emerged from the house. "I don't mean
to be rude, but I don't think your Magda knows how to use the com-
post," she said as Julia scrambled to push on her sunglasses. She

would rather die than have Betsy know she had been crying. "I just saw her throw a napkin into there."

Julia looked to the kitchen window, from which she could see Magda peering out with a nonplussed expression. "She knows how to use it."

"Do napkins go in the bin?"

"If they've been wiping food, yes. They can go in."

"Oh. Well."

Betsy sat on the blanket. An almost admirable quality of Charlie's mother was her unwavering confidence in her own popularity; even if you were rude, as Julia had been earlier, she assumed it had nothing to do with her.

Betsy glanced around, assessing the greenery. She fingered the rosemary bush, rubbing and then sniffing. "How big is this yard?"

"I don't know."

"Does Charlie come out a lot? He used to like big open spaces when he was a boy."

"Not much." The last time Julia could recall was when the ceramic grill was delivered. Charlie had ordered it from Osaka, along with an accompanying table made of Hinoki wood. Both the table and the grill now sat by the pool, the latter resembling a giant dinosaur egg. Charlie had never used it.

"Your son is cheating on me," Julia said. The words were an accident; they simply slipped out. She didn't look at Betsy but from the side she heard a sharp breath. She wondered what Charlie's mother would say: if she would rejoice, say it was Julia's fault, that she hadn't done nearly enough, and didn't she regret now being such a bitch about the lemon chicken?

"Oh," Betsy said. "Oh, oh. I'm so disappointed. He's ruined his life if that's so." And then, to Julia's shock, she encircled her with her arms; the two of them sat, slowly rocking, the sounds of the garden around them.

# 27

# LEAH

Leah Connolly was having a good quarter.

For starters, she was dating again. For a long while she'd been near celibate, because trying to find love in Silicon Valley was a nightmare of sorts, a market failure of inaccurate pricing and lopsided supply and demand. But after too long on her own she became miserable, not just in her own feelings, but also a more miserable *person*, and so she'd resolved to try. For her last date, she had met an Iranian named Dana at Evvia in Palo Alto; Dana had both paid and refrained from asking to share Leah's galaktoboureko, upon which they'd returned to Dana's, a cute three-bedroom cottage in Waverly Park. By the next morning, Leah was at her own apartment, where she microwaved a day-old cup of coffee before signing on to Navient and making her final $1,800 payment. Her four years at Georgetown now free and clear.

Hell, Leah thought, I'm having a good year.

Her professional streak had begun six months earlier. She'd been on a different squad then, financial crimes, on an insider trading case with some finance directors at a software company. The finance guys (and one woman) were "closers," which meant they were responsible for the numbers reported to Wall Street each quarter. During this period they were barred from trading, but that didn't mean there weren't other methods of getting out the information. One of the directors, a mid-level controller, lived next door to a man named Reddy Sahib. Reddy was a real estate investor with properties in San Jose and Sacramento and an expensive lifestyle he buttressed through options trading.

"I've got tenants," Reddy said in the interview room. Not even bothering to sit before talking, clearly shitting himself at the idea of prison. "I've got drug dealers in my buildings, I've got all kinds of criminals."

"Oh yeah?" Leah had said. She paused. "What makes you think they're criminals?"

He had caught himself then, stopped talking. Gauging her. As they both knew what he'd been about to say: because my tenants are Black; because they are Mexican; because they are undocumented, pay in cash; because they look "ghetto." When she first started this job, there were few things that turned her off more—some quip about white extinction, and instantly Leah would categorize the person: *fucking useless.* But she'd since learned that racists could be savvy in other areas. They could even be intelligent—just one of the many inelegant, inconvenient aspects of her job.

She saw Reddy sneak a look at her complexion, technically a medium beige, NC35 at the MAC counter. Just a regular white lady with a tanning habit? Or something else? He made a decision. "I've got a guy. A white guy."

"Oh, a *white* guy." She made a jerk-off motion. "We don't have any of *those*."

"No, I'm serious. There's something wrong with this one. He pays in cash, right? For my most expensive place. Each month, five thousand dollars. I ask him once, what does he do? You know what he says?"

"What," Leah said, though she was already bored. People were always convinced their neighbors were secretly depraved. Mostly, she thought, because they hoped others believed interesting things about them.

"He's a waiter. A *waiter*! You know who lives in my apartments? I got Google, Uber guys. Not drivers. Corporate. With RSUs. I don't got waiters."

"Okay, so he has rich parents."

"No, no." Reddy shook his head. "He don't look the type."

"What's the type?" Leah asked, before deciding she didn't care anyway. "Never mind. If that's all you've got, a waiter who can live in one of your tacky apartments and pays his rent on time—"

"I promise!" Reddy had screamed. "I promise, there is something wrong! You don't believe, but I know people. If you follow him you will see!"

"Fine," Leah said. "We'll take a look." And then tossed him over to the SEC anyway.

It was something in Reddy's agitation, Leah would later decide, that made her think of his tenant when she moved to the Russia squad; the distress in his eyes, the tenor and depth of his outrage. It certainly wasn't what he *said*, because by now she'd met countless people who thought they "knew" human behavior—an unfortunate by-product of all those serial killer podcasts and shows on TV.

Now Leah was waiting. In a parking lot, in the shade, in the back corner of a strip mall that contained a Whole Foods and two exercise studios and a Starbucks. If you spent too long in certain Bay Area suburbs, it was easy to believe daily life was all variations of the same: hot yoga and overpriced prepared foods never more than a few miles away. Even though she'd spent her childhood in Mattapan—being walked to elementary school by a ten-year-old uncle, buying her breakfast at the bodega, waiting as the cashier made change behind bulletproof glass—sometimes now Leah was annoyed when she had to drink the shitty coffee, not the good kind. When the Pilates instructor was too hyper. That was how easy it was to get used to a nicer life. She thought about this as she sat half dozing in the car; it wasn't her own but rather a gray Honda Odyssey, and in this lot there were at least four of the same color and model.

She watched the Whole Foods. Leah calculated the doors opened on average once per minute. A woman was leaving now, late thirties, with the brown splotch of a birthmark on her cheek. No style. Limp hair. Large eyes a little too wide-set. The woman carefully returned her shopping cart and then went and grabbed two others that had rolled off, pushing them into the row. Leah stared at her.

It was only when she was in her early twenties, just starting at the bureau, that Leah really discovered she loved women. Bad timing, because by her mid-twenties she hated them. Women being such deceitful, unpleasant creatures: giving their children to pornographers; blowing up their lives for the worst kinds of love; setting rapists free because it wasn't their fault, not when bad women teased and taunted and made spectacles of themselves . . .

But still, they were usually better than the men.

The one she'd been waiting for came into view. Oblong shaped, pleasant-faced like a roadside daisy. Chester wasn't his real name, but Leah still liked to call him that. He was the only Chester she knew. He slid open the door.

"So," Leah said. She looked to confirm he'd shut the door, and then climbed from the front seat into the other captain's chair in the back.

"Yeah," Chester returned. He was in a similar getup as when she last saw him, a gray tee and black jeans.

"I'd like to ask you some questions."

"You ask, I come, right? That is the deal."

That was what Leah liked about the Chesters of the world: they knew the rules, how to behave when someone else held the leverage. She'd just happened to be following him when he parked in front of a UPS Store and spent what she considered an inordinate length of time inside. From the store's footage, obtained via FISA warrant, he'd been scanning documents onto a USB stick, the papers later revealed as having been stolen from a components manufacturer. Pure dumb luck, because even though she'd decided to tail him that morning, she could have used those hours in a myriad of other ways, as the bureau didn't possess nearly enough resources to manage surveillance on all their targets. Leah herself had over two hundred identified persons of interest operating in the Bay Area, and received dozens of tips a month. So when she'd been passed Sean's name she hadn't thought much, just another rich dick to pacify so that he didn't go squalling off and making things difficult. She happened to have another errand in Berkeley that day, and missed Cheese Board, so thought: Why not?

But then that name: *Jefferson Caine*. Caine's handler on the FBI end, Scott Seton, had been one of Leah's instructors. He'd called after it happened, asking her to watch for the name. "He'd started talking to some of his old friends," Scott said. "Even though I *told* him . . ." Leah said she was glad to assist, surprised to hear the unsteadiness in Scott's voice before he thanked her and hung up.

Chester was calm, his breath steady. Some in his position couldn't handle the pressure: they were swarmed by guilt, they had to spill, Poor me, my life is so complicated! Chester, however, was cool. Nerves of steel actually, given that his lazy tradecraft would certainly get him censured, if not detained in some nasty place like Lefortovo back home—but he accepted his exposure, continued to clock in at the Rosewood, no problems there. He was a low-level get, and he knew it: Leah had met with him only twice and his residence and person weren't actively monitored. Their second rendezvous he'd even brought her some leftover mushroom flatbread. She'd thanked him and set the box in the back, thinking she should get it tested; by the end of their hour the aroma had gotten to her, and she'd ended up eating it all.

She was slightly disappointed he had brought her nothing today.

"I'd like to go over our situation so far, if that's all right with you," she said. As if he had a choice. "You've been working as an intelligence asset for the SPB in the United States for eight years. Prior to that, you were trained in Donetsk, on the edge of Ukraine."

Nothing.

"You came over on a tourist visa and, through marriage to an American, Deborah Griffin, obtained citizenship." Poor Deborah. In the beginning, there'd been the theory she was in on the deal. She was a real estate agent, specializing in Burlingame and Hillsborough, with wealthy clients. She'd been innocent, though, had apparently truly married Chester for love, wringing from him three torrid years before he abruptly dropped her. Based on her emails, Deborah still held hopes for a reconciliation; occasionally she messaged, asking if they could meet, did he need anything, a home-cooked meal, some money, honey?

He smirked. "Yes."

"You communicate on a regular schedule with your handlers."

"With the account," Chester corrected.

"Oh, right. The *account*." This useless "account" he claimed: some generic email address Chester supposedly received orders from and sent intelligence to, with no other communication, as if he were sticking little scrolls into glass bottles and shoving them out to sea. Normally Leah would press but she wanted to keep the conversation light, flowing. "And what have the requests been lately, from this *account*?"

"The usual." He bit a loose piece of nail off his thumb. "To observe in my job, identify those easy to compromise."

"And how do you identify who is easy to compromise?"

"I listen to conversations. What they speak of, if they are interested to have more power or money. Who is having an argument, who is there with their mistress. Or mistresses. You know. Sometimes, the men, they like to bring two."

She knew he was trying to disgust her. "And how often do candidates crop up?"

"Every day," Chester said evenly.

Silicon Valley, Leah thought. You're going to destroy us all. She checked the clock: twenty minutes until the end of the hour. Reaching into her bag, she removed a Givenchy lipstick. She took her time applying, checking her accuracy in the cap's small mirror. "And what," she asked, still staring at her reflection, "do you know about the Golden Hand Spa?"

She'd surprised him, she noted. "What's that? Hand Spa? I don't know. Sounds like a massage place, yes?"

"So you think it's just massages there?"

"Are you a client? Perhaps you could tell me."

Leah groaned. "We know you own it. Or that your name is listed as an investor."

"If you already know, why are you asking?"

"I was wondering how forthright you'd be. And I have to say: not an encouraging response, Chester."

They sat in companionable silence. Emerging from the store was either a young grandmother or an old mother—in the Bay Area, one had to be careful—leading two sisters; the girls had matching pigtails, their hair like bicycle handlebars.

"How long have you known about the spa?" Chester's voice was unconcerned, but Leah knew the fact that he was asking meant that somewhere there was a worry.

"About a year." She couldn't have sat on the knowledge much longer—the place was trafficking too many girls, the ADA would have to move.

"Ah." His face returned to its earlier blankness. "Your people, they're watching?"

Why, was there something interesting? It would be almost comical, Leah thought, if Julia was meeting her handler at the Golden Hand—actually, it would be extremely funny, if not for a huge fuckup with their surveillance. They'd obtained a FISA for both video and sound, only to realize too late that the team had merely covered the little-utilized front entrance, next to a Panera Bread. Even now, when she considered the miss, Leah still raged.

Chester was watching her, his fingers stroking the underside of his seat. Leah decided now was the time, when he was distracted:

"Are there any SPB operations currently in play at Tangerine?"

Chester froze. For less than a second, but it was enough. "What's this? Tangerine?"

"Yes, the company. Not the fruit, just to be clear."

"Where did you hear this? Who tells you?"

"I didn't know this was a conversation. I thought we had an agreement: I ask, you answer."

"Huh." He kicked his legs against the front seat. "I don't hear anything."

"About Tangerine at all? I don't know, Chester, that seems like a miss. They're a big company. It would almost be negligent not to target them."

"A company. There are too many companies here. I don't know such things."

The van was becoming warm: multiples bodies, no open windows. Leah reached into the front seat for two bottles of sparkling water. "I think possibly you've been mistaken about the nature of our relationship," she said, uncapping one. She offered Chester the other bottle, but he waved it away. "You believe we're friends. Colleagues, maybe. You think that because you still have your job, because you operate with some freedom, because the FBI isn't on your ass, I'm doing you a favor. Is that right?"

"You're not doing me a favor. You know I am too small for you to care. You do not have, what do you call it, the manpower."

That even Chester knew of their strained resources was painful. "You're lying about Tangerine. I know, and you know. So now you're going to tell me what you *do* know, otherwise I'm going to speak with the district attorney and have you charged."

"You cannot do such a thing."

"Uh, yeah I can." What did he think, that she was a paralegal or something? "You're a citizen now, aren't you? That means the diplomatic processes aren't in place, and I can do what I like. As I would with any petty burglar or carjacker. And you know what else? I can also put it out that you've turned, that you came in voluntarily. That you've become a believer in the American way, as it were. I'll do it subtle. Send a message through some of our looser cables. Real storyteller style."

For the first time she saw fear. Yes, that's right, start sharing, or else you can say goodbye to the free flatbread, Reddy Sahib's $5,000 apartment, random bangs with crumpled ex-wives at the Rosewood. Come clean, little Chester, otherwise I'll put out the video of your idle ass in the UPS Store, and we'll see what the SPB thinks about that . . . This was when people broke, it was coming, she could *feel* it—

Chester bent forward, elbows on knees. "I don't know anything. You can do what you want."

And then, furious, Leah told him to get out of the car; once he was gone, she went into Whole Foods and bought the first full-fat ice cream she saw, a single serving of strawberry. Opened it in her car, savoring it, but still watching the clock, as she had only a few minutes. Because there was always some other task waiting for her.

# JULY 2019

# 28

# ALICE

**W**e have a problem," Leah said.

They were in a hotel suite in Cupertino. The space was large though not luxurious, decorated soullessly in shades of blue. Alice sat near the window by Sean, who was looking not at her or Leah but at the intersection below. By now she'd learned this was his usual state, a spaced-out inertia where he pondered various lewd entertainments and the answers to difficult crosswords, all while his brain awaited more worthwhile interaction.

"Have you heard of the term 'hands on keyboard'?" Using a fork, Leah gently arranged a row of miniature pickles on the paper plate on which she'd set a pastrami sandwich. She'd brought in lunch for the group, three bags from a local deli, from which a meaty smell was now filling the room.

"No," said Sean. After a prolonged deliberation he had not taken a sandwich, only an unripe banana smeared with green. "No, I have not."

"It means we have to catch Julia with her hands on her keyboard, actually passing intelligence, for us to move." Leah coughed. "The evidence we have isn't enough, otherwise."

Alice and Sean exchanged a look. She could tell they shared the same thought: Why, exactly, was this their issue? They had already given Leah everything they knew—had stated it all in exhaustive detail, in multiple follow-ups with her and her colleagues.

"But don't you have the searches?" Alice asked before Sean could interject. He seemed to almost enjoy antagonizing Leah; there had been a moment, last week in the FBI's conference room, when Alice thought Leah might smack him as she had, right across his face. "I'm sure if you asked for the server files, they would confirm everything I've said. All the FreeTalk data, too."

"We'd have to get a FISA warrant first. For an individual, that might be feasible. But a company like Tangerine? That's a whole new level of difficulty. And what you have to understand is that even if we obtained a warrant, none of it ties to Julia. The way I gather the data was accessed—through this other login, all of it done online— she could easily argue it was a hacker or someone using her credentials."

"Can't you just follow her? You know . . . catch her doing something?"

Leah directed a small, doleful smile at Alice and bit into her sandwich. As she ate, Alice could see Sean stealthily reaching for the sealed Faraday bag in which Leah had stowed their phones. She kicked him in warning, and he dropped his head into his hands and groaned.

Leah swallowed. "No. In terms of surveillance, Julia's a complete nightmare. You guys have both worked at Tangerine—you know how hard it is to get on campus. Even if we managed it, Julia's surrounded by private security, and most likely her office is swept for equipment. You said she asked you to her roundtable, right?" Leah wiped her mouth. "But you don't have any other interaction?"

Alice shook her head. She could attempt a conversation, but knew it'd be impossible. In the ecosystem of Tangerine, Julia was like a magnificent alpha, gliding through the halls. Surrounding her at nearly all times was a phalanx of middle managers who'd built their careers on proximity; any attempt by Alice to engage would be immediately noticed and blocked.

"I could go," Sean offered. "Say I want to present something. A new start-up."

"What's that going to do?" Leah opened a bottle of water. "You planning to hang after, chat about God Mode?"

"At least she'd let me into the building." Sean stood. "*And* meet with me. You think the same goes for you?"

Leah didn't respond. She dipped back her head, water disappearing down her throat. "I thought she hated you," she said coolly.

"No." Sean went to the window, where he peered out at the street below. "I said I disliked her business methods, in a blog post. Not exactly an op-ed in the *Times*. Julia's a pro." He turned to face them. "She knows that if I want to meet, I've got something good."

"Oh, brother," Leah muttered. But after another second she went to her bag. "All right," she said, retrieving a pen and paper and then returning to her chair. "Let's say Sean can get me in. It's got to be more than just me, for starters. I'm going to need a team. And we still need Julia to be passing intelligence at the exact time we're in the room. That's the hard part. How do we know when she's doing work for the SPB?"

"*Wellll*—" Sean began.

"We don't," Leah overrode, "unless we manufacture a situation."

Sean looked at Alice. Mouthing: *What the fuck?*

"We have a person," Leah said. "A sort of . . . involuntary source, if you will." She looked at them and then quickly nodded, as if she'd just decided something. "His name is Chester. Last week, while Chester was at work, we were able to access his locker for a quick peek at his phone. Where we found FreeTalk installed, with the username HELPER. And the name of the sole other account in HELPER's contacts list? Our dear friend User 555."

The room dissolved into silence. Alice tried to make sense of what Leah had just said. HELPER was such a friendly name, she thought. Like something Tangerine's marketing team would dream up for an electronic assistant.

"We think likely Julia's messaging him to pass off data," Leah continued. "Though from what I understand, Chester's mostly an errand boy. Probably they haven't even met. He may not even know who she is. *If*, however, we could access Chester's account, messaging Julia as HELPER at the same time she's meeting with us . . ." She looked at Alice.

It took Alice a few seconds to understand. "You're asking me to take over his account?"

"Yup."

"I can't. I'd be fired." Then, embarrassed by her cowardice: "Plus it's not possible, anyway." Which was true. Years back a customer service employee had done just this, giving notice and then on her last day logging in to a prominent politician's account—who had then seemingly announced himself as a war criminal and a "fucking stupidhead" on his official Tangerine page, with abject apologies for all his earlier environmental policies. In the resulting furor, the ability to take over customer accounts had been removed. Employees could pause accounts, or close them, but not message or post.

"God Mode can't do it?" Leah pressed.

"God Mode only lets you see things. Not change them." Much like an actual god, Alice thought, though she supposed it depended on which kind.

"What about from the back end?"

Alice considered this. "You'd have to have what's referred to as Level Zero access. Level Zero means you have the power to shut down Tangerine's site entirely, or make the home page purple. I definitely don't have that. The only person I imagine would is Julia."

The room went quiet again. Leah rose and began to pace. Alice could almost physically feel the agent's agitation, and in turn was distressed herself. She absentmindedly scratched at her lower arm, while thinking that there had to be a solution. It was what she'd been taught in school, that there was always a remedy. And in fact Tangerine had extolled the same, at the monthlong mandatory Fast Rope training all incoming engineers had to attend—Pierre droning on in a video about how you had to own your code, own your problems. Had Julia been in any of the videos? Alice tried to recall.

"Surely," Sean was saying. "Surely you must have something else. What is the FBI even doing if you can't manage anything about *Julia Lerner* being a spy?"

"Do you understand we are under attack?" Leah said. "Constantly, as a country. To the level where Julia and your worst nightmares about Tangerine are just a blip. Do you know how often threads are dropped, threats allowed to move forward? Do you understand how much we in the FBI *know*, versus how much we can *do*?"

"What *are* you doing, then? What exactly are my taxes—of which I pay a great deal—going to? Christ, I'd heard about government inefficiencies, but this is incredible! Because I can show you what I've worked on. You can open the FreeTalk app right now on your phone."

"Yeah, you did that work and then you sold it," Leah shot back. "For something like ten billion dollars, right? You understand that's more than the agency's entire budget for the year?"

Sean appeared genuinely surprised by this. He paused, tapping his fist against his chest, and then walked back to Leah, stopping an arm's length away. "I am not the expert on domestic security. She"—Sean pointed at Alice—"is not the expert. You are the expert."

They both looked at Alice. She knew she had to say something, but the idea hadn't come, it was somewhere in her brain, just hovering for her to capture—

And then she had it. *You have to own your code. Own your problems.*

"There's someone else with Level Zero," Alice said.

# 29

# PIERRE

Pierre Roy didn't have kids.

This was something he was proud of, that he'd managed to go so long without them—though sadly it wasn't the same with marriages, as he'd done the big wedding with Susie, flown all their friends and family to Necker Island, and then, a year later: *kabloom!*

Though he wasn't ashamed. Pierre thought it was rather nice that he was always falling in love, especially since he'd never had to beg for sex to begin with. By the time Tangerine went IPO he'd had his first actress proposition him; this had been back in the old days, when they didn't understand private valuations and move earlier. He'd faced Elodie at dinner, marveling at her perfect bone structure, her eyes blue like clear water; they'd slept together that first night, and then again, a few weeks later, when he flew her to Boston. Closing out the restaurant at the Four Seasons, filthy talk, her tongue on his neck—and then they'd gone to his room, and right as he rolled toward the nightstand, she grabbed his hand: "No. I want to feel you *completely* inside of me."

A decade earlier, such a statement would have been enough for Pierre Jr. to let it go right there—five-years-younger Pierre would have tried to hold out, but capitulated in a few seconds, max. Would have given Elodie all that she asked and then afterward stroked her hair, having fallen in love (again); would have proposed, invested in her beauty line, given her a production company, seed money, whatever.

Post-IPO Pierre, though?

He reached over and tucked a strand of hair behind her ear. "You're sweet," he said. And then put on the condom. And took it with him, after.

Really it was the children, Pierre thought, who messed up most things, a theory he'd first begun to germinate around the Cameron Ekstrom era. So many lost souls, trapped with their useless husbands, vapid wives, mooching in-laws. And the kids themselves weren't so great, either! Sure, some were okay, pretty cute, but he'd met a few who were fucking lunatics, the sort who really shouldn't be allowed in public, and then there were also just the plain unpleasant and boring ones. Of course he did one day want some himself—when he was finally ready there'd be a whole army of mini Roys that he'd spawned with his super-hot but also surely super-smart wife. He'd heard that the whole mortality-depression thing that came about in your forties was a real bitch, and he thought it'd be good to have some posterity by then.

But that wouldn't be for a while.

Lately, Pierre had a secret: he was getting sick of work. Well, it wasn't really so much a secret as a pebble with sharp edges rolling around in his head—work was so *useless*, and really just doing the same thing, over and over. Making money, making plans to make more money, not pissing off the government, not pissing off the public: cycle, rinse, repeat. At his last lunch with Julia, inside the new restaurant he'd poached, this time from Emeryville (vegan Hawaiian), he'd nearly spilled his guts: said that maybe she should take over as CEO; he could move over to special projects, do his thing. In fact, he'd been pondering blurting exactly this—all while avoiding the stares of employees walking past (he was beginning to think of them as rats, rats who wanted to eat his body) and admiring the plated symmetry of his jalapeño and pineapple toast—when Julia said: "I'm not feeling well."

Pierre studied her. He realized she truly did look bad: there were dark crescents under her eyes, and her lips were flaky and pale. It took him a moment to realize she was bare-faced—it was always confusing when a woman who took great pains to look like she didn't need makeup actually went without it.

"What's the problem?"

She scooted her pineapple to the side of her plate. "Do you re-member the first time we met?"

Pierre thought and then he did. Back at the old office, the build-ing with the brick. "The VisionMatch meet."

Her smile was hooded. "Did you ever imagine we'd still be here together?"

"No." In truth, he'd assumed Julia would be like the rest of his overpaid acqui-hires: lucky once, and then quickly discarded. But somehow, through all his purges, Julia had stayed on the winning side. "I was lucky. To have come across you." There. Let that be her motivation for the week.

"We've known each other a decade."

"Right." His impatience rising. What was this, a retrospective?

"We know each other's secrets. Like pretending to disable God Mode."

"Uh-huh." There chimed the low interior hum of potential danger.

"We've lied together. To investors. To Congress."

He cut her off. "Julia, what's going on?" Pierre calculated she'd lasted a decade without some sordid scandal or going to rehab, so he was overdue for some crazy. Though he didn't like it. Mental stability was a genetic gift, just like good looks—you were capable of accomplishing so much more if you were able to keep yourself from going bonkers. "I love the work you do. And I trust you more than anyone in the company. I hope we spend another ten years together."

She pitched forward and grabbed his hand, not romantically but rather as if he were on top of a mountain and she dangling off its cliff. "Say it again."

"What, the 'loving your work' part? Or all of it?" Pierre looked around nervously. And then he repeated himself, assuring Julia of her importance while she held him in her grip. He was confused, unmoored, and then at the end, when she let go, he recalled he had meant to speak with her about taking over as CEO. But by that point the atmosphere had changed; he didn't say anything about retirement after all.

NOW IT WAS WEDNESDAY. AND Pierre was going to yoga. Not to a studio on campus, though they had a few—he would occasionally pass and surreptitiously eye the women stretching inside, asses high and tight in the air. In very private rooms, in very private conversations, Pierre would occasionally opine that he didn't fully "get" sexual harassment, especially when it seemed some of the victims so clearly wished to be harassed! He'd just had to fire Eli Moskowitz, a move-fast-and-break-things kind of guy, after a married manager of Eli's had come forward, claiming they'd had an inappropriate relationship. Eli had texts of her *begging* for it, explicit photos, reams of her demands to meet, to fuck, but at some point she'd changed her mind and said she'd felt pressured. In the following days Pierre met with PR and legal, who wore at him with their risk-assessment this and bad-press that, and in the end he'd been forced to cut Eli loose with a $9 million parachute, upon which he'd just been snatched up by Google. A complete waste of a good engineering VP, but what could you do?

So, no company ink on his quill. He didn't even need to mine the Bay Area these days, given the plane, but on occasion he still liked to stroll the neighborhood. Shop local.

Normally, when Pierre went out, it was with security. He'd resisted it at first, hated the feeling of being tracked, as if he were one of his Tangerine cookie crumbs, scuttling across the web—but he'd acquiesced after the board insisted and too many incidents of randoms trying to paw at him. It was as if people thought physical proximity to success might improve their own dismal lots. *Learn to code*, he wanted to shout. And don't fucking touch me!

He was with two of his regulars today, both ex–Israeli special forces, Ben and Itai. Pierre hopped out of the Sprinter and sent them for coffee.

The yoga studio was cute. Hanging plants, a squat bookshelf with chairs. Cute instructor. Cute students. A dozen women and two men: one older gentleman who sat cross-legged in the back, and a younger one in the front giving Pierre the stink-eye.

The instructor was one of those unnaturally attractive sorts, a Jordanian chick with a great body and the kind of aura that said she just did this for fun, she had other things going on, like a wellness start-up. Pierre never went out of his way to speak to such women: they had it too easy, the Valley was too ugly, the conversations half-depressing as they inevitably arrived at the issuance of some "provocative" statement—"I think big tech is *toxic*"—the predictable challenge in their face.

"All right," the instructor said. "Let's start." They began with seated meditation and then transitioned to chair pose. Pierre half closed his eyes, idly scanning the room. The best one, he'd already determined, was a brunette in pink in the back. Early thirties but with good genetics, a little generic but only if gorgeous was generic, long limbs, actually a little too long, and now she'd seen him looking and he glanced away.

Afterward, Pierre lingered. He liked the end of class, when the instructor would come and touch their foreheads with oils; it was here, lying on his back and breathing in the cold sting of eucalyptus, that he'd had some of his most significant breakthroughs. Pierre knew Julia liked to imply in public that she was the one who ideated, and he let her have it. After all, so many of his competitors were now struggling with the politically inconvenient problem of all-male executive teams: "Where's the Julia?" had become an actual rallying cry. Pierre had lots of good ideas, but only one Julia. And she was back to normal behavior, after that lunch. It usually bored Pierre to consider the motivations of others (does a tiger lose sleep over the opinion of sheep, etc.), but Julia had been so consistent that the aberration was strange. Was there anything else to consider there? Something to beware?

"You looked good in class," a voice said from above. Pierre opened his eyes. The brunette had a thin towel draped over her neck.

He rose. "Hey. Thanks." Pierre received compliments from females with such frequency that he unconsciously sorted them into two categories: earnest, issued by unattractive women blessed with supportive parents, and begrudging, served by girls used to being worshipped. This one before him, he understood, was the latter. "You looked good too."

Usually this was all that was needed to conjure some warmth—assurance to the beautiful and busty that even with billionaires, their aesthetic currency still held at near parity. To his surprise however, she seemed almost irritated. "Do you want to go for a coffee? I'm Ava." That she still seemed to dislike him while inviting him out was intriguing. He technically had a meeting in Menlo Park at eleven, but that left twenty minutes.

They exited together. Down the street was a new French café, Patisserie Jacques, which served bad croissants but at high prices, which Pierre knew for a girl like Ava was all that mattered. Pierre himself ate only between noon and four P.M., but he could order some rose pistachio croissants to go, Itai would like those . . .

Ava abruptly turned toward the parking lot behind the studio. "I need to drop my bag," she apologized. Pierre followed her to the car, a white SUV.

Ava opened the front passenger door and tossed in her duffel. She bent and began to rummage through the items, eventually returning with a bottle of burgundy liquid. "Want to try?" she asked, shaking. "It's good. Veggie."

"No, thanks." Ava had removed her top, and was now clad only in her leggings and sports bra. Instead of mashing down her breasts, as such garments often ruinously did, this one pressed them into perfect twin globes, each rimmed with sweat. Up close, her skin was creamy, unblemished—he guessed her not the sort to bake in the sun but rather to sit in the shade with a big hat (Pierre's mother was a dermatologist).

She gave a slow smile. "Looking," she said, not a question.

"Appreciative."

"You want to hang in the car? I have good music . . ." Her expression promising they wouldn't just be imbibing beet kombucha and listening to Top 40.

Pierre was tempted. The last time he'd had car sex had been in the Susie days, and he didn't think doing it on a massage table in the Sprinter in standstill traffic, waiting for a manic-depressive to complete his business on the Bay Bridge, was the same as real car sex. Junior year, with Janie Hoffman, her skirt hiked as she straddled him in her dad's Miata . . . Sometimes Pierre thought that as you aged, all your pleasures became so diluted that it just took so much more—more money, more effort, more time—to feel the way you did back in high school.

He looked around. The lot wasn't completely empty; there was a gray van two spaces down. "I have to be somewhere soon. We still have time for a coffee though, right? And you can even stay in the bra."

Instead of laughing or agreeing—both of which he expected—Ava held open her door. "Please get in."

His psycho alert issued a ping. "Uh. No."

"Yes. Now."

Ava had seemed like a nine at first, close to a ten, but something in the way she'd adjusted her stance, her aggro questioning, was turning her slightly mannish. He reduced her to a six. "No, let's end here." He wanted to walk away but thought it better not to turn his back to her. He'd tell Ben and Itai to come get him here instead. He checked his phone. Why didn't he have reception?

"Get in the car." Ava was tapping her ear now, in a way that made her look crazy. The door to the gray van slid open. A group came out, and now Pierre knew something was wrong. It was how they were dressed (business casual), their walk (stiff), how they looked at him. He had to move, to run, this could not be happening, oh God, never to him—

A dark-haired woman broke off and moved toward him faster than the rest. "You look like you're about to freak out," she said. "I just need to talk. Don't do something dumb like start yelling, okay?"

He stared at her hand. There was something in it, a badge and ID, and though his mind registered familiarity the panic was already near breach. "Hello?" the woman said. "Seriously, stay calm, all right? I need to speak with you, it's an emergency. Please come with me."

Pierre shut his eyes and began to scream.

From: Sean@Whispernet.to
To: Julia@Tangerine
Subject: Meeting?

Julia,

Saw your recent interview on 60 Minutes—great work. Very insightful comments on motherhood.

I'm about to go out for funding on a new project. Partnering with some old friends on AI. Tangerine interested? Thursday afternoon would work best. Assume I should go through you.

Sean


From: Julia@Tangerine
To: Sean@Whispernet.to

Sean,

Always excited to see what you're up to. Thanks for giving us a preview. Thursday works, my office will set it up. Nicole's on copy—let her know your coffee order.

JL

## 30

# LEO

**M**aybe it was fine, Leo thought. Two trips to Moscow in half a year. It was more than he'd ever done, but some made such journeys each month. The husband of the loathsome Mrs. Jeffries, who worked for Apple, apparently traveled to China every two weeks—Leo had once heard him brag through their shared wall that he now qualified to book business class. *Business class,* Mrs. Jeffries shouted back. *What a husband. While I wait at home.*

*You'd understand if you got off your ass and did some business of your own,* the husband snarled, and then from behind the wall there'd been no more.

Leo's first night in Moscow, he went to eat at an old favorite: Pasha, off Tsvetnoy Boulevard. The restaurant was a little glitzy, the kind with bored hostesses in slip dresses executing half-hearted face control. The prices were high, but not enough to be insulting, and he ordered his usual plov and lamb dumplings and beer. As he ate, he found the flavors softer and more savory than he'd recalled and was filled with regret. What was he doing in America? How much longer could he stand it?

The group on the sofas next to him, two men and their young

girlfriends dressed in what appeared to be identical gold dresses, were getting drunk. The smoke from their shisha was sweet, and Leo inhaled the plumes of mint and strawberry. Within an hour Leo was full and the smoke was in his hair and clothes. The women next to him had disappeared somewhere, and the men were discussing them.

"Mine talks too much," one said.

"Then shove a dick in her mouth." The two of them laughed. They saw him looking their way and stopped, a challenge in their faces. After a moment Leo looked off, surprised by how much he missed California.

THE NEXT MORNING, LEO LEFT the hotel two hours before his meeting. In the past, with Vera, this was always how early they departed—like most in their circle, Vera would rather sit in traffic, fixing her makeup, talking, listening to music, than walk or take the Metro. Leo had Californian habits now however, the dead guilt after a big meal of requiring exercise (Julia patting her waist after asparagus risotto—"I'll have to play some *tennis*!"), so he walked until he found a café with a window from which he could observe if he'd been followed. Once satisfied he was clear, he left through a back exit and proceeded to the destination. The same building in Shchukino District, the same apartment, Ivan at the door with greetings.

"Aaron has left for Berlin," Ivan said, once he'd ushered Leo inside. He fussed with the espresso maker, an expensive hematite-colored model Leo had also seen at Julia's. "His interviews were deemed satisfactory and he left last night."

"Okay." Leo sat on a stool. "Good."

"Very unfortunate about the photos. Aaron maintained he had no idea how the paper procured them. They must have come from somewhere, I said. Such things don't just magically appear! Was there some slip on his part, you think?"

Leo paused, as if he needed to ponder this. "No. Only bad timing." He unclenched his fingers from underneath his stool. "The way of the world," he then added. Ivan nodded. It was a truth they both acknowledged—that it was the natural order for things to go wrong, for the universe to move toward entropy, and that no matter how much you might plot or try, you could only ever stop a little of it.

"I'm told you helped with his placement," Ivan said.

"Yes." Leo had furnished the introduction, to an executive at a municipal transport company in Saxony. Given Aaron's new minor notoriety, the plan was to place him back within Independence Alliance. That Aaron himself was reportedly morose over this move was not met without sympathy by Leo—while the political extremists, religious zealots, and gun nuts were useful in small doses, almost no one wished to live among them long term.

"Before he left, Aaron wrote a memorandum." Ivan turned and pushed a small porcelain cup across the counter.

"A memorandum," Leo repeated, taking the cup and standing.

"Yes." Ivan made a pressing motion to sit. "A letter. Three pages, handwritten. Could you ever believe the man would have such patience?"

"To whom?" Leo strained to keep the urgency from his voice. This was the most important part, even more crucial than the contents of the letter. In their organization, words were both expensive and cheap: there were so many, saying so much, but the most important people, those making the decisions, still only heard from a few.

"Just me. So far." Ivan sipped his espresso, his hand stroking a pink paper box on the counter. "It's a well-written report. Aaron makes some recommendations, including that we integrate our news outlets with Tangerine's algorithm, so our articles appear as if from trusted sources. Aaron claims he had begun such a project but that he wasn't able to complete it, due to interference from

MINERVA." Ivan swallowed the last of his drink. "He describes it as sabotage."

The air went stale. Ivan was watching him carefully now, Leo saw—a keen alertness in his face. And yes, Ivan was rich and indulged and liked to eat, but one didn't survive so long in the SPB, as he had, without a survival instinct.

Leo selected his words, heart pounding. "MINERVA claims Aaron was aggressive to her. That he threatened her."

Ivan raised an eyebrow. "It could be."

"If so, could it not also be possible that Aaron was the inappropriate party? You know what the man is like. He would have an incentive to want MINERVA sidelined."

Ivan looked thoughtful. He rose and went to his bag. Leo straightened and clasped his hands, before recalling that this had also been Julia's stance at the Golden Hand, and switched to leaning on the counter.

"Just a minute," Ivan said, still rifling. "I thought I had it. Ah, here we go." He returned holding his reading glasses and a folder.

"'MINERVA demonstrates little interest in the current events of Russia, which, given their position, is acceptable and may even be encouraged,'" Ivan read, squinting and holding the page farther from his face. "'MINERVA also holds what I initially thought to be sympathetic feelings toward their adopted country, but which I now believe to be a single-minded focus on preserving an expensive lifestyle in which they enjoy many perks and power. I believe that were MINERVA to be recalled, or instructed to take action detrimental to their employment, they would choose to preserve their own self-interests. I do not make a recommendation but report what I believe to be a conflict of interest.'"

*We all want to live here. We all want to have this life.*

"Obviously," Ivan said, setting down the paper, "this is of concern."

To buy time, Leo rose and went to the box on the counter. "Go on, go on," Ivan said, taking off his glasses and cleaning them on his shirt. "The Star's bakery, the best. Unfortunately, I'm on a diet." He patted his stomach.

Leo selected an almond croissant and placed it on a dish with a napkin. "Aaron and MINERVA had poor dynamics. They should not have been placed together. I accept responsibility for the failure."

Ivan waved away the apology. "I would eliminate ten Aarons and ship them to file paper in Novaya Zemlya in exchange for another MINERVA." He eyed Leo's croissant with a slightly proprietary air; a plump hand crept toward the plate. "What I am most concerned about are Aaron's intimations. He recommends her responsibilities be curtailed."

"I'm sure he would say such a thing. Once you're no longer on the plane, who cares if it crashes to the ground, yes? Here," Leo said, pushing his plate toward Ivan. "I don't know why I chose this, I already ate. We shouldn't be wasteful."

Ivan made an anticipatory smack, claiming the croissant. "These politics, the letter, it's all such a pain in the head." He licked his lips, buttery flakes falling from his chin. "All I want is another year of peace. I have to know MINERVA won't embarrass us. You are sure she is safe? That her character is trustworthy?"

He should be honest, Leo knew. He should tell the truth, because Ivan had been kind to him, multiple times in his career. His abrupt declaration of "pneumonia" and prolonged absence, after Natalia's death; the weeks following his divorce, in which he'd operated half-distracted, mindlessly shuffling paper at his chair. Ivan's hand on his shoulder, exhorting him to go home, rest—each time Leo showed weakness, Ivan had lent the great canopy of his protection.

So who has been protective of you, Julia? Leo thought. Who has been kind? He assumed he'd been, back in that warehouse in Mitino. But of course he'd wanted something from her, and maybe this was where they'd both gone wrong, because now everyone wanted something from her. And so could she truly be blamed, for wanting to ensure she might have so much that she'd never run out?

"I have full confidence in MINERVA," Leo said.

# 31

# ALICE

It was cold in the Bowhead Whale.

Really cold. Colder than in the rest of the building. Alice wondered if it was deliberately kept this way, if Julia liked her environment icy. She couldn't recall any details from the roundtable—as she'd repeatedly told Sean and Leah, she barely remembered anything about the room, not that they cared.

She crouched, much like she'd done before, in Sean and Johan's office. Again she was underneath a table, this time Julia's acrylic ten-seater. She'd dressed absurdly, all in black, thinking it'd be discreet, and now felt like a cartoon bank robber. The camera had to be placed behind the head of the table, where Julia always sat; it was very *important*, Leah said, it was to establish their *case*, and thus Alice had to do it.

"I'm already messaging Julia," Alice had protested in the back room of the Milpitas Library, where Leah had asked yesterday to meet. As it'd been determined that it had to be Alice to take over HELPER's account, since Pierre's credentials would work only within Tangerine's internal employee network. The details of this assignment had kept Alice from sleep every night this week; she'd pressed Leah, how did such people *talk*, was there some sort of *spy* dictionary she could access? But Leah seemed unconcerned. "A few words of greeting, after we get in the room. Then we grab her. What's the big deal? It's simple."

Simple for you, Alice had thought. Alice, who'd been taught to always prepare for the worst-case scenario, that she had to work twice as hard if she wanted to succeed, and even then maybe she wouldn't. She'd spent all of last week streaming a well-reviewed series about a husband and wife sleeper cell in Berlin. The night before, she'd also finished the penultimate episode of a spy drama set in Queens, one in which the innocent fishmonger who'd inadvertently tipped off authorities was found with his head severed in his own product. As the credits rolled Alice had shut off the TV and gone to her laptop, where she watched animal videos in a loop. She'd woken at three A.M. from a nightmare, one in which Julia laughed and drew her nails across her face.

Desperate for more information on Julia, Alice had then thought to look up her husband. Sure, Julia might have firewalled herself from God Mode, but what about those around her? She'd found Charlie Lerner's FreeTalk messages with Mandy Lewis within minutes, and as she read, Alice felt a deep frisson of unease. That Julia's husband was either cheating or engaging in some tremendously inappropriate flirtation was so unnecessary, Alice thought. So unnecessary and ordinary and crude. She knew Leah would be interested in Mandy, though so far Alice hadn't mentioned her. But this too seemed wrong, and in agitation she ran her knuckles against the camera bag.

Leah, mistaking her anxiousness, had leaned across the table. "You'll have plenty of time, okay? I promise. Just install the device in Julia's conference room and wait until you see us come in. Then log in to HELPER and message Julia. You'll see. It's easy."

"We check for electronic interference," Alice told her. "It's one of the intrusions we monitor for. Independent wireless signals, especially from unknown equipment. Like a camera."

"The wireless feed from the camera will only be on for an hour. Two, max."

"I'm going to get fired."

Leah regarded her without pity. "Even if you do, you can get another job. You understand the resources we've put into this? Not to mention Pierre. We've already *got* Pierre, as you know."

"Yes." Which Alice also found disturbing. That they had taken Pierre, a *very important person*—seized him right off the street, though Leah claimed he had come willingly, after some "light discussion." "Where *is* Pierre?"

"Pierre's fine. In a safe place."

Alice fingered the camera bag. "Does he know anything? That it's Julia?"

"No. We described the situation as terrorism related. A threat to Tangerine. And possibly his life. He was happy to cooperate after that." It was clear Leah considered the description justified.

"And he's given you access."

"Yes. Starting tomorrow morning. But he thinks we're only gathering data, using his back end to nab some faraway criminals with socialist designs." Leah laughed. "After all, why would we know anything about God Mode or Level Zero, right?"

Alice's panic began to rise again. "What if I get caught?"

Leah looked unconcerned. "You won't."

THE KIT WAS IN HER hand now. The camera itself was tiny, dime sized; it was the battery and transmitter that took up space. The entire contraption resembled a whiteboard eraser, which was its intention. The ends were matted and dingy, as if it'd been used often.

Thankfully today was barbecue Thursday, and most of the floor was outside for lunch. Alice studied the whiteboard. It was off center— she'd have to position the eraser just right so that it would capture the view from Julia's chair. At least from what Sean said, Julia always sat in the same seat: like a royal court, there was observed protocol.

Alice had just begun to move when a pair of legs entered her sight line. She shuffled back under the table. She recognized the legs, which had now stopped outside the door, as belonging to Nicole, Julia's admin. Alice dropped the camera into her backpack.

The door was opening.

"Excuse me," Nicole asked from the doorway. "What are you doing?"

Julia's assistant was like a mini facsimile of her—a racially ambiguous, extremely frightening version, who spoke in person like she was better than you, which she was. Alice forced herself to move languorously and with confidence, like a villainous DMV employee. "Fixing the phones."

She sensed the woman's scrutiny. "Are they broken?"

"Yup."

"You work for tech support?"

"Yup," Alice said again, and flashed her badge, even though it had only her photo and employee number.

"Okay." Nicole looked at her watch. "She has a meeting in there at one, so."

Yeah, Alice thought. I know.

After Nicole moved off, Alice rose. In half an hour Sean, Leah, and whoever else Leah was bringing would be in this room. She forced herself to breathe, to be still and concentrate. What was about to happen was only the culmination of all Alice had tried to do these past months, the *right thing*, as she'd repeatedly told herself. But still there was a regretful piece of her heart, because it was hard enough for Julia to be who she was in this unfair and shitty world.

I am angry—

I am remorseful—

I am a hypocrite—

Alice rose and went to the whiteboard. She set the eraser and walked out.

## 32

# LEO

There was a moment, as he stood in the lobby of the Hilton Moscow Leningradskaya, when Leo was afraid he'd not be allowed to leave. That the dinner at Pasha, the conversation with Ivan, all of it had been a trick, the players arranged like palm trees in a mirage. But he checked out of the Hilton with no issue, the Azeri concierge handing him his paper folio; the hotel car returning him to Sheremetyevo in under an hour, the light traffic a near miracle, and the next morning Leo was at his apartment.

Before he could change his mind, he went to Miriam's. In his hand was a carrier bag from duty free containing a Hungarian dessert wine and a nesting doll. The dolls were everywhere in Moscow, in both the traditional patterns and modern formats, like footballers and reality stars. Next to the Hilton had even been a shop where you could print your own image, which Leo thought an apt stand-in for Americans, the layers of their face being revealed with each step, until you arrived at the very last, removing it to find nothing but air.

He knocked on Miriam's door. There was no immediate answer, and he thought with a lurch that she wasn't home. But then she opened the door, and he looked up with relief.

"Hi," Miriam said. She appeared (he thought) pleased to see him. There was no mention of his earlier rudeness, and within seconds Patrick had ambled forward in basketball shorts. Leo said hello and offered the boy the nesting dolls and a medal he'd retrieved from the storage locker he kept near the Dubrovka Metro. He had a whole collection of medals, though most were from the SPB and thus secret. This one was a particular favorite however, with a green-and-red ribbon, and had been presented to him upon his graduation from the Institute of Foreign Languages. For the week after he received it, Leo had slept with the medal by his bed. Only for it to eventually become commonplace, and after depositing it into storage he had not thought of it at all, or of any of his other prized possessions, since moving to California.

"Cool," Patrick said. Leo thought he might add something more—the medal was the sort of item he would have loved as a child—but Patrick only tucked it into his pocket and then left with the dolls, studying the outermost closely.

Miriam invited him to the next block for coffee. "So," she said as they walked. She seemed to know Leo was disappointed by Patrick's reaction. As he'd held the medal, she'd made dramatic oohing and aahing sounds, as if encouraging her son to echo. "You went to Moscow, is that right? Did you have fun?"

"Yes."

"What about your troublesome employee?"

At first Leo was confused, but then he recalled their earlier conversation. "Actually, I had the opportunity to—to have the employee sent away. Back to headquarters, as it were."

"Did you?"

"No."

"Why not?"

"I suppose I still like working together."

"Good for you," Miriam said, slapping him on the back.

What Miriam claimed was coffee was in fact one of those Chinese tea shops that seemed to be everywhere. Walking up to its doors, Leo asked himself why he'd never come before, especially as he'd often driven past and wondered what was inside. When had he decided that the possibility of even mild disappointment was enough not to try?

They entered and stood in line. When it was Miriam's turn she said she was still deciding and pushed him forward. "You first."

"Taro tea," Leo said quickly, the last menu item he'd been looking at, even though he didn't know what it was.

"Percent sweetness?"

"Full?" And then, right after, Miriam chose 15 percent, which to Leo sounded like a made-up figure, but the teenager nodded and punched numbers into his screen.

They spent an hour outside. Leo's drink was the color of lilacs, with a fat green straw. He found it so sweet as to be nearly acrid, and yet kept drinking. His conversation with Miriam was so easy and humorous that initially its waning came as a surprise—the laughter fading, replaced by an overriding sensation that they had attempted too much, strayed too far from the limitations of their friendship. Miriam had finished her tea and was now methodically sucking out each of the remaining pearls as she rotated her cup; she waved at the plumes of cigarette smoke from a nearby group of teenagers, who ignored her.

"I guess we should go," Miriam said. She stood and threw her cup into the recycling bin. "Though we should hang out again. You want to come for dinner with me and Patrick?"

Happiness, blinking on as quick as a light—this was normal, this was human, this was what breathing was like.

"Yes. Please tell me what I can bring."

They had just started to walk back when Miriam decided to bring Patrick a drink. There was a longer line now, and as they waited, Miriam chattered on about her weekend plans, a new hummus place she liked, a colleague she bafflingly described as a *mansplainer*. "Speaking of weird work stuff. You know who came and saw me the other day there?"

"Who?" Leo was looking at the menu. Should he get something to help with jet lag? What on earth was cream cheese tea? Did it have caffeine?

"The FBI!"

"The FBI," Leo repeated. The air in the café suddenly thinner, the machines louder.

"Yuh. I'm ashamed to say my first thought was my ex. I don't know if I ever told you, but he works at a venture fund. Foreign money. Not that there's anything wrong with that. But they didn't care about him, only asked if I knew anyone in technology."

"What did you say?" Leo pictured the star above Miriam's head and concentrated on breathing, slowly drawing a line from top to bottom.

"Well, yeah. I know a ton. Video games are technology. Half our building works in the industry."

"So you told them that."

"Yeah," Miriam said again, and he was briefly maddened as she moved away to examine an order that had just come out, a paper bag that smelled of fried chicken. "Should I get one of those?"

"How many people from the FBI were there?"

She looked at him curiously. "Two."

"And then what happened? Did they tell you what they wanted?" Leo worried he was pressing too much, but Miriam shrugged.

"It was unclear. They asked if I'd had any contact with foreign entities, if I was contracting or advising in my private hours. I was like, you guys are welcome to come take a look at my apartment, does it *look* like I've got big money coming in? But they were apologetic, said they were only doing a routine check. It was like they were going down a list or something." She stepped to the register. "A honeydew milk, please. To go."

*A list. A list.* The words reverberated in Leo's head.

Miriam turned. "What do you want? You want something?"

"Yes," Leo said automatically. The boy behind the register waved at him to speak. Leo tried to respond, but his head was still stuck on the lists. The lists. Like the lists he'd given to Julia. The lists on which he'd once put Miriam's name.

"Can I have your order?" The cashier was impatient now.

"Hey." Miriam nudged him. "Hey, are you *okay*? Breathe in and out. No, don't do anything, you need to stay still."

But Leo was already moving, running outside; sprinting until he was a distance away, hands fumbling for his phone.

# 33

# JULIA

Pierre wasn't answering his phone.

That wasn't in itself a concern—he often did this, left the grid, didn't ring back when he said he would. None of it mattered because he'd always had Julia. Could trust her to perform.

And she had. Because she loved it. Because this was who she was and it had long since stopped being pretending. Though some might say her being here was a cheat, Julia thought it was really everyone else who were the cheaters. The born rich, the parentally educated and loved—who went from private high schools to Ivy legacies to jobs with friends of the family. Who said they "hated the word 'privilege'" and insisted that they were who paid their mortgage each month. Yeah, but who put forth the *down payment*, Julia wanted to ask, how much did they *give*?

Though it was strange that even Pierre's secret number, the one not given to his girlfriends (or wife, when he'd had one) but only to Julia and Ron Murphy, Tangerine's in-house counsel, was going to voicemail. Out of habit Julia logged in to God Mode, before recalling that she and Pierre had long ago removed God Mode's permissions to their accounts. So next she had Nicole go to Pierre's assistant, Thora Clark—a pair of Warriors tickets in hand as tribute, as Thora considered herself queen of the admins—only for Nicole to return, minutes later, and report: "He's unaccounted for."

Hmm. Interesting.

Pierre had been gone more often as of late, Julia noticed. Had been distracted, and she knew him well enough to understand he was bored with the power, the work and the pressure of it all. Because he took it for granted, and it wasn't that he *hadn't* worked hard, but he'd acquired it so young and as such had no idea what it was like. To want it so bad that once you had it, you knew better than to ever loosen your grip.

Though it wouldn't be so bad, if he gave it to her.

She knew he'd been thinking about it. Of making her CEO. At that lunch, Julia had a feeling he was about to offer, but she lost control of the moment.

She was going to hire a divorce lawyer.

After that, the next priority was a weekend nanny.

And then. The next time she saw Pierre. She would tell him she wanted it, the CEO position, and if he didn't give it to her she'd leave.

There were a dozen other companies that would jump at her. A dozen famous names who would put her at the top. Names big enough, entrenched enough, to make Leo happy. Because she was *Julia fucking Lerner*.

Or maybe she'd go back to Kall. Why not?

Julia was in the Bowhead Whale, after some barbecue. Had endured her weekly *Executives—We're Just Like You!* showing in the courtyard outside, milling among the employees. She was in her usual seat now, having just opened Net-a-Porter on her phone, when there was a knock on the door. She looked at the time, 12:55, and called without looking up: "Room's private."

"I know," said a familiar voice, and Julia looked up and saw Sean.

Julia quietly swore. Sean had never been early when he reported to her—in fact it was as if he and Johan had made a special point of being late, just to show they didn't give a shit.

"You're early," she called.

"Wow wow wow. I'm sorry."

The rest of his group filed in. Julia made a quick scan of the faces, not recognizing any. And now this was interesting, it wasn't the usual lineup of model minorities in their dowdy fleece, but rather what appeared to be a pack of accountants in suits—and even two women! One obviously pretty, with long legs, while the other bore a severe look, like that of a disappointed governess. Julia was going to be pissed if Sean brought his B team. Where were the engineers?

"Right," she said. "Why don't we start?" The minions began to scramble. Julia sat, pen in hand: she would take notes; it was important to be organized when managing a snake like Sean.

It was during the third slide—the laughably titled Ten-Year Plan!—that the message blinked on her phone.

Julia checked the notification. The message was from HELPER to her User 555 account. Huh. HELPER had never messaged her before. It'd only ever been a one-way communication, Julia signaling out. Out of muscle memory she swiveled, to ensure no one was behind her. The eraser on the whiteboard looked grungy; she'd ask Nicole to order more.

As Sean droned on, Julia opened the message.

Hi.

*Hi?* What the fuck? She decided it was a misfire and closed the app.

Another slide. Sean was proposing some AI tool, a shit hot sector and he knew it—though before she gave him any money, she wanted to see the engineers and scientists. Engineers and scientists: the national anthem of their industry, their huge stock packages the redress for the formerly oppressed, unloved, unseen.

Another notification.

HELPER: Can you speak?

Can you speak? Jeez, what do you think? The only thing Julia knew about her dead-drop gofer was that she thought he was a man—though she had no real evidence of this, only a feeling. And when possible—when the price wasn't too high—Julia usually followed her feelings.

She didn't respond.

HELPER was typing something again. The little bubble went on too long, as if there was a hesitation, and Julia exited the screen.

Sean cleared his throat: "Now, we've got a quick demo . . ." He fumbled about his laptop, characteristically underprepared. In the interruption, a woman, the slightly mean-looking one wearing red lipstick, approached: "I have to say how much I admire you. I've followed your entire career. It's amazing, what you've achieved."

"Thank you," Julia said. The woman didn't move. "I appreciate you coming," Julia added, smiling. You mean something to me, her smile said. You are special, you are female. *Now fuck off.*

Julia's phone lit up. But before she could see what had been written, likely again from the malfunctioning HELPER, the device rang in her hand.

It was strange: it was as if the sound of it sucked away all other noise in the room. Conversation stopped. Julia realized she hadn't silenced it. She usually did so at the start of a meeting, but Sean's early arrival had distracted her. She stared at the screen. Why would Leo be calling, it must have something to do with HELPER . . .

"Ooh," Sean said. "Who *is* it?" The beautiful woman to his right shot him a homicidal look.

"I need a few minutes," Julia said, standing. Beatific nods all around. She unlocked the screen, to a new message from HELPER.

It is urgent.

Oh yeah? Isn't everything? Julia tightened her hand on her phone, she would leave now and call Leo—

About Mandy Lewis.

Julia stopped. Breath short, brain reshuffling. Could Mandy be a plant? No, likely something more basic and sordid, your run-of-the-mill star fucker trying to wrest her bit of glory. So what was it, Charlie Lerner's in love with me, now make me famous?

Julia hovered over the message, deciding. She sat. Quickly she wrote: Need details.

"If you don't mind, I've just made a video call to my mother," the red lipstick woman was saying. "Could you say hi? A quick wave, I know you're so, so busy."

Julia suppressed the urge to hit her. As if she'd ever bother a man like this! But you couldn't go your whole time comparing your deal to men's—it would only drive you crazy. She raised her head and prepared a quip about women in entrepreneurship—and her glance happened to land on the room across the hall, in which stood . . . who was that? She searched and then the name arrived: Alice Lu. Their eyes met, Alice looked away; Julia's senses pinged, and at the same moment she felt the invasion of her space, the movement of bodies, and before she could react, her notebook was gone, her phone yanked, and she knew, with an animal instinct, what it was that had just happened to her.

# AUGUST 2019

## 34

# ALICE

Alice knew Julia would be gone. And yet when Monday came and Julia wasn't in her office, there was still a part of Alice that thought Julia was just home with a cold, or maybe away, in Aspen or Kauai. She made multiple trips to the fourth floor: Nicole sitting at her desk, typing with perfect posture, and for a bizarre moment Alice wondered if Julia had existed at all.

This strangeness was highlighted by Pierre's return on the day after. Normally Alice was unaware of Pierre's movements, tech support not being executive stomping grounds, but he was obvious as he strolled the floor, security trailing. "You're the third team I'm going to be adding," Pierre said, hands in pockets. "Because I don't want burnout. Coverage for the coverage and all that. I expect everyone to make observations on the environment, analyze potential holes, because I'm not tolerating anything less than Secret Service shit."

As he passed Alice's chair, a skittish energy rolled off him, and Alice realized that while she'd assumed Pierre wouldn't be told of her involvement, this had not actually been promised or stated in any way. It would be extremely upsetting, she thought, to go through all this only to still end up fired—and her anxiety amplified until

she called Leah, who didn't respond for three days, finally directing
Alice to Cuesta Park in Mountain View.

"Pierre doesn't know anything," Leah said as they walked. "Not
about you. Not about Julia. Our story was always that we'd received
credible intelligence of an attack. I may have hinted that the attack
had Pierre as a target, not that I was far off, if you think about it.
I mean, a Russian agent running Tangerine? You know what that
would do to the stock? Pierre was upset, obviously. I've heard he's
increased his protection detail *considerably*."

Alice didn't mention that she'd seen Pierre with new security.
This struck her as gossipy, and in a way she thought Pierre justified,
given that were Alice to have billions at her disposal she'd likely do
the same, after having been snatched off the street and informed
people wished to kill her. "Are you sure he doesn't know about me?"

"Yes. Everything's fine. Everything's back to the way it was earlier."

Everything except for Julia, Alice thought, and she knew Leah
was thinking the same. A day earlier, Alice had watched from the
lobby monitors as Pierre had gone onstage at Moscone Center to
present the latest road map. She couldn't recall a time when Julia
had not also been at the event, and she found she almost resented
his solo presence.

"I'm going to get a hot dog," Leah announced, nodding toward
a stand on the far hill. She waved, as if she thought the cart might
leave otherwise. "You want anything?"

"Yeah, sure." The proprietor watched dispassionately as they
huffed toward him. June and Lincoln had always instructed Alice to
greet customers with extreme enthusiasm: ("To Americans, this is
just regular friendliness," June had explained once.)

"I thought you weren't hungry," Alice said. She'd originally invited Leah for lunch at Tangerine, at the Mongolian BBQ located
next to the content moderation team, an area never visited by executives and thus safe from Pierre. Alice had thought Leah would be

interested in seeing the campus again, but the agent had declined, suggesting the park instead.

"I can't accept free meals." Leah took a step back from the cart, a hand shielding her forehead as she assessed her options. A handwritten sign advertised chocolate chip cookies and madeleines, both of which Alice recognized as being from Costco.

"Really?"

"Technically I can. Twice a year."

"Wow," Alice said stupidly. She wondered if she should offer to pay. But as she deliberated whether this would seem patronizing, Leah was already handing over the cash. I have to be a faster person, Alice thought. I shouldn't always live in my head, because otherwise that's where I'll drown.

Alice paid for her food and they took their hot dogs and sat on a bench. The scent of meat mixed with ketchup reminded her of family holidays: downtown Reno, vanilla ice cream molded into a star and covered in chocolate. Lincoln handing over the bills, he and June shaking their heads: No, no, we don't want any. It was only later that Alice understood that her parents didn't want to spend the money, that it was in her pleasure that they derived the most satisfaction.

"I'm going on vacation," Alice said. "At the end of the year. I'm taking my parents to Spain."

"Hey. That's cool. Your treat, huh? Glad you don't talk to *my* mom. Her dream is Argentina." Leah opened a bag of chips. "So there's a name I need to ask about. Logan Schiller."

Alice swallowed. "Yes," she said after a moment.

"Is that name familiar?"

"Yes," Alice said again as she tried to quell the flipping of her stomach. A Chinese couple was walking past; they held hands, and Alice thought that they must have lived in America a long time. She had never seen June and Lincoln demonstrate physical affection.

"We've been going through Julia's records," Leah said. "Slowly.

Carefully. We've started on her phone and email; that's easy for us to get, without a big fuss. We've also got her notebook, which is fascinating. Like those interviews with rich people, where you see what their day is like. Though I would describe it as eighty percent lists. On one page however, we saw your name. And right above yours, Julia wrote Logan Schiller."

Alice's heart beat, hard and fast; her hands were clammy and she wiped them against her jeans. Of course she was already aware that Julia knew who she was—but that Julia also knew of her searches made her feel horribly exposed. And then as her indignation rose Alice remembered what she'd written as HELPER: *It's about Mandy Lewis.* The way Julia had looked back at her before being led out, striding forth as if she were the one wanting to leave, and the FBI only following.

Leah studied her, eyes porous in the light. When Alice didn't respond, Leah sighed and went into her bag, retrieving a pair of sunglasses. "The name showed up when Julia logged in to God Mode one day," she said, pushing the glasses on top of her head. "She was already on alert, had seen your name when you flagged one of her servers. She wasn't certain if it was you using God Mode, since she couldn't figure out how you got her password. Still can't figure it out, actually."

"The password was in a plain text file, to which almost all employee passwords are saved." So Julia had found her through the servers. Despite her trepidation, Alice felt a quick thrill at having been right. "When Julia created the User 555 account, the system automatically captured its information. But she wouldn't know about something like that, way too low-level."

"Fucking Tangerine." Leah laughed. "What a mess. It's only our lives, right?" She paused. "You should be aware of another thing. Even though she can't figure out how you accessed her account, Julia does believe you were involved. Because she saw you that day in her conference room."

Alice waited for Leah to scold her. To say that she shouldn't have let Julia see her, or used God Mode, done the Very Bad Thing that Julia was currently being accused of. But Leah said nothing.

"What else did Julia say?" Alice finally asked.

"She said if it was you on God Mode, she assumed Logan was an ex. Or someone you were in love with."

"No. No to either."

"Right." Leah was eyeing the Chinese couple, on their second loop through the park. "You know what's strange? We have questions for Julia, many questions. I thought she'd have many in return. But that's one of the few she's asked. Who Logan was to you."

"Did you tell her? Why I looked for him." Alice didn't know if Leah was able to access Logan's history.

"Yes. In broad strokes." Leah looked apologetic. "Apparently he never bothered to seal his juvenile records. I guess it was so long ago that he assumed it wouldn't matter. Or forgot about it altogether."

Alice was surprised by the sting of this. She bit her lip and squeezed shut her eyes. "What'd Julia say? After she found out. That Logan wasn't a friend." *But rather someone I hate*, Alice meant to add. But as she thought it the hurt simultaneously faded and she knew it was no longer true; she didn't hate Logan, he was a memory from a former world, one already gray and dying. After Julia was taken, Alice had looked him up a final time: his profile read "Separated," with a solo shot of him skiing in Tahoe, while Carolyn's still featured her and Logan and the girls. *Snow bunnies*, Carolyn had written. *Love this dude!*

"Was Julia disappointed?" Alice asked, opening her eyes. "About Logan."

Leah hesitated. She glanced again at Alice and then back out at the park. "She seemed kind of happy."

BACK AT TANGERINE, ALICE'S COWORKERS had already returned from lunch: Sam sat at his desk, humming and picking the crust off of his pear tart, while Larry conducted a furtive inventory of the office supplies in his cabinet.

"Hey," Alice said. Larry's headphones weren't yet on.

Larry swiveled. "Yes?"

"You're a good worker. I mean, good coworker. I'm happy you sit next to me."

"Eh?"

"Thanks for helping me. Earlier."

"Yes." He rolled his eyes.

Alice gathered her things. It was her weekly one-on-one with Tara, and Alice thought she could even learn to appreciate this—because it meant Tara cared, didn't it? At least enough to dedicate to her a half hour each week. Alice vowed to be a happier person going forward. A more thankful person.

Tara's desk was the barest Alice had ever seen it, empty save for her laptop and a manila folder in her acrylic tray. "Come in."

"Hi," Alice said cheerfully.

Tara pushed the folder at her. "We're letting you go."

Alice was still in the dreamy haze of newly avowed optimism; she took a step back and tried to right herself against the chair. "What?"

Tara stood and pressed her palms against the desk. "This will be your last day at Tangerine. Here are the details of your termination."

# 35

# JULIA

The room was soiled and small but she was familiar with filthy spaces, cramped rooms; the walls were white and there was a single red door locked from the outside. Through the door's window she glimpsed people pass. But only their shadows, through a screen.

They did not want anyone to see her.

She'd been brought by plane. A short flight, though she hadn't known it, and when the hood was dropped over her head it was the closest she'd come to terror. The black fabric against her face, Leo's voice—*they will strip you hurt you humiliate you*—echoing as she stared into the dark. The woman's voice against her ear like rough paper. And then, at the end, adding softly: "Shall I put the earmuffs on now?"

Julia had tried hard not to cry.

But so far none of it had happened. There had been no torture, no photographs; she had been stripped, but the guards were female, and they handled her cautiously but without feeling, like movers transporting an unwieldy antique.

She lay on the bed and counted the ridges above. It was a popcorn ceiling, which over her time in California she'd learned was actually tacky: something to do with them being cheap and old and all the other qualities that made something undesirable in America. But as she stared she found the jagged peaks and blotches striking. She tried to match them to countries she'd visited. China. Mauritius. Iceland. After she tired of this she went to the sink, where she wet the cloth and scrubbed at the toilet and floors, the wiped metal sparkling against the light.

At midday there was a knock, and one of the women from Sean's presentation entered. "Nice to see you," Julia said, and the woman raised her head, surprised by either the pleasantry or the sight of Julia kneeling at the toilet. She jerked a hand to indicate down the hall, and Julia retrieved her slippers from under the bed. After they'd left Tangerine she'd been allowed to go home, pack a bag, though there'd been two agents with her the entire time. Luna pushing Emily into her arms, Julia desperately kissing Emily's hair; she'd been determined not to cry, had wanted their parting to seem ordinary, and so after a minute she'd gently returned Emily to Luna. "I'll be back," Julia said, and she struggled to recall if these had been Nina's last words.

She told Charlie she had to leave. For a business trip. An inverse of what she'd emailed Pierre: *Will need some time off. Personal matters.*

"How long?" Charlie asked.

"Maybe a week. Or longer. I'm sorry," she added. Meaning it. It seemed incomprehensible that just that morning she'd daydreamed of leaving him. Why hadn't she said sorry more often, Julia had then wondered. What had she believed she'd be giving away? Maybe if she'd apologized more, given in to Leo more, Charlie more, she wouldn't be in such a miserable position. Then again, she couldn't go by how she felt at any one particular moment—she knew that misery, like happiness, could be a trick.

The woman walked her to the room. The walls were clean, carpet thin, *left, right, left, right*, twenty-eight steps in total. Having spent so long in her room, examining each crevice, in this space Julia was now overwhelmed; she didn't even look at the person, so much did she want to save the interaction. She started with the ceilings, also popcorn, the door behind her, also red. But here were some new details: a metal table with rounded corners, two metal chairs; she ran her hand underneath her seat, to see if this metal felt warmer than in her room. They kept Julia's room cool, the air conditioner running throughout the night. Her blanket was thin but she wore the cashmere sweater and pants they'd allowed her. Mixed signals.

On top of the table was a yellow pad, a recorder, two pens. And then, behind the table: Leah. Not a bad-looking woman, if rather brittle; Julia would have pegged her as difficult at work but submissive at home, with a brutish husband. Though there was the undertone of something else that threw off the calculation.

"And how are we doing," Leah said. Her lipstick was slick and red. Julia inhaled—Leah was wearing perfume again, with neroli undertones.

"I'm fine."

"Anything I can get you?"

"No."

"Maybe call your lawyer?"

"No. Funny, though." There was a moment when Julia had thought to call Paolo at Quinn Emanuel. She imagined sitting across from her attorney, a compact and handsome Mexican Princetonian whom so far she'd utilized only for her prenup, and asking him to get her off from espionage. Even the accusation would be enough to ruin her future. Hers and Emily's.

"I would like to reiterate," Leah said, "that you, Julia Lerner, formerly Julia Kall, are a United States citizen, with all the rights accorded to such. That you are here today of your free will, with the understanding that you may request to leave at any time, and that your request will be granted."

"Yes."

"And you acknowledge this has been the case since your arrival."

"Yes." Though Leah left the kicker unsaid. That were Julia to leave they would immediately pursue legal action, charge her—they had already played for her the video from her conference room. Julia was using her questions sparingly, to avoid ceding accidental ground, but she was desperate to know: Where was Leo? And HELPER? Who else had been taken, what else was known?

"I've been thinking," Leah said. "About how it's hard to do the right thing once you get cynical. You know what I mean?"

Julia smiled but said nothing, like one of those pleasant mutes who occasionally arrived at the institute. There had been one in particular, a pretty fox-like girl named Taya, who enjoyed helping Sophia sweep and mop; seeing her in domestic action, an Australian couple had adopted her, and last Julia heard, Taya had burned their house to the ground.

"I used to hate in high school when the girls said one day we'd die and get all heavy about it," Leah went on. "Typical juvenile shit. If you keep thinking there's no way to cheat death, what's the reason for anything, right? I've accepted I'm going to die and put it out of my mind. Only focus on the near and present term. That's the best way, in my opinion." She played with the yellow pad, flipping it over and over. "You've been gone for six days so far." Looking up. "Is that going to be a problem?"

Julia knew what Leah was asking. Not whether it'd be an issue for her family, or Tangerine, but for the SPB. The answer was possibly, but she couldn't be sure. And still, what defined a problem? As she'd faced worse.

"Not necessarily. Depending on how it is managed."

It had taken Julia some time to work it out. Why they hadn't yet touched her. There was more to it than just fame, she knew: Americans worshipped celebrity, but only second to the joy they took in tearing it down. There were promotions to be had from her arrest, news cycles, political careers. And yet so far no perp walk, no attorney generals; from the flight time she guessed she was in another state, possibly Oregon or Nevada.

I am the COO of Tangerine, she reminded herself. In many ways, I'm more powerful than anyone in this building.

As if she were aware of Julia's thoughts, Leah smiled. "I'd like for this to be a relationship. And I'm aware that in all relationships, there's got to be some give-and-take. So why don't I start with some give? We haven't taken HELPER, for one. I know that's something you've likely been wondering. Whether or not we've actually grabbed them, in which case your superiors at the SPB would be alerted, and you'd be screwed. Correct?"

Some inner pocket of tension released. Though Julia kept silent.

"You can keep it all, Julia. Your family, your money, your job. All you've got to do is change the people you work for. Don't you want to be on the right side? The *good* side."

"Don't be patronizing," Julia snapped. "It's disappointing."

She could see she'd managed to sting: satisfying, if potentially foolish. Leah put a fist to her lip. When she brought it down, her knuckle held a smear of red. "You chose to live here, right? You could have gone anywhere. But you chose to live in America."

Julia studied her fingers. "I didn't choose my life. Not all of us are so lucky."

"I didn't think you'd say that. Play the victim. Now I'm the one feeling disappointed." Leah rose, and out of reflex Julia moved to stop her from leaving.

Leah returned to her seat, satisfied in her victory. "I don't know what kind of life it is you had in Russia. I can't imagine you want to share."

"No."

"No," Leah repeated. "But I can assume it's better here than wherever you came from. So now I've got a question: Where do you want your daughter to live, Julia? *How* do you want her to live? All the wealthy in your former country, the oligarchs, the securocrats, where do they send their children? Volgograd? Their old mining towns? Or, you know, do they send them someplace else, somewhere with reliable sunshine, the freedom to speak their opinion without falling out of a window, good democratic processes . . ."

The day she finally left the institute, Julia hadn't said goodbye. She'd anticipated the moment for years, had studied how it happened for others. Sophia, now the institute's director, arriving that morning with the customary stipend; Julia's clothes and pencil box and the few textbooks she'd been allowed to keep all packed inside the blue parachute bag. Julia surprising herself the most when at the end she started to sob. She didn't understand why, because who did she love that she was leaving? Not even Misha had come to wish her farewell, and as a parting gift he'd given her nothing but some old magazines, had not even spared her one of his toy planes.

"But you don't even like planes or aviation," he'd said when she asked him for one. "You never did. You won't appreciate them."

"I will," she said, surprised by his resistance. "Besides, you don't even use them anymore. You haven't played with them in years."

"Why do you have to take something from me just because you'll miss me?" he asked, and she hadn't known what to say.

"Why don't we start with something easy," Leah said. Her voice slow and inviting and gentle. "Your handler. How did you meet?"

Julia lightly scratched at the metal surface of the table and didn't respond.

"I understand you might feel some loyalty. Honestly, it's only natural. Admirable, even. But I think you know the choice before you. It's the best one, the most logical one. And from what I know of you, Julia, you always make the logical decision, don't you?"

Was there a way to recover, Julia thought. Or when you moved to a new phase of life, did you always have to shed some part of yourself, leave some precious item behind? She hadn't known until she was leaving that she'd wanted a plane from Misha—to clutch in her palm when she wished to visit that stowed part of herself. And now she was back in Moscow, Leo before her, saying he was going to change her life. If he were next to her now, she knew he'd tell her she couldn't save him, she couldn't even save herself.

Julia took a deep breath. She exhaled. "Ned Daly."

"What?" For a second Leah's gaze went over her shoulder. "Who's that again? The semiconductor guy?"

"Yes. I'm certain he's given information to the SPB. Or is working for them directly. The same with Dmitri Marin."

"Okay," Leah said. "Okay, okay." She was trying to remain calm, but her excitement was obvious; she punched a button on the recorder and drew the legal pad toward her. From behind the reflective glass of the window and the halls beyond, Julia could sense noise, movement. She cleared her throat and sat even straighter.

"Dmitri Marin," Julia repeated. "Ned Daly. There's more. If we work this out, if you let me go, if you let me return to my daughter, I could get you them. All of them."

# 36

# ALICE

Some mornings when Alice woke she still thought she was employed.

In the weeks after she had been fired ("walked to the door") from Tangerine, the sun would creep over her face as she lay in bed and Alice would open her eyes and reach for her phone. Checking the weather, the news, her work email, before recalling with a lurch she no longer had a job. No more staff meetings, syncs with Larry, or weekly security checks that she used to dread; now her phone served mostly as a receptacle for store promotional emails, which, given the recent and total elimination of her income, she deleted en masse.

Amazingly, given that it'd been a long-standing fear of hers, there were many downsides she'd never considered to getting fired. Yes, the act itself was humiliating, the loss of income terrible (and what was she going to do about rent, and loans, and oh my God); but there were also the other parts, the pits of depression it left in your soul. As her savings evaporated so did her good habits. Her diet had gone to hell: nearly every afternoon she would make instant ramen—mixing in an egg and scallions if she had them, to increase the dish's nutritional value—and then allow herself unlimited sips of the oily soup, only for a hot, dirty feeling to linger in her stomach after. And yet by the end of the night she would again be dreaming of noodles, and the next day open another pack. Since its initial download she had not signed on to the Spanish learning app she'd paid forty-nine dollars for "unlimited" access to; she was also not bathing much.

At least the apartment was clean. The stripes of mold underneath the shower grout, the scary rust behind the toilet, the black stains around the lip of the kitchen sink: Alice attacked each with vigor. One afternoon, after a bowl of udon she'd made from powdered stock, she decided to go after the calcified rust on the bathroom fixtures with a pair of Bobbi Brown tweezers she'd found in the garbage. She was nearly done, making her final revolutions around the right tap, her unwashed hair heavy with grease against her scalp, when Cheri appeared. Surprised, as she'd thought her cousin was out, Alice slipped and jabbed her hand.

"Are you okay?" Cheri asked.

"Yes." Alice looked at her palm. Where the metal had bit, her flesh was already pulsing; there were red specks coming to the surface, and she was curious if blood would eventually break through.

"Did you get fired?"

"Yes," Alice repeated dully, still watching her hand. It was a relief, actually, to say it. Should she say it *more*? Post it on Tangerine?

"Are those my tweezers?"

"Uh-huh." Then, slightly defensive, because she'd found them in Cheri's garbage, which she'd searched only to see if Cheri had eaten her Ritter Marzipan (verdict: possibly innocent), Alice asked, "Did you still want them?"

"No. I got a new pair. I don't like those so much. I meant to throw them out." Cheri slowly moved forward and raised a hand, as if demonstrating friendly intentions to a skittish animal. "You know, I have some savings. I'm sure we'll get through this. I just mean you can count on me and everything. Oh come on, Alice, don't be a baby, please don't cry." But once she began Alice found she couldn't stop: she cried and cried and cried. She cried because she had ruined everything and yet still her life was better than many others and so she shouldn't be crying; she cried because she knew she had triumphed and yet still she was lonely and humiliated. She cried until she thought she had lost interest in crying forever, she couldn't do it anymore, the act had lost all meaning, and then she cried some more.

And then the next morning the call came, and Alice went back to work.

THE SPACE WAS SMALLER, LESS grand and hip than she'd expected. The first floor of a commercial building in San Jose, the second and third floors filled with psychiatrists and lawyers. Often when Alice arrived the small lot would already be filled, forcing her to park on the street.

"We're going to have to move," Sean said as she entered, keeping pace with her as she walked. Alice was late, having scheduled a dental cleaning as soon as she received confirmation of health insurance. Arriving to work, she had struggled to parallel park between a Tesla and an oversize Infiniti, as nearby construction workers observed with a mix of anticipation and horror. "I think that this is going to be a very successful company, very soon."

Alice picked up a discarded energy bar wrapper. "Yeah?"

When Sean had first called, asking if she'd come interview, Alice had slapped her leg, in case it was either a nightmare or a dream. She'd never thought she would work at a start-up, liking the stability of a large corporation, but then Tangerine hadn't been so stable in the end, had it? As she sat on the floor of her room, her stomach upset from a new super-spicy brand of ramen, she'd listened to Sean describe the open positions at his company. After they hung up, Alice ran her hand underneath her bed, in an area she was certain she'd searched earlier, and found the missing Ritter bar. She ate half and then showered for the first time in a week.

As Alice reached her chair, Sean abruptly veered off, back to the office he shared with Johan, who sat starchily at his desk. The building's owner had banned visits from Johan's Saint Bernard; photos of Tintin, his brown-and-white face cocked to the camera, sat adjacent to framed portraits of Johan's children. Through the glass, Alice could see Sean pacing, motioning to Johan. Suddenly he stopped.

"Hey!" he said, rushing to the doorway. "Hey, *Alice.* Get over here."

"What?" Alice returned. She wasn't used to speaking to her bosses so casually, though admittedly she did not find Sean a formidable authority figure.

"*Hurry!*" Sean said. Which could signal an emergency ranging from a technical meltdown to a celebrity breakup. When Alice reached his office, he pushed her inside and shut the door. "Look."

He pointed to the TV. Julia was on, speaking live.

SHE LOOKED GOOD. RESTED AND calm, with great hair. Tangerine had just reported record earnings, and now she was on CNBC for the victory lap, discussing the results and Tangerine's newly announced international expansion.

"You haven't been in these places before," the interviewer was saying. "Pakistan. Parts of the Middle East. Because as we understand, your employee base has expressed some concerns over human rights and surveillance."

"Correct," Julia said as the camera drew back to a wide angle. Her navy dress, which came down to the floor, had a slit that showed a sleek line of tanned leg.

"She said she just came back from vacation," Sean muttered. "Turks and Caicos, *veerrrrrry* relaxing."

"Shh," Alice said.

"So what's changed in your strategy?" the interviewer asked. Andrew Waller, typically smug from the brief snippets Alice had seen of him before, though he seemed almost ingratiating now. His face had the concentration of someone listening carefully, trying hard not to make a mistake.

"Well, I wouldn't say *changed*," Julia said, "so much as *evolved*. And as a company, we're always evolving. The same as people. We believe that what we do here at Tangerine—developing tools for humans to communicate and share—is fundamentally good. But the truth is, there's bad stuff going on all over the world, including right here in the United States. So we started to ask ourselves: Are we saying that in these places—Iran, for example—we're simply not going to participate? Are we saying we're going to cut off large swaths of the human population, just because they live under a different system of government, some of which local citizens may have had no part in selecting?"

"And what about those employees who've historically had problems with such positions?"

Julia smiled. There was a new hardness to her, like with an expensive jewel, that hadn't been there before. "We respect all opinions. That said, there are many places to work."

Andrew blinked. "It's quite a change. Earlier, it had been posited that it was Pierre who wanted to expand—and that it was you who held him back."

"Funny. I hadn't heard that."

He tried again: "Pierre recently started an aerospace company, did he not? Outer Horizon? Is that its name?"

"Outer Horizon is a private concern, unrelated to Tangerine."

"Still, CEO of two companies at the same time . . . that's a lot, for any person. No matter how exceptional. There have been rumors Pierre may step down from Tangerine, upon which you'd be the natural candidate to replace him. Any comment?"

"No," Julia said, and then they cut away.

Sean muted the TV. Alice stood, heart thudding.

Johan appeared next to her. "It's a good move. Expanding, especially as their existing ad business has reached a saturation point."

"Uh." Alice tried to think of a useful response. Johan made her nervous. They rarely spoke, and she still didn't know if he recalled she'd once fixed his phones.

Johan scratched his head. "You came from Tangerine too, right?"

"Yes."

"Well. I can see why you left. Why you had to run from that *vile* woman."

Suddenly Alice was furious. As if Johan would ever call Pierre vile! Or himself, because certainly he and Sean had been part of it, had taken Tangerine's money and now that they were far away they could preach how they wanted. She started to speak, her throat emitting a strangled noise, and Sean poked her hard in her ribs. "You know, I really—" Alice began.

"Let's go eat," Sean said, nearly dragging her out.

THEY WALKED A QUARTER MILE to India Dreams, which served a well-frequented buffet lunch from its corner in a strip mall. The proprietor recognized them as recent regulars, extending his hand to indicate that they could pick any seat.

"So she's out," Sean said, after they'd found a table outside. The owner's wife was already moving away, having deposited a plastic basket of naan.

Alice reached for the bread. "She must have made an agreement with Leah. You know. A deal, or whatever."

"A *deal*? What do you think this is? Some mafia movie?"

Alice huffed, irritated by the insinuation that she was being dramatic. "I'm trying to be logical. We were there. She was caught. Now she's back at work. It's the only thing that makes sense."

Sean shaped a tiny mound of rice with his spoon. "The fact that she's out there, walking around. It doesn't seem right."

"We don't know everything the FBI is doing. You remember what Leah said, that it's ongoing." Leah had reminded them of this just last week, after they'd signed yet another set of national security letters prohibiting them from speaking about Julia. She'd looked amused to learn that Alice and Sean were working together, though she still had not replied with available dates for Alice's proposed group lunch. "Maybe she had to give up all her money."

"You think *money* is what matters to Julia?"

"It's a big deal if you don't have it."

"At Julia's level, you don't care about that. It's the other stuff you think about."

"Well I wouldn't know, would I? So then what do you care about?"

"Status. You know, never having to wait, everyone kissing your ass. Thousands of worker bees at your command." Sean looked wistful; the start-up had only twelve employees so far, and none were particularly deferential. All except Alice were already millionaires from the original FreeTalk sale to Tangerine, and had known Sean and Johan for years.

"Well, maybe that goes away. Like with Bernie Madoff. I'm sure that guy's suffering."

"You saw Julia just now. Did you see any suffering? Whose idea do you think it was to expand to Egypt and Iran? Julia's worth way more to the U.S. government in charge of Tangerine than sitting in prison or anywhere else." Using a napkin, Sean ripped the last piece of naan and placed half on Alice's plate. "I don't know. I'd like to see *something*. Something more. I don't think it's quite fair that this should be the end for her."

"But this isn't the end of anything," Alice said.

AFTER LUNCH, ALICE WALKED BACK to the office alone. Sean had left first, shouting into his headset about the latest round of financing—there was so much to starting a company Alice had never thought of, and she realized Sean had done all this before, with FreeTalk.

She reached into her pocket. India Dreams kept a glass bowl of candied fennel seeds by the register, which Alice liked to obsessively eat in a repeating pattern of green, pink, and white. She deposited one in her mouth and, realizing she'd forgotten to mark its color, took out her phone to check it on her tongue. Green.

The phone vibrated in her hand. Alice saw the sender's name on the message and stopped. She stared at the locked screen as she stood on the sidewalk, cars whizzing past her, and then she forced herself to shove her phone into her pocket and walk on.

Ten minutes later, she was at the office. Instead of going inside Alice walked around to the back of the building, to a small patch of concrete Sean had requisitioned as an outdoor meeting area. Around a garbage can were three plastic folding chairs, left over from the last tenants.

Using the back of her sleeve, Alice wiped the dirt and cigarette ash from one of the seats. She took out her phone and then, at last, allowed herself to read:

From: Julia@Tangerine
To: AliceLu1984@gmail.com

Alice,

I was sorry to hear about your separation from Tangerine, which I only learned of when I returned. Truly unfortunate, given your numerous talents. The individual responsible for the employment action has been counseled.

I enjoyed our conversation at the roundtable and know that you are a bright young woman with an even brighter future.

Please know if you ever wish to return to the company, my door is open. I look forward to speaking soon.

Best,

Julia

After she'd read the message, and read it again, Alice set her phone on the ground. Despite her efforts a smile crept onto her face; it stretched and tugged until she finally gave in and laughed.

She leaned back into the chair. An arm's length away was a window, and through it she could see into the office: her new coworkers at their desks; Sean pacing near the front, still on the phone. The clock on the far wall read five minutes before the end of the hour. Why go in early? She settled against her seat and closed her eyes, letting the sun wash her face as she dreamed.

# SEPTEMBER 2019

# 37

# JULIA

She'd been home a month. The first minute nearly stumbling, so eager was she to get through the door; Julia had promised herself she'd be calm, steady, and nonhysterical, but as the car approached the driveway her anticipation was so great that she feared she might vomit. Entering the nursery, she'd scooped Emily into her arms. Kissing her on her head, her hands, her feet, her cheeks, until finally—perhaps due to the overstimulation—Emily burst into tears.

As Emily wailed, Charlie had come into the room. He gave Julia a kiss on the cheek, which after a second she returned. That night, as she sat before her computer and entered Charlie's name, she wondered what God Mode would yield. She had divided the potential outcomes into two categories:

*My wife knows, this is over, this was a terrible mistake . . .*

Or maybe: *My wife knows, but don't worry, I won't let us be apart.*

I'm ready, she thought. Hoping. Dreading. But in the end, she discovered Charlie had written nothing. Instead, there was only a series of messages, days apart, from Mandy:

Hello?

Are you there?

Hello?

Hello?

Hello, Julia thought now. Hello. She had woken suddenly, as had been her habit these last weeks. The window was dark and from her fatigue she thought it around three A.M. Since her return she'd begun thrashing in her sleep; she would be in a dream she could never remember, and wake to her hand slamming the board behind her.

She turned to her side. Charlie was breathing at his usual unencumbered pace. She had the impulse to knock on his back. Hello, how are you, was it just a mistake? Can I trust you, and either way I suppose I'll have to. For a while.

Charlie opened his eyes. He stretched and rubbed his fist against his face.

"Did I wake you?" Julia asked.

He yawned. "You were kicking, earlier."

"Sorry."

Charlie stretched again. Julia assumed he'd turn and go back to sleep, but instead he reached his hand toward her. "Hey," he said, gently cupping her cheek. "I know it's been a little crazy. I'm sure we've both said things we regretted."

*We?* Though Julia didn't argue. "Yes."

"I haven't wanted to talk to you about it because I know you've been stressed. It's been hard to find time." He placed his other hand on top of hers. "I love our life together. I love our daughter. And I love you."

Julia closed her eyes; her mind went blank and she let herself be held. His embrace was warm and she was safe and comfortable and then at some point she began to feel hot. She could hear that Charlie had fallen asleep behind her; his arms were heavy and she tried, very gently, to wriggle out of them. But she must not have been as careful as she thought, because Charlie suddenly grunted—and then, since he was awake anyway, she pushed him to his side of the bed. She unfurled her arms and extended her legs, taking up her half of the space. Her husband raised his head and looked at her.

"I love you, too," Julia said.

FOUR HOURS LATER, JULIA GOT up and dressed. She told Charlie, who was still half-asleep in bed, that she was leaving for work and went to the nursery and kissed Emily. And then drove to Santa Cruz. To the boardwalk, a place she'd never been but planned to visit once Emily was older—one of the many assumptions dotted on her mental calendar, since she'd be here a long time.

The rest of her life, if she could manage it. If she wanted.

It was a cold Tuesday morning, and the boardwalk was almost empty. Patches of seniors, a few tourists. The actual spread of rides was shorter than she'd thought, and interspersed with carnival games and ice cream stands. It took her only ten minutes to walk through, but then how much more did you need?

Julia went to a bench on the edge of the wooden walkway. The beach itself wasn't appealing: the water was gray, and chunks of seaweed and debris littered the shore. From farther away, a man was walking in her direction.

"Let's go over how you started with the SPB," Leah had said. After Julia offered Ned Daly, after they'd settled the first part of her agreement, they'd kept her in the room until night. The dinner they brought in (sushi and cheeseburgers) had obviously been purchased out of optimism—a sort of advance payment for the bounty expected to come. But Julia stayed careful.

"I was originally contacted by a person in Moscow." The same story she'd already told Leah and her colleagues twice before. "We had limited interaction."

"A man or woman?"

"Woman."

"What was their name?"

Julia paused. "Raisa."

"And what happened when you got to California?"

"I waited for further instruction. The goal was for me to live my life. Until the next contact."

Leah was tired, Julia could tell. She was tired and yet kept her back straight and for this Julia liked her. "Then how did you arrive at your present situation? Because I've got to say, it's quite a rise you've had. Improbable, some might believe. Who helped your ascent?"

Julia crossed her arms. "No one," she said icily. "Myself."

"And who has been your handler since you moved to California?"

"I receive information through an account. I've never met a real person."

Leah scrawled a note. "An account. Huh. Funny, I've heard that before." She looked up. "Which account?"

"A different one each time."

"What accounts? Do you have names?"

"I delete the messages right after I receive them. As per protocol. I don't remember any." Looking almost insulted that they'd believe the SPB to be so reckless as to give her a live contact, the same person to interact with each time.

She couldn't protect him forever, of course. The FBI knew she was lying. Knew it but couldn't prove it, at least not without a lot of work. And while there were many tools in their toolbox, Julia also knew she wasn't the sort you took a hammer and chisel to. Yet. Though they constantly reminded her of the power dynamic: You have already *crossed*, Leah saying in a voice too loud, you are now working for the United States government.

"Okay," Julia said. "Right." Upon which Leah looked away.

A bird cawed from above, a gray-and-blue scrub jay. Julia looked to the beach and watched Leo approach, the same as she'd done back at the institute. Observing him then, Julia had thought: Here is someone interesting. Possibly even good. On days she felt hopeful, she would tell herself that one day he might return . . . but he hadn't, and she'd thought: Ah well.

But then he'd come back for her.

Leo stood at the water's edge and then came up the stairs and sat to her right.

"You know I've been here before," he said.

Julia stopped in her greeting, surprised. She had expected him to start angry, ask where the hell she'd been. She'd put off calling Leo to meet, wondering when he'd make contact, before finally giving in, and when he answered his voice had been neutral: "Okay," he'd said, and she'd set down the phone.

"You have?" she asked. "To the boardwalk?"

"Yes. There's a lot you don't know about me or my time here, Julia. About what I do when I'm not with you. Just like I don't know what you were doing those seven days you were gone, unreachable."

He knew. He'd spoken calmly, had not moved or glanced at her, but still Julia knew that he knew. She understood she ought to say something, that she had to defend herself, but she was so tired. She touched her hand to her chest, where it almost felt as if her heart was splitting.

"What happened?" Leo asked.

Julia sighed. Looked at him and then back to the water.

And told.

Afterward, Leo was still, his hands in his lap. As Julia waited, she watched the few children playing on the shore.

"Were you followed?" Leo asked at last, not looking at her.

"No. I was careful. On the way I took an earlier exit, and then looped back and drove on side streets. Santa Cruz is good for that, especially in the morning. Not a lot of traffic. All the cars, anyone on foot is visible. You know." Her voice caught. "Everything you taught."

"The first time I went to Santa Cruz was right after I'd moved," Leo said. His voice was neat, even, as if she'd interrupted him in the middle of a narration. "I'd heard California had good nature, and thought I might as well see. But when I came, I didn't like it. I didn't know about the different beaches then, all I saw were these rides, the candy shops and bowling alleys. I went home and said I wouldn't come again. But eventually I did, and then at some point I was surprised to find that I liked it. Did you know that in Big Sur, there are cafés where you can drink a cup of coffee and watch whales? A friend took me to such a place the other day. There were five other people inside and even though I didn't know any of them, I felt in that moment we had something in common, because we were all doing the same thing, searching the ocean for a whale."

Julia tried to make sense of what he was saying. "Leo. Do you like it so much here? Do you ever think you could make it your home?"

He exhaled. "Of course not."

She deflated. Julia had never cried in front of Leo before. She'd not wanted to give him the satisfaction, though now it simply seemed to her that she'd squandered her self-control in all the wrong places.

Leo watched as she dabbed at her eyes with a tissue. "I want you to listen to me," he said quietly. "I had a nice drive on the way here. Did you look out your window as you were driving, at the view? If you didn't, you wasted it."

Julia's nose was runny. "I—"

He raised a hand, stopping her. "When I was young, I thought I could plot out everything. Mark all the bits and pieces I wanted in life, hit each of them as if charting a train journey. I suppose I'm middle-aged now, and the funny thing is sometimes I still believe this, even though I know it isn't true. I thought I would be sadder about it all, the things I haven't managed to accomplish or failed at, but I'm not."

She was having trouble understanding him again. "What do you want me to do?"

He turned. "When the Americans took you. They said if you didn't cooperate, you would lose your life here. Your daughter."

"Yes." It came out a whisper.

"And when they said that, you knew from your training that an option was to keep quiet. Return to Russia. We would have found a way to get you out, eventually. But you didn't. Because in the end, you wanted to stay."

Julia swallowed. She tried to prepare in her head some excuse. But Leo knew her as well as any parent could know a child; more than Nina or Karl ever had, by magnitudes.

He stretched, pointing his fingers. "I want to stay, too. For now."

Julia took a deep breath. She tried to think of why Leo might want to stay, and realized he was right: She knew so little about him. Nothing except that perhaps he might care for her, and what did it matter if in his care he expected things from her as well? Only a fragment of love was truly unconditional, but that didn't mean the rest was bad for you, it was just that the other person had to survive, too.

Intermixed with her hope was caution. "What if something goes wrong?"

"We fix it," Leo said.

"How?"

"I don't know yet. But don't you think it is worth it to try?"

Julia pressed the tissue against her face. Tipped back her head and thought of the last time she'd seen Nina. She didn't know what had happened after: whether Nina had given up or tried. She imagined it could be either way. And then Julia straightened and sat watching the waves with Leo, waiting to hear where it was they'd next go.

# ACKNOWLEDGMENTS

With thanks to Kate Nintzel and the team at HarperCollins; Michelle Brower and the team at Aevitas Creative Management; Kassie Evashevski, Ryan Wilson, and the team at Anonymous Content; Danya Kukafka and Emily May, who read early drafts; Cathi Hanauer and John Jay Osborn, for your friendship; my mom, for being my mom; and Tom, Daniel, and Vivienne for your love and encouragement—there's no three people I'd rather spend a pandemic with.